QUEEN OF BABBLE

and

QUEEN OF BABBLE
IN THE BIG CITY

Meg Cabot has lived in Indiana and California, USA, and in France. In addition to her adult novels *The Guy Next Door*, *Boy Meets Girl*, *Every Boy's Got One* and *Size 12 Is Not Fat*, the first novel in the new Heather Wells mystery series, she is the author of the highly successful series of children's books, *The Princess Diaries*. Meg and her husband divide their time between New York City and Key West.

Be sure to check out Meg's websites:

www.megcabot.com
www.megcabotbookclub.com

QUEEN OF BABBLE

and

QUEEN OF BABBLE
IN THE BIG CITY

MEG CABOT

PAN BOOKS

Queen of Babble first published 2006 by William Morrow,
an imprint of HarperCollins Publishers, New York.
First published in Great Britain in paperback 2006 by Pan Books
Queen of Babble, In the Big City first published 2007 by William Morrow,
an imprint of HarperCollins Publishers, New York
First published in Great Britain in paperback 2007 by Pan Books

This omnibus first published 2008 by Pan Books
an imprint of Pan Macmillan Ltd
Pan Macmillan, 20 New Wharf Road, London N1 9RR
Basingstoke and Oxford
Associated companies throughout the world
www.panmacmillan.com

ISBN 978-0-330-50789-9

Grateful acknowledgement is made to reprint the lyrics from
"(I've Had) The Time of My Life" by WordSong, Inc., and by Sony/ATV Music
Publishing, LLC. "(I've Had) The Time of My Life © 1987 Sony/ATV Songs LLC,
R.U. Cyrius Publishing, Knockout Music Company and Donald Jay Music LTD.
All rights on behalf of Sony/ATV Songs LLC administered by Sony/ATV Music Publishing,
8 Music Square West, Nashville, TN 37203. All rights reserved. Used by permission.

Queen of Babble is a work of fiction. The characters, incidents, and dialogue
are drawn from the author's imagination and are not to be construed as real.
Any resemblance to actual events or persons, living or dead, is entirely coincidental.

1 3 5 7 9 8 6 4 2

A CIP catalogue record for this book is available from
the British Library.

Printed in the UK by CPI Mackays, Chatham ME5 8TD

QUEEN OF BABBLE

For Benjamin

Many thanks to all the extremely generous people who helped with the writing of this book, including Beth Ader, Jennifer Brown, Megan Farr, Carrie Feron, Michele Jaffe, Laura Langlie, Laura McKay, Sophia Travis and especially Benjamin Egnatz

Part One

Part One

Clothing. Why do we wear it? Many people believe that we wear clothing out of modesty. In ancient civilizations, however, clothing was developed not to cover our private parts from view, but merely to keep the body warm. In other cultures, clothing was thought to protect its wearers from magic, while in still others clothing served merely ornamental or display purposes.

In this thesis, I hope to explore the history of clothing—or fashion—starting with ancient man, who wore animal hides for warmth, to modern man, or woman, some of whom wear small strips of material between their buttocks (see: thong) for reasons no one has yet been able to adequately explain to this author.

History of Fashion
SENIOR THESIS BY ELIZABETH NICHOLS

can't believe this. I can't believe I don't remember what he looks like! How can I not remember what he *looks* like? I mean, *his tongue has been in my mouth*. How could I forget what someone whose tongue has been in my mouth *looks* like? It's not like there've been that many guys who've had their tongues in my mouth. Only, like, three.

And one of those was in high school. And the other one turned out to be gay.

God, that is so depressing. Okay, I'm not going to think about that right now.

It isn't like it's been THAT long since I last saw him. It was just three months ago! You would think I'd remember what someone I've been dating for THREE MONTHS looks like.

Even if, you know, for most of those three months we've been in separate countries.

Still. I have his photo. Well, okay, you can't really see his face in it. Actually, you can't see his face at all, since it's a photo of his—oh God—naked ass.

Why would anyone send someone something like that? I didn't

ask for a photo of his naked ass. Was it supposed to be erotic? Because it so wasn't.

Maybe that's just me, though. Shari's right, I've got to stop being so inhibited.

It was just so shocking to find it in my in-box, a big photo of my boyfriend's naked ass.

And okay, I know they were just goofing around, he and his friends. And I know Shari says it's a cultural thing, and that the British are much less sensitive about nudity than most Americans, and that we should strive as a culture to be more open and carefree, like they are.

Also that he probably thought, like most men do, that his ass is his best feature.

But still.

Okay, I'm not going to think about that right now. Stop thinking about my boyfriend's ass. Instead, I'm going to look for him. He has to be here somewhere, he swore he'd be here to pick me up—

Oh my God, that can't be him, can it? No, of course it's not. Why would he be wearing a jacket like that? Why would ANYONE be wearing a jacket like that? Unless they're being ironic. Or Michael Jackson, of course. He is the only man I could think of who would wear red leather with epaulets. Who isn't a professional break-dancer.

That CAN'T be him. Oh, please God, don't let that be him . . .

Oh no, he's looking this way . . . he's looking this way! Look down, look down, don't make eye contact with the guy in the red leather jacket with the epaulets. I'm sure he's a very nice man; it's a shame about his having to shop for coats from the 1980s at the Salvation Army.

But I don't want him to know I was looking at him, he might think I like him or something.

And it's not that I'm prejudiced against homeless people, I'm not, I know all about how many of us are really only a few paychecks away from being homeless ourselves. Some of us, in fact, are less than a paycheck away from being homeless. Some of us, in fact, are so broke that we still live with our parents.

But I'm not going to think about all that right now.

The thing is, I just don't want Andrew to get here and find me talking to some homeless guy in a red leather break-dancing jacket. I mean, that is so not the first impression I want to give. Not that, you know, it will be his FIRST impression of me, since we've been dating for three months and all. But it will be the first impression he'll have of the New Me, the me he hasn't met yet . . .

Okay. Okay, it's safe, he's not looking anymore.

Oh God, this is awful, I can't believe this is how they welcome people to their country. Herding us down this walkway with all these people LOOKING at us . . . I feel like I'm personally disappointing each and every one of them by not being the person they're waiting for. This is a very unkind thing to do to people who just sat on a plane for six hours, eight in my case if you count the flight from Ann Arbor to New York. Ten if you count the two-hour layover at JFK—

Wait. Was Red Break-dancing Jacket just checking me out?

Oh my God, he WAS! Red leather jacket with the epaulets totally checked me out!

Oh God, this is so embarrassing. It's my underwear, I KNOW it. How could he tell? That I'm not wearing any, I mean? It's true I don't have any visible panty lines, but for all he knows, I could be wearing a thong. I SHOULD have worn a thong. Shari was right.

But it's so uncomfortable when they go up your—

I KNEW I shouldn't have picked a dress this tight to get off the plane in—even if I did personally modify it by hemming the skirt to above the knee so I'm not hobbled by it.

But for one thing, I'm freezing—how can it be this cold in AUGUST?

And for another, this silk is particularly clingy, so there's the whole panty line thing.

Still, everyone back at the shop said I look great in it . . . though I wouldn't have thought a mandarin dress—even a vintage one— would actually work on me, seeing as how I'm Caucasian and all.

But I *want* to look good, since he hasn't seen me in so long, and I did lose those thirty pounds, and you wouldn't be able to tell I'd lost all that weight if I got off the plane in sweats. Isn't that always what celebrities are wearing when they show up on *Us Weekly*'s "What Were They Thinking?" page? You know, when they get off a plane in sweats and last year's Uggs, with their hair all crazy? If you are going to be a celebrity, you need to LOOK like a celebrity, even when you're getting off a plane.

Not that I'm a celebrity, but I still want to look good. I went to all this trouble, I haven't had so much as a crumb of bread for three months, and—

Wait. What if he doesn't recognize me? Seriously. I mean, I did lose thirty pounds, and with my new haircut and all—

Oh God, could he be here and not recognize me? Did I already walk right by him? Should I turn around and go back down that walkway thingie and look for him? But I'll seem like such an idiot. What do I do? Oh my God, this is so not fair, I just wanted to look good for him, not be stranded in a foreign country because I look so different my own boyfriend doesn't recognize me! What if he thinks I haven't shown up and just goes home? I don't have any money—well, twelve hundred bucks, but that has to last me until my flight home at the end of the month—

RED LEATHER JACKET IS STILL LOOKING THIS WAY!!! Oh God, what can he want from me?

What if he's part of some kind of airport white slavery ring? What if he hangs out here all the time looking for naive young tourists from Ann Arbor, Michigan, to kidnap and send to Saudi Arabia to be some sheikh's seventeenth bride? I read a book where that happened once ... although I have to say the girl seemed to really enjoy it. But only because at the end the sheikh divorced all his other wives and just kept her because she was so pure and yet so good in the sack.

Or what if he just holds girls for ransom instead of selling them? Except that I am so not rich! I know this dress looks expensive, but I got it at Vintage to Vavoom for twelve dollars (with my employee discount)!

And my dad doesn't have any money. He works at a cyclotron, for crying out loud!

Don't kidnap me, don't kidnap me, don't kidnap me—

Wait, what is this booth? Meet Your Party. Oh, great! Customer service! That's what I'll do! I'll have Andrew paged. And that way, if he's here, he can come find me. And I'll be safe from Red Leather Break-dancing Jacket; he won't dare kidnap me and send me to Saudi Arabia in front of the pager guy—

"Hullo, love, you look lost. What can I do for you, then?"

Oh, the booth guy is so nice! And such a cute accent! Although that tie was an unfortunate choice.

"Hi, I'm Lizzie Nichols," I say. "I'm supposed to be picked up by my boyfriend, Andrew Marshall. Only he doesn't seem to be here, and—"

"Want me to page him for you, then?"

"Oh! Yes, please, would you? Because there's a guy following me, see him over there? I think he might be a kidnapper or the operator of a white slavery ring—"

"Which one?"

I don't want to point, but I do feel I have a duty, you know, to report Red Leather Break-dancing Jacket to the authorities, or at least to the Meet Your Party booth attendant, because he DOES look very odd in that jacket, and he IS still staring at me, really rudely, or at least suggestively, like he still wants to kidnap me.

"Over there," I say, nodding my head toward Red Leather Break-dancing Jacket. "That one in the hideous jacket with the epaulets. See him? The one staring at us."

"Oh, right." The Meet Your Party booth attendant nods. "Right. Very menacing. Hold on, then, I'll have your boyfriend over here, giving that git the thrashing he so richly deserves, in a second. ANDREW MARSHALL. ANDREW MARSHALL, MISS NICHOLS IS WAITING FOR YOU AT THE MEET YOUR PARTY BOOTH. ANDREW MARSHALL, PLEASE FIND MISS NICHOLS AT THE MEET YOUR PARTY BOOTH. There? How was that?"

"Oh, that was great," I say encouragingly, because I feel a little sorry for him. I mean, it must be hard to sit in a booth all day, yelling over a loudspeaker. "That was really—"

"Liz?"

Andrew! At last!

Only when I turn around, it's Red Leather Break-dancing Jacket. Except.

Except that it WAS Andrew, all along.

And I just didn't recognize him, because I was distracted by the jacket—the most hideous jacket I've ever seen. Plus he seems to have had his hair cut. Not very flatteringly.

Sort of menacingly, in fact.

"Oh," I say. It is extremely difficult to hide my confusion. And dismay. "Andrew. Hi."

Behind the glass of the Meet Your Party booth, the attendant bursts into very, very loud laughter.

And I realize, with a pang, that I've done it.

Again.

The first woven material was made of vegetable fibers such as bark, cotton, and hemp. Animal fibers were not employed until the Neolithic period, by cultures that—unlike their nomadic ancestors—were able to establish stable communities near which sheep could graze, and in which looms could be constructed.

Nevertheless, the ancient Egyptian refused to wear wool until after the Alexandrian conquest, obviously citing its itchiness in warm climates.

History of Fashion
SENIOR THESIS BY ELIZABETH NICHOLS

Gossip isn't scandal and it's not merely malicious.
It's chatter about the human race by lovers of the same.
—*Phyllis McGinley (1905–1978), U.S. poet and author*

Two Days Earlier Back in Ann Arbor
(or maybe three days—wait, what time is it in America?)

You're compromising your feminist principles." That's what Shari keeps saying.

"Stop it," I say.

"Seriously. It's not like you. Ever since you met this guy—"

"Shari, I love him. Why is it wrong that I want to be with the person I love?"

"It's not wrong to want to be with him," Shari says. "It's wrong to put your own career on hold while you wait for him to finish his degree."

"And what career would that be, Shar?" I can't believe I'm even having this conversation. Again.

Also that she would station herself next to the chips and dip like this when she knows perfectly well I'm still trying to lose five more pounds.

Oh well. At least she's wearing the fifties black-and-white Mexican swing skirt I picked out for her at the shop, even though she claimed it made her butt look too big. It so doesn't. Except maybe in a good way.

"You know," Shari says. "The career you could have, if you would just move to New York with me when you get back from England, instead of—"

"I told you, I'm not arguing with you about this today," I say. "It's my graduation party, Shar. Can't you let me enjoy it?"

"No," Shari says. "Because you're being an ass, and you know it."

Shari's boyfriend, Chaz, comes over to us and scoops up some onion dip with a barbecue-flavored potato chip.

Mmm. Barbecue-flavored potato chips. Maybe if I just had one . . .

"What's Lizzie being an ass about now?" he asks, chewing.

But you can never have just one barbecue-flavored potato chip. Never.

Chaz is tall and lanky. I bet he's never had to lose five more pounds before in his entire life. He even has to wear a belt to hold up his Levi's. It's a mesh leather weave. But on him, mesh leather works.

What doesn't work, of course, is the University of Michigan baseball cap. But I have never successfully managed to convince him that baseball caps, as an accessory, are wrong on everyone. Except children and actual baseball players.

"She still plans to stay here after she gets back from England," Shari explains, plunging a chip of her own into the dip, "instead of moving to New York with us to start her real life."

Shari doesn't have to watch what she eats, either. She's always had a naturally fast metabolism. When we were kids, her school sack lunches consisted of three peanut butter and jelly sandwiches and a pack of Oreo cookies, and she never gained an ounce. My lunches? A hard-boiled egg, a single orange, and a chicken leg. And I was the blimp. Oh yes.

"Shari," I say, "I have a real life here. I've got a place to stay—"

"With your parents!"

"—and a job I love—"

"As an assistant manager of a vintage clothing store. That's not a *career*!"

"I told you," I say for what has to be the nine hundredth time, "I'm going to live here and save my money. Then Andrew and I are moving to New York after he gets his master's. It's just one more semester."

"Who's Andrew again?" Chaz wants to know. And Shari hits him in the shoulder.

"Ow," Chaz says.

"You remember," Shari says. "The R.A. at McCracken Hall. The grad student. The one Lizzie hasn't stopped talking about all summer."

"Oh, right, Andy. The British guy. The one who was running the illegal poker ring on the seventh floor."

I burst out laughing. "That's not Andrew! He doesn't *gamble*. He's studying to be an educator of youth so that he can preserve our most precious resource . . . the next generation."

"The guy who sent you the photo of his naked ass?"

I gasp. "Shari, you *told* him about that?"

"I wanted a guy's perspective," Shari says with a shrug. "You know, to see if he had any insights into what kind of individual would do something like that."

Coming from Shari, who'd been a psych major, this is actually a fairly reasonable explanation. I look at Chaz questioningly. He has lots of insights into lots of things—how many times around Palmer Field make a mile (four—which I needed to know back when I was walking it every day to lose weight); what the number 33 on the inside of the Rolling Rock bottle means; why so many guys seem to think man-pris are actually flattering . . .

But Chaz shrugs, too. "I was unable to be of any aid," he says, "not ever having taken a photo of my bare ass before."

"Andrew didn't take a photo of his own ass," I say. "His friends took it."

"How homoerotic," Chaz comments. "Why do you call him Andrew when everybody else calls him Andy?"

"Because Andy is a jock name," I say, "and Andrew isn't a jock. He's getting a master's in education. Someday he'll be teaching children to read. Could there be a more important job in the whole entire world than that? And he's *not* gay. I checked this time."

Chaz's eyebrows go up. "You *checked*? How? Wait . . . I don't want to know."

"She just likes pretending he's *Prince* Andrew," Shari says. "Um, so where was I?"

"Lizzie's being an ass," Chaz helpfully supplies. "So wait. How long's it been since you saw this guy? Three months?"

"About that," I say.

"Man," Chaz says, shaking his head, "there is going to be some major bone-jumping when you step off that plane."

"Andrew isn't like that," I say warmly. "He's a romantic. He'll probably want to let me get acclimated and recover from my jet lag in his king-size bed and thousand-thread-count sheets. He'll bring me breakfast in bed—a cute English breakfast with . . . Englishy stuff on it."

"Like stewed tomatoes?" Chaz asks with feigned innocence.

"Nice try," I say, "but Andrew knows I don't like tomatoes. He asked in his last e-mail if there are any foods I dislike, and I filled him in on the tomato thing."

"You better hope breakfast isn't all he brings you in bed," Shari says darkly. "Otherwise what is the point of traveling halfway around the world to see him?"

That's the problem with Shari. She's so unromantic. I'm really surprised she and Chaz have gone out as long as they have. I mean, two years is really a record for her.

Then again, as she likes to assure me, their attraction is almost purely physical, Chaz having just gotten his master's in philosophy and thus, in Shari's opinion, being virtually unemployable.

"So what would even be the point of hoping for a future with him?" she often asks me. "I mean, eventually he'll start to feel inadequate—even though he's got his trust fund, of course—and consequently suffer from performance anxiety in the bedroom. So I'll just keep him around as a boy toy for now, while he can still get it up."

Shari is very practical in this way.

"I still don't get why you're going all the way to England to see him," Chaz says. "I mean, a guy you haven't even slept with yet, who obviously doesn't know you very well if he isn't aware of your aversion to tomatoes and thinks you'd enjoy seeing a photograph of anyone's naked ass."

"You know perfectly well why," Shari says. "It's his accent."

"Shari!" I cry.

"Oh, right," Shari says, rolling her eyes. "He saved her life."

"Who saved whose life?" Angelo, my brother-in-law, moseys over, having discovered the dip.

"Lizzie's new boyfriend," Shari says.

"Lizzie's got a new boyfriend?" Angelo, I can tell, is trying to cut back on his carbs. He's only dipping celery sticks. Maybe he's on South Beach to control his belly fat, which is not enhanced by the white polyester shirt he is wearing. Why won't he listen to me and stick to natural fibers? "How did I not hear about this? The LBS must be on the fritz."

"LBS?" Chaz echoes, his dark eyebrows raised.

"Lizzie Broadcasting System," Shari explains to him. "Where have you been?"

"Oh, right," Chaz says, and swigs his beer.

"I told Rose all about it," I say, glaring at all three of them. Someday I'm going to get my sister Rose back for that Lizzie Broadcasting

System thing. It was funny when we were kids, but I'm twenty-two now! "Didn't she tell you, Ange?"

Angelo looks confused. "Tell me what?"

I sigh. "This freshman on the second floor let her potpourri boil over on her illegal hot plate and the hall filled with smoke and they had to evacuate," I explain. I am always eager to relate the story of how Andrew and I met. Because it's superromantic. Someday, when Andrew and I are married and live in a ramshackle and tomato-free Victorian in Westport, Connecticut, with our golden retriever, Rolly, and our four kids, Andrew Jr., Henry, Stella, and Beatrice, and I'm a famous—well, whatever I'm going to be—and Andrew's the headmaster at a nearby boys' school, teaching children to read, and I get interviewed in *Vogue*, I'll be able to tell this story—looking funky yet fabulous in vintage Chanel from head to toe—while laughingly serving a perfect cup of French roast to the reporter on my back porch, which will be decorated entirely in tasteful white wicker and chintz.

"Well, I was taking a shower," I go on, "so I didn't smell the smoke or hear the alarm going off or anything. Until Andrew came into the girls' bathroom and yelled '*Fire!*' and—"

"Is it true the girls' bathrooms in McCracken Hall have gang showers?" Angelo wants to know.

"It's true," Chaz informs him conversationally. "They all have to shower together. Sometimes they soap each other's backs while gossiping about their girlish hijinks from the night before."

Angelo stares at Chaz, bug-eyed. "Are you shitting me?"

"Don't pay any attention to him, Angelo," Shari says, going for another chip. "He's making it up."

"That kind of thing happens all the time on *Beverly Hills Bordello*," Angelo says.

"We didn't shower all together," I say. "I mean, Shari and I did sometimes—"

"Tell us more about that, please," Chaz says, opening a new beer with the church key my mom had provided near the cooler.

"Don't," Shari says. "You'll just encourage him."

"Which bits were you washing when he came in?" Chaz wants to know. "And was there another girl with you at the time? Which bits was *she* washing? Or was she helping to wash *your* bits?"

"No," I say, "it was just me. And naturally, when I saw a guy in the girls' shower, I screamed."

"Oh, naturally," Chaz said.

"So I grabbed a towel and this guy—I couldn't really see him all that well through the steam and the smoke and all—goes, in the cutest British accent you ever heard, 'Miss, the building's on fire. I'm afraid you'll have to evacuate.'"

"So wait," Angelo says. "This dude saw you in the raw?"

"In her nudie-pants," Chaz confirms.

"So by then the halls were all smoky and I couldn't see, so he took my hand and guided me down the stairs and outside to safety, where we struck up a conversation—me in my towel and everything. And that's when I realized he was the love of my life."

"Based on one conversation," Chaz says, sounding skeptical. But then, having a philosophy master's degree, he is skeptical about everything. They train them to be that way.

"Well," I say, "we made out the rest of the night, too. That's how I know he's not gay. I mean, he got a full stiffy."

Chaz choked a little on his beer.

"So, anyway," I say, trying to steer the conversation back on track, "we made out all night. But then he had to leave the next day for England, because the semester was over—"

"—and now, since Lizzie's finally done with school, she's flying to London to spend the rest of the summer with him," Shari finishes for me. "Then coming back here to rot, just like her—"

"Come on, Shar," I interrupt quickly. "You promised."

She just grimaces at me.

"Listen, Liz," Chaz says, and reaches for another beer, "I know this guy's the love of your life and all. But you have all next semester to be with him. Are you sure you don't want to come to France with us for the rest of the summer?"

"Don't bother, Chaz," Shari says. "I already asked her eighty million times."

"Did you mention we're staying in a seventeenth-century French château with its own vineyard, perched on a hilltop overlooking a lush green valley through which snakes a long and lazy river?" Chaz wants to know.

"Shari told me," I say, "and it's sweet of you to ask. Even if you're not exactly in a position to be inviting people, because doesn't the château belong to one of your friends from that prep school you went to, and not you?"

"A trifling detail," Chaz says. "Luke would love to have you."

"Ha," Shari says, "I'll say. More slave labor for his amateur wedding franchise."

"What're they talking about?" Angelo asks me, looking confused.

"Chaz's childhood friend from prep school, Luke," I explain to him, "has an ancestral home in France that his father rents out during the summer sometimes as a destination wedding spot. Shari and Chaz are leaving tomorrow to spend a month at the château for free, in exchange for helping out at the weddings."

"Destination wedding spot," Angelo echoes. "You mean like Vegas?"

"Right," Shari says. "Only tasteful. And it costs more than one ninety-nine to get there. And there's no free breakfast buffet."

Angelo looks shocked. "Then what's the *point*?"

Someone tugs on the skirt of my dress and I look down. My sister Rose's firstborn, Maggie, holds up a necklace made of macaroni.

"Aunt Lizzie," she says. "For you. I made it. For your gradutation."

"Why, thank you, Maggie," I say, kneeling down so that Maggie can drop the necklace over my head.

"The paint's not dry," Maggie says, pointing to the red and blue splotches of paint that have now been transferred from the macaroni to the front of my 1954 Suzy Perette rose silk party dress (which wasn't cheap, even with my employee discount).

"That's okay, Mags," I say. Because, after all, she's only four. "It's beautiful."

"There you are!" Grandma Nichols teeters toward us. "I've been looking for you everywhere, Anne-Marie. It's time for *Dr. Quinn*."

"Grandma," I say, straightening up to grasp her spool-thin arm before she can topple over. I see that she has already managed to spill something all down the green crepe de chine 1960s tunic top I got her at the shop. Fortunately the paint stains from the macaroni necklace Maggie made for her are somewhat hiding the stain. "It's Lizzie. Not Anne-Marie. Mom's over by the dessert table. And what have you been drinking?"

I seize the Heineken bottle in Grandma's hand and smell its contents. It should, by prior agreement with the rest of my family, have been filled with nonalcoholic beer, then resealed, due to Grandma Nichols's inability to hold her liquor, which has resulted in what my mom likes to call "incidents." Mom was hoping to head off any "incidents" at my graduation party by letting Grandma have only nonalcoholic beer—but not telling her it was nonalcoholic, of course. Because then she would have raised a fuss, telling us we were trying to ruin an old lady's good time and all.

But I can't tell if the beer in the bottle is of the nonalcoholic variety. We had stashed the faux Heinekens in a special section of the cooler for Grandma. But she may have managed to find the real thing somewhere. She's crafty that way.

Or she could just THINK she's had the real thing, and consequently thinks she's drunk.

"Lizzie?" Grandma looks suspicious. "What are you doing here? Shouldn't you be away at college?"

"I graduated from college in May, Grandma," I say. Well, sort of, anyway. Not counting the two months I just spent in summer school getting my language requirement out of the way. "This is my graduation party. Well, my graduation-slash-bon voyage party."

"Bon voyage?" Grandma's suspicion turns to indignation. "Where do you think you're going?"

"To England, Grandma, the day after tomorrow," I say. "To visit my boyfriend. Remember? We talked about this."

"Boyfriend?" Grandma glares at Chaz. "Isn't that him right there?"

"No, Grandma," I say. "That's Chaz, Shari's boyfriend. You remember Shari Dennis, right, Grandma? She grew up down the street?"

"Oh, the Dennis girl," Grandma says, narrowing her eyes in Shari's direction. "I remember you now. I thought I saw your parents over by the barbecue. You and Lizzie going to do that song you always do when you get together?"

Shari and I exchange horror-filled glances. Angelo hoots.

"Hey, yeah!" he cries. "Rosie told me about this. What song was it you two used to do? Like at the school talent show and shit?"

I give Angelo a warning look, since Maggie is still hanging around, and say, "Little pitchers." It's clear from his expression that he has no idea what I'm talking about. I sigh and begin steering Grandma toward the house.

"Better come on, Grandma," I say, "or you'll miss your show."

"What about the song?" Grandma wants to know.

"We'll do the song later, Mrs. Nichols," Shari assures her.

"I'm going to hold you to that," Chaz says with a wink. Shari mouths *In your dreams* at him. Chaz blows a kiss at her over the top of his beer bottle.

They're so cute together. I can't wait until I'm in London and Andrew and I can be that cute together, too.

"Come on, Grandma," I say. "*Dr. Quinn*'s starting now."

"Oh, good," Grandma says. To Shari, she confides, "I don't care about that dumb Dr. Quinn. It's that hunk who hangs out with her—him I can't get enough of!"

"Okay, Grandma," I say quickly as Shari spurts out the mouthful of Amstel Light she's just taken. "Let's get you inside before you miss your show—"

We hardly get a few yards down the deck, however, before we're waylaid by Dr. Rajghatta, my dad's boss at the cyclotron, and his pretty wife, Nishi, beaming in a pink sari at his side.

"Many congratulations on your graduation," Dr. Rajghatta says.

"Yes," his wife agrees. "And may we say, you are also looking so slim and lovely?"

"Oh, thank you," I say. "Thank you so much!"

"And what will you be doing now that you have your bachelor's degree in . . . what is it again?" Dr. R wants to know. It's unfortunate about the pocket protector he's wearing, but then I haven't been able to wean my own father from the habit, so it's unlikely I'll ever make any headway with his boss.

"History of fashion," I reply.

"History of fashion? I was not aware this school offered a major in that field of study," Dr. R says.

"Oh, it doesn't. I'm in the individualized major program. You know, where you make your own major?"

"But fashion history?" Dr. Rajghatta looks concerned. "There are many opportunities available in this field?"

"Oh, tons," I say, trying not to remember how just last weekend I picked up a copy of the Sunday *New York Times* and saw that every fashion-related job in the want ads—besides merchandising—either didn't exactly require a bachelor's degree, or did require years of experience in the field, which I don't have. "I could get a job in the Costume Institute of the Metropolitan Museum of Art." Sure. As a janitor. "Or as a costume designer on Broadway." You know, if all the other costume designers in the world suddenly died at the same time. "Or even as a buyer for a major high-end fashion retailer like Saks Fifth Avenue." If I had listened to my dad, who'd begged me to minor in business.

"What do you mean, a buyer?" Grandma looks scandalized. "You're going to be a designer, not a buyer! Why, she's been ripping her clothes apart and sewing them back together all weird since she was old enough to pick up a needle," she tells Dr. and Mrs. R, who look at me as if Grandma has just announced I like to salsa naked in my spare time.

"Huh," I say with a nervous laugh. "It was just a hobby." I don't mention, of course, that I only did this—reinvented my clothing—because I was so chubby I couldn't fit into the fun, flirty clothes in the junior department, and so I had to somehow make the stuff Mom got me from the women's department look younger.

Which is, of course, why I love vintage clothes so much. They're so much better made—and more flattering, no matter what your size.

"Hobby my ass," Grandma says. "See this shirt here?" Grandma points at her stained tunic. "She dyed it herself! It was orange, and now look at it! And she hemmed the sleeves to make them sexier, just like I asked!"

"It's a very beautiful top," Mrs. Rajghatta says kindly. "I'm sure Lizzie will go very far with such talents."

"Oh," I say, feeling myself blush beet red. "I mean, I could never . . . you know. For a living. It's just a hobby."

"Well, that's good," her husband says, looking relieved. "No one should spend four years at a top college just so that she can sew for a living!"

"'That would be such a waste!" I agree, deciding not to mention to him that I'd be spending my first semester out of college continuing in my assistant shop manager position while waiting for my boyfriend to graduate.

Grandma looks annoyed. "What do you care?" she asks, giving me a poke in the side. "You went for those four years for free anyway. What does it matter what you do with what you learned there?"

Dr. and Mrs. Rajghatta and I smile at one another, all equally embarrassed by Grandma's outburst.

"Your parents must be so proud of you," Mrs. Rajghatta says, still smiling pleasantly. "I mean, having the confidence to study something so . . . arcane when so many qualified young people can't even find jobs in today's market. That is very brave of you."

"Oh," I say, swallowing down the little bit of vomit that always seems to rise into my throat when I think about my future. Better not to think about it right now. Better to think about the fun I'm going to have with Andrew. "Well, I'm brave all right."

"I'll say she's brave," Grandma chimes in. "She's going to England day after tomorrow to hump some guy she barely knows."

"Well, we have to be going inside now," I say, grabbing Grandma's hand and tugging her along. "Thanks so much for coming, Dr. and Mrs. Rajghatta!"

"Oh, wait. This is for you, Lizzie," Mrs. Rajghatta says, slipping a small gift-wrapped box into my hand.

"Oh, thank you so much," I cry. "You didn't have to!"

"It's nothing, really," Mrs. Rajghatta says with a laugh. "Just a book light. Your parents said you were going to Europe, so I thought, if you are reading on a train or something—"

"Well, thank you very much," I say. "That will come in handy all right. Bye now."

"Book light," Grandma grumbles as I hurry her away from Dad's boss and his wife. "Who the hell wants a book light?"

"Lots of people," I say. "They are very handy things to have."

Grandma says a very bad word. I'll be happy when I get her safely tucked in front of the rerun of *Dr. Quinn*.

But before I can do that, there are several more obstacles we have to hurdle, including Rose.

"My baby sister!" Rose cries, looking up from the infant she's got in a high chair by the picnic table, into whose mouth she's shoveling mashed peas. "I can't believe you're graduating from college! It just makes me feel so old!"

"You *are* old," Grandma observes.

But Rose just ignores her, as is her custom where Grandma is concerned.

"Angelo and I are just so proud of you," Rose says, her eyes filling with tears. It's a shame she didn't listen to me about the length of her jeans. The cropped look just doesn't work unless you've got legs as long as Cindy Crawford's. Which none of us Nichols girls do. "Not just for the graduating thing, but for—well, you know. The weight loss. Really. You just look terrific. And . . . well, we got you a little something." She slips a small gift-wrapped package in my hand. "It isn't anything much . . . you know, with Angelo out of work, and the baby in day care and all . . . But I thought you might be able to use a book light. I know how much you love to read."

"Wow," I say. "Thank you so much, Rose. That was really thoughtful of you."

Grandma starts to say something, but I squeeze her hand, hard.

"Ow," Grandma says. "Stab me next time, why don't you?"

"Well, I have to get Grandma inside," I say. "Time for *Dr. Quinn*."

Rose looks down her nose at Grandma. "Oh God," she says. "She didn't talk about her lust for Byron Sully in front of everyone, did she?"

"At least *he's* got a job," Grandma begins, "which is more than I can say for that husband of—"

"Okay," I say, grabbing Grandma and heading for the sliding doors. "Let's go, Grandma. Don't want to keep Sully waiting."

"That is no way," I hear Rose wail behind us, "to talk about your grandson-in-law, Gram! Wait till I tell Daddy!"

"Aw, go ahead," Grandma retorts. Then, as I drag her away, she complains, "That sister of yours. How could you stand her all these years?"

Before I can form a reply—that it wasn't easy—I hear my other sister, Sarah, call my name. I turn around and see her staggering toward us, a casserole dish in her hands. Sadly, she is in a pair of white stretch capris that are far too tight on her.

Will my sisters never learn? Some things *need* to be left a mystery.

But I guess since that's the look that won Sarah her husband, Chuck, she's sticking with it.

"Oh, hey," Sarah says, not very distinctly. She's clearly been hitting the Heineken herself. "I made your favorite for you, in honor of your big day." She whisks the plastic wrap off the casserole dish and waves it under my nose. A wave of nausea grips me.

"Tomato ratatouille!" Sarah shrieks, laughing uproariously. "Remember that time Aunt Karen made that ratatouille and Mom told you you had to eat it to be polite and you threw up over the side of the deck?"

"Yes," I said, feeling like I was about to throw up over the side of the deck all over again.

"Wasn't that funny? So I made it for old times' sake. Hey, what's the matter?" She seems to notice my expression for the first time. "Oh, come on. Don't tell me you still hate tomatoes! I thought you grew out of that!"

"Why should she?" Grandma demands. "I never did. Why don't you take that stuff and put it up—"

"Okay, Gram," I say quickly. "Let's go. *Dr. Quinn's* waiting . . ."

I hustle Grandma away before punches are thrown. Inside the sliding doors stand my parents.

"There she is," Dad says, brightening when he sees me. "The first of the Nichols girls actually to finish college!"

I hope Rose and Sarah don't overhear him. Even though it is, technically, true.

"Hi, Dad," I say. "Hi, Mom. Great par—" Then I notice the woman standing next to them. "Dr. Sprague!" I cry. "You came!"

"Of course I came." Dr. Sprague, my college adviser, gives me a hug and a kiss. "I wouldn't have missed it for the world. Look at you, so skinny now! That low-carb thing really worked."

"Aw," I say, "thanks."

"Oh, and here, I even brought you a little going-away present . . . sorry I didn't have time to wrap it," Dr. Sprague says, stuffing something into my hands.

"Oh," my father says. "A book light! Look at that, Lizzie! Bet you'll find a use for that."

"Absolutely," Mom says. "On those trains you'll be taking across Europe. A book light always comes in handy."

"Jesus H. Christ," Grandma says. "Was there a sale on 'em somewhere?"

"Thank you so much, Dr. Sprague," I hurry to say. "That was so thoughtful of you. But you really didn't have to."

"I know," Dr. Sprague says. She looks, as always, coolly professional in a red linen suit. Although I'm not sure that particular red is the right color for her. "I was wondering if we could talk privately for a moment, Elizabeth?"

"Of course," I say. "Mom, Dad, if you'll excuse us. Maybe one of you can help Grandma find the Hallmark Channel? Her show is on."

"Oh God," my mother says with a groan. "Not—"

"You know," Grandma says, "you could learn a lot from Dr.

Quinn, Anne-Marie. She knows how to make soap from a sheep's guts. And she had twins when she was fifty. Fifty!" I hear Grandma cry as Mom leads her toward the den. "I'd like to see you having twins at fifty."

"Is something wrong?" I ask Dr. Sprague, guiding her into my parents' living room, which has changed very little in the four years since I've been living in a dormitory more or less down the street. The pair of armchairs in which my mom and dad read every night—him, spy novels, her, romance—are still slipcovered against Molly the sheepdog's fur. Our childhood photos—me looking fatter in each consecutive one, Rose and Sarah slimmer and more glamorous—still line every inch of available wall space. It's homey and threadbare and plain and I wouldn't trade it for any living room in the world.

With the possible exception of the one in Pam Anderson's Malibu beach house, which I saw last week on *MTV Cribs*. It was surprisingly cute. Considering.

"Didn't you get my messages?" Dr. Sprague wants to know. "I've been calling your cell all morning."

"No," I say. "I mean, I've been busy running around helping Mom set up the party. Why? What's the matter?"

"There's no easy way to say this," Dr. Sprague says with a sigh, "so I'll just say it. When you signed up for the individualized major, Lizzie, you did realize one of the graduation requirements was a written thesis, didn't you?"

I stare at her blankly. "A what?"

"A written thesis." Dr. Sprague, apparently seeing by my expression that I have no idea what she's talking about, sinks with a groan into my dad's armchair. "Oh God. I knew it. Lizzie, didn't you read *any* of the materials from the department?"

"Of course I did," I say defensively. "I mean . . . most of it, anyway." It was all so *boring*.

"Didn't you wonder why, at commencement yesterday, your diploma tube was empty?"

"Well, sure," I say. "But I thought it was because I hadn't finished my language requirement. Which is why I took both summer sessions—"

"But you had to write a thesis, too," Dr. Sprague says, "summarizing, basically, what you learned about your field of concentration. Liz, you haven't officially graduated until you turn in a thesis."

"But"—my lips feel numb—"I'm leaving for England day after tomorrow for a month. To visit my boyfriend."

"Well," Dr. Sprague says with a sigh, "you'll have to write it when you get back, then."

It's my turn to sink into the armchair she's just vacated.

"I can't believe this," I murmur, letting all of my book lights fall into my lap. "My parents put on this huge party—there must be sixty people out there. Some of my teachers from high school are coming. And you're saying I'm not even really a college graduate?"

"Not until you write that thesis," Dr. Sprague says. "I'm sorry, Lizzie. But they're going to want at least fifty pages."

"Fifty pages?" She might as well have said fifteen hundred. How am I going to enjoy having English breakfast in Andrew's king-size bed knowing I have fifty pages hanging over my head? "Oh God." Then a worse thought hits me. I'm no longer the first of the Nichols girls actually to finish college. "*Please* don't mention this to my parents, Dr. Sprague. *Please.*"

"I won't. And I'm really sorry about this," Dr. Sprague says. "I can't imagine how it happened."

"I can," I say miserably. "I should have gone to a small private college. In a huge state university, it's so easy to get lost in the shuffle and turn out not to have actually graduated after all."

"But an education at a small private college would have cost you thousands of dollars, which you'd have to be worrying about paying back now," Dr. Sprague says. "By attending the huge state university in which your father works, you got a superior education for absolutely nothing, and so now, instead of having to get a job right away, you can flit off to England to spend time with—what's his name again?"

"Andrew," I say dejectedly.

"Right. Andrew. Well." Dr. Sprague shoulders her expensive leather purse. "I guess I'd better be going now. I just wanted to drop by to give you the news. If it's any comfort to you, Lizzie, I'm sure your thesis is going to be just *great.*"

"I don't even know what to write it *on,*" I wail.

"A brief history of fashion will suffice," Dr. Sprague says. "To show you learned something while you were here. And," she adds brightly, "you can even do some research while you're in England."

"I could, couldn't I?" I'm starting to feel a little better. The history of fashion? I *love* fashion. And Dr. Sprague is right—England would be the perfect place to research this. They have all sorts of museums there. And I could go to Jane Austen's house! They might even have some of her clothes there! Clothes like they wore in *Pride and Prejudice* on A&E! I *loved* those clothes!

God. This might even turn out to be fun.

I have no idea whether Andrew is going to want to go to Jane Austen's house. But why wouldn't he? He's British. And so is she. Naturally he's going to be interested in his own country's history.

Yeah. Yeah, this is going to be great!

"Thanks for coming by personally to deliver the news, Dr. Sprague," I say, getting up and showing her to the door. "And thanks so much for the book light, too."

"Oh," Dr. Sprague says, "don't mention it. I shouldn't say this, of course, but we're going to miss you around the office. You always made such a splash whenever you'd show up there, in one of your, um"—I notice her gaze drop to the macaroni necklace and my paint-splashed dress—"*unusual* outfits."

"Oh," I say with a smile. "Well, thank you, Dr. Sprague. Any time you want me to find you an unusual outfit of your own, just stop by Vintage to Vavoom, you know, over in Kerrytown—"

Just then my sister Sarah bursts into the living room, her anger over the tomato ratatouille incident apparently forgotten, since she's laughing a little hysterically. She's followed by her husband, Chuck, my other sister, Rose, her husband, Angelo, Maggie, our parents, the Rajghattas, various other party guests, Shari, and Chaz.

"Here she is, here she is," Sarah yells. She, I can tell right away, is drunker than ever. Sarah grabs my arm and starts dragging me toward the landing—the one we used to use as a stage, when we were little, for putting on little plays for our parents. Well, the one Rose and Sarah used to push ME onto, to put on little plays for our parents. And for them.

"Come on, graduate," Sarah says, having a little trouble with the word. "Sing! We all want you and Shari to sing your little song!"

Only it comes out sounding like, *Shing! We all want you and Shari to shing your liddle shong!*

"Uh," I say, noticing that Rose has Shari in a grip about as tight as Sarah's on me. "No."

"Oh, come *on*," Rose cries. "We want to see our baby sister and her little fwiend do their song!" And she throws Shari hard against me, so that the two of us stumble and almost fall across the landing.

"Your sisters," Shari grumbles in my ear, "have the worst cases of sibling envy I have ever seen in my life. I can't believe how much they resent you because you, unlike them, did not become impregnated by a bohunk your sophomore year and have to drop out and stay home all day with drooling sprog."

"Shari!" I am shocked by this assessment of my sisters' lives. Even if it is, technically, accurate.

"All college gwaduates," Rose continues, apparently unaware that she's using baby talk while speaking to adults, "have to shing!"

"Rose," I say. "No. Really. Maybe later. I'm not in the mood."

"All college graduates," Rose repeats, this time with dangerously narrowed eyes, "have to *sing*!"

"In that case," I say, "you're going to have to count me out."

And then I turn to face thirty dumbfounded expressions.

And realize what I've just let slip.

"Kidding," I say quickly.

And everyone laughs. Except for Grandma, who's just come in from the den.

"Sully's not even in this episode," she announces. "Goddammit. Who's going to get an old lady a drink?"

Then she topples over onto the carpet and lets out a gentle snore.

"I love that woman," Shari says to me as everyone rushes forward to attempt to revive my grandmother, completely forgetting about Shari and me.

"So do I," I say. "You have no idea how much."

The ancient Egyptians, who invented both toilet paper and the first known form of birth control (lemon rind as cervical cap, plus alligator dung, which made an effective, if pungent, spermicide), were extremely hygienic, preferring fine linen to any other material, as it was easily washable—a not entirely surprising attitude, considering the alligator dung.

History of Fashion
SENIOR THESIS BY ELIZABETH NICHOLS

3

Anyone who has obeyed nature by transmitting a piece of gossip experiences the explosive relief that accompanies the satisfying of a primary need.

—*Primo Levi (1919–1987), Italian chemist and author*

I thought that was you!" Andrew gushes in that cute accent that had all the girls in McCracken Hall swooning—even if his *th*'s do sound like *f*'s. "What's the matter? You walked right past me!"

"She thought you were a kidnapper," the guy from the Meet Your Party booth explains between guffaws.

"Kidnapper?" Andrew looks from the guy in the booth to me. "What's he talking about?"

"Nothing," I say, grabbing Andrew's arm and rushing him away from the booth. "Nothing, really. Oh my gosh! It's good to see you!"

"Good to see you, too," Andrew says, putting an arm around my waist and giving me a hug—so tight that the epaulets from his jacket dig into my cheek. "You look fucking fantastic! Did you lose weight or something?"

"Just a little," I say modestly. No need for Andrew to know that no starch whatsoever—not so much as a French fry or even a lousy crumb of bread—has touched my lips since he waved good-bye to me last May.

Then Andrew notices me looking at an older bald man who has

come up to us and is smiling politely at me. He is wearing a navy-blue windbreaker and a pair of brown corduroy pants. In August.

This is not a good sign. I'm just saying.

"Oh, right!" Andrew cries. "Liz, this is my dad. Dad, this is Liz!"

Oh, how sweet! He brought his dad to meet me at the airport! Andrew really MUST be taking our relationship seriously if he would go to so much trouble. I've already forgiven him for the jacket.

Well, almost.

"How do you do, Mr. Marshall?" I say, putting out my hand to shake his. "It's so nice to meet you."

"Nice to meet you, too," Andrew's father says with a nice smile. "And please, call me Arthur. Don't mind me, I'm just the chauffeur."

Andrew laughs. So do I. Except—Andrew doesn't have his own car?

Oh, but wait, that's right. Shari said things are different in Europe, that lots of people don't own cars because they're so expensive. And Andrew *is* trying to get by on a teacher's salary . . .

I've got to stop being so judgmental about other cultures. I think it's just cute as can be that Andrew doesn't have a car. So environmentally conscious! Besides, he lives in London. I imagine lots of people in London don't have cars. They take public transportation, or they walk, like New Yorkers. Which is why there are so few fat people in New York. You know, because they're all such healthy walkers. Probably there aren't many fat people in London, either. I mean, look at Andrew. He's thin as a toothpick, practically.

And yet he's got those marvelous grapefruit-size biceps . . .

Although now that I look at them, they seem sort of more orange-size.

But how could anybody really tell beneath a leather jacket, anyway?

It's sweet he has such a close relationship with his dad, too. I mean, that he could ask him to come with him to pick up his girl-friend at Heathrow. My dad is always too busy working to take time out for things like that. But then, his job at the cyclotron is very important, since they're always smashing atoms up there and things. Andrew's dad is a teacher, like Andrew wants to be. Teachers get summers off.

Dr. Rajghatta would laugh his head off if my dad ever asked for a summer off.

Andrew takes my bag, which has wheels, so it's actually the lightest thing I'm carrying. My carry-on is way heavier, since it has all my makeup and beauty supplies in it. I wouldn't mind so much if the airline lost my clothes, but I would totally die if they lost my makeup. I look like a total beast without it. I have eyes that are so small and squinty without liner and mascara I actually resemble a pig . . . even if Shari, who's lived with me for the past four years, swears this isn't true. Shari says I could get away without makeup if I wanted to.

But why would I want to when makeup is such a brilliant and helpful invention for those of us cursed with piggy eyes?

Still, makeup does weigh an awful lot, at least when you have as much of it as I do. Not to mention all of my hairstyling equipment and products. Having long hair is no joke. You have to bring about nine tons of stuff with you in order to keep it properly shampooed, conditioned, tangle-and-frizz-free, dry, shiny, and full of body. Not to mention all the different adapters I had to bring for my hair dryer and curling iron, since Andrew was remarkably unhelpful in describing what British electrical outlets look like ("They look like *outlets*," he kept saying on the phone. Isn't this just like a guy?), so I had to bring every different kind I could find at CVS.

But maybe it's just as well Andrew is pulling the wheelie bag and not carrying my carry-on. Because then if he asks what's inside and why it's so heavy, I'll have to tell him the truth, as I have resolved this relationship will not be founded on artifice, like the one with that guy T.J. I met at the McCracken Hall Movie Night, who turned out to be a practicing warlock—which would have been all right, I totally respect other people's religions . . .

Except that he also turned out to be a chubby-chaser, as I learned when I caught him making out in the quad with Amy De Soto. He tried to tell me his familiar *made* him sleep with her.

Which is why I plan to always tell the truth to Andrew, because T.J. did not give me even that much respect.

But that doesn't mean I'm not going to go out of my way to avoid having to tell him the truth, if I can. Like, there is absolutely no reason he needs to know that the reason my carry-on bag is so heavy is because it's filled with approximately seventy-five billion Clinique cosmetic samples; a container of astringent pads (because I shine so much, thanks to Mom's side of the family); a family-size container of Tums (because I've heard English food isn't necessarily the best); a family-size container of chewable fiber tablets (because ditto); the aforementioned curling iron and hair dryer; the clothes I wore on the plane before I changed into my mandarin dress; a Game Boy loaded with Tetris; the latest Dan Brown (because you can't go on a transatlantic flight with nothing to read); my mini iPod; three book lights; Sun-In for my highlights; all of my pharmaceuticals, such as aspirin, Band-Aids for the blisters I am undoubtedly going to get (from strolling hand in hand with Andrew through the British Museum, soaking in all the art), and prescriptions, including my birth control pills and antibiotic acne medication; and of course the notebook in which I've begun my senior thesis. I had to repack my sewing kit—for emergency clothing repairs—into my suitcase because of the stitch scissors and seam ripper.

There is no reason at this point in our relationship for Andrew to find out I wasn't actually born this good-looking—that a great deal of artifice goes into it. What if he turns out to be one of those guys who like naturally pink-cheeked beauties like Liv Tyler? What kind of chance do I stand against an English rose like that? A girl has to have *some* secrets.

Oh, wait, Andrew is talking to me. He's asking how my flight went. Why is he wearing that jacket? He can't seriously think it looks good, can he?

"The flight was great," I say. I don't tell Andrew about the little girl in the seat next to mine who ignored me throughout the flight when I was just wearing my jeans and T-shirt, with my hair in a ponytail. It wasn't until after I came back from doing my hair and makeup and changing into my silk dress a half hour before we landed that the kid did a double take, and the next thing I knew she was asking shyly, "Excuse me. But are you the actress Jennifer Garner?"

Jennifer Garner! Me! This kid thought *I* was Jennifer Garner!

And okay, she was only like ten or whatever, and wearing a shirt with Kermit the Frog on it (surely she meant this ironically and is not actually a current viewer of *Sesame Street,* as she seemed a bit old for it).

But still! No one has ever mistaken me for a movie star in my life! Let alone a skinny one like Jennifer Garner.

And the thing is, with my makeup on and my hair done, I guess I *do* look a bit like Jennifer Garner . . . you know, if she hadn't quite lost all the baby fat. And had bangs. And was only five feet six.

I guess it never occurred to the kid that Jennifer Garner would hardly be flying coach, by herself, to England. But whatever.

And before I could stop myself, I was going, "Why, yes. I AM Jennifer Garner," because, whatever, I'm never going to see this kid again in my life. Why not give her a thrill?

The kid's eyes practically bugged out, she was so excited.

"Hi," she said, bouncing a little in her seat. "I'm Marnie! I'm your biggest fan!"

"Well, hi, Marnie," I said. "It's nice to meet you."

"Mom!" Marnie turned to whisper to her dozing mother. "It IS Jennifer Garner! I TOLD you!"

And the little girl's drowsy mother looked over at me, her eyes still bleary with sleep, and went, "Oh. Hello."

"Hi," I said, wondering if I sounded Jennifer Garnery enough.

But I guess I did, since the next words out of the kid's mouth were, "I just loved you in *13 Going on 30.*"

"Why, thank you," I said. "I do consider that some of my best work. Besides *Alias,* of course."

"I'm not allowed to stay up late enough to watch that," Marnie said mournfully.

"Oh," I said. "Well, maybe you can see it on DVD."

"Can I have your autograph?" the little girl wanted to know.

"Of course you can," I said, and took the pen and the British Airways cocktail napkin she offered me and scrawled *Best wishes to Marnie, my biggest fan! Love, Jennifer Garner* on it.

The little girl took the napkin reverently, as if she couldn't believe her good fortune. "Thanks!" she said.

I just knew she was going to take that napkin back to America when she got home from her fun European vacation and show it to all of her friends.

I didn't really start feeling bad until then. Because what if one of Marnie's friends has an autograph from the REAL Jennifer Garner and they compare the handwriting? Then Marnie is going to be all suspicious! And she might even ask herself why Jen wasn't with her publicist or even why she was flying commercial. And then she'll realize I wasn't the REAL Jennifer Garner, and that I was lying the whole time. And that could shake her faith in the goodness of humankind. Marnie could develop serious trust issues, like the kind I myself developed when my prom date, Adam Berger, told me he had to go home and paint the ceiling instead of taking me to the after-party, when really he went ahead and attended the after-party with skinny-as-a-stick Melissa Kemplebaum after dropping me off.

But then I told myself that it didn't matter, since I'd never see Marnie again. So who even cared?

Still, I don't mention the incident to Andrew because, seeing as how he's getting a master's in education, I highly doubt he approves of lying to young children.

Also, the truth is, I am feeling kind of sleepy, even though it is eight o'clock in the morning in England, and I am wondering how far it is to Andrew's apartment, and if there's any chance at all he might have some diet Coke there. Because I could totally use one.

"Oh, not too far at all," is what Andrew's dad, Mr. Marshall, says when I ask Andrew how far he lives from the airport.

It's kind of strange that Andrew's dad answered, and not Andrew. But then again, Mr. Marshall's a teacher and answering questions is basically his job. He probably can't help it, even when he's off duty.

It's such a good thing there are men like Andrew and his dad who are willing to undertake the education of our youth. The Marshalls are truly a dying breed. I'm so glad I'm with Andrew and not, say, Chaz, who chose to pursue a philosophy degree solely so that he could argue more effectively with his parents. How is *that* supposed to help future generations?

Whereas Andrew has purposefully chosen a career that will never make him much money, but that will ensure that young minds don't go unmolded.

And isn't that the noblest thing you've ever heard of?

It's a long, long way to Mr. Marshall's car. We have to go through all of these hallways, where, along the walls, there are advertisements for products I've never heard of. Chaz had been complaining, last time he'd gone to visit his friend Luke—the one with the château—about the Americanization of Europe and how you couldn't go anywhere without seeing a Coca-Cola ad.

But I don't see any Americanization here in England. So far. I don't see anything even vaguely American. Not even a Coke machine.

Not that this is a bad thing. I'm just saying. Although a diet Coke wouldn't be so bad right about now.

Andrew and his dad are talking about the weather, and how lucky I am to have come at a time when it's so nice out. But when we step out of the building and into the parking garage, I realize it's maybe sixty degrees, at most, and that the sky—what I can see of it at the end of the garage level—is gray and overcast.

If this is good weather, what do the British consider bad? And, granted, it's certainly cold enough for a leather jacket. But that doesn't excuse the fact that Andrew is wearing one. Surely there's some rule somewhere—like the one about no white pants before Memorial Day—about no leather in August.

We're almost to the car—a small red compact, exactly what I'd expect a middle-aged teacher to drive—when I hear a shriek, and look around to see the little girl from the plane standing next to an SUV with her mother and an older couple I can only assume are her grandparents.

"There she is!" Marnie is screaming, pointing at me. "Jennifer Garner! Jennifer Garner!"

I keep walking, my head down, trying to ignore her. But both Andrew and his father are looking over at her, bemused smiles on their faces. Andrew does look a bit like his dad. Will he, too, be totally bald when he's fifty? Is baldness a trait passed on by the mother's side of the family or the father's? Why didn't I take a single bio course while I was designing my own major? I could have squeezed in at least one . . .

"Is that child speaking to you?" Mr. Marshall asks me.

"Me?" I glance over my shoulder, pretending to notice for the first time that a small child is shrieking at me from across the garage.

"Jennifer Garner! It's me! Marnie! From the plane! Remember?"

I smile and wave at Marnie. She flushes with pleasure and grabs her mother's arm.

"See?" she cries. "I told you! It really *is* her!"

Marnie waves some more. I wave back while Andrew wrestles my suitcase into the small trunk, swearing a bit. Since he's been wheeling it along the whole time, he had no idea how heavy it is until he bent to lift it.

But really, a month is a long time. I don't see how I could have packed less than ten pairs of shoes. Shari even said she was proud of me for being sensible enough not to bring my lace-up platform espadrilles. Although I did manage to squeeze them in at the last minute before I left.

"Why is that child calling you Jennifer Garner?" Mr. Marshall wants to know as he, too, waves at Marnie, whose grandparents, or whoever they are, still haven't succeeded in herding her into the car.

"Oh," I say, feeling myself begin to blush. "We sat next to each other on the plane. It's just a little game we were playing, to pass time on the flight."

"How kind of you," Mr. Marshall says, waving even more energetically now. "Not all young people realize how important it is to treat children with respect and dignity instead of condescension. It's so important to set a good example for the younger generation, especially when one considers how unstable many of today's family units really are."

"That's so true," I say in what I hope sounds like a respectful and dignified manner.

"Christ," Andrew says. He's just tried to pick up my carry-on bag from where I've set it on the ground. "What have you got in here, Liz? A dead body?"

"Oh," I say, my respectful and dignified demeanor threatening to crumble, "just a few necessities."

"I'm sorry my chariot isn't more stylish," Mr. Marshall says, opening the driver's door to his car. "It's certainly not what you're used to, I'm sure, back in America. But I hardly use it, since I walk to the school where I teach most days."

I am instantly charmed by the vision of Mr. Marshall strolling down a tree-lined country lane in a herringbone jacket with leather elbow patches—rather than the extremely uninspired windbreaker he is currently wearing—and perhaps a cocker spaniel or two nipping at his heels.

"Oh, it's fine," I say about his car. "Mine isn't much bigger."

I wonder why he's just standing there by the door, instead of getting in, until he goes, "After you, er, Liz."

He wants *me* to drive? But . . . I just got here! I don't even know my way around!

Then I realize he isn't holding open the driver's door at all . . . it's the passenger side. The steering wheel is on the right side of the car.

Of course! We're in England!

I laugh at my own mistake and sit down in the front seat.

Andrew slams down the trunk and comes around to see me sitting in the passenger seat. He looks at his dad and says, "What, I'm supposed to sit in the boot, then?"

"Mind your manners, Andy," Mr. Marshall says. It seems so strange to hear Andrew called Andy. He is such an Andrew to me. But evidently not to his family.

Although truthfully, in that jacket, he looks a bit more like an Andy than an Andrew.

"Ladies in the front seat," Mr. Marshall goes on with a smile at me. "And gentlemen in the back."

"Liz, I thought you were a feminist," Andrew says (only it comes out sounding like, *Liz, I fought you were a feminist*). "Are you going to stand for this kind of treatment?"

"Oh," I say. "Of course. Andrew should sit in front, he's got longer legs—"

"I won't hear of it," Mr. Marshall says. "You'll muss your pretty Chinese dress, climbing about." Then he shuts my car door, firmly, for me.

Next thing I know, he's come around the right side and is holding the driver's-side seat back for Andrew to crawl behind. There's a brief argument I can't really hear, and then Andrew appears. I don't really know any other word I can use to describe the expression on Andrew's face except peevish.

But I feel bad for even *thinking* Andrew might be feeling peevish about me getting to sit in the front seat. Most likely he's just embarrassed about not having his own car to pick me up in. Yes, that's probably it. Poor thing. He probably thinks I'm holding him to American standards of capitalist materialism! I'll have to find some way to assure him that I find his poverty extremely sexy, seeing as how all the sacrifices he's making, he's making for the children.

Not Andrew Jr., Henry, Stella, and Beatrice, of course. I mean the children of the world, the ones he'll be teaching someday.

Wow. Just thinking about all the little lives Andrew's going to improve with his sacrifices in the teaching profession is making me kind of horny.

Mr. Marshall climbs into the driver's seat and smiles at me. "Ready?" he asks cheerfully.

"Ready," I say, and I'm filled with a spurt of excitement despite my jet lag. England! I'm in England at last! I'm about to be driven along the English countryside, into London! Maybe I'll even see some sheep!

Before we're able to pull out, however, an SUV drives up behind us, and a back window powers down. Marnie, my little friend from the plane, leans out the window to yell, "Good-bye, Jennifer Garner!"

I roll down my own window and wave. "Bye, Marnie!"

Then the SUV pulls away, Marnie beaming happily in the back.

"Who in heaven," Mr. Marshall asks as he backs out, "is this Jennifer Garner?"

"Just some American film star," Andrew says before I can say anything.

Just some American film star? Just some American film star who happens to look exactly like your girlfriend! I want to shriek. *Enough so that little girls on airplanes want her autograph!*

But I manage to keep my mouth shut for once, because I don't want Andrew to feel inadequate, knowing he's dating a Jennifer Garner look-alike. That could be really intimidating, you know, for a guy. Even an American one.

In contrast to Egyptian costume, in which there was a distinct division in style between the sexes, the Greek costume during this same period did not vary between men and women. Large rectangles of cloth of different sizes were draped across the body and fastened only with a decorative brooch.

This garment, which is called a toga, went on to become a favorite costume of college fraternity parties, for reasons this author cannot fathom, as the toga is neither flattering nor comfortable, especially when worn with control-top underwear.

History of Fashion
SENIOR THESIS BY ELIZABETH NICHOLS

Men have always detested women's gossip because they suspect the truth: their measurements are being taken and compared.

—Erica Jong (1942–), U.S. educator and author

I don't see any sheep. It turns out Heathrow airport isn't exactly that far out in the country. As if I can't tell I'm not in Michigan anymore from the way the houses look (many of them are attached, like in that movie *The Snapper* . . . which, come to think of it, was actually set in Ireland, but oh well), I definitely know it from billboards that flash by us. I can't tell, in many cases, what the product is that they're trying to sell—one of them shows a woman in her underwear with the word *Vodafone* beneath her, which could be an ad for a phone-sex service.

But it could just as easily be an ad for panties.

But when I ask, neither Andrew nor his father is able to tell me which it is, since the word *panties* causes them to dissolve into peals of laughter.

I don't mind that they find me so (unintentionally) hilarious, though, since it means Andrew's mind has been taken off being in the backseat.

When we finally turn onto the street I recognize as Andrew's from the care packages I've been sending him all summer—boxes filled with his favorite American candy, Necco wafers, and Marlboro Lights, his preferred brand of cigarettes (though I don't smoke myself, and assume Andrew will quit well before the first baby is born)—I'm feeling much better about things than I had been back in the parking garage. That's because the sun has finally put in an appearance, peeking shyly out from behind the clouds, and because Andrew's street looks so nice and Europeany, with its clean sidewalks, flowering trees, and old-fashioned town houses. It's like something out of that movie *Notting Hill*.

I have to admit, it's something of a relief: I had been wavering between picturing Andrew's "flat" as being as high tech as Hugh Grant's in *About a Boy*, or a garret, like in *A Little Princess* (which looked very cute once that old guy fixed it up for her), only in a seedier part of town, overlooking a wharf. I'd just been assuming I wouldn't be able to go walking around his neighborhood by myself after dark for fear of being set upon by heroin addicts. Or Gypsies.

I'm glad to see it's actually somewhere between the two extremes.

We are, as Mr. Marshall assures me, just a mile away from Hampstead Heath, the park where a lot of famous stuff happened, none of which I actually remember at this current time, and where people go today to have picnics and fly kites.

I'm happily surprised to see that Andrew lives in such a nice, upscale neighborhood. I didn't think teachers made enough to rent apartments in town houses. No doubt his flat is at the top of one—just like Mickey Rooney's in *Breakfast at Tiffany's*! Maybe I'll get to meet Andrew's wacky but bighearted neighbors. Maybe I can have them—and Andrew's parents, to thank Mr. Marshall for the ride from the airport—over for a small supper to show my American hospitality. I can make Mom's spaghetti due (pronounced doo-ay). It tastes complicated, but nothing could be simpler to make. It's just pasta, garlic, olive oil, hot pepper flakes, and Parmesan cheese. I'm sure even England would have all the ingredients.

"Well, here we are," Mr. Marshall says, pulling into a parking space in front of one of the brown-brick town houses and turning off the ignition. "Home sweet home."

I'm a little surprised that Mr. Marshall is getting out with us. I would have thought he'd have dropped us off and gone on to his own house somewhere—well, wherever Andrew's family lives, a family that consists, from what I remember him saying in his e-mails, of a teacher father, a social worker mother, two younger brothers, and a collie.

But maybe Mr. Marshall wants to help us with my bags, seeing as how Andrew probably lives on the top floor of the charming town house we're parked in front of.

Except that when we get to the top of the long flight of steps that leads up to the front door, it's Mr. Marshall who takes out a key and unlocks it.

And is greeted by the inquisitive gold and white muzzle of a beautiful collie.

"Hello," Mr. Marshall calls into what I can clearly see is not the foyer of an apartment house, but the entrance to a single-family home. "We're here!"

I am lugging my carry-on bag while Andrew pulls my wheelie bag up the stairs, not even bothering to lift it, but dragging it up one step at a time—*thonk, thonk, thonk*. But I swear I nearly drop the bag—hair dryer be damned—when I see that dog.

"Andrew," I whisper, whirling around, since he's coming up the steps behind me. "Do you live . . . at home? With your parents?"

Because, unless he's dog-sitting, that's the only explanation I can think of for what I'm seeing. And even that isn't a very good one.

"Of course," Andrew says, looking annoyed. "What did you think?"

Only it comes out sounding like, *What did you fink?*

"I thought you lived in an apartment," I say. I am really not trying to sound accusatory. I'm not. I'm just . . . surprised. "A flat, I mean. You told me, in school last May, that you were getting a flat for the summer when you got back to England."

"Oh, right," Andrew says. Since we've paused on the steps, he seems to think (fink) this is a good time for a cigarette break and pulls out a pack and lights up.

Well, it *was* a long trip from the airport. And his father *did* tell him he couldn't smoke in the car.

"Yeah, the flat didn't work out. My mate—you remember, I wrote you about him? He was going to loan me his place, since he got a gig on a pearl farm in Australia. But then he met a bird and decided not to go after all, so I moved in with the parentals. Why? Is that a problem?"

Is that a problem? IS THAT A PROBLEM? All of my fantasies about Andrew bringing me breakfast in bed—his king-size bed, with the thousand-count sheets—crumble into bits and float away. I won't be making spaghetti due for the neighbors and Andrew's parents. Well, maybe his parents, but it won't be the same if they just come down the stairs for it, as opposed to from their own place . . .

Then I have a thought that causes my blood to run cold.

"But, Andrew," I say, "I mean, how are you—how are you and I going to—if your parents are around?"

"Ah, don't worry about that," Andrew says, blowing smoke out of one side of his mouth in a manner I have to admit to finding thrillingly sexy. No one back home smokes . . . not even Grandma, since that time she lit the living-room carpet on fire. "This is London, you know, not Bible Belt America. We're cool about that kind of thing here. And my parents are the coolest."

"Right," I say. "Sorry. I was just, you know. Sort of surprised. But it really doesn't matter. As long as we can be together. Your parents really won't mind? About us sharing a bedroom, I mean?"

"Yeah," Andrew says, sort of distractedly, giving my suitcase a yank. *Thonk.* "About that. I don't actually have a bedroom in this house. See, my parents moved here with my brothers this past year, while I was in America. I'd told them I wouldn't be coming home summers, you know, but that was before I had those troubles with my student visa . . . Anyway, they figured, you know, I'd basically moved out, so they only got a three-bedroom. But don't worry, I'm—how do you say it in the States? Right, bunking up—I'm bunking up with my brother Alex—"

I look at Andrew on the step below me. He's so tall that even when he's standing below me, I still have to tilt my chin up a little to look into his gray-green eyes.

"Oh, Andrew," I say, my heart melting. "Your other brother's given up his room for me? He shouldn't have!"

A strange look passes across Andrew's face.

"He didn't," Andrew says. "He wouldn't. You know kids." He gives me a crooked grin. "But don't worry, though. My mom's a whiz at do-it-yourself projects, and she's rigged up a loft bed for you—well, for me, actually. But you can use it while you're here."

I raise my eyebrows. "A loft bed?"

"Yeah, it's fantastic. She's made the whole thing out of MDF, in the laundry room. Right over the washer/dryer!" Andrew, seeing my expression, adds, "But don't worry. She's strung a curtain up between the laundry room and the kitchen. You'll have plenty of privacy. No one goes back there anyway, except the dog. That's where his food bowl is."

Dog? Food bowl? So . . . instead of sleeping with my boyfriend, I'll be sleeping with the family dog. And its food bowl.

That's okay, though. That's fine. Educators like Andrew's dad—and social workers like his mom—don't make a lot of money, and real estate in England is expensive. I'm lucky they have any room at all for me! I mean, they don't even have a room for their own eldest child, and they've found a way to squeeze in a bed for me!

And why would one of Andrew's brothers give up his room for

me? Just because back home I always had to give up MY room for whatever out-of-town guest was coming to stay doesn't mean Andrew's family necessarily does things the same way . . .

Especially since I'm not even an important visitor. I'm only Andrew's future wife, after all.

Well, in my mind.

"Come on now," Andrew says. "Get a move on. I have to change for work."

I'm about to climb another step when I freeze all over again. "Work? You have to go to work? *Today?*"

"Yeah." At least he has the grace to look apologetic. "But it's no big deal, Liz, I just have to do the lunch and dinner shifts—"

"You're . . . you're a *waiter?*"

I don't mean to sound pejorative. I don't. I have nothing against people who work in restaurants, I really don't. I did my stint in food service just like everybody else, wore the polyester pants with pride.

But . . .

"What happened to your internship?" I ask. "The one at the prestigious primary school for gifted children?"

"Internship?" Andrew flicks ash off his cigarette. It falls in the rosebushes below. But ash is often used as fertilizer so this doesn't necessarily count as littering. "Oh, *that* turned out to be a disaster of epic proportions. Did you know they weren't going to pay me? Not a fucking cent."

"But—" I swallow. I can hear birds singing in the treetops along the street. At least the birds sound the same here as they do back in Michigan. "That's why it's called an internship. Your pay is all the experience you get."

"Well, experience won't pay for pints with my mates, will it?" Andrew jokes. "And of course it turned out they had two thousand applications for the position . . . a position that doesn't even pay! It's not like it is back in the States, either, where you've got an edge over everybody else if you've got a British accent, since you Yanks are convinced anyone who says 'tomahto' over 'tomato' is somehow more intelligent . . . The truth is, Lizzie, I didn't even bother applying. What would have been the point?"

I just stare at him. What happened to taking on a job for the pure challenge and experience of it? What happened to teaching the children to read?

"Besides," he adds, "I want to work with *real* kids, not posh little geniuses . . . kids who actually *need* positive male role models in their lives . . ."

"So," I say, my heart lifting, "you applied to teach in some inner-city schools for the summer?"

"Oh, fuck no," Andrew says. "Those positions paid shit. The only way you can make ends meet in this town is in food service. And I've got the best shift, eleven to eleven. In fact, I've got to run right now if I'm going to make it there in time . . ."

But I've just gotten here! I want to cry. *I've just gotten here, and you're leaving? Not just leaving, but leaving me alone with your family, whom I've never met—for TWELVE HOURS?*

But I don't say any of these things. I mean, here Andrew is, inviting me to stay, rent-free, in his family's home with him, and I'm freaking out over his having to work—and the *kind* of work he's doing. What kind of girlfriend am I, anyway?

Except I guess my expression must have given away the fact that I am less than enthusiastic about the situation, since Andrew says, reaching out to wrap an arm around my waist and bringing me up close against him, "Look, don't worry, Liz. I'll see you tonight when I get off work."

Suddenly he's grinding the cigarette beneath his heel and his lips are against my throat.

"And when I do," he murmurs, "I'm going to show you the best time you ever had. All right?"

It's very hard to think properly when a cute guy with a British accent is nuzzling your neck.

Not that there's anything to think about, really. My boyfriend obviously adores me. I'm the luckiest girl in the world.

"Well," I say, "that sounds—"

And the next thing I know, Andrew's mouth is on mine, and we're making out on the front steps of his parents' house.

I hope the Marshalls don't have any easily startled little old ladies as neighbors, and that if they do, they aren't actually looking out their windows right now.

"Fuck," Andrew breaks off our kiss to say, "I have to go to work. But look, I'll see you tonight, yeah?"

My lips are still tingling from where his razor stubble chafed them. They're probably about as swollen as Angelina Jolie's by now, from all the pressure on them.

Not that I mind. I don't have a lot of experience in the kissing department.

But I think Andrew may just be the best kisser in the world.

Plus I can't help noticing that there appears to be something going on in the vicinity of the crotch of Andrew's jeans that I also like very much.

"Do you really have to go to work?" I ask him. "Can't you blow it off?"

"Not today. But I've got tomorrow off," he says. "There's something I've got to do in the city. But after that, we'll do whatever you like. Oh God." He kisses me a few more times, then rests his forehead against mine. "I can't believe I'm doing this. You'll be all right, yeah?"

I stare at him, thinking how good-looking he is, in spite of the hideous jacket, and how sweet and unassuming he is as well. I mean, he's just so determined to follow in his father's footsteps and teach all those children to read. Only he's not going to settle for just any situation. He's waiting for the right one to come along . . .

I am so lucky that I was taking a shower at the *exact* moment that girl's potpourri caught on fire and that Andrew happened to have been the R.A. on duty at the time.

I think of the first time he kissed me, outside McCracken Hall (with me in my towel and him in those Levi's that were faded in just the right places), his breath smoky—but from cigarettes, not the fire—and hot in my mouth.

I remember all the phone calls and e-mails between us since. I remember the fact that I blew all my money on a plane ticket to England, since I'm not moving to New York with Shari and Chaz, so I can live at home and be near Andrew in the fall instead.

And I say with a big smile, "I'll be fine."

"Cheers, then," Andrew says. And gives me one last kiss.

And then he turns around and leaves.

One of the earliest known female arbiters of fashion was the Byzantine empress Theodora, the daughter of a bear trainer who beat out thousands of other girls for the hand of Emperor Justinian. Rumor had it she was helped in no small part during the talent portion of the Empress Hunt by her background in dancing and acrobatics.

Though it took a special act of legislation to allow Justinian to marry one of such lowly stature, Theodora proved herself a worthy empress, commissioning two royal spies to sneak into China and steal silkworms so that she could drape herself in the manner in which she felt she could become accustomed. If Theodora couldn't get to Chanel, well, she just had Chanel brought to her.

History of Fashion
SENIOR THESIS BY ELIZABETH NICHOLS

5

"I never repeat anything." That is the ritual phrase of society
people, by which the gossip is reassured every time.
—*Marcel Proust (1871–1922), French novelist, critic, and essayist*

I'm here! I'm finally here, in England!

And okay, it's not *exactly* what I'd expected. I really did
think Andrew had his own place.

But it's not like he LIED to me.

And maybe this is better than if the two of us had just holed
up in his flat, making sweet love all night and day. This way, I'll be
forced to interact with his family. We can sort of test each other
out, the Marshalls and I, and see if we are compatible. After all, you
don't want to marry into a family that hates you.

Plus, while Andrew's out working, I can start my thesis. Maybe
one of the Marshalls will let me borrow a computer. And I can do
some research at the British Museum. Or whatever it's called.

Yes, honestly, it's much better this way. I'll really get to know Andrew and his family, and I'll get a good solid start on my thesis.
Maybe I can even get it done before I get home! That would be so
great! My parents will never even know there was a slight delay in
my actual graduation.

Mmm . . . I smell something coming from the kitchen. I wonder
what it is. It smells good . . . sort of. It doesn't smell a bit like the
scrambled eggs and bacon that are my mom's specialty. Really, it's

just so kind of Mrs. Marshall to make breakfast for me. I told her she didn't have to . . . She seems so nice, with her sandy-brown bob. She told me to call her Tanya—though of course I never will. Her eyes got kind of wide when I walked in and Mr. Marshall introduced me. But whatever it was that was freaking her out about me, she didn't let on.

I certainly hope she didn't guess about my underwear. Or lack thereof. What if THAT'S why she'd stared at me like that? She's probably thinking, Of all the girls in America for my son to bring home, he had to pick a slut. I knew I should have worn something different getting off the plane. And I'm so cold in this stupid dress, I know I must have had some nipple action going on. Maybe I should change into something a little less . . . thin. Yes, that's what I'll do. I'll change into some jeans and my beaded sweater set—even though I was saving that for evenings, when I thought it might be a bit cooler . . .

Little did I know it's evening cool here all day long.

Okay. Wow, whatever Mrs. M is cooking in there sure smells—strongly. I wonder what it is? Also why it seems familiar.

You know, my MDF bed isn't so bad. It's kind of cute, really. It's like the kind of bed Ty Pennington would make for some kid who has cancer on that *Extreme Makeover: Home Edition* show.

Only his version would be shaped like a heart ventricle, or a spaceship, or something.

Okay, there, I'm ready. Just give the hair a little toss, and—hmm, too bad there's not a mirror in here. Oh well, British people clearly aren't as vain as we are in the U.S. Who cares if my mascara is smudged or whatever? I'm sure I look fine. Okay. I'll just throw the curtain back, and—

"Oh my," Mrs. Marshall says brightly. "I thought you were going to have a bit of a lie-down."

Had *that* been what she'd been saying to me a little while ago? I couldn't really understand her. Oh, *why* did Andrew have to go off to work? I clearly need a translator.

"I'm sorry," I apologize. "I'm just way too excited to sleep!"

"Is this your first time in England, then?" Mrs. M wants to know.

"It's my first time outside of the U.S. ever," I say. "Whatever you're cooking smells delicious." This is a slight lie. What she's cooking just . . . smells. Still, it will *probably* be delicious. "Is there anything I can do to help?"

"Oh no, dear, I think I've got it under control. How are you liking your bed, then? Not too hard? It's all right?"

"Oh, it's great," I say, slipping onto a stool at the end of the kitchen counter. I can't tell what's sizzling in the pans on the stove in front of her because they all have lids. But it sure smells . . . a lot. The kitchen is tiny, more of a galley than an actual kitchen. There is a window at the end of it that looks out onto a bright, sunlit garden bursting with rose blossoms. Mrs. M looks like a rose herself, all pink-cheeked and shiny in jeans and a peasant top.

Although the peasant top doesn't appear to be from this season's crop of them. In fact, it might actually be a peasant top from all the way back when peasant tops first made an appearance in serf-free society, way back in the days of Haight-Ashbury!

Now I know why Andrew thinks it's okay to go around in a break-dancing jacket. But while some vintage pieces—like Mrs. Marshall's blouse—are great, other examples—such as Andrew's jacket—aren't. Clearly the Marshall family needs to be brought into the vintage-know.

It's a good thing they have me to help. I'll have to be very sensitive to the fact that they don't have a lot of money to spend on clothes. But I'm living proof you don't have to spend a lot in order to look great. I got this sweater set on eBay for twenty dollars! And my stretch Levi's are from Sears. And okay, they came from the juniors department . . . but how thrilled was I at being able to *fit* into something from the juniors department?

Not that, in our weight-obsessed society, this is something to brag about. Why should women have to fit into child sizes in order to be considered desirable? That is both sick and depressing.

Although . . . they're nines! I fit into a nine! I never fit into a nine, even back when I was the age I was supposed to wear one.

"That's a very pretty top," Mrs. M says about my sweater set.

"Thanks," I say. "I was just admiring yours!"

She laughs when she hears this. "What, this old thing? It must be thirty years old if it's a day. Very likely older."

"That's neat," I say. "I love old clothes."

This is so cool! Andrew's mother and I are bonding. Maybe later we can go shopping, just Mrs. M and me. She probably doesn't have many opportunities for girl talk, having three sons and all. Maybe we can get manis and pedis and go to Harrods for champagne! Wait—do people in England get manis and pedis?

"I just can't tell you how great it is to meet you, after hearing about you for so long," I say. I'm not trying to suck up, either. I really mean it. "I'm so excited to be here!"

"How nice," Mrs. Marshall says, looking genuinely pleased for me.

I can see that her fingernails are square and strong-looking and completely without polish. Well, she probably doesn't have time for frivolities like manicures, being a busy social worker. "And what do you look forward to seeing most here, then?"

For some reason my mind flashes to the picture of Andrew's naked ass. I can't believe I thought of that! It must be the jet lag.

I say, "Oh, Buckingham Palace, of course. And the British Museum." I don't mention that the only parts of the museum I'm interested in touring are the rooms where they keep the historical costumes. If they even have any rooms like that. I can see boring old art back home anytime I want. I'm moving to New York City after Andrew gets his master's, anyway. He already agreed.

"Oh, and the Tower of London." Because I hear that's where they keep all the fancy jewels. "And . . . oh, Jane Austen's house."

"Oh, you're a fan, are you?" Mrs. Marshall looks a bit surprised. Clearly none of Andrew's previous girlfriends had such sophisticated taste in literature. "Which one's your favorite, then?"

"Oh, the A&E version with Colin Firth, of course," I say. "Although the costumes in the Gwyneth Paltrow one were really nice, too."

Mrs. Marshall looks at me a bit oddly—maybe she can't understand my Midwestern accent any easier than I can understand her British one. But I'm really trying to enunciate clearly. Then I realize what she means and say, "Oh, you mean of the *books*? I don't know. They're all so good." Except there aren't nearly enough descriptions of what the characters are wearing.

Mrs. Marshall laughs and asks, "Would you like to help yourself to some tea? I'm certain you must be parched after your trip."

What I'd really like, of course, is a diet Coke. But when I ask if the Marshalls have any, Mrs. Marshall gives me another odd look and says she'll have to pick some up at "the market."

"Oh no," I say, mortified. "Really, it's all right. I'll just have some tea."

Mrs. Marshall looks relieved. "Oh, good," she says. "Because I don't like the thought of your putting all those nasty, unnatural chemicals into your body. They can't be good for you."

I smile at her, even though I have no idea what she's talking about. Diet Coke does not contain nasty chemicals. It contains lovely and delicious carbonation, caffeine, and aspartame. What's unnatural about that?

But I'm in England now, so I will do as the English do. I pour myself some tea from the ceramic pot sitting by the electric kettle and, at Mrs. M's urging, put milk in it, because that is apparently how British people drink it, instead of with honey or lemon.

I'm surprised to discover that it's actually quite good that way. Which I mention out loud.

"What's good?" A sandy-haired boy, maybe fifteen or sixteen, wearing a dark-rinse jean jacket with acid-washed jeans (ouch— although beneath the jacket he's got on a Killers T-shirt, which redeems him a bit), has come into the kitchen, then freezes when he sees me.

"Who's *that*?" he wants to know.

"What do you mean, who's that?" Mrs. M demands tartly. "This is Liz, your brother Andy's girlfriend from America—"

"Oh, c'mon, Mum," Alex says, grinning. "What do I look like? That's not her. She's not—"

"Alex, this is Liz," Mrs. M interrupts even more tartly. She doesn't look as much like a rose now. Or I guess she does, just one whose thorns are showing. "Say hello to her properly, please."

Alex, looking sheepish, sticks his right hand out. I shake it.

"Sorry," he says. "Pleased to meet you. It's just that Andy said—"

"Alex, please take this out to the table," Mrs. M says, shoving a handful of knives and forks at her youngest son. "Breakfast will be ready soon."

"Breakfast? It's nearly time for lunch, isn't it?"

"Well, Liz hasn't had breakfast yet, so that's what we're having."

Alex takes the silverware from his mother and goes out into the dining room. Geronimo, which is what they named their collie— isn't that the cutest?—who had been pressing against the side of my legs the whole time I'd been sitting down, trails after him, apparently in hopes of coming across a stray piece of food.

"Do you have any brothers, Liz?" Mrs. M asks me, all prickliness gone now that her son has left the room.

"No," I say. "Just two older sisters."

"Your mother was very fortunate," Mrs. M says. "Boys are quite a handful." Then she turns off the oven and calls, "Alex, tell your dad breakfast is ready. Give a shout to Alistair as well."

Andrew, Alistair, and Alexander. I love the names Andrew's parents picked out for their three boys! How cute to give them all *A* names . . . just like Paul Anka did, only he had daughters—Alexandra, Amanda, Alicia, Anthea, and Amelia.

And how cute that they all call me Liz and not Lizzie. Nobody ever calls me Liz. Nobody except Andrew, of course. Not that I ever told him to. He just . . . does.

"Well," Mrs. Marshall says, smiling at me. "Why don't you have a seat, Liz? Then we can eat."

"Let me help you bring things to the table," I say, sliding down from my stool.

But Mrs. Marshall shoos me out of the kitchen, saying she doesn't need any help. I go into the dining room—which is really just part of an L off the living room, where the family's dining table is. Geronimo is already sitting next to the chair at the head of the table, alert for any scraps that might fall his way.

"Where should I sit?" I ask Alex, who, in typical teen fashion—I guess it's universal—shrugs.

Just then Mr. Marshall walks in and pulls out a chair for me with gallant flair. I thank him and sit in it, trying to remember when my own father ever pulled out a chair for me, and failing.

"Here we are," Mrs. Marshall says, emerging from the kitchen with several platters that are steaming. "In honor of Andy's friend Liz's first visit to this country, a genuine English country breakfast!"

I sit up a bit straighter in my seat to show how excited and flattered I am. "Thank you so much," I say. "You really didn't have to go to so much—"

Then I see what's on the platters.

"Tomato ratatouille," Mrs. Marshall says proudly. "Your favorite! And our own very English interpretation of the same dish, stewed tomatoes. Also stuffed tomatoes, and an egg and tomato omelet. Andy told me how much you love tomatoes, Liz. I hope this meal will make you feel right at home!"

Oh. My. God.

"Liz?" Mrs. Marshall, I realize, is looking down at me with concern on her rosy face. "Are you all right, dear? You look a little . . . peaked."

"I'm fine," I say. And take a big gulp of my milky tea. "It looks great, Mrs. Marshall. Thanks so much for going to all this trouble. You didn't have to."

"It was my pleasure," Mrs. Marshall says, beaming as she takes a seat in a chair across the table from mine. "And please, call me Tanya."

"Right. Tanya," I say, hoping my eyes don't look as wet as they feel. How can he have made such a mistake? Did he not even READ my e-mails? Was he not even *listening* that night of the fire?

"Who's missing?" Mrs. Marshall asks, looking at the empty chair across from Andrew.

"Alistair," Alex says, reaching for a piece of toast. Toast! I can eat toast. No, wait, I can't. Not if I want to stay a junior size nine. Oh God. I'm going to have to eat something. The egg and tomato omelet. Maybe the egg will drown out the taste of the tomato.

"ALISTAIR!" Mr. Marshall bellows.

From somewhere deep in the house, a male voice calls, "Oy! I'm coming!"

I take a bite of the omelet. It's good. You can barely taste the—

Oh no. Yes you can, actually.

The thing is, it was an honest mistake. About the tomatoes, I mean. Anyone could get something like that mixed up. Even a soul mate.

And, I mean, at least he remembered I'd *mentioned* tomatoes. He may not have remembered what I actually said about them. But he obviously knows I said *something*.

And it's not like he's not busy, teaching the children to read and all.

And waitering, apparently.

Seeing that no one is looking at me, I knock some of the omelet on my plate and down onto the napkin on my lap. Then I look over at Geronimo, who has left Mr. Marshall's side, apparently sensing he's not going to be scoring any scraps over there.

The collie meets my gaze.

Next thing I know, I have dog nose in my crotch.

"What's this now?" A boy who must be Andrew's second-youngest brother, Alistair, appears in the doorway. Unlike his mom and two brothers, Alistair's hair is bright, coppery red—probably the same color his dad's had been, before he lost it all . . . judging from his eyebrows, anyway.

"Oh, hullo, Ali," Mrs. Marshall says. "Take your seat. We're having a traditional English breakfast to welcome Andrew's friend Liz from America."

"Hi," I say, looking up at the redhead, who appears to be just a year or two younger than me. He is dressed from head to toe in Adidas apparel . . . Adidas warm-up pants, jacket, T-shirt, and shoes. Perhaps they've asked for his personal endorsement. "I'm Lizzie. Nice to meet you."

Alistair stares at me for a minute. Then he bursts out laughing.

"Right!" he says. "Come off it, Mum. What kind of joke is this supposed to be, anyway?"

"It's not a joke at all, Alistair," Mr. Marshall says in a cold voice.

"But," Alistair bleats, "she can't be Liz! Andy said Liz is a fatty!"

Little is known about costume from the period of the second century until well into the 700s, thanks to barbarian invasions by the Goths, Visigoths, Ostrogoths, Huns, and Franks. We do know, thanks to these invasions, that few people had time to think about fashion, as they were busy fleeing for their lives.

It isn't until Charlemagne came to rule in 800 that we have any sort of detailed description of wardrobe at the time, which included cross-gartered trousers that came to be known as braies, or breeches, that garment so well beloved by historical romance authors around the world.

History of Fashion
SENIOR THESIS BY ELIZABETH NICHOLS

6

But speak the truth, and all nature and all spirits help you with
unexpected furtherance. Speak the truth, and all things alive or
brute are vouchers, and the very roots of the grass underground
there do seem to stir and move to bear you witness.

—Ralph Waldo Emerson (1803–1882),
U.S. essayist, poet, and philosopher

It takes five rings before Shari answers. For a minute I'm worried she won't pick up at all. What if she's asleep? I know it's
only nine o'clock after all, Europe time, but what if she hasn't
adjusted to the time difference as well as I have? Even though she's
been over here longer. She was supposed to have gotten to Paris two
days ago, stayed one night in a hotel there, then traveled down to
the château the next day.

But then again, she's Shari—great at school stuff, not so good at
everyday life stuff. She's dropped her cell phone in the toilet more
times than I can count. Who knows if I'll even get through to her?

Then, to my relief, she finally picks up. And it's clear I haven't
wakened her—because there is music blaring in the background. A
song in which the refrain, *Vamos a la playa,* plays over and over, to
a Latin beat.

"Liz-ZIE!" Shari yells into the phone. "Is that YOOOOOU?"

Oh yes. She's drunk.

"How are yooooouuuuu?" she wants to know. "How's London?
How's hot, hot, hot Andrew? How's his aaaaaaaassssssssssss?"

"Shari," I say in a low voice. I don't want the Marshalls to hear
me, so I'm running the water in the bathtub. I'm not wasting it. I

really do plan to take a bath. In a minute. "Things are weird here. Really weird. I need to talk to someone normal for a minute."

"Wait, let me see if I can find Chaz," Shari says. Then she cackles. "Just kidding! Oh my God, Lizzie, you should see this place. You'd die. It's like *Under the Tuscan Sun* and *Valmont* combined. Luke's house is HUGE. HUGE. It has a name—Mirac. It has its own VINEYARD. Lizzie, they make their own champagne. THEY MAKE IT THEMSELVES."

"That's great," I say. "Shari, I think Andrew told his brothers I was fat."

Shari is silent for a moment. I am urged once again to *Vamos a la playa*. Then Shari explodes.

"He fucking said that? He fucking said you were fat? Stay where you are. Stay right where you fucking are. I'm getting on the Chunnel train thingie and I'm coming over there and I'm going to cut his balls off—"

"Shari," I say. She is yelling so loudly I'm worried the Marshalls might hear her. Through the closed door. Over the TV and the running water. "Shari, wait, that isn't what I meant. I mean, I don't *know* what he said. Things are just really weird. I got here, and the very first thing, Andrew took off for work. Which was okay. I mean it was fine. Because the truth is"—I can feel the tears coming. Oh, great—"Andrew isn't working with children. He's a waiter. He works from eleven in the morning until eleven at night. I didn't even know that was *legal*. Plus, he doesn't even have his own place. We're staying with his parents. And his little brothers. Who he told I was fat. Also, he told his mom that I like tomatoes."

"I take it back," Shari says, "I'm not going there. You're coming here. Buy a train ticket and get over here. Be sure to ask for a youth pass. You'll have to change trains in Paris. Buy a ticket there for Souillac. And then just call me. We'll pick you up at the station."

"Shari," I say, "I can't do that. I can't just *leave*."

"Like fuck you can't," Shari says. I hear another voice in the background. Then Shari is saying to someone else, "It's Lizzie. That fucker Andrew works all day and all night and is fucking making her stay at his parents' and eat tomatoes. And he said she was fat."

"Shari," I say, feeling a twinge of guilt, "I don't know that he said that. And he's not—who are you telling this to, anyway?"

"Chaz says get your far-from-fat ass on a train in the morning. He will personally pick you up at the train station tomorrow night."

"I can't go to *France*," I say, horrified. "My return ticket home is from Heathrow. It's nonreturnable and nontransferable and non—everything."

"So? You can go back to England at the end of the month and fly home from there. Come on, Lizzie. We'll have SO MUCH fun."

"Shari, I can't go to France," I say miserably. "I don't *want* to go to France. I love Andrew. You don't understand. That night outside McCracken Hall . . . it was magical, Shar. He saw into my soul, and I saw into his."

"How could you?" Shari demands. "It was dark."

"No it wasn't. We had the glow of the flames from that girl's room to see by."

"Well, then maybe you just saw what you wanted to see. Or maybe you just *felt* what you wanted to *feel*."

She's talking, I know, about Andrew's stiffy. I stare blindly down at the water splashing into the tub.

The thing is, I am generally a very happy person. I even laughed after Alistair said that thing at the table, about me being a fatty. Because what else are you supposed to do when you find out your boyfriend's been going around telling people you're fat?

Especially since the last time Andrew saw me, I *had* been fat. Or at least thirty pounds heavier than I am now.

I *had* to laugh, because I didn't want the Marshalls to think I'm some kind of oversensitive freak.

I think I succeeded, too, because all Mrs. Marshall did was shoot her son an outraged look . . . Then, since I guess I didn't appear to be offended, she seemed to forget about it. So did everyone else.

And Alistair turned out to be quite nice, offering to let me use his computer in order to start my thesis, which I then worked on for the rest of the day, until breaking for a "curry supper" from the "takeaway" shop on the corner with the two elder Marshalls, the boys having gone out. We ate while watching a British mystery show, during which I only understood approximately one word out of every seven, due to the actors' accents.

The thing is, I was *determined* not to let the fat thing get me down. Because despite what my sisters might think—and they were always more than happy to let their feelings on the matter be known to me, growing up—weight doesn't matter. It really doesn't. I mean, it does if you're a model or whatever.

But in general being a few pounds overweight hasn't ever kept me from doing what I wanted to. Sure, there were all those times I was the last one picked for volleyball in gym class.

And the occasional mortification of having to appear in front of a guy I had a crush on in a bathing suit at the lake or whatever.

And then there were the dumb frat guys who wouldn't look twice at me because I was heavier than the kind of girls they preferred.

But who wants to hang around *frat guys*? I want to be with guys who have more on their minds than where the next keg party is. I want to be with guys who care about making this world a better place—the way Andrew does. I want to be with guys who know that what's important isn't the size of a girl's waistband but the size of her heart—like Andrew. I want to be with guys who are able to see past a girl's outward appearance, and into her soul—like Andrew.

It's just that . . . well, based on Alistair's remark, it seems like maybe Andrew *didn't* see into my soul that night outside Mc-Cracken Hall.

The tomato thing, too. I TOLD Andrew—or wrote to him, actually—that I hate tomatoes. I told him it's the one single food I totally can't stand. I even went on, at great length, about how horrible it was, growing up in a household that was half Italian, hating tomatoes. Mom was always brewing up huge batches of tomato sauce to use in her pastas and lasagnas. She had a huge tomato garden in the backyard that I was in charge of weeding, since I wouldn't touch the ugly red things and so was no help in the picking or cleaning department.

I *told* Andrew all this, not just in my reply to his question about what foods I liked, but that night we spent together as well, three months ago, me in my towel and him in his Aerosmith T-shirt—it must have been laundry day—and R.A. badge, under the stars and smoke.

And he didn't listen. He hadn't paid a bit of attention to a word I'd said.

But he *had* managed to let his family know I was a—what was it again? Oh yes—"fatty."

Is it possible I've made a mistake? Is it possible—as Shari once suggested—that the reason I love Andrew is not because of who he actually is, but because I've projected onto him the personality I *want* him to have?

Could she be right that I've stubbornly refused all along to see him for what he really is, because making out with him had been so much fun (and I'd been so flattered by his full stiffy) I don't want to admit my attraction to him is merely physical?

I hadn't spoken to Shari for nearly two hours after she said this, it had made me so mad, and she'd finally apologized.

But what if she's right? Because the Andrew I knew—or felt like I knew—wouldn't have told his brother I'm fat. The Andrew I know wouldn't even have noticed I was fat.

"Lizzie?" Shari's voice crackles over the phone I'm pressing to my cheek. "Did you die?"

"No, I'm here," I say. I can still hear rock music booming in the background. Shari, it's clear, isn't a bit jet-lagged. Shari's boyfriend isn't at work. Or, rather, he is. But they're working together. "I just . . . Look, I gotta go. I'll call you later."

"Wait," Shari says. "Does this mean you'll be coming to New York with me in the fall after all?"

I hang up. It's not that I'm mad at her, exactly. I'm just . . .

So tired.

I don't even remember bathing or changing into my pajamas and dragging myself into bed. All I know is, it seems like it's about a million o'clock when Andrew gently shakes me awake. But it's really only midnight—at least according to the watchface he shows me when I groggily ask what time it is.

I never realized he wears a glow-in-the-dark digital watch. That's kind of . . . not sexy.

But maybe he needs it. For telling time when he's slaving away in that dark, candlelit restaurant . . .

"Sorry to wake you," he says. He is standing beside my loft bed, which is just high enough off the ground that he doesn't even have to stoop to whisper to me. "But I wanted to make sure you were all right. You don't need anything?"

I squint at him in the semidarkness. The only light is the moonlight that streams through the laundry room's single narrow window. Andrew, I can see, is wearing black jeans and a white shirt—a waiter's uniform.

I don't know what makes me do it. Maybe because I've been so lonely and depressed all evening. Maybe because I'm still half asleep.

Or maybe because I truly do love him. But the next thing I know, I'm sitting up and, my fingers entwined in his shirtfront, I'm whispering, "Oh, Andrew, everything's so awful! Your brother Alistair—he said something today about your having said I was a fatty. That's not true, is it?"

"What?" Andrew is laughing into my hair as he nuzzles my neck. He is quite a neck nuzzler, I'm finding out. "What are you talking about?"

"Your brother, Alistair. He acted all shocked when he met me, because he said you'd told him I was fat."

Andrew stops nuzzling my neck and peers down at me in the moonlight.

"Wait," he says. "He said that? Are you taking the mickey?"

"I don't know anything about Mickey," I say. "But, yes, he really did say he'd been expecting me to be fat. 'A fatty' were his exact words."

I realize, a little belatedly, that Andrew might possibly become a little ticked off with his brother for having said this—especially if it's not true. Which it can't be. Right? Andrew would never say something like that . . .

"Oh, Andrew, I'm sorry," I say, wrapping my arms around his neck and kissing him tenderly. "I can't believe I even brought it up. Forget I said anything. Alistair was obviously pulling my leg. And I fell for it. Let's just forget the whole thing, all right?"

But Andrew doesn't seem willing to forget it. His arms tighten around me, and he uses some very choice adjectives to describe his brother, which he whispers against my lips. Then he says, "I think you look fucking fantastic. I always have. Sure, when we first met, you were a bit plumper than you are now. When I first saw you coming out of Customs at the airport in that little Chinese dress, I didn't even recognize you. I couldn't stop staring. I kept wondering who the lucky bloke was who was meeting such a hot little number."

I can only blink at him. Somehow his words are not as encouraging as I think he means them to be.

Maybe it's because of his seeming inability to pronounce his *th*'s as anything but *f*'s, so his *thinks* come out as *finks*.

"Then, when I got the page, and I came over and saw you were—well, *you*—I realized *I* was the lucky bloke," Andrew goes on. "I'm sorry everything has been such a cock-up so far—my mate's flat falling through, and your not having a proper bed, and my arsehole of a brother, and my fucking work schedule. But you have to know"—here he snakes an arm around my waist—"I'm over the moon that you're finally here." This is where he leans down and kisses my neck some more.

I nod. Much as I am enjoying the neck kissing, there is still something weighing on my mind. So I say, "Andrew. Just one more thing."

"Yeah, what's that, Liz?" he wants to know as his lips approach my ear.

"The thing is, Andrew," I say slowly, "I really . . . I . . ."

"What is it, Liz?" Andrew asks again.

I take a deep breath. I have to do this. I *have* to say it. Otherwise it will be hanging over our heads for my entire stay.

"I really hate tomatoes," I say all in a rush, to get it over with.

Andrew raises his head to look at me blankly. Then he throws back his head and laughs.

"Oh God!" he whispers. "That's right! You wrote me that! Mum asked me what you particularly liked, so she could be sure to have it for your arrival breakfast. But I couldn't remember. I knew you'd said something about tomatoes—"

I try not to take it personally that he remembered I'd said something about tomatoes, but not WHAT I'd said about them. Like that I hated them more than anything in the world.

Andrew is guffawing now. I'm glad he finds the situation so uproarious. "Oh, you poor girl. Don't worry, I'll drop a hint. Come here, let me kiss you again—" He does so. "You really *are* a keeper, aren't you?"

I hadn't been aware there'd been any doubt on that score.

But I know what he means.

Or I think I do, anyway. It's hard to tell what I think while he's kissing me, except *Hooray! He's kissing me!*

And then there's no whispering at all for a while, as we kiss.

And I can tell that Andrew's brother is wrong—he *doesn't* think I'm a fatty . . . unless he means fatty in a *good* way. He likes me. RE-ALLY likes me. I can feel that like pressing against me through his waiter pants.

Which I feel duty-bound to help him remove. Because they seem so binding.

When he's laughingly scrambled up into my loft bed with me—thank God it holds. Or, I should say, thank you, Mrs. Marshall—and the two of us are in each other's arms again, I see why. The pants were so binding, I mean.

"Andrew," I whisper, "have you got any condoms?"

"Condoms?" Andrew whispers the word back like it's foreign. "Aren't you on the pill? I thought all American girls were on the pill."

"Well," I say uncomfortably, "I am. But—you know, the pill doesn't protect you against diseases."

"Are you suggesting I have a disease?" Andrew demands—not in a joking way, either.

Oh dear. Why can't I ever learn to keep my mouth shut?

"Um," I say, thinking fast. Which is hard to do when I'm so tired. And horny. "No. But, um, *I* might have one. You never know."

"Oh," Andrew says with a chuckle. "Right. You? Never. You're too sweet." And he goes back to nuzzling my neck.

Which is very nice. But he still hasn't answered my question.

"Well?" I ask. "Have you got one?"

"For God's sake, Liz," Andrew says, sitting up. He fumbles around and finally produces a Trojan from the pocket of his waiter pants, which are wadded up at the end of the bed. "Happy now?"

"Yes," I say. Because I am. Happy, I mean. Even though my boyfriend apparently goes to work with a condom in his pocket, which might make one ask oneself, if one were of a suspicious nature (which I am not), just what he intended to do with said condom. I mean, considering that his girlfriend is at home, and not at his place of work.

But that is not the point. The point is that he has a condom, and now we can get down to business.

Which we proceed to do without further delay.

Except.

Well, things are going the way I suppose they should, given that my experience in these matters is pretty much limited to some awkward fumblings in an extralong dorm bed with Jeff, my only long-term boyfriend (three months), whom I dated sophomore year and who later that semester tearfully confessed that he was in love with his roommate, Jim.

Still, I have read enough issues of *Cosmo* to know every girl is responsible for her own orgasm—just like every guest is responsible for her own good time at a party . . . no hostess can control EVERYTHING! I mean, you really can't leave this kind of thing up to a guy. He's just going to mess it up or, worse, not even bother to give it a try (unless, of course, he's like Jeff, who was very interested in my orgasms . . . just as he was very interested in my circa 1950 Herbert Levine pumps with the rhinestone buckle, as I discovered when I caught him admiring himself in them).

But while I might have taken care of my own good time, Andrew is apparently having some trouble with his own. He's abruptly stopped what he was doing and has flopped back onto the bed.

"Um, Andrew," I say, filled with concern, "is everything all right?"

"I can't fucking come," is his romantic reply. "It's this fucking bed. There's not enough room."

I am, to put it mildly, astonished. I have never heard of a man who can't come. While I know that to some people—Shari, for instance—a man who is perpetually hard would be a godsend, for me it is merely inconvenient. I have already taken care of my own good time, as *Cosmo* advised. The truth is, I'm not sure how much longer I can hold out down there. I'm starting to chafe.

Still, it's wrong to think of yourself when the person next to you is in so much agony and pain. I can't imagine how Andrew must be feeling.

Feeling very bad for him, I kiss him and ask, "Well, is there anything I can do to help?"

I soon learn that there is. At least if the way Andrew starts pushing my head in a southerly direction is any indication.

The thing is, I've never given one of *those* before. I'm not even sure I know how . . . although that girl Brianna from my dorm floor did try to teach me once, using a banana.

Still. This is really not how I pictured the two of us consummating our relationship.

And yet these are the kinds of things you do for the people you love when they are in need.

I make him change the condom first, though. I don't love anybody THAT much. Not even Andrew.

The Crusades weren't all about one culture trying to inflict their religious views on another. They were also about fashion! Returning Crusaders brought back to their womenfolk not only their vanquished enemy's gold, but also beauty tips from the ladies of the Orient, including pubic shaving (not heard of in most parts of Europe since the age of the early Roman Empire).

Whether or not English ladies adopted this practice from their sisters in the Far East can be left to the imagination of the reader, but we do know from portraits of that era that many of them took matters a little too far, plucking and shaving all the hair from their heads—including eyelashes and eyebrows. As most of them could not read or write at the time, it is no small wonder they got the message wrong.

History of Fashion
SENIOR THESIS BY ELIZABETH NICHOLS

Keep your own secret, and get out other people's.
—*Philip Dormer Stanhope, fourth Earl of Chesterfield (1694–1773),*
British statesman

I wake up with a feeling of deep and utter contentment, even though I'm sleeping alone, Andrew having stumbled to his own bed after an attempt at sleeping together in the narrow MDF bed failed miserably, thanks to his long legs and my tendency to sleep with my knees curled up to my chest.

Still, he left grateful and happy. I saw to that. I may be a beginner, but I learn quickly.

As I stretch, I replay the night before over in my head. Andrew is lovely. Well, not lovely, because you can't really call a guy lovely. But sweet. All that worry over him thinking I was fat . . . I can't believe I wasted so much time over something so silly! Of course he never thought I was fat, or said anything about that to his family. His brother probably got me mixed up with some other girl.

No, Andrew is the perfect boyfriend. And I'll soon have him weaned off the red leather jacket. Maybe, to make it up to him, I'll even get him a new one while we're out shopping today—because this is what Andrew had promised me (during our postcoital chitchat last night) that we'd do today—shop and see the sights (once he'd completed a quick errand he had to do in the city).

Of course, the sights I'm most interested in seeing—besides Andrew, of course—are the Oxfams where I can find some undiscovered treasure, and maybe this place I've heard about called Topshop, which is like the British equivalent of T.J. Maxx, or maybe H&M, which we don't actually have in Michigan, but that I've heard about, of course, as a fashion lover's mecca.

Only I don't mention this to Andrew, because of course I want to seem more intellectual than that. I should be interested in his country's history, which is incredibly rich and goes back many thousands of years . . . or at least two hundred, as far as interesting fashion goes. Andrew is so sweet. All of his family has been so lovely, fatty remark aside—I wish there were some way I could show my appreciation for their kindness to me . . .

And then it comes to me, as I'm shaving my legs in the bathtub a little while later, Andrew not being up yet, and the rest of the family appearing to have gone off to their various jobs: I'll do it with food! Yes! Tonight I'll show my appreciation to the Marshall family for all their hospitality by making them my mother's famous spaghetti due! I'm sure they probably have all the ingredients right here in the house—it's just pasta, garlic, oil, Parmesan, and hot pepper flakes, after all.

And if there's something they don't have—like a nice crusty baguette, which you really need, to sop up the delicious oil—Andrew and I can stop on our way home from sightseeing to pick it up!

Imagine how surprised and happy Mr. and Mrs. Marshall will be to come home from a long day of work to find supper already waiting for them!

Superpleased with my scheme, I put on my makeup, and am just applying an extra layer of topcoat to my pedicure—since I'll be traipsing around the city in open-toed shoes, and I want to protect my French tips—when Andrew finally stumbles down the stairs, blinking groggily. We have a very nice good-morning lovemaking session in the MDF bed before I throw on my fun 1960s Alex Colman sundress with the leaf pattern (I have a cashmere sweater that matches . . . thank God I brought it along at the last minute, since I'm going to need it) and urge Andrew to get dressed so we can get started on our many activities for the day. I still have to change money, and he has his appointment downtown.

My first proper day in London—yesterday doesn't count, because I was so sleepy I hardly remember any of it—has already started out so well (a tomato-free breakfast; a leisurely bath; sex) that I can hardly hope for it to get better, but it does: the sun is shining, and it's too hot for Andrew to wear his break-dancing jacket!

We leave the Marshalls' house hand in hand—Geronimo gazing sadly after us ("That dog really likes you," Andrew observes. Yes! I've won over the family pet through the surreptitious slipping of food! Can the actual family be far behind?) through the glass door—and head for the Tube. I am traveling on the London Tube for the very first time!

And I am not at all frightened of being blown up, because if you let that kind of fear consume you, you have allowed the terrorists to win.

Still, I keep a sharp eye out for young men (and women—it's as wrong to profile by sex as it is by race) wearing bulky coats on such a gorgeous day. While I look for terrorists, I can't help noticing how much better dressed everyone in London is than they are back in Ann Arbor. It is a terrible thing to say about one's own country, but it appears that Londoners simply care about how they look more than people back home. I haven't seen a single person—except for Alistair, who is, after all, a teenager—in sweats, or even an elastic waistband.

Granted, no one appears to be as vastly overweight here as many people back in America are. What makes Londoners so slim? Could it be all the tea?

And the ads! The ads they have on the walls of the Tube station!

They're so . . . interesting. I don't really understand what it is they're advertising in many cases. But this might be because I have never seen topless women used to sell orange juice before.

I guess Shari is right. The British are much less inhibited about their bodies—although they dress them better—than we are.

When we finally reach the stop where Andrew's got his appointment—he says there's a bank close by where I can change money—we scramble back out into the sunshine—and I catch my breath . . .

I'm in London! The town center! The place where so many significant historical events have taken place, including the introduction of the punk movement (where would we be today if Madonna hadn't donned that first bustier, and Seditionaries on Kings Road hadn't introduced the world to Vivienne Westwood?) and that black evening gown Princess Diana (still only Lady Diana then) wore the night of her engagement party?

But before I can really absorb the richness of it all, Andrew drags me into a bank, where I stand in line (or in the queue, as Andrew calls it) to exchange some of my traveler's checks for British pounds. When I get to the teller, she asks to see my passport and I hand it over, and she eyes my photo suspiciously.

Well, and why not? I was thirty pounds heavier when I had that photo taken.

When she returns my passport to me, Andrew asks to see it, and he has a good chuckle over the photo.

"I can't believe you were ever that fat," he says. "Look at you now! You look like a model. Doesn't she look like a model?" he asks the teller.

The teller says, "Uh, yuh," in a noncommittal way.

It is always nice, of course, to be told you look like a model. But I can't help wondering—did I really look that bad before? I mean, when Andrew first saw me that night of the fire, I was thirty pounds heavier than I am now, but he was still attracted to me. I know. I felt his stiffy.

And okay, I was dressed in a towel since the fire department wouldn't let us back into the building. But still.

I am distracted from thinking about all this when the teller finally hands me my money—it's so pretty! So much prettier than American money, which is just so . . . green. And it comes in so many sizes—the British pound coin looks and feels like gold in my hand.

I am completely excited to go out and spend some of my new British money, so I urge Andrew to hurry up and get his appointment over with so we can get to Harrods (I've already mentioned that this is where I want to go first. I don't want to buy anything there, though . . . I just want to see the shrine the owner, Mohamed Al Fayed, has erected to his son, who was killed in the car crash with Princess Diana).

Andrew says, "Let's go then," and we head toward a very dull-looking office building with Job Centre (it's so cute how the British spell everything wrong!) written across the entrance, where Andrew gets in a long line with a lot of other people because, he says, he has to "sign on" for work, or something like that.

I am very interested in all things British, of course, because once Andrew and I are married, this could become my adopted country, the way Madonna has made it hers, so I pay attention to the signs we are passing as the line moves along. The signs all say things like: Ask Us About New Deal for Jobseekers—Part of the Department for Work and Pensions and Thought About Working in Europe? Ask Us How.

And I think how strange it is that in England they call Europe Europe like they aren't a part of it, but in the U.S. we all think of England as part of Europe. Probably incorrectly.

And that the man behind the counter is asking Andrew if he's looked for work, and Andrew says he has but he hasn't found any.

What? What is he talking about, hasn't found work? That's all he's been doing since I got here: working.

"But, Andrew," I hear myself cry, "what about your waitering job?"

Andrew goes pale. Which is an accomplishment for him since he's already so pasty. In a sexy way . . . like Hugh Grant.

"Ha," Andrew says to the man behind the counter. "She's kidding."

Kidding? What is he *talking* about?

"You were there all day yesterday," I remind him. "Eleven to eleven."

"Liz," Andrew says in a strained voice, "don't joke with the nice man. He's busy working, can't you see?"

Of course I can see that. The question is, why can't Andrew?

"Right," I say. "Like you were busy yesterday at the waitering job you had to get because the school thing didn't pay enough. Remember?"

Could Andrew be on drugs? How could he not remember the fact that the very day I arrived for my first-ever trip to England, he was working?

A glance at his face, however, reveals that he not only remembers but doesn't seem to be on drugs. Not if the look he gives me—a look that could kill—is any indication.

Well. It's clear I've done something wrong. But what? I'm only telling the truth.

So I say, to Andrew, "Wait. What's going on here?"

That's when the man behind the counter at the Job Centre picks up a phone and says, "Mr. Williams, I have a problem. Yeah, be right there."

Then he plops a Closed sign down in front of him and says, "Come with me, please, Mr. Marshall, miss," while holding up the partition in the counter so we can pass through it.

Then he escorts us into a little room—empty except for a desk, some shelves with nothing on them, and a chair—in the back of the Job Centre office.

On the way there, I can feel the gazes of everyone else—both in line and working behind the counter—burning into the back of my neck. Some people are whispering. Some of them are laughing.

It takes a good five seconds before I finally realize why.

And when I do, my cheeks go as red as Andrew's had gone pale a minute earlier.

Because that's when I know that I've done it again. Yes. Opened my big, fat, stupid mouth when I should have kept it closed.

But how was I to know that a Job Centre is where British people go to sign up for unemployment benefits?

And what is Andrew doing, anyway, signing up for unemployment benefits when he ISN'T UNEMPLOYED?

Except that Andrew doesn't seem to see it that way—you know, as illegal. He keeps opening his mouth to bleat, "But everybody does it!"

But that's not how the Job Centre people seem to feel, if the look the man gives us before he leaves to find his "superior" is any indication.

"Look, Liz," Andrew says to me the minute the Job Centre man is out of the room, "I know you didn't mean to, but you've completely cocked things up for me. It'll be all right, though, if, when the bloke comes back, you just tell him you made a mistake. That we had a little misunderstanding and I wasn't working yesterday. All right?"

I stare at him, confused.

"But Andrew—" I can't believe this is happening. There has to be some mistake. Andrew—MY Andrew, who's going to teach the children to read?—can't be a welfare cheat. That's just not possible.

"You *were* working yesterday," I say. "I mean . . . weren't you? That's where you told me you were. That's why you left me alone with your family for the whole day and most of the night. Because you were waitering. Right?"

"Right," Andrew says. He is, I notice, sweating. I've never seen Andrew sweat before. But there is a definite sheen along his hairline. Which, I notice, is receding just a little. Will he be as bald as his father someday? "Right, Liz. But you've got to tell a little lie for me."

"Lie for you," I say confusedly. It's like . . . I realize what he's saying. I understand the words.

I just can't believe Andrew—MY Andrew—is saying them.

"It's just a white lie," Andrew elaborates. "I mean, it's not as bad as you're thinking, really, Liz. Waiters make SHIT here, it's not like back in the States, where they're guaranteed a fifteen percent tip. I swear to you, every single waiter I know is on the dole as well—"

"Still," I say. I can't believe this is happening. I really can't. "That doesn't make it right. I mean, it's still . . . it's kind of dishonest, Andrew. You're taking money from people who actually NEED it."

How could he not realize this? He wants to teach underprivileged children . . . the very people that welfare money he seems to feel so entitled to is actually *for*. How could he not know this? His mother is a social worker, for crying out loud! Does she know how her son comes by his extra cash?

"*I* need it," Andrew insists. He's sweating harder now, even though it's actually quite pleasant, temperaturewise, in the little office. "*I'm* one of those people. I mean, I've got to live, Liz. And it's not easy, finding a decent-paying job when everyone knows you're going to be leaving in a few months to go back to school, anyway—"

Well . . . he's right about that. I mean, the only way I managed to work my way up to assistant manager at Vintage to Vavoom is because I live in town year-round.

Also because I'm so good at what I do.

But still . . .

"And I wasn't doing it just for me, you know. I wanted to show you a nice time while you were here," he goes on, darting a nervous glace at the open office door. "Take you nice places, have some nice meals. Maybe even take you . . . I dunno. On a cruise or something."

"Oh, Andrew!" My heart swells with love for him. How could I have thought—well, what I was thinking about him? He may have gone about it the wrong way, but his intentions were in the right place.

"But Andrew," I say, "I have tons of money saved up. You don't have to do this for me—work all these hours, and . . . um, collect the dole, or whatever it is. I have plenty of money. For the both of us."

Suddenly he doesn't look quite so sweaty.

"You do? More than what you changed today, at the bank?"

"Of course," I say. "I've been saving my earnings from the shop for ages. I'm happy to share." I really mean it, too. After all, I'm a feminist. I have no problem supporting the man I love. No problem at all.

"How much?" Andrew asks quickly.

"How much have I got?" I blink at him. "Well, a couple thousand—"

"Honestly? Brilliant! Can I borrow a bit, then?"

"Andrew, I told you," I say. "I'm more than happy to pay for us to go out—"

"No, I mean, can I borrow a bit in advance?" Andrew wants to know. He's stopped sweating, but his face has taken on a bit of a pinched look. He keeps looking at the doorway where the man behind the counter's supervisor is due to appear at any moment. "See, I haven't paid my matriculation fees for school yet—"

"Matriculation fees?" I echo.

"Right," Andrew says. Now he's grinning sort of sheepishly, in the manner of a child with his hand caught in a cookie jar. "See, I had a bit of a cock-up myself just before you got here. Did you ever go to any of the Friday poker nights, back at McCracken Hall?"

My head is spinning. Seriously. "Poker nights? McCracken Hall?" *What is he talking about?*

"Yeah, there was a whole group of residents who played Texas Hold'em every Friday night. I used to play with them, and I got to be quite good . . ."

The British guy, Chaz had said about someone . . . someone I now realize was Andrew. *The one who was running the illegal poker ring on the seventh floor.*

"That was *you?*" I'm staring at him. "But . . . but you're an R.A. Gambling in the dorms is illegal."

Andrew shoots me an incredulous look.

"Right," he says. "Well, maybe, but everybody did it . . ."

If everybody suddenly started wearing epaulets, would you do it, too? I start to ask . . . then stop myself just in time.

Because, of course, I know the answer.

"Anyway," Andrew says, "I got involved with a game here not long ago, and . . . well, the stakes were a bit higher than I'm used to, and the players a bit more experienced, and I—"

"You lost," I say flatly.

"I told you I was a bit overconfident and thought I could clean up at that game I got into . . . but instead I got my arse kicked, and lost the money for my matriculation fees for next semester. That's why I was working so much, see? I can't tell my parents what happened to their money—they're dead set against gambling, and they'd probably kick me out of the house . . . I've barely got a bed there as it is, as you well know. But if you can spare it . . . well, then I'm golden, right? I won't have to work, and then we can be together all day"—He snakes out an arm, wrapping it around my waist and pulling me to him—"and all night, too," he adds with a suggestive wag of his eyebrows. "Wouldn't that be *brilliant*?"

My head is still spinning. Even though he's explained, somehow none of this is making sense . . . or rather, it *is* . . .

But I don't think I like the sense it's making.

I blink at him. "A few hundred? To pay your matriculation fees?"

"Two hundred quid or so, yeah," Andrew says. "Which is . . . what, five hundred dollars? Not so much if you consider it's all going to my future . . . *our* future. And I'll make it up to you. If it takes me the rest of my life, I'll make it up to you." He lowers his head to my neck, to nuzzle it. "Not," he adds into my hair, "that spending the rest of my life making it up to a girl like you will be such a hardship."

"Um," I say, "I guess I can spare it . . ." Inside my head, though, a voice is screaming something entirely different. "We could . . . we could go wire it to the university after we leave here."

"Right," Andrew says. "Listen, about that . . . It might just be better if you gave me the cash and I sent it. There's a bloke I know at work, he can get it there for nothing, no fees, no nothing . . ."

"You want me to give you cash," I repeat.

"Right," Andrew says. "It'll be cheaper than if we wired the money from here in town. They kill you with fees . . ." Then, hearing footsteps in the hallways outside the little office, he says quickly, "Listen, tell that wanker, when he gets in here, that you were wrong about my having a job. That you misunderstood. All right? Can you do that for me, Liz?"

"Lizzie," I say in a sort of daze.

He looks at me blankly. "What?"

"Lizzie. Not Liz. You always call me Liz. No one calls me that. My name's Lizzie."

"Right," Andrew says. "Whatever. Look, he's coming. Just tell him, will you? Tell him you made a mistake."

"Oh," I say, "I will."

But the mistake, I realize, was not about Andy's employment status.

While the Elizabethan age is considered by many historians to be one of enlightenment, given the rise of such geniuses as Shakespeare and Sir Walter Raleigh (see: cape in the mud, etc.), there is no question that Elizabeth, toward the end of her reign, began to behave in an unpredictable and skittish fashion. Many believe this may have been due to the copious amount of white foundation she wore upon her face in order to give it what was then considered a youthful appearance. Unfortunately for Queen Elizabeth, there was lead in her face paint, which may have caused lead poisoning, affecting her brain.

Elizabeth I is not the last to suffer hardship in the pursuit of beauty (see: Jackson, Michael).

History of Fashion
SENIOR THESIS BY ELIZABETH NICHOLS

I don't know what made me do it.

One minute I was asking Mr. Williams—the supervisor of the man who'd escorted us to the little back office—if he could direct me to the ladies' room (although here in England they apparently call it a toilet, since it took some seconds before I could make anyone understand what it was that I needed), and the next I was making a run for it.

That's right. I left. I left the Job Centre—and Andrew. I pretended like I was going to the women's toilet.

But instead I exited the building, hurrying out onto the busy London streets with no idea where I was going, let alone how to get there.

I don't know why I did it. I'd said what Andrew had told me to say—that I'd been mistaken about his having been at work. I suppose that since Andrew gets paid under the table, the Job Centre people have no way to check on whether this is really true. So it wasn't as if Mr. Williams could really *do* anything to Andrew . . . like have him arrested.

In fact, all Mr. Williams was doing when I interrupted to ask where the bathroom was was giving Andrew a lecture on how wrong it is for people who don't truly need the welfare system to abuse it.

That's when I left.

And I never returned.

Which is why I'm wandering the streets of London, with no idea where I am. I don't have a guidebook or a map or anything. All I have is a purseful of British money and a sinking feeling that Andrew isn't going to be too pleased to see me when I get back to his parents' house—if I can even figure out *how* to get back there.

Maybe I should have stayed. It was wrong of me just to leave like that. Andrew's right, it really *is* hard for students to make ends meet . . .

Although obviously it doesn't help if they gamble away their savings.

And what about the money? I promised him five hundred dollars for his matriculation fees and then I just . . . left. How could I walk out like that? If Andrew doesn't pay his matriculation fees, he won't be able to come back to school in the fall. How could I just turn my back on him like this?

But how could I stay?

It isn't the money. It *isn't*. I'd gladly give him every cent I have. Because the truth is, I really can put up with the fact that he thought I was fat.

And I can put up with the fact that he apparently complained about my fatness to his family.

And I can put up with the gambling, and even with the fact that he pretended like he couldn't come so I would give him a blow job.

But defrauding poor people? Because that is basically what someone who takes unemployment while having a paying job is doing.

That I cannot tolerate.

And he wants to be a teacher! A TEACHER! Can you imagine a man like that molding the minds of impressionable young people?

I'm such an idiot. I can't believe I fell for his whole "I want to teach the children to read" thing. It was all so obviously just an act so he could get into my pants—and, later, my wallet. Why didn't I see the signs? I mean, what kind of man who wants to teach the children to read—really and sincerely—also e-mails photos of his naked butt to innocent American girls?

I'm so stupid. How could I have been so blind?

Shari's right, of course. It was his accent. That has to be it. I was completely swayed by his accent. It's just so . . . charming.

But now I know that just because a guy sounds like James Bond doesn't mean he's necessarily going to ACT like him. Would James Bond collect unemployment while also working? Of course not.

Oh God, and to think I wanted to MARRY him!!! I wanted to marry and support him for the rest of my life. I wanted to have children with him—Andrew Jr., Henry, Stella, and Beatrice. And a dog! What was the dog's name?

Oh, never mind.

I'm the biggest idiot this side of the Atlantic. Possibly both sides. God, I wish I'd figured that out before I gave him that blow job. I can't believe I did that.

You know what? I want that blow job back. Andrew Marshall isn't worthy of a blow job by me. That blow job was special. It was my first. And it was meant for a teacher, not a welfare fraud!

Or a dole fraud. Or whatever they call it here.

What am I going to do? It's only two days into my trip to visit my boyfriend and I've already decided I never want to see him again. And I'm staying with his *family*! It's not like I can avoid him there.

Oh God. I want to go home.

But I can't. Even if I could afford it—even if I could call home right now and have them buy me a ticket—I'd never hear the end of it. Sarah and Rose—Mrs. Rajghatta—even my mother—everyone. They'll never let me live it down. They all told me—ALL OF THEM—not to do this, not to go all the way to England to visit a guy I hardly knew, a guy who'd, yeah, okay, saved my life . . .

But chances are I wouldn't have died. I mean, eventually I'd have noticed the smoke and gotten out on my own.

They will never let me forget the fact that they were right. God! They were all right! I can't believe this. They've never been right about *anything*. They all said I'd never graduate . . . well, I have.

Well, okay, almost. I just have to write one little paper.

And they all said I'd never lose my baby fat.

Well, I did. Except for those last five pounds. But they're hardly noticeable to anyone but me.

They said I'd never get a job or an apartment in New York—well, I'm going to prove them wrong about that. I hope. Actually, I can't think about that right now or I'll throw up.

All I know is, I can't go back home. I can't let them think they were right about this.

But I can't stay, either! Not after walking out like that—Andrew will never forgive me. I mean, I just *left*. It was like my feet developed little brains all their own and just took off, trying to put as much distance between Andrew and me as they could.

It isn't his fault. Not really. I mean, gambling is an addiction! If I were a decent person, I would have stayed and tried to help him. I'd have given him the money so he could come back in the fall and make a fresh start . . . I'd have *been* there for him. Together, we could have worked to lick it . . .

But instead I just *left*. Oh, good job, Lizzie. Some girlfriend you are.

My chest feels tight. I think I might be having a panic attack. I've never had one before, but Brianna Dunleavy, back in the dorm, used to get them all the time, and end up at the student health center, where they'd give her a note to get out of her exams.

I can't have a panic attack on the street. I can't! I'm wearing a skirt. Supposing I fall down and everyone sees my underwear? It's true they're the cute polka-dot ones with the bows from Target. But still. I need to sit down. I need to—

Oh—a bookshop. Bookshops are excellent for panic attacks. At least, I hope so, never having had one before.

I plunge past the latest releases and the checkout counter, deep into the bowels of the store. Then, spying a leather chair in the self-help section, which is otherwise empty (British people evidently don't feel the need for much self-help. Which is too bad, because some of them—namely Andrew Marshall—really need it), I sink down into it and put my head between my knees.

Then I breathe. In. Out. In. Out.

This. Can't. Be. Happening. I. Can't. Be. Having. A. Panic. Attack. In. A. Foreign. Country. My. Boyfriend. Can't. Have. Lost. All. His. Grad. School. Money. Playing. Texas. Hold'em.

"Pardon me, miss?"

I lift up my head. Oh no! One of the bookstore clerks is looking down at me curiously.

"Um," I say, "hi."

"Hullo," he says. He seems nice enough. He is wearing jeans and a black T-shirt. His dreadlocks are very clean. He doesn't seem like the kind of person who would kick a woman who is having a panic attack out of his shop.

"Are you all right?" he wants to know. A tag on his shirt says his name is Jamal.

"Yes," I squeak. "Thank you. I'm just . . . I'm not feeling very well."

"You don't look well," Jamal confirms. "Would you like a glass of water?"

I realize then how incredibly thirsty I am. A diet Coke. That's what I really need. Is there no diet Coke in this benighted country?

But I say, "That would be so nice of you," to Jamal's offer of water.

He nods and goes off, looking concerned. Such a nice person. Why can't I be dating him instead of Andrew? Why did I have to fall in love with a guy who claims he WANTS to teach children to read, as opposed to one who really is helping them to do it?

Well, okay, Jamal doesn't work in the children's department.

But still. I bet there are children who have been in this shop that he's encouraged to read.

But maybe I'm just projecting. Again. Maybe I'm just believing what I *want* to believe about Jamal.

Just like I wanted to believe that Andrew is really an Andrew and not an Andy. When in reality he's the biggest Andy I've ever met.

Not that there's anything wrong with the name Andy. It's just that—

Suddenly I know what I need, and it's not water.

I don't want to. I really don't want to. But I realize I have to hear my mother's voice. I simply *have* to.

With trembling fingers, I dial my house. I won't tell her about Andrew, I decide, and how he's turned out to be an Andy. I just need to hear a familiar voice. A voice that calls me Lizzie instead of Liz. A voice—

"Mom?" I cry when a woman picks up the phone on the other end and says hello.

"What the hell are you doing calling so early in the morning?" Grandma demands. "Dontcha know what time it is here?"

"Grandma," I say. I close my eyes. My chest still feels tight. "Is Mom there?"

"Hell no," Grandma says. "She's over at the hospital. You know she helps Father Mack give out communion on Tuesdays."

I don't dispute this, even though it isn't Tuesday. "Well, is Dad there, then? Or Rose? Or Sarah?"

"What's the matter, I'm not good enough for you?"

"No," I say. "You're fine. I just—"

"You sound like you're coming down with something. You catching one of those avian flus over there?"

"No," I say. "Grandma . . ."

And that's when I start to cry.

Why? WHY??? I'm too angry to cry. I already told myself that!

"What's with the waterworks?" Grandma wants to know. "You lose your passport? Don't worry, they'll still let you come home. They let anybody in here. Even people who want to blow us all to kingdom come."

"Grandma," I say, "I think . . ." It's hard to whisper when I'm sobbing, but I try. I don't want to disturb the bookstore customers and get kicked back out onto the street. I know Jamal will be coming back with my water at any moment. "I think I made a mistake in coming here. Andrew . . . he isn't the person I thought he was."

"What did he do?" Grandma wants to know.

"He . . . he . . . told his family I was fat. And he gambles. And he's defrauding the government. And he . . . he . . . he said I liked tomatoes!"

"Come home," Grandma says. "Come home right now."

"That's just it," I say. "I c-can't come home. Sarah and Rose—everybody—they all told me this was going to happen. And now it has. If I come home, they'll all just say they told me so. Because they did. Oh, Grandma." Now the tears are coming even faster. "I'm never going to get a boyfriend! A real one, I mean, who loves me for me, and not my savings account."

"Bullshit," Grandma says.

Startled, I say, "W-what?"

"You're going to get a boyfriend," Grandma says. "Only unlike your sisters, you're choosy. You're not going to marry the first asshole who comes along who tells you he likes you, then knocks you up."

This is a very sobering assessment of my older sisters' relationships. It has the effect of drying up my tears instantly.

"Grandma," I say, "I mean, really. Isn't that a little harsh?"

"So this latest one turned out to be a dud," Grandma goes on. "Good riddance. What are you going to do, stay with him anyway until your flight leaves?"

"I don't see what choice I have," I say. "I mean, I can't just . . . leave him."

"Where is he now?"

"Well," I say, "he's back at the Job Centre, I guess." Would he have come looking for me?

Yes, of course. I have his five hundred dollars.

"Then you already left him," Grandma says. "Look. I don't get what the big deal is. You're in Europe. You're young. Young people have been going to Europe on a shoestring for a hundred years. Use your head, for God's sake. What about your friend Shari? Isn't she over there somewhere?"

Shari. I forgot all about her. Shari, who is right across the English Channel, in France. Shari, who actually invited me, just last night, to come stay with her at—what was it called again? Oh yes. Mirac.

Mirac. The word might as well mean heaven, it sounds so magical right now.

"Grandma," I say, climbing out from my chair, "do you really think . . . I mean . . . should I?"

"You said he gambles?" Grandma asks.

"Apparently," I say, "he has a fondness for Texas Hold'em."

Grandma sighs. "Just like your uncle Ted. By all means stay with him if you want to live the rest of your life trying to bail him out financially. That's what your aunt Olivia did. But if you're smart—and I think you are—you'll get the hell out now, while you still can."

"Grandma," I say, choking back tears, "I . . . I think I'll take your advice. Thank you."

"Well," Grandma says flatly, "this is an occasion. One of you girls actually listening to me for a change. Somebody needs to break out the champagne."

"I'll toast you in absentia, Grandma," I say. "And now I'd better call Shari. Thank you so much. And, um, don't tell anyone about this conversation, okay, Grandma?"

"Who would I tell?" Grandma grumbles, and hangs up.

I hang up as well and hurriedly dial Shari's number. Shari. I can't believe I didn't think of SHARI! Shari's in France. And she said I could come see her. The Chunnel. Didn't she say something about taking the Chunnel? Can I really do this? *Should* I?

Oh no. It goes to Shari's voice mail. Where *is* she? Out in the vineyard squishing grapes between her toes? Shari, where are you? I need you!

I leave a message: "Hi, Shar? It's me, Lizzie. I really need to talk to you. It's really important. I think . . . I'm pretty sure Andrew and I are breaking up." I flash back to the expression on his face as he was telling me about his friend from work who could wire my money to the States with no fees.

My heart twists.

"Um, in fact, I think we've *definitely* broken up. So could you call me? Because I'm probably going to need to take you up on your France offer. So call me back. Right away. Well. Bye."

Saying the words out loud makes it suddenly seem much more real. My boyfriend and I are breaking up. If I had just kept my mouth shut about his waitering job, none of this would have happened. It's all because of me. Because of my big mouth.

Really, I have put my foot in it before. But never this big.

On the other hand . . . if I hadn't said anything, would he ever have told me? About the gambling, I mean? Or would he have tried to keep a secret from me for the rest of our lives together—as he seemed to have done, pretty successfully, for the past three months? Would we have ended up like Uncle Ted and Aunt Olivia—bitter, divorced, financially insolvent, and living in Cleveland and Reno, respectively?

I can't let that happen. I *won't* let that happen.

I can't go back to the Marshalls' house. That's all there is to it. I mean, obviously, I have to, in order to get my things. But I can't sleep there tonight. Not in the MDF bed, the same bed Andrew and I made love in . . . the bed I gave him that blow job in.

The blow job I want back.

And, I realize, I don't *have* to sleep there tonight. Because I have somewhere to go.

I stand up so suddenly that I get a head rush. I am staggering around, clutching my head, when Jamal comes back with a glass of water for me.

"Miss?" he says worriedly.

"Oh," I say, seeing the water. I snatch it from him and down the glass's contents. I don't mean to be rude, but my head is pounding. "Thanks so much," I say when I'm done drinking. And hand the glass back to him. I'm feeling better already.

"Is there someone I can telephone for you?" Jamal wants to know. Really, he is so kind. So attentive! I almost feel like I'm back in Ann Arbor. Except for the English accent.

"No," I say. "But there is something you can help me with. I need to know how to get to the Chunnel."

Part Two

The French Revolution in the late 1700s wasn't just an uprising of common people overthrowing the monarchy in favor of democracy and republicanism. No! It was also about fashion—the haves (who favored powdered wigs, fake facial moles, and hooped skirts, sometimes as much as fifteen feet wide) versus the have-nots (who wore stout boots, narrow skirts, and plain cloth). In this particular uprising, as history shows, the peasants won.

But fashion lost.

History of Fashion
SENIOR THESIS BY ELIZABETH NICHOLS

9

Good talkers are only found in Paris.
—*François Villon (1431–1463), French poet*

I'm pulling my wheelie bag down the aisles of the Paris-Souillac train, and I'm trying not to cry.

Not because of the bag. Well, sort of because of the bag. I mean, the aisle is very narrow, and I have my carry-on bag over my shoulder, and I sort of have to walk sideways, like a crab, in order not to bang people in the head with it as I search—apparently fruitlessly—for a front-facing first-class seat in a nonsmoking car.

If I smoked and I didn't mind facing backward, I'd be all set. Except that I don't smoke, and I'm afraid if I ride facing backward, I might throw up. In fact, I am *sure* I will throw up, because I have felt like throwing up ever since I woke up in Paris—having conked out in my comfy seat on the train from London, like Grandma after too much cooking sherry—and realized what I'd done.

Which is, pretty much, set off by myself through Europe, with no idea whether I am actually going to find the place, much less the person, I'm looking for. Especially since Shari still isn't answering her cell phone, much less calling me back.

Of course, part of the reason why I feel like throwing up might be that I am so incredibly hungry I can hardly see. All I've had to eat since breakfast is an apple I bought at Waterloo Station, since that was the only nutritious food I could find for sale there that didn't have tomatoes on it. If I'd wanted a Cadbury bar or an egg and tomato sandwich, I'd have been all right.

But since I didn't, I was out of luck.

I'm hoping there'll be a dining car on this train. But before I can go look for it, I need to find a decent seat where I can dump my stuff.

And that's proving difficult. My bag is so wide and awkward that it keeps bumping people in the knees as I go by them, and even though I'm apologizing like crazy—"*Pardonnez-moi*," I say to them, when I'm not "*Excusez-moi*"-ing them—nobody seems to appreciate my apologies very much. Maybe because they're all French and I'm American and no one here seems to like Americans. At least, judging by the way the kid next to me in the backward-facing smoking seat I found—but consequently had to abandon—had gone, "*Êtes-vous américaine?*" in a disgusted voice when he overheard me leaving yet another message for Shari on my cell.

"Um," I said, "*oui?*"

And he made a face and pulled out an iPod, inserted his earphones, and turned his face to the window so he wouldn't have to look at me again.

Vamos a la playa, screamed the song I could plainly hear from his earphones. *Vamos a la playa.*

I know that song is going to be stuck in my head for the rest of the day. Or night, I should say, since it's already afternoon and my train won't be arriving at the station in Souillac for six hours.

That's another reason I'm going in search of a new seat. How am I supposed to spend six hours next to a snot-nosed seventeen-year-old in an Eminem T-shirt who listens to Europop, hates Americans, and *smokes*?

Of course, now it's looking like that seat was actually the last vacant one on this train.

Can I stand for six hours? Because if so, I'll be golden. There's

plenty of space for me and my gargantuan bags in the spaces between the cars.

How can this be happening to me? It all seemed so simple when
Jamal, back at the bookshop, explained what I'd have to do to get to
France. He'd been so knowing and kind, it had sounded as if getting
from London to where Shari is was going to be a snap.

He didn't mention, of course, the fact that the minute you open
your mouth to speak to anyone in this country and they realize
from your accent that you're American, they just answer you in
English anyway.

And usually not very nicely, either.

But still. I was able to follow most of the signage at the Gare du
Nord. Enough to get my ticket, anyway—which I'd reserved over
the phone—out of the machines. Enough to find my train. Enough
to stumble onto the first car I reached and plop down into the first
available seat.

Too bad I didn't notice the smoke—and the fact that I was facing
the wrong way—until the train actually started moving.

It's hard not to feel like this whole thing was a very bad idea. Not
the moving-to-the-different-seat thing—I already know THAT was
a bad idea. But the coming-to-France thing. I mean, what if I never
get ahold of Shari? What if her cell phone fell into the toilet again,
the way it did that time back in the dorm, and she can't afford a
new one or there's no cell phone store nearby and she's just going
without one for the rest of her trip? How will I ever find her?

I suppose I could ask people, when I get to Souillac, if they know
where Château Mirac is. But supposing they've never heard of Château Mirac? Shari didn't say how far the château was from the train
station. What if it's really, really far?

And it's not like I can call Shari's parents and ask them if they
know where she is and how I can get in touch with her. Because
then they'll want to know why I want to know, and if I tell them,

they'll tell my mom and dad, and then they'll know things didn't work out with Andrew—I mean, Andy—and tell my sisters.

And then I will never hear the end of it.

Oh God, how did I get myself into this? Maybe I should have just stayed at Andy's. What's the worst that would have happened? I could have gone to Jane Austen's house by myself and just used Andy's house as a sort of home base. I didn't have to leave. I could have just been like, "Look, Andy, it's not working out between us, because you're not who I thought you were. I have a thesis to write, so let's just agree to ignore each other the rest of the time I'm here and I'll do my thing and you do yours."

I could have just said that to him. Of course, it's too late now. I can't go back. Not after that note I left him when I took that taxi back to his house—best fifteen pounds I ever spent—to get my stuff. Thank GOD no one had been home . . .

. . . and thank God Andy had thought to give me my own key this morning before we'd left, which I'd dropped into the Marshalls' mailbox on my way out.

Oh my God. A seat! An empty seat! Facing the right way! In a nonsmoking car! And it's next to a window!

Okay, be calm. It might be taken and the person just got up to use the bathroom or whatever—oh jeez, I bonked that lady in the head with my bag—"*Je suis désolée, madame,*" I say. That means "I'm sorry," right? Oh, who cares. A seat! A seat!

Oh my God. A seat next to a guy who looks to be about my age, with curly dark hair, big brown eyes, and a gray button-down shirt that is actually tucked into his faded-in-all-the-right-places Levi's. That he is wearing with a mesh weave leather belt.

It is possible that I have died. That I have passed out in the aisles of the train—and died of hunger, dehydration, and heartache.

And that this is heaven.

"*Pardonnez-moi*," I say to the totally hot guy. "*Mais est-ce que . . . est-ce que—*"

"Is that seat next to you taken?" is what I want to ask. Only in French, obviously. Only I can't remember the word for seat. Or taken. In fact, I don't think we ever covered this phrase in French 101 or 102. Or maybe we did but I was too busy daydreaming about Andrew—I mean, Andy—that I wasn't paying attention that day.

Or maybe it's just that this guy is so good-looking I can't think of anything else.

"Do you want to sit here?"

That's what the guy in the aisle seat asks, indicating the empty window seat beside him.

In perfect English. In perfect AMERICAN English.

"Oh my God!" I burst out. "Are you American? Is that seat really not taken? Can I sit there?"

"Yes," the guy says with a smile that reveals perfect white teeth. Perfect white AMERICAN teeth. "To all three."

And he gets up to let me into the window seat.

Not only that, but he actually leans over, grabs my gargantuan wheelie bag that has just popped a thousand French kneecaps during its long drag through several train cars, and says, "Let me help you with this."

And, seemingly without effort, he lifts the bag and shoves it up onto the rack above our heads.

Okay. *Now* I'm crying.

Because this is not a hallucination. I am not dead. This is really happening. I know because I've just slung my carry-on bag down from my shoulder and put it under the seat in front of mine, and my entire right side has gone numb from the weight not being there anymore. If I were dead, would I feel numb?

No.

I sink down into the seat—the soft, cushiony seat—and just sit there, blinking at the buildings flashing by so unbelievably quickly, completely unable to believe my good fortune. How could my luck, which has been so totally rotten lately, have taken such an incredible turn for the better? This can't be right. There has to be a catch. There just has to be.

"Water?" the guy next to me asks, holding out a plastic bottle of Evian.

I can barely see him through my tears. "You're . . . you're giving me your water?"

"Um," he says, "no. They come with the seats. This is first class. Everyone gets one."

"Oh," I say, feeling stupid (so what else is new?). I hadn't noticed the water at my last seat. Probably that French kid had bogarted mine. He looked like the type who would steal someone else's water.

I take the water from my new—and vastly improved—seatmate.

"Thank you," I say. "I'm sorry. It's just . . . it's been a long day."

"I can see that," he says. "Unless you always cry on trains."

"I don't," I say, shaking my head and sniffling. "Really."

"Well, that's good to know," he says. "I've heard of fear of flying, of course. But I've never heard of a fear of trains."

"I've had the worst day," I say, opening the water. "Really. You have no idea. It's so nice to hear an American accent. I can't believe how much everybody here hates us."

"Oh," the guy says with another flash of those perfect white teeth, "they aren't so bad. If you saw how the typical American tourist acted, you'd probably feel the same way about us that the French do."

I've chugged most of my water. I'm starting to feel a little better—not so much like death warmed over. Although I'm sure I probably look it. Which is great since now that I have an even closer view of him, I can see that my seatmate isn't just handsome. His face is filled with kindness, intelligence, and good humor as well.

Unless that's just the starvation talking.

"Well." I reach up to dab at my eyes with my wrist. I wonder if my mascara is running down my cheeks in streaks. Did I wear the waterproof kind? I can't even remember. "I'll just have to take your word for it."

"Your first time in France?" he asks sympathetically. Even his *voice* is nice. Sort of deep, and very understanding.

"My first time anywhere in Europe," I say. "Well, except for London, where I was this morning."

And then, like a dam bursting, I'm crying again.

I try not to do it loudly. You know, without sobbing or anything. I just can't think about London—I never even got to go to Topshop!—without tearing up.

My seatmate nudges my elbow with his. When I open my streaming eyes, I see that he is holding a plastic bag in front of me.

"Honey-roasted peanuts?" he asks.

I am overwhelmed by hunger. Without a word, I dive my hand into the bag, grab a handful of nuts, and stuff them into my mouth. I don't care if they're honey-roasted and jam-packed with carbs. I'm starved.

"Do . . . do they come with the seats, too?" I ask between sniffles.

"No," he says, "they're mine. Help yourself to more, if you want some."

I do. They are the best thing I have ever tasted. And not just because I haven't had sugar in so long.

"Thanks," I say. "I . . . I'm s-sorry."

"For what?" my seatmate asks.

"For s-sitting here crying like this. I'm not usually like this. I swear."

"Travel can be very stressful," he says. "Especially in this day and age."

"It's true," I say, taking some more nuts. "You can just never tell. I mean, you meet people and they seem perfectly nice. And then it turns out that all along they were just lying to you to get you to pay their matriculation fees because they lost all their money in a game of Texas Hold'em."

"I was actually referring to terrorist alerts," my seatmate says somewhat dryly. "But I guess what, er, you mentioned could be troubling as well."

"Oh, it is," I assure him through my tears. "You have no idea. I mean, he just outright lied to me—telling me that he loved me and all of that—when all along I think he was just using me. I mean, Andy—that's the guy I left, back in London—he seemed so nice, you know? He was going to be a teacher. He said he was going to devote his life to teaching little children to read. Have you ever heard of anything that noble?"

"Um," my seatmate says, "no?"

"No. Because who even does that in today's day and age? People our age—how old are you?"

"I'm twenty-five," my seatmate says, a little smile on his lips.

"Right," I say. I open my purse, fishing inside it for some tissue. "Well, haven't you noticed that people our age . . . all they seem to think about is making money? Okay, not everyone. But a lot of them. No one wants to be a teacher anymore, or even a doctor . . . not with HMOs and all of that. There's not enough money in it. Everyone wants to be an investment banker, or a corporate headhunter, or a lawyer . . . because that's where the money is. They don't care if they're doing anything good for mankind. They just want to own a McMansion and a BMW. Seriously."

"Or pay back their student loans," says my seatmate.

"Right. But it's like, you don't *have* to go to the world's most expensive college in order to get a good education." I've managed to locate a wadded-up piece of tissue at the bottom of my purse. I use it to mop up some of my tears. "Education is what you *make* out of it."

"I never actually thought of it that way," says my seatmate. "But you could have a point."

"I think I do," I say. The buildings that had been whizzing past my window have turned to open fields. The sky is a golden red as the sun begins to slide down toward the western horizon. "I mean, I've been out there. I've seen it for myself. If you're studying something like—I don't know. History of fashion or something—people think you're a freak. No one wants to pursue anything creative anymore, because that's too risky. They may not get the kind of return on the financial investment they've made in their education that they think they should. So they all go into business or accounting or law or . . . or they look for stupid American girls to marry so they can live off them."

"You sound as if you're speaking from personal experience," my seatmate observes.

"Well, what else am I supposed to think?" I'm babbling. I know I'm babbling. But I can't seem to stop myself. Any more than I can stop the tears that continue to flow down my cheeks. "I mean, what kind of person—you know, who wants to be a teacher—works as a waiter, and ALSO collects the dole?"

My seatmate seems to consider this. "A financially needy one?"

"You would think that," I say, sniffling into the tissue. "But what if I told you that this was also a person who lost all his money playing Texas Hold'em, then asked his girlfriend to pay his matriculation fees, and then, as if that were not enough, also told his entire family that . . . she's . . . I mean, I'm . . . a fatty?"

"You?" My seatmate sounds suitably stunned. "But you're not. Fat, I mean."

"Not now," I say with a little sob. "But I was. When we met. But I lost thirty pounds since the last time I saw him. But even if I *was* fat—he shouldn't go around telling people that! Not if he really loved me. Right? If he really loved me, he wouldn't have *noticed*

I was fat. Or he would have, but it wouldn't have mattered. Not enough to tell his family."

"That's true," my seatmate says.

"But he did. He told them I was fat!" New tears erupt. "And when I got there, they were all, 'You're not fat!' Which is how I knew he'd said something about it. And then he goes and gambles away the money his parents—his hardworking parents—gave him for school! I mean, his mother—his poor mother! You should have seen her. She's a social worker, and she made me a giant breakfast and everything. Even though I don't like tomatoes, and every single thing she made had tomatoes in it. Which is another sign Andy never loved me at all—I specifically told him I don't like tomatoes, and yet he didn't pay any attention. It was like he didn't even know me at all. I mean, he e-mailed me a picture of his naked butt. What would make a guy think a girl would WANT to see a picture of his naked butt? I mean, seriously? Why would he think that was an okay thing to do?"

"I really couldn't say," my seatmate says.

I blow my nose. "But see, that's just typical cluelessness on Andy's part. The scariest part is, I felt *sorry* for him. Seriously. I didn't know about the welfare fraud or that he was going around calling me fat, or that he was using me just to pay his gambling debts. And the worst part is . . . Oh God, I can't be the only one this has ever happened to, can I? I mean, haven't you ever thought you loved someone and done things you regretted with that person? And then wished you could get them back, only you can't? I mean, haven't you?"

"What kind of things are we talking about?" my seatmate wants to know.

"Oh," I say. It's amazing, but I'm starting to feel a little bit better. Maybe it's the comfortable seat, or the golden glow flooding the train car as well as the tranquil countryside we're passing. Maybe it's the fact that I finally got some liquids into me. Maybe it's the sugar from the peanuts.

Or maybe, just maybe, it's that saying all of this out loud is restoring my faith in myself. I mean, anyone might have been tricked by as smooth an operator as Andrew—I mean, Andy. ANYONE. Maybe not my seatmate, since he's a guy. But any girl. ANY girl.

"You know the kinds of things I'm talking about," I say. I look around to make sure no one is listening. All the other passengers appear to be dozing, listening to things through headphones, or too French to understand me anyway. Still, I lower my voice. *Blow job,* I mouth meaningfully.

"Oh," my seatmate says, both of his dark eyebrows going up. "*That* kind of thing."

The thing is, he's American. And he's my age. And he's *so* nice. I feel totally comfortable talking about this with him, because I know he's not going to make any judgments about me.

Besides, I'm never going to see him again.

"Seriously," I say, "guys have no idea. Oh, wait, maybe you do. Are you gay?"

He nearly chokes on the water he is sipping. "No! Do I seem gay?"

"No," I say. "But then my gaydar isn't the best. My last relationship before Andy was with a guy who dumped me for his roommate. His MALE roommate."

"Well, I'm not gay."

"Oh. Well, the thing is, unless you've given one, you can't know. It's a major deal."

"What is?"

"*Blow job,*" I whisper again.

"Oh," he says. "Right."

"I mean, I know you guys all want them, but they're not easy. And the thing is, did he so much as attempt to give me anything in return? No! Of course not! Not that I didn't take care of, you know. Myself. But still. That's just impolite. Especially since I only did it out of pity for him."

"A . . . pity blow job?" My seatmate has the strangest expression on his face. Sort of like he's trying not to laugh. Or that he can't believe he's having this conversation. Or maybe a combination of both.

Oh well. Now he'll have a funny story to tell his family when he gets back home. If he is from the kind of family where it's okay to talk about blow jobs. Which I am definitely not. Except with Grandma, maybe.

"Right," I say. "I did it out of pity for him because he couldn't come. But now I realize that the whole couldn't-come thing was just a ruse. He was faking it! So I'd blow him! I feel so used. I'm telling you . . . I want it back."

"The . . . blow job?" he asks.

"Exactly. If only there was a way I could take it back."

"Well," my seatmate says, "it sounds like you did. You left. If that's not taking a blow job back, I don't know what is."

"It's not the same thing," I say dejectedly.

"*Billets.*" I see someone in a uniform standing in the aisle. "*Billets, s'il vous plaît.*"

"Do you have your ticket?" my seatmate asks me.

I nod, and open my purse. I manage to locate my ticket, and the guy next to me takes it. A second later the conductor moves on, and my seatmate says, "You're going to Souillac, I see. Any particular reason? Do you know someone there?"

"My best friend, Shari," I say. "She's supposed to meet me there. At the station. If she gets my message. Which I don't even know if she did, since she doesn't seem to be picking up her phone. Which she's probably dropped in the toilet again. Because she's always doing things like that."

"So . . . Shari doesn't even know you're coming?"

"No. I mean, she invited me. But I said no. Because back then I thought I could work things out with Andy. Only it turned out I couldn't."

"Well, not through any fault of your own."

I look at him then. The sun, sliding into the car, has outlined his profile in gold. I notice that he has really long eyelashes. Sort of like a girl. Also that his lips are very full and squishy-looking. In a good way.

"You're really nice," I say to him. My tears have totally dried up now. It's amazing how therapeutic telling all your problems to a total stranger can be. No wonder so many of my peers are in therapy. "Thanks for listening to me. Although I must sound completely psychotic to you. I bet you're wondering what you did to deserve having such a total wack job sit down next to you."

"I think you've just been through a rotten time," my seatmate says with a smile. "And so you have every right to sound psychotic. But I don't consider you a wack job. At least, not a total one."

"Really?" He also has, in addition to the lovely eyelashes and lips, really nice-looking hands. Strong and clean—tanned, too—with just a light spatter of dark hair on the back of them. "I just don't want you to think I go around giving blow jobs to all the guys I feel sorry for. I really don't. That was my first one. Ever."

"You don't? That's too bad. I was going to tell you about how I was raised in a Romanian orphanage."

I stare at him. "You're Romanian?"

"That was a joke," he says. "To make you feel sorry for me. So you'll—"

"I get it," I say. "Funny."

"Not really," he says with a sigh. "I suck at jokes. I always have. Hey, listen. Are you hungry? Want to go to the dining car? It's a long way to Souillac, and you've eaten all my nuts."

I look down at the empty plastic bag in my lap.

"Oh my God," I say. "I'm so sorry! I was starving—yes, let's go to the dining car. I'll buy you dinner. To make up for the nuts. And the crying. And the thing about the blow job. I'm really sorry about that."

"I'll take *you* to dinner," he says gallantly. "To make up for your recent mistreatment at the hands of one of my gender. How's that?"

"Um," I say, "okay. But ... I don't even know your name. I'm Lizzie Nichols."

"I'm Jean-Luc de Villiers," he says, holding out his right hand. "And I think you should know, I'm an investment banker. But I don't own a McMansion or a BMW. I swear."

I automatically take his hand, but instead of shaking it, I just stare at him, momentarily flustered.

"Oh," I say, "I'm sorry. I didn't mean ... I'm sure not *all* investment bankers are bad—"

"It's okay," Jean-Luc says, giving my hand a squeeze. "Most of us are. Just not me. Now come on. Let's go eat."

His fingers are warm and just slightly rough. I gaze up at him, wondering if the rosy glow all around him is really just caused by the setting sun, or if he is, by some chance, an angel sent down from heaven to rescue me.

Hey. You never know. Even an investment banker could be an angel. God moves in mysterious ways.

The "Empire waist"—a waistline beginning just beneath the bust—was popularized by Napoléon Bonaparte's wife, Joséphine, who, during her husband's reign as emperor beginning in 1804, favored the "classical" style of Greek art, and emulated the togalike robes worn by figures on ancient pottery from that time.

In order to better simulate the look of the pottery figures, many young women dampened their skirts so that their legs, beneath the sopping garments, were more apparent. It is from this tradition that the modern-day "wet T-shirt contest" is believed to have derived.

History of Fashion
SENIOR THESIS BY ELIZABETH NICHOLS

The way to get a man interested and to hold his interest was to talk about him, and then gradually lead the conversation around to yourself—and keep it there.
—*Margaret Mitchell (1900–1949), U.S. author*

He isn't an angel. At least, not unless angels are born and raised in Houston, which is where he's from.

Also, angels don't have degrees from the University of Pennsylvania, the way Jean-Luc does.

Also, angels don't have parents who are going through an acrimonious divorce, the way Jean-Luc's are, so that when they want to come visit their father—the way Jean-Luc's taken a few weeks off from his job at the investment firm of Lazard Frères to do—they have to come all the way to France, since that's where Jean-Luc's dad, a Frenchman, lives.

Also, angels tell better jokes. He wasn't lying about the joke thing. He really does suck at them.

But that's okay. Because I would rather be with a bad joke-teller who remembers I hate tomatoes than with a gambling welfare cheat who doesn't.

Because Jean-Luc does—remember about the tomatoes, I mean. When I come back from the ladies' room (picturesquely referred to on French trains as the "toilet"), where I went to repair the damage done to my face by my tears—fortunately, nothing a new application of eyeliner, undereye cover-up, lipstick, and powder couldn't cure, along with some hair combing—I find the waiter already at our table, taking our order. Jean-Luc does all the talking because, being half French, he speaks the language fluently. And quickly. I can't catch everything he says, but I hear *"pas de tomates"* several times.

Which even I, with my summer-school French, know means "no tomatoes."

It is all I can do to keep from bursting into tears all over again. Because Jean-Luc has renewed my faith in men. There *are* nice, funny, totally good-looking guys out there. You just have to know where to look . . . and apparently, where NOT to look. Which is in the ladies' shower of your dorm.

Of course, I've found this one on a train . . . which means after I get off this train, I'll probably never see him again.

But that's okay. It's fine. I mean, what did I expect, to walk out of one relationship right into another? Right. Like that's even healthy. Like it would have had a chance of lasting, since I'm so obviously on the rebound from Andy.

Plus, you know. The whole two-ships-passing-in-the-night thing.

Oh, and the fact that I told him about the blow job. (WHY? WHY DID I DO THAT??? WHY DO I HAVE TO HAVE THE BIGGEST MOUTH IN THE ENTIRE UNIVERSE???)

Still. He's just so . . . cute. And not married—no ring. Maybe he's got a girlfriend—actually, no guy this cute could *not* have a girlfriend—but if so, he certainly isn't talking about her.

Which is good. Because why would I want to sit here and listen to this totally cute guy talk about his girlfriend? I mean, obviously, if he talked about her I *would* listen, since he listened so patiently when I was talking about Andy.

But, you know. I'm glad he's not.

He orders wine to go with dinner, and when it arrives and the waiter pours it out for us, Jean-Luc lifts his glass, clinks it with mine, and says, "To blow jobs."

I nearly choke on the bread I'm scarfing down. Because even though we're on a train, we're on a train in *France*, so the food is incredible. At least the bread is. So incredible there's no possible way I can resist it after I take a tiny nibble from a roll in the basket on the table. Perfectly crunchy crust with a warm, soft middle? How can I abstain? Sure, I'll regret it later, when my size nine jeans won't zip up.

But for right now, I'm still in heaven. Because, for such a bad joke-teller, Jean-Luc is still pretty funny.

And I've missed bread. I've really, really missed it.

"To blow jobs we want *back*," I correct him.

"I can only pray," Jean-Luc says, "there's no woman out there wishing she could take back one she's given me."

"Oh," I say, gently laying a curl of salted butter on top of the center of my roll and watching it melt into the warm bread, "I'm sure there's not. I mean, you don't seem like a user to me."

"Yes," he says, "but then neither did—what's his name again? Blow-job boy?"

"Andy," I say, blushing. God, why did I ever open my big mouth about that? "And my instincts were off about him. Because of the accent. And his wardrobe. If he'd been American, I never would have fallen for him. Or his lies."

"His wardrobe?" Jean-Luc asks as the waiter brings over my pan-seared pork medallions and his poached salmon.

"Sure," I say. "You can tell a lot about a guy from what he's wearing. But Andy was British, so that threw everything off a little. I mean, until I got there, I just figured everyone in England wore Aerosmith T-shirts, like Andy was wearing the night we met."

Jean-Luc's dark eyebrows go up. "Aerosmith?"

"Right. Obviously, I assumed he was being ironic, or possibly that it was laundry day. But then I got to London and I saw that is how he really dresses. There was nothing ironic about it. If things had worked out between us, I might eventually have gotten him into decent clothes. But . . ." I shrug. Which is a very French thing to do, I notice. All the other ladies in the dining car are shrugging as well, and saying, *"ouais,"* which is French slang for *oui,* at least according to the copy of *Let's Go: France* I bought from Jamal and skimmed before I zonked out in the Chunnel.

"So you're saying," Jean-Luc says, "that you can tell what someone is like just by the clothes they're wearing?"

"Oh, absolutely," I say, digging into my pork tenderloin. Which, I might add, is totally delicious, even by non-train-food standards. "What someone wears reveals so much about themselves. Like you, for instance."

Jean-Luc grins. "Okay. Hit me."

I squint at him. "Are you sure?"

"I can take it," Jean-Luc assures me.

"Well . . . all right, then." I study him. "I can tell by the fact that you tuck your shirt into your jeans—which are Levi's; I doubt you own any other brand—that you're confident about your body and also that you care about how you look, but you aren't vain. You probably don't think much about how you look, but you glance in the mirror in the morning to shave and maybe make sure no tags are sticking out. Your mesh leather belt is casual and understated, but I bet it cost a lot, which means you're willing to spend money on quality, but you don't want it to look show-offy. Your shirt is Hugo—not Hugo Boss—which means you care, just a little, about not looking like everybody else, and you have on Cole Haan driving shoes with no socks, which means you like to be comfortable, aren't impatient about waiting in lines, don't mind having weird girls you've never met before sit next to you on trains and cry, and that you don't suffer from any sort of glandular foot-odor problems. Oh, and you're wearing a Fossil watch, which means you're athletic—I bet you run to stay in shape—and that you like to cook."

I laid down my fork and look at him. "How am I? Close?"

He stares at me across the bread basket.

"You got all that," Jean-Luc says incredulously, "just from what I'm wearing?"

"Well," I say, taking a sip of wine, "all that and the fact that you don't suffer from feelings of sexual inadequacy, because you aren't wearing cologne."

He says, "I got my belt for two hundred dollars, Hugo Boss fits weird on me, socks make my feet feel hot, I run three miles a day, I hate cologne, and I make the best cheese and scallion omelets you've ever tasted."

"I rest my case," I say, and dive into the mesclun salad the waiter's just brought us. It is loaded with blue cheese and candied walnuts. Mmm, candied walnuts.

"But seriously," Jean-Luc says, "how'd you do that?"

"It's a talent," I say modestly. "Something I've always been able to do. Except, obviously, it doesn't always work. In fact, it seems to always fail me when I need it most—if a guy is ambivalent about his sexual orientation, I totally can't tell by what he's wearing. Unless, you know, he's in something of mine. And like I said—Andy was a foreigner. That threw me off. I'll know better next time."

"Next British guy?" Jean-Luc asks, the eyebrows going up again.

"Oh no," I say. "There will be no more British guys. Unless they're members of the royal family, of course."

"Wise strategy," Jean-Luc says.

He pours me more wine as he asks me what I have planned for after I return to the States. I tell him about how I was going to stay in Ann Arbor and wait for Andy to get his degree. But now . . .

I don't know what I'm going to do.

Then I find myself telling him—this stranger who is buying me dinner—my concerns about how if I go ahead and go with Shari to New York, she is going to ditch me eventually to go live with her boyfriend, since Chaz is going to be heading off to NYU to get a Ph.D. in philosophy, and then I'll have to room with total strangers. And also how I don't really have my degree yet since I haven't finished (or actually started) my thesis, so I probably won't even be able to get a job in my chosen field in New York—if jobs for history of fashion majors even exist—and will probably end up having to work at the Gap, my personal idea of hell on earth. All those capped-sleeved T-shirts, each one exactly the same as the other, and people mixing their denim rinses. It might actually kill me.

"Somehow," Jean-Luc says, "I can't quite picture you working at the Gap."

I look down at my Alex Colman sundress and say, "No. You're right. Do you think I'm insane?"

"No, I like that dress. It's kind of . . . retro."

"No. I mean about how I was going to stay in Ann Arbor until Andy was done with his degree and live at home. Shari says I was compromising my feminist principles, doing that."

"I don't think it's compromising your feminist principles," Jean-Luc says, "to want to stay close to someone you really love."

"Okay," I say. "But what am I going to do now? I mean, is it insane to move to New York without a job or a place to live first?"

"Oh no. Not insane. Brave. But then you seem like a fairly brave girl."

Brave? I nearly choke on a sip of wine. No one's ever called me fairly brave before.

And outside the dining car, the sun is still setting—it stays light out so late in France during the summer!—turning the sky behind the green hills and woods we're hurtling through a luscious, sultry pink. Around us, the waiters are passing out plates of assorted cheeses and chocolate truffles and tiny glasses of digestifs, and over in the smoking section our fellow diners have lit up, enjoying a lazy after-supper cigarette, the secondhand smoke from which, in this romantic setting, doesn't smell anywhere near as foul as it might coming out of, say, my ex-boyfriend's nostrils.

And I feel as if I'm in a movie. This isn't Lizzie Nichols, youngest daughter of Professor Harry Nichols, recent college nongraduate, who spent her whole life in Ann Arbor, Michigan, and has only been out with three guys her entire life (four if you count Andy).

This is Elizabeth Nichols, fairly brave (!), cosmopolitan world traveler and sophisticate, dining in a train car with a perfect (and I do mean perfect!) stranger, enjoying a cheese course (cheese course!) and sipping something called Pernod as the sun sets over the French countryside whizzing past—

And suddenly, in the middle of Jean-Luc's description of his own senior thesis, which has to do with shipping routes (I'm trying hard not to yawn—but then the history of fashion probably wouldn't light his fire, either), my cell phone chirps.

I snatch it up, thinking it must be Shari at last.

But the caller ID says Unknown Number. Which is weird, because no one Unknown *has* my cell number.

"Excuse me," I say to Jean-Luc. Then, ducking my head, I answer. "Hello?"

"Liz?"

Static crackles. The connection is terrible.

But it's unmistakably the last person in the world I want to hear from.

I don't know what to do. Why is he calling me? This is terrible. I don't want to talk to him! I have nothing to say to him. Oh dear.

"Just a minute," I say to Jean-Luc, and I leave our table to take the call in the open area beside the sliding door to the next train car, where I won't disturb the rest of the passengers.

"Andy?" I say into the cell phone.

"There you are!" Andy says, sounding relieved. "You have no idea how glad I am to hear your voice. Didn't you get my calls? I've been ringing your mobile all day. Why didn't you pick up?"

"I'm sorry, did you call? I never heard it ring." This is true. Cell phones don't work in the Chunnel.

"You have no idea what I've been through," Andy goes on, "coming out of that horrible office and finding you gone like that. The whole way home, I kept thinking, What if she's not there? What if something happened to her? I tell you, I must really love you, eh, if I was that scared something might have happened!"

I give a weak laugh. Even though I don't feel like laughing. "Yes," I say, "I guess you must."

"Liz, Christ," Andy goes on. Now he sounds . . . tense. "Where the fuck *are* you? When are you coming home?"

I gaze up at what looks, in the slanting rays of the sun, like a castle on a hillside. But that, of course, is impossible. Castles don't sit out in the middle of nowhere. Even in France.

"What do you mean, when am I coming home?" I ask him. "Didn't you get my note?" I left a note for Mrs. Marshall and the rest of Andy's family, thanking them for their hospitality, and a separate note for Andy, explaining that I was very sorry, but that I had unexpectedly been called away and would not be seeing him again.

"Of course I got your note," Andy says. "I just don't understand it."

"Oh," I say, surprised. I have excellent penmanship. But I was crying so hard maybe my handwriting was shakier than I'd thought. "Well . . . like I said in the note, Andy, I'm really very sorry, but I just had to go. I really am—"

"Look, Liz. I know what happened this morning at the Job Centre upset you. I hated having to ask you to lie like that. But you wouldn't have had to lie if you'd just kept your mouth shut in the first place."

"I realize that," I say. Oh God, this is awful. I don't want to do this. Not now. And certainly not here. "I know it's all my fault, Andy. And I really am sorry. I hope I didn't get you into trouble with Mr. Williams."

"Well, I won't lie to you, Liz," Andy says. "It was close. Very close. But . . . Wait a sec. Why are you calling me Andy?"

"Because it's your name," I say, moving out of the way of some people who've come through the sliding door from another car and are looking for an empty table.

"But you never call me Andy. You've always called me Andrew."

"Oh," I say. "Well, I don't know. You just seem like more of an Andy to me now."

"I'm not sure I like the sound of that," Andy says in a rueful tone. "Look, Liz . . . I know I made a fuck-all of everything. But you didn't have to *leave*. I can fix this, Liz. Really. Things didn't get off on the right foot between us, but everyone feels gutted about it, especially me. I'm done with Texas Hold'em . . . I swear it. And Alex has given up his room—he says you and I can share it. Or, if you like, we can go somewhere else . . . somewhere we can be alone. Where was it you wanted to go? Charlotte Brontë's house?"

"Jane Austen," I correct him.

"Right, Jane Austen's house. We can leave right away. Just tell me where you are and I'll come fetch you. We'll patch things up. I'll make it up to you—all of it—I swear it."

"Oh, Andy," I say, feeling guilt-ridden. Jean-Luc, over at our table, is paying the bill to make room at the table for the new passengers who've come in. "That just . . . I mean, it won't be possible for you to come fetch me. Because I'm in France."

"You're WHAT?" Andy sounds a bit more surprised than is necessarily flattering. I guess he doesn't consider me fairly brave, the way Jean-Luc does. At least, not brave enough to get to France on my own. "How did you get *there*? What are you *doing* there? Where are you? I'll join you."

"Andy," I say. This is terrible. I *hate* confrontations. It's so much easier to walk away than it is to have to explain to someone that you never want to see them again. "I want . . . I *need* to be by myself for a bit. I just need some time alone to think."

"But for God's sake, Liz, you've never been in Europe before. You don't have the slightest idea what you're doing. This isn't funny, you know. I'm really worried. Just tell me where you are and I'll—"

"No, Andy," I say softly. Jean-Luc is coming toward me, looking concerned. "Listen, I can't talk right now. I really have to go. I'm so sorry, Andy, but . . . like you said, I made a mistake."

"I forgive you!" Andy says. "Lizzie! I forgive you! Just—listen. What about the money?"

"The . . . what?" I am so stunned I nearly drop the phone.

"The money," Andy says urgently. "Can you still wire me the money?"

"I can't talk about that right now," I say. Jean-Luc has reached my side. He is, I note, really very tall—taller, even, than Andy. "I'm so sorry. Good-bye."

I hang up, and for a second or two my vision swims. I would not have thought it possible to have any tears left, but apparently I do.

"Are you all right?" I hear—since I cannot see—Jean-Luc ask gently.

"I will be," I assure him, more heartily than I actually feel.

"Was that him?" he wants to know.

I nod. It's feeling a little hard to breathe. I can't tell if it's because of my barely repressed tears or Jean-Luc's proximity . . . which, given how often the swaying of the train occasionally causes his arm to brush mine, is considerable.

"Did you tell him you were here with your attorney," Jean-Luc wants to know, "and that he was busy drawing up your demand for your blow job back?"

I am so shocked by this I forget about not being able to breathe. Instead I find myself grinning . . . and the tears mysteriously drying up in my eyes.

"Did you let him know that if he can't see fit to return your blow job immediately, you will have no choice but to sue?"

Now the tears in my eyes are from laughter.

"You said you can't tell jokes," I say accusingly when I've stopped laughing long enough to catch my breath.

"I can't." Jean-Luc looks grave. "That was a horrible one. I can't believe you laughed."

I'm still giggling as I collapse back into my seat beside him, feeling pleasantly full and more than a little sleepy. I struggle to stay awake, however, keeping my gaze on the window on the far side of the car, just behind Jean-Luc's head, where the sun—still not quite sunk—seems to be silhouetting another castle. I point at it and say, "You know, it's so weird. But that looks like a castle over there."

Jean-Luc turns his head. "That's because it *is* a castle."

"It is not," I say drowsily.

"Of course it is," Jean-Luc says with a laugh. "You're in *France*, Lizzie. What did you expect?"

Not castles, just sitting there for anyone to see by train. Not this breathtaking sunset, filling our car with this rosy light. Not this perfectly kind, perfectly lovely man sitting next to me.

"Not this," I murmur. "Not this."

And then I close my eyes.

The so-called Empire dresses worn by women at the dawn of the nineteenth century were often as sheer as today's nightgowns. To keep warm, women wore flesh-toned pantaloons, made of stockinette (a closely woven cotton) and reaching all the way to the ankles or to just below the knee. This is why, when seen in paintings of the era, women in Empire gowns often appear to be wearing no underwear at all, though the idea of "going commando" would not actually occur to anyone for at least two more centuries.

History of Fashion
SENIOR THESIS BY ELIZABETH NICHOLS

We feel safer with a madman who talks than with one who
cannot open his mouth.
—E. M. Cioran (1911–1995), Romania-born French philosopher

I wake up to someone saying my name and gently shaking
me.

"Lizzie. Lizzie, wake up. We're at your station."

I open my eyes with a start. I'd been dreaming about New York—
of Shari and me moving there, and finding no better place to live
than a cardboard refrigerator box on some kind of highway merid-
ian, and my having to get a job folding T-shirts—miles and miles of
capped-sleeved T-shirts—at the Gap.

I am startled to find I am not in New York but on a train. In
France. That is stopped at my station. At least if the sign outside the
window, silhouetted against the night sky (when did it get so dark
out?), which says Souillac, is any indication.

"Oh no," I cry, hurtling out of my seat. "Oh. No."

"It's all right," Jean-Luc says soothingly. "I've got your bags here."

He does. My wheelie bag is down from the overhead rack, and he
passes me the handle, along with my carry-on bag and purse.

"You're fine," he says with a chuckle at my panic. "They won't
leave with you still on board."

"Oh," I say. My mouth tastes awful, from the wine. I can't believe
I fell asleep. Had I been breathing on him? Had he smelled my dis-

gusting wine breath? "I'm so sorry. Oh. It was so nice to meet you. Thank you so much for everything. You're so nice. I hope to see you again someday. Thanks again—"

Then I barrel from the train, saying, *"Pardon, pardon,"* the French way to everyone I bang into on my way out.

And then I'm standing on the platform. Which appears to be in the middle of nowhere. In the middle of the night.

All I can hear is crickets. There is a faint scent of woodsmoke in the air.

Around me, the other passengers who got out at the same time I did are being greeted by excited family members and escorted to waiting cars. There is a bus purring nearby that other passengers are climbing onto. The sign in the bus's windshield says Sarlat.

I have no idea what Sarlat is. All I know is the town of Souillac isn't much of a town. It appears, in fact, to be merely a train station.

Which is currently closed, if the locked door and dark windows are any indication.

This is not good. Because, despite the numerous messages I left informing her of my arrival time, Shari is not here to pick me up. I am stranded on a train platform in the middle of the French countryside.

All alone. All alone except for—

Someone beside me clears his throat. I spin around and smack—almost literally—into Jean-Luc. Who is standing behind me. With a big grin on his face.

"Hello again," he says.

"What—" I stare at him. Is he a figment of my imagination? Can blood clots form in your legs on trains and then travel to your brain? I'm almost sure not. They are from the air pressure in planes, right?

So he really is here. Standing in front of me. With a long, extremely bulky gray garment bag in his hands. As the train pulls away.

"What are you *doing* here?" I shriek. "This isn't your stop!"

"How do you know? You never even asked where I was going."

This is totally true, I realize belatedly.

"But—but," I stammer, "you saw my ticket. You knew I was getting off at Souillac. You didn't say you were, too."

"No," Jean-Luc says, "I didn't."

"But . . . *why*?" I'm suddenly seized with a horrible thought. What if charming, handsome Jean-Luc is some kind of serial killer? Who woos vulnerable American girls on foreign trains, lulls them into a false sense of trust, then kills them when they get to their destinations? What if he's got some kind of scythe or garrote in that garment bag? He totally could. It looks awfully bulky. Way too bulky to be a suit jacket or hemmed trousers.

I look around and see that the last car in the parking lot is pulling away—along with the Sarlat bus—leaving us alone on the platform. Totally alone.

"I wanted to tell you I was getting off at Souillac," Jean-Luc is saying when I am able to focus on him, and not my complete and utter lack of recourse if he starts trying to kill me, "but I was afraid you'd feel embarrassed."

"About what?" I ask.

"Well," Jean-Luc says. He's starting to look a little sheepish in the bright glare of the streetlamp, around which moths are throwing themselves about as noisily as the crickets are chirping. Why does he look sheepish? Because he realizes he has to kill me now and I'm probably not going to like it? "I haven't exactly been honest with you . . . I mean, you thought I was just some random stranger on a train you could pour out all your problems to . . ."

"I'm really sorry about that," I say. My God, what kind of person would kill another person just because she told her life story to him on a train? This is totally unreasonable. All he had to do was pull out a book and pretend to read or something, and I'd have shut up. Probably. "I was very upset—"

"But it was so entertaining," Jean-Luc says with a shrug. "I have to tell you. I've never had a girl sit down next to me and start talking about—well, what you did. Ever."

This can't be happening. Why did I tell a total stranger so much about my personal life? Even a totally cute one in a Hugo shirt?

"I think you've got the wrong idea about me," I say, backing slowly toward the train platform's stairs. "I'm not that type of girl. I'm really not."

"Lizzie," Jean-Luc says. He takes a step toward me. He is not letting me back away toward the steps. "The reason I didn't tell you I was getting off at Souillac—besides the fact that you didn't ask—is because I'm *not* some random stranger you met on a train."

Oh, great. This is the part where he starts telling me something psychotic about how we knew each other in a past life. It's like T.J. from my freshman year all over again. Why am I such a weirdo magnet? WHY?

And he seemed so great back on the train! Really! He said I was fairly brave! He totally restored my faith in men! Why does he have to turn out to be a murdering psycho? WHY?

"Really," I say. This is all Shari's fault, of course. If she would just answer her freaking cell phone once in a while, none of this would be happening. "What do you mean?"

"I mean, I'm actually your host. Jean-Luc de Villiers? Your friend Shari's staying at my father's place, Mirac."

I stop backing up. I stop staring at the garment bag. I stop thinking about my imminent death.

Mirac. He said Mirac.

"I never told you the place I was going was called Mirac," I say. Because, while it's true I'd babbled almost nonstop to him, I don't remember ever saying the word *Mirac*. Which I'd actually forgotten until that very moment.

"No, you didn't," Jean-Luc says. "But that's where your friend Shari is staying, isn't it? With her boyfriend, Charles Pendergast?"

Charles Pendergast? He knows Chaz's real name! I *know* I never told him that. No one ever uses Chaz's real name, because he tells hardly anyone what it is.

Who would know Chaz's real name? Only someone who knew him. Well.

"Wait," I say, my mind lurching for some—*any*—reasonable explanation for what's happening. "You're . . . Luke? *Chaz's* friend Luke? But . . . you said your name was Jean-Luc."

"Well," Luke—or Luc—or Jean-Luc—or whatever his name is—says, still looking sheepish, "that's my full name. Jean-Luc de Villiers. But Chaz has always just called me Luke."

"But . . . but aren't you supposed to be at Mirac with Chaz and Shari?"

He swings the garment bag off his shoulder. "I had to go into Paris for the day to pick up my cousin's wedding gown. She didn't trust the shop's courier to get it here in one piece. See?"

He unzips the bag a little and a froth of white lace—unmistakably bridal—spills out. He tucks it back in and rezips.

"I never thought in a million years, when you sat down next to me, that you were the Lizzie I've heard so much about from Shari and Chaz. But then when you said Shari's name, I knew it. But by that time you'd already mentioned . . . you know." Now he looks more embarrassed than sheepish. "And I knew you'd only done that because you thought you were never going to see me again . . ."

"Oh," I say, feeling suddenly sick to my stomach. Since that's exactly what I HAD thought to myself. "My. God."

"Yeah," Luke says with a very French shrug. For an American.

Which makes sense. Since he's half French. "Sorry about that. Although you have to admit . . . it's kind of funny."

"No," I say, "it's really not."

"Yeah." He sighs, not smiling anymore. "I sort of guessed you'd see it that way. That's why I didn't tell you."

"So you knew," I say, feeling my cheeks heating up. "You knew all along we'd be seeing each other again. A lot. And you didn't try to stop me. You just let me go on and on like that. Like a moron."

"No, not like a moron," he says, *really* not smiling anymore. In fact, he looks a little worried. "Nothing like that. I thought you were really charming. And funny. That's why I didn't try to stop you. I mean, in the first place, I didn't know, until you were almost through with your—um, venting—who you were. I just knew you needed to vent, and so I let you, because I actually enjoyed it. I thought you were sweet."

"Oh God!" I want to throw his garment bag over my head and hide in it. "*Sweet?* Talking about how I gave my boyfriend a blow job?"

"You talked about it in a very sweet manner," Luke assures me.

"I'm going to kill myself," I say from between my fingers, since I've buried my burning face in my hands.

"Hey."

I hear footsteps, then feel hands go around my wrists. I look up, startled, and find that Luke has laid the garment bag across my suitcase and is standing very, very close to me, looking down into my face while gently pulling my hands from my eyes.

"Hey," he says again, his voice as gentle as his touch. "Seriously. I'm sorry. I wasn't thinking. I didn't . . . I didn't know what to do. I wanted to tell you, but then I thought . . . well, I thought it would be a funny joke. But. Like I said. Jokes aren't really my thing."

I am intensely aware of how dark his eyes are—as dark as the tree branches behind the train station, silhouetted against the navy-blue sky—and how kissable his lips look. Especially since they're only just a few inches away from mine.

"If you tell anyone," I hear myself say in a voice that has gone strangely throaty, "about what I told you on the train—especially Chaz—I will kill you. About my not finishing my thesis yet AND the other thing. The you-know-what. You can't tell *anyone*. Do you understand? I will *kill* you if you do."

"I totally understand," Luke says, his grip on my wrists even firmer now that I've dropped my hands from my face. He's essentially holding them in his big warm hands. And it feels nice. Really nice. "You have my complete and total word. I won't say a thing. Your blow job is totally safe with me."

"Ack!" I cry. "I mean it! Don't mention those words again!"

"What words?" he asks. Now his dark eyes are as lit up as the smattering of stars I see winking down at us, like sequins on a blue cashmere sweater set. "Blow job?"

"Stop it," I say, and let myself sway toward him.

Just in case, you know, he wants to kiss me.

Because I'm starting to realize that the fact that Luke is Jean-Luc is hardly what anyone can call bad news. Considering that now I don't have to worry about getting hold of Shari. And about where I'm going to stay tonight.

Not to mention the fact that he's the nicest, hottest guy I've met in a really long time. Who doesn't have an addiction to Texas Hold'em . . . that I know of, anyway.

And that he seems to like me.

And that I'm going to be spending the rest of the summer with him.

And that he's holding my hands.

Suddenly things are looking up. Way up.

"So," Luke says, "am I forgiven?"

"You're forgiven," I say. I can't help smiling up at him like the moron he claims I'm not. He's just so . . . cute.

And not just cute, either. He's nice, too. I mean, he bought me dinner.

And he was totally sympathetic when I was crying like a maniac.

Plus he's an investment banker. He's working hard to . . . protect rich people's money. Or something.

And he made me laugh instead of cry after I got off the phone with Andy.

And I'm going to be with him. All summer. All—

"Good," Luke says. "Because I'd hate for you to think you were wrong. You know, about my character assessment. The one you made based on my clothes."

"I don't think," I say, lowering my gaze to the opening of his shirt, where I see a few promising-looking chest hairs poking out, "that I'm wrong."

"Good," he says again. "I think you're really going to like Mirac."

I *know* I'm going to like it, I think—but for once restrain myself from saying out loud—if *you're* there, Luke.

"Thanks," I say. And wonder if he's going to kiss me now.

And then we both hear a car coming and Luke says, "Oh, great. Here's our ride." And abruptly drops my wrists.

And an ancient butter-yellow convertible Mercedes pulls into the parking lot, driven by a honey-colored blonde who calls out in a French accent, "Sorry I'm late, *chéri!*"

And I know, even before he hurries down to kiss her, who she is.

His girlfriend.

It so figures.

Women were not the only ones who were interested in showing off their figures in the early 1800s. This period saw the introduction of the "dandy," followers of the fashion icon George "Beau" Brummell, a gentleman who insisted his trousers fit tightly as a second skin and could not abide a wrinkle in his waistcoat. A dandy's neckwear consisted of a collar so high he could not turn his head from side to side.

It is not known how many gentlemen met their deaths from stepping out in front of oncoming carriages they failed to see.

History of Fashion
SENIOR THESIS BY ELIZABETH NICHOLS

Because of course he has a girlfriend. He's way too fabulous not to—that little keeping-his-true-identity-a-secret-from-me thing aside.

The thing is, she seems really nice. She's definitely gorgeous, with all that hair and her slim tanned shoulders and long, equally tanned legs. She's wearing a very simple black tank top and a longish peasant skirt (new, not vintage, and expensive-looking, too) with jeweled flip-flops. She's definitely in vacation mode.

Although my fashion radar may be off, because Dominique Desautels—that's her name—like Andy, is foreign. She's Canadian. *French* Canadian. She works at the same investment banking company in Houston that Luke does.

And they've been going out for six months.

At least that's what I'm able to gather from my careful questioning of them both from the backseat of the Mercedes before my voice dies.

Because it's very hard to concentrate on gathering information about the two of them when we're whizzing past such beautiful scenery. The sun has set, but the moon's rising, so I can still make out enormous oaks, their branches twisting across the road to make a sort of canopy of leaves above us. We're careening down a twisting two-lane country road that winds alongside a wide, burbling river. It's hard to tell, judging by the scenery, where, exactly, we are.

Or even *when* we are. Judging by the lack of telephone poles and streetlights, this could be *any* century, not just the twenty-first. We even pass an old-fashioned mill—a mill! With one of those big paddle wheels on the side of it!—with a thatched roof and beautiful garden.

There are electric lights on in the windows of the mill, though, indicating that this isn't the 1800s.

Still, I see a family in there, sitting down to dinner.

In a millhouse!

It's very hard to remember that I am depressed about my boyfriend turning out to have a gambling problem when the scenery whizzing past me is so picturesque.

Then we pass out from beneath the canopy of trees and I see towering cliffs above us, with castles on top of them, and Luke explains that this area of France (known as the Dordogne, after the river) is famous for its castles, having over a thousand of them, as well as for its caves, on the walls of some of which are paintings dating back to 15,000 BCE.

Then Dominique adds that Périgord, which is the part of the Dordogne we are in, is also known for its black truffles and foie gras. I am barely listening, though. It's hard not to be distracted by the sight of a set of high-fortified walls—Luke says they belong to the ancient medieval village of Sarlat, and that we can go there to shop if I want to.

Shop! They couldn't possibly have a vintage store there. But maybe a thrift shop . . . God, could you imagine the finds just waiting for someone like me? Givenchy, Dior, Chanel . . . who KNOWS?

Then we turn off the road onto what appears to be a very steep gravel-covered mountain track, barely wide enough for the car to pass. Branches, in fact, are whipping the side of it—and nearly me, as well, until I move into the middle of the backseat.

Dominique notices when I move and says, "You've got to get the men to trim that back before your mother gets here, Jean-Luc. You know how she is."

Luke says, "I know, I know," and then, to me, says, "You all right back there?"

"I'm good," I say, clutching the back of the seats in front of me. I am being bounced around quite a bit. The driveway—if that's what it is—needs some maintenance.

And then, just when I think the shuddering car can't take it anymore—and am starting to wonder if we'll ever reach the top of this hill, or if tree limbs are going to whip our heads off first—we burst through the last of the trees onto a wide, grassy plateau overlooking the valley below. Bright torches line the driveway, leading up to what appears to be—if my eyes are not deceiving me—the same house Mr. Darcy lived in in the A&E version of *Pride and Prejudice.*

Only this mansion is bigger. And more elegant-looking. With more outbuildings.

And it has electric light, which is making what looks like hundreds of windows blaze brightly against the blue satin sky. Arcing out from the circular driveway is a wide lawn dotted with huge, elegant oak trees, a massive swimming pool—lit up and gleaming like a sapphire in the night—and a scattering of white wrought-iron lawn furniture.

It is the most perfect place for a wedding that I have ever seen. The entire well-manicured lawn is fenced in with a low stone wall. All I can see beyond the wall, which appears to drop off into thin air, is a vast expanse of moonlit trees, far below, and then, off in the distance, another cliff like the one we're on, topped by a château that could be a sister to this one, its own lights blazing in the night sky.

It is breathtaking. Literally. I find I've stopped breathing, gazing at it all.

Luke pulls the car into the circular driveway and switches the motor off. All I can hear is crickets.

"Well?" he says, turning around in his seat. "What do you think?"

I am, for the first time in my life, speechless. It is an historic occasion, but Luke doesn't even know it.

The crickets sound very loud in the silence that follows Luke's question. I still can't breathe.

"Yes," Dominique says, getting out of the car and heading toward the château's massive oak doors, the garment bag with the wedding gown in it in both her hands. "It tends to have that effect on people. It's pretty, isn't it?"

Pretty? *Pretty?* That's like calling the Grand Canyon big.

"It's," I say, not finally finding my voice until Dominique has gone inside and Luke is helping me pull my suitcases from the trunk, "the most beautiful place I've ever seen."

"Really?" Luke looks down at me, his dark eyes hooded in the moonlight. "Do you think so?"

He keeps saying he's bad at telling jokes. But he has to be kidding me. There can't be any more beautiful place on the entire planet.

"Completely," I say, though even that seems like a total understatement.

And then I hear familiar voices from the grassy terrace overlooking the valley.

"Is that Monsieur de Villiers, returned from Paris?" Chaz, striding out from the shadows of one of the massive trees, demands. "Why, yes, it is. And who is that with him?"

Then, midway across the circular drive, Chaz stops, recognizing me. It's hard to tell, with the moon at his back—and the bill of his University of Michigan baseball cap pulled low over his eyes, as always—but I think he's smiling.

"Well, well, well," he says in a pleased way. "Look what the cat drug in."

"What?" And Shari appears behind him. "Oh, hi, Luke. Did you get the—"

Then her voice trails off. And a second later she shrieks, "LIZZIE? IS THAT YOU?"

Then she's leaping across the driveway and all over me, and shouting, "You came! You came! I can't believe you came! How did you get here? Luke, where did you find her?"

"On the train," Luke says, smiling at the panicky look I throw him over Shari's shoulder as she's hugging me.

But he doesn't elaborate. Just like I'd asked him not to.

"But that's amazing," Shari cries. "I mean, that you two, of all people, would run into each other—"

"Not really," Chaz says mildly. "I mean, considering they were probably the only two Americans heading for Souillac—"

"Oh, not another one of your philosophical speeches on the nature of randomness," Shari says to Chaz. "PLEASE." To me, she cries, "But why didn't you call? We'd have met you at the station."

"I *did* call," I say. "About a hundred times. But I kept getting your voice mail."

"That's impossible," Shari says, pulling her cell phone out of the pocket of her shorts. "I have my . . . Oh." She squints at the screen in the moonlight. "I forgot to turn it on this morning."

"I figured you'd dropped it in the toilet," I said.

"Not this time," Chaz says, wrapping an arm around my shoulders to give me a quick welcoming hug. As he does so, he whispers, "Is there anybody back in England that I have to beat up? Because, with God as my witness, I'll go over there and kick his scrawny naked ass for you. Just say the word."

"No," I assure him, laughing a little painfully. "It's okay. Really. It's as much my fault as it is his. I should have listened to you. You were right. You're always right."

"Not always," Chaz says, dropping his arm. "It's just that the times I'm wrong don't register in your memory with as much clarity as the times I'm right. Still, go right ahead thinking I'm always right if you want to."

"Cut it out, Chaz," Shari says. "Who cares about what happened in England, anyway? She's here now. It's okay if she stays, right, Luke?"

"I don't know," Luke says teasingly. "Can she pull her weight? We don't need any more slackers around here. We've already got this one." He slaps Chaz on the shoulder.

"Hey," Chaz says, "I'm helping out. I'm testing all the alcohol for purity and freshness before Luke's mom gets here."

Shari shakes her head at her boyfriend and says, "You're insufferable." To Luke, she says, "Lizzie's superhandy. Well, with a needle. If you've got any seamstressy stuff to do . . ."

Luke seems surprised to learn that I can actually sew. Most people are. It's not something many people know how to do anymore.

"I just might," he says. "I'll check with, ahem, Mom when she gets here tomorrow. But right now I think we have more pressing concerns—helping Chaz with the alcohol testing."

"This way, ladies," Chaz says, indicating, with a courtly bow, the path to the outdoor bar he's apparently set up, "and gentleman."

Shari and I follow the guys into the cool, slightly damp grass. As we get closer to the low stone wall, I glance over it and see the valley stretched below, the river—just as Chaz promised—winking in the moonlight like a long, silver snake. It is so beautiful my throat catches. I feel as if I am in a daze. Or a dream.

And I am not the only one.

"I can't believe this," Shari whispers, still hanging on to my arm. "What happened? I know I was pretty drunk last time I talked to you, but I thought you said you were going to try to work things out with Andy."

"Yeah," I whisper back. "Well, I did try. But then I found out—well, it's a long story. I'll tell you sometime when"—I nod my head in Luke and Chaz's direction—"*they're* not around."

Although of course Luke already knows most of it.

Well, okay. All of it.

And I do mean *all*.

"Was it bad?" Shari asks, concern creasing her pretty face. "Are you okay?"

"I'm fine," I assure her. "Really. I wasn't before, but . . ." I glance in Luke's direction again. "Well, I had a very sympathetic shoulder to cry on."

Shari's dark-eyed gaze follows mine. I see her eyebrows go up beneath her curly bangs. I wonder what she's thinking. Not, I hope, *Oh, poor little Lizzie, in love with a guy so out of her league.*

Because I'm not. In love with him, I mean.

But all she says is, "Well, I'm glad about that. So your heart's not broken?"

"You know," I say thoughtfully, "I don't think it is. A little bruised, is all. Is it really all right that I'm here? What's Chaz talking about, Luke's mom coming tomorrow?"

Shari grimaces. "Luke's mom and dad are getting divorced, but apparently she—Mrs. de Villiers—promised her niece a long time ago that she could get married at Mirac. So she—Mrs. de Villiers, I mean—is arriving tomorrow, with her sister, the niece, the groom—the whole family. It should be a helluva party. Especially considering Luke's parents are barely speaking, and he's caught up in the middle of the whole thing. According to Chaz, Luke's mom is some kind of battle-ax."

I wince, remembering Dominique's warning about Luke needing to get the brush along the driveway cleared before his mom's arrival.

"So they won't want me here," I whisper, to make sure Luke doesn't overhear us. I say *they,* but I mean Luke, of course. "I mean, I don't want to crash—"

"Lizzie, it's *totally* okay," Shari says. "This place is huge, and there's plenty of room. Even with Luke's entire extended family here, there are rooms to spare. And there'll be plenty to do. It's actually good you're here. We could use the help. Apparently this niece—Luke's cousin, Vicky—is some kind of Texas socialite. She already browbeat Luke into making the trip to Paris and back just to pick up her dress from the fancy Parisian seamstress who made it, and she's not even here yet. Plus, she's apparently invited half of Houston for this wedding, including her brother's garage band, who just got some kind of recording contract and are supposed to be the Next Hot Thing. So it's not exactly going to be intimate."

"Oh," I say. "Well, good. Because I really couldn't think what else to do other than come here. I couldn't go home—"

"Of course you couldn't," Shari says, sounding horrified. "Your sisters would have had a field day!"

"I know," I say. "So I just figured . . . well, you'd said it was okay to come here—"

"I'm so glad you did. I mean, look at the two of them." She nods toward her boyfriend and Luke, who've drifted over to one of the wrought-iron tables and are mixing up some kind of concoction in fluted champagne glasses. "They're like long-lost twins. All they do is yak, yak, yak about everything under the sun—Nietzsche, Tiger Woods, beer, the probability of coincident birth dates, the good old days at prep school. I've been feeling like a total third wheel." She puts her arm around me. "But now I've got my own friend to yak with."

"Well," I say with a grin, "you know I'm always good for a bit of yaking. But what about Luke's girlfriend, Dominique? You can't yak with her?"

Shari makes a face. "Sure. If you want to yak about Dominique."

"Oh," I say. "I sort of got the idea, what with the flip-flops."

"Really?" Shari looks interested. She's always valued my fashion analyses. "They give you a bad vibe?"

"No," I say hastily. "Nothing like that. Just sort of like she's trying too hard. But then she's Canadian. I think my radar is off when it comes to foreigners."

Shari winces. "You mean Andy? Yeah, well, I always did wonder what you saw in him. But you're not wrong about Dominique. Those flip-flops? They're Manolo Blahniks."

"No!" Manolo Blahnik flip-flops, I know from my *Vogue* perusing, can cost upward of six hundred dollars. "Gosh. I always wondered who bought them—"

"Hey, you two." Chaz strolls across the moonlit grass toward us. "No shirking your duties. There's alcohol to inspect."

"Hang on." Luke is one step behind him. "I've got their first test subjects here." He hands each of us a champagne flute filled with sparkling liquid. "Kir royales," he says, "with champagne made right here at Mirac."

I don't know what a kir royale is, but I'm game to try one. Dominique reappears and lays claim to a glass as well.

"What shall we drink to?" she asks, raising her glass.

"How about," Luke says, "to strangers meeting on a train."

I smile at him across the few feet of grass separating us.

"Sounds good to me," I say, and clink glasses with everyone. Then I take a sip.

It is like drinking liquid gold. The mingled flavors of berry, sunlight, and champagne dance on my tongue. Kir royale turns out to be champagne with a sort of liqueur in it—cassis, Shari explains, which is a type of berry.

"Now *you* explain something to me," Shari says when she's through with her cassis commentary.

"Hmm?" I am pretty fairly convinced by now that this is all just a dream from which I'm going to wake up eventually. But until that moment, I plan on enjoying myself. "What's that?"

"What did Luke mean with that toast? Strangers on a train and all that?"

"Oh." I glance over at him, where he's laughing with Chaz. "I don't know. Nothing."

Shari narrows her eyes at me. "Don't you nothing me, Lizzie. Spill. What happened on that train?"

"Nothing!" I cry, laughing a little myself. "Well, I mean, I was upset—you know, about Andy. And I cried a bit. But like I said . . . he was very sympathetic."

Shari just shakes her head. "There's more to this story. Something you aren't telling me. I know it."

"There's not," I assure her.

"Well," Shari says, "if there is, I know I'll find out eventually. You've never kept a secret in your life."

I just smile at her. There are a couple of secrets I've managed to keep from her so far. And I don't plan on spilling them anytime soon.

But all I say is, "Really, Shari. Nothing happened."

Which is, basically, the truth.

A little while later, I stroll toward the low stone wall and stand there, trying to take it all in—the valley; the moon rising over the roof of the château across from ours; the starry night sky; the crickets; the sweet smell of some kind of night-blooming flower.

It's too much. It's all too much. To go from that horrible little office in the Job Centre to this, all in one day . . .

Beside me, Luke, who has somehow managed to break away from Chaz and Dominique for a minute, asks softly, "Better now?"

"Getting there," I reply, smiling up at him. "I can't thank you enough for letting me stay here. And thanks for . . . you know. Not telling them. Anything."

He looks genuinely surprised. "Of course," he says. "What else are friends for?"

Friends. So that's what we are.

And somehow, there in the moonlight? That's more than enough.

The Romantic movement of the 1820s brought back a yearning for narrow-waisted heroines like the ones in the novels of Sir Walter Scott (the Dan Brown of his day—though Sir Walter would not have dared dress a French heroine in a big sweater and black leggings, as Mr. Brown did poor Sophie Neveu in *The Da Vinci Code*), and corsets gained popularity while skirts became wider. So beloved was Sir Walter that a brief craze for tartan overtook a few of the less sensible ladies of the time, though thankfully they soon realized the error of their ways.

History of Fashion
SENIOR THESIS BY ELIZABETH NICHOLS

I should not talk so much about myself if there were anybody else whom I knew as well.
—*Henry David Thoreau (1817–1862),*
U.S. philosopher, author, and naturalist

When I wake up the following morning, I look around the tiny, low-ceilinged room I'm in, with its bright white walls and dark wood rafters, in confusion. The curtains—cream-colored, with large pink roses splotched on them—are drawn across the room's single window, so I can't see outside. For a second I can't remember where I am—whose bedroom, or even what *country*.

Then I see the old-fashioned door, with its latch you press down on instead of turn—like the latch to a garden gate—and I realize I'm at Château Mirac. In one of the dozen attic bedrooms—which, in the château's glory days, housed the serving staff—and which now house Shari, Chaz, and myself—not to mention Jean-Luc and his girlfriend, Dominique.

That's because the château's formal bedrooms, below us, are reserved for the wedding party—and guests—that are due to arrive this afternoon. While renting out the main house, Luke's father—whom Shari refers to as Monsieur de Villiers—stays in a small thatched-roofed cottage near the outbuildings, where he keeps the oak casks of his wine before it's ready for bottling. Shari told me last night, as we climbed the seemingly hundreds of stairs to our rooms after four—or was it five?—more kir royales, that birds regularly nest in the thatch and have to be chased away lest their waste eat through the roof.

Somehow a thatched roof will never seem picturesque to me again.

After blinking groggily at the cracks in the ceiling above, I realize what's wakened me. Someone is knocking on the door.

"Lizzie," I hear Shari say, "are you up yet? It's noon. What are you going to do, sleep all day?"

I throw back the duvet and rush to the door to hurl it open. Shari is standing there in a bikini and a sarong holding two enormous, steaming mugs. Her hair, which is normally dark and curly, is looking enormous, a sure sign that it's hot outside.

"Is it really noon?" I ask, freaking out that I slept so long and wondering if people—okay, Luke—are going to think I'm a rude slacker.

"Five after," Shari says. "I hope you brought a swimsuit. We've got to try to catch as many rays as we can before Luke's mom and her guests arrive and we have to start setting things up for the meals and wine tastings. That only gives us about four hours. But first"—she thrusts one of the steaming mugs at me—"cappuccino. Lots of aspartame, just the way you like it."

"Oh," I say appreciatively as the milky steam bathes my face. "You are a lifesaver."

"I know," Shari says, and comes into the room to make herself comfortable on the end of my rumpled bed. "Now. I want to know everything that happened with Andy. And with Luke, on the train. So spill."

I do, settling in beside her. Well, I don't tell her *everything*, of course. I've still never told her the truth about my thesis, and I'm definitely never telling her about the blow job. Of course, I told a total stranger on a train about both. But somehow that was much easier than telling my best friend, who would, I know, only disapprove of both—especially the latter. I mean, a blow job, without reciprocation, is the height of antifeminism.

"So," Shari says when I'm through, "you and Andy are really over."

"Definitely," I say, sipping the last of my delicious cappuccino.

"You told him that. You told him it's over."

"Totally," I say. Didn't I? I think I did.

"Lizzie." Shari gives me a hard look. "I know how much you hate confrontation. Did you *really* tell him it's over?"

"I told him I need to be alone," I say . . . realizing, a little belatedly, that that's not the same thing as telling someone it's over.

Still, Andy got the message. I *know* he did.

But just in case, maybe I won't pick up if he calls again.

"And you're really okay with that?" Shari wants to know.

"Mostly," I say. "I mean, I guess I feel pretty guilty about the money—"

"What money?"

"The money he wanted to borrow," I say. "For his matriculation fees. I probably should have given it to him. Because now he's not going to be able to go to school in the fall—"

"Lizzie," Shari says in tones of disbelief, "he *had* the money . . . he gambled it away! If you'd given him more, he just would have gambled that away, too. You'd have been enabling him to continue his destructive behavior. Is that what you want? To be an enabler?"

"No," I say mournfully, "but, you know. I did really love him. You can't turn love on and off, like a faucet."

"You can if the guy's trying to take advantage of your generous nature."

"I guess." I sigh. "I really shouldn't feel bad. He *was* getting unemployment money while being employed."

One corner of Shari's mouth turns up. "I love how, to you, that's obviously the worst thing he did. What about the gambling? What about the fat thing?"

"But cheating the government is way worse than either of those."

"Okay. If you say so. Anyway, good riddance to him. Now will you stop being such a pain in my ass and just move to New York with me and Chaz?"

"Shari," I say. "Really. I just—" How can I tell her the truth? That I can't possibly go job-hunting in New York City without a college degree, and I don't know if I'll be done with my thesis by the time she and Chaz are ready to leave. Also the whole even-if-I have-a-degree-I'm-not-so-sure-I-can-make-it-in-the-big-city thing.

"Fine," Shari says, clearly misinterpreting my reluctance. "I get it. It's a big step. You need time to adjust to the idea. I know. Well, what about the other thing?"

"What other thing?"

"About you and Luke. On that train."

"Shari, I already told you. Nothing happened. I mean, come on. I just got out of a disastrous relationship with a guy I hardly knew. You think I'm going to rush into another one right away? Give me some credit. Besides, have you had a good look at his girlfriend? Why would a guy who has that go for a girl like me?"

"I can think of a few reasons," Shari says darkly.

But before I have a chance to ask what she means, she says, "All right, listen. I know you've been through a lot the past couple days, so I won't bug you about the New York thing for a while. How about you take some time off from worrying about the future? God knows you deserve it. Consider the next few days a well-earned vacation. We'll revisit the subject later, when you've had a chance to recover from finding out that the man of your dreams was actually more of a nightmare. Now"—she smacks me on the leg—"throw on your suit and meet me at the pool. We have tanning to do."

I don't argue. I hurry to grab my beauty supplies so I can have a quick wash before hitting the pool.

"And hurry up," she says before stomping away. "Prime tanning hours are a-wasting."

I rush to comply, since Shari doesn't like having her orders disobeyed. I dart across the hall into an ancient bathroom that comes complete with a massive claw-foot tub and a toilet with a wooden seat and one of those chain-pull flushers. After a quick bath and makeup application, I pull on my bikini—the first time I've ever worn one in my life. My sisters used to mock me mercilessly every time I tried to put a two-piece on, back in my pre-weight-loss days.

Of course, that might have been because all my bathing suits were vintage one-pieces, many of which had built-in little skirts and had a distinct Annette Funicello flare to them.

Still, while I may have been the chubbiest girl at the pool, I was always the most originally dressed . . . or, as Rose used to put it, the biggest "fashion freak."

My new suit doesn't make me look like a freak at all. At least, I don't think so. It's a two-piece, but it's vintage, too . . . vintage Lilly Pulitzer, from the sixties. Sarah used to say it was gross to wear someone else's old swimsuit, but it's actually perfectly hygienic if you wash it a few times before you wear it.

Now, checking out my reflection in the somewhat dim but otherwise fairly reliable mirror on the back of the bathroom door, I think I look . . . all right. I'm no Dominique, of course. But then, who among us can be?

Except, of course, for Dominique.

I hurry back to my room, tug a matching Lilly Pulitzer sundress over my suit, and hurriedly make my bed, pausing to throw back the rose curtains, then open the small diamond-shaped window so I can let in some fresh air . . .

And catch my breath, struck by what I see out my window . . .

Which is nothing less than the daylight view of the valley stretching out below the château. Green velvet treetops and rolling hills, pale brown cliffsides and, high above it all, the bluest, most cloudless sky I have ever seen.

And it's all so beautiful. I can see, seemingly, for miles, nothing but trees, and the silver river winding through them, dotted by tiny village hamlets, with the occasional château or castle perched on a cliffside above. It's like something out of a book of fairy tales.

How can Luke, I wonder, go back to Houston after having spent any amount of time here? How can anyone go *anywhere* else?

But I don't have time to mull over this. I have to meet Shari at the pool or face her wrath.

It's no joke, trying to find my way back downstairs through the myriad hallways and staircases that seem to make up Château Mirac, but I manage somehow to end up in the marble foyer, and slip outside into the soft, sweetly scented summer air. Somewhere in the distance I hear the whine of a motor—possibly a lawn mower, judging by the smell of freshly cut grass—and the tinkle of . . . cowbells? It can't be.

Or can it?

I don't pause to investigate. I put on my rhinestone-studded sunglasses, then hurry across the driveway, and finally across the lawn to the pool, where I see Shari, Dominique, and another girl all stretched out across chaise longues with blue-and-white striped cushions. The chaise longues face the valley, and the sun. Dominique and the other girl are already brown—this is undoubtedly not the first day they've spent lying out. Shari, I can see, is determined to gain on them before the summer is over.

"Good morning," I say to Dominique and the other girl, who is on the chubby side and looks like a teenager. She's in a blue one-piece Speedo while Dominique, beside her, is in a black Calvin Klein string bikini.

And the strings don't seem to be tied very tightly.

"*Bonjour,*" the teenager says to me cheerfully.

"Lizzie, this is Agnès," Shari says. Only she pronounces it the French way, which is *Ahn-yes.* "She's staying here for the summer as the resident au pair. Her family lives in the millhouse down the road."

"Oh!" I cry. "I saw the millhouse! It's so beautiful!"

Agnès continues to smile at me pleasantly. It's Dominique who says, "Don't bother. She doesn't understand a word of English. She claimed she did when she applied to work here, but she doesn't, beyond hello, good-bye, and thank you."

"Oh," I say. And smile back at Agnès. "*Bonjour! Je m'appelle Lizzie,*" which pretty much exhausts what French phrases I know, with the exception of *Excusez-moi* and *J'aime pas des tomates.*

Agnès says a lot of stuff back to me, none of which I understand. Shari says, "Just smile and nod and you two'll get along fine."

And so I do. Agnès beams at me, then hands me a white towel and a bottle of cold water from a cooler she's brought with her. I wonder if there's any diet Coke in the cooler, but a glimpse before she closes the lid tells me there's not. Do they even HAVE diet Coke in France? They must. It's not the Third World, for crying out loud.

I thank Agnès for the water and spread the towel out on the chaise longue between hers and Dominique's. I peel off my dress, then kick off my sandals. Then I lie back against the comfy cushion and find myself gazing at a cloudless blue sky.

This, I realize, is something I could get used to. Fast. England, and its cool, moist air, seems a long time ago.

So, for that matter, does Andy.

"That's an . . . unusual swimsuit," Dominique says.

"Thank you," I say, even though I have a sneaking suspicion she didn't mean it as a compliment. But I'm probably just projecting again, on account of the six-hundred-dollar flip-flops. "So where are Luke and Chaz?"

"Trimming the branches along the driveway," Shari says.

"Ouch," I say. "Don't they have—I don't know. A tree-trimming company who does that?"

Dominique shoots me a very sarcastic look from behind her Gucci sunglasses.

"Certainly—if someone had thought to call them in time. But as usual, Jean-Luc's father waited until the last minute and couldn't get anyone. So now Jean-Luc has to do it, if he doesn't want Bibi to have a fit when she arrives."

"Bibi?"

"Jean-Luc's mother," Dominique explains.

"Mrs. de Villiers is kind of . . . particular, from what I understand," Shari says tonelessly from her chaise longue.

Dominique lets out a delicate snort. "You could say that," she says. "You could also say, of course, that she's merely frustrated by her husband's complete and total absentmindedness. All he thinks about are his stupid grapes."

"Grapes?"

Dominique waves a hand behind us, toward some of the château's outbuildings behind which I'd seen some kind of orchard stretching.

"The vineyard," she says.

So it was a vineyard, not an orchard! Of course!

"Oh," I say. "Well, shouldn't Monsieur de Villiers think about his grapes? This place is primarily a vineyard, isn't it? Isn't the wedding thing just sort of a side business?"

"Of course," Dominique says, "but Mirac hasn't had a decent harvest in years. First there were the droughts, then a blight . . . anyone else would take this as a hint to move on, but not Jean-Luc's father. He says the de Villiers family has been in the wine business since the 1600s, when Mirac was first built, and he's not going to be the one to give up on it."

"Well," I say admiringly, "that's kind of . . . noble. I mean, isn't it?"

Dominique makes a disgusted noise. "Noble? It is a total waste. Mirac has got such tremendous potential, if only Jean-Luc and his father would see it."

"Potential?" What is she talking about? It's gorgeous the way it is. The perfect grounds, the beautiful house, the frothy cappuccino . . . what needs changing?

Dominique has a few suggestions, it turns out.

"Well, it's obviously in terrible need of updating. The place needs a total renovation—particularly the bathrooms. We need to replace those tacky claw-foot tubs with Jacuzzis . . . and pull-chain toilets! My God. They have to go as well."

"I kind of like the pull-chain toilets," I say. "I think they're sort of . . . charming."

"Well, yes, of course *you* would think that," Dominique says, and raises an eyebrow meaningfully in the direction of my swimsuit. "But most people do not. The kitchen, too, needs a total overhaul. Do you know they still have a—what do you call it? Oh yes. A larder. Ridiculous. No chef in his right mind could be hired who would work under the current conditions."

"Chef?" I say. And even as I think of cooking food, my stomach rumbles. I'm starving. I know I've missed breakfast, but when's lunch? Is there really a chef? Did he make the cappuccino?

"But of course. In order to turn Mirac into a true world-class hotel, it will need a five-star Michelin chef."

Oh. So . . .

"Turn it into a . . ." I sit up and stare down at Dominique. "Wait. They're thinking of turning this place into a *hotel*?"

"Not yet," Dominique says, reaching for a bottle of water she has sitting by her chaise longue. "But as I keep telling Jean-Luc,

they ought to. Just think of the fortune that could be made in corporate retreat and convention business alone! And then, of course,
there's the spa route—they could easily get rid of the vineyards—
turn them into jogging paths or horseback-riding trails—and
convert the outbuildings into massage, acupuncture, and hydro-
therapy rooms. The plastic surgery recovery industry is booming
right now—"

"The what?" I interrupt. I'm sorry to say I yelled it, too. But I was
just so shocked at the idea of anyone wanting to turn this fabulous
place into a *spa*.

"The plastic surgery recovery industry," Dominique repeats,
looking annoyed. "People who've recently undergone liposuction
or a face-lift need a place to recover, and I've always thought Mirac
would be outstanding in that capacity—"

I can't help it. I have to look over to see what Shari thinks about
all this.

But she merely holds the book she is pretending to read even
closer to her face, in order to hide her expression.

Still, I can see her shoulders shaking. She can't stop laughing.

"Really," Dominique goes on, taking another sip of her water.
"The de Villiers family has failed to see the entrepreneurial potential of this property. By hiring trained professional servers—instead
of the local riffraff—and offering services such as broadband and
satellite television—installing air-conditioning, and perhaps even a
home movie theater—they will attract a much wealthier clientele.
And turn over a much bigger profit than Jean-Luc's father's puny
wine business ever has."

Before I can make any sort of reply to this horrifying speech, my
stomach chooses to do my talking for me, letting out an extremely
loud gurgle of hunger. Dominique ignores it, but Agnès sits up and
babbles something that sounds like a question. I do hear the word
goûter, which I know means "to taste."

"She wants to know if you want her to get you something to eat," Dominique translates in a bored voice.

I say, "Oh. Uh . . ."

Agnès babbles some more, and Dominique says in the same bored voice, "It's no trouble. She's getting herself a snack anyway."

"Oh," I say. "Then, yes, thank you, I'd love one." I beam at Agnès and say, *"Oui, merci."* Then I add, *"Est-ce que vous . . . Est-ce que vous . . ."*

"What are you trying to ask her?" Dominique asks—a little waspishly, I think. But maybe I'm projecting, because of the liposuction thing. I'm still having a hard time believing that she really wants to turn this beautiful place into one of those hotels where they send contestants on *The Swan* after they get their new noses.

"I wanted to know if they've got any diet Coke," I say.

Dominique makes a face. "Of course not. Why would you want to put those kinds of terrible chemicals in your body?"

Because they're delicious, I want to say. But instead I say, "Oh. Okay. Then . . . nothing."

Dominique snaps something at Agnès, who nods, leaps up from her towel, stuffs her feet into a pair of rubber clogs—which seem like the appropriate footwear for walking through gravel and grass. WAY more appropriate than suede Manolos—grabs her sarong, and takes off for the house.

"Wow," I say. "She's so nice."

"She's *supposed* to do what you say. She's the *help*," Dominique says.

I look over at Shari. "Um . . . but aren't we, too? The help, I mean?"

"But you aren't expected to fetch and carry for people," Dominique says. "And you mustn't *vous* her."

"I'm sorry." I shake my head. "I mustn't *what*?"

"You *vous*'d her," Dominique says. "When you tried to speak

French to her just now. That isn't proper. She's younger than you, and she's a servant. You should *tu* her—the informal version of *you*—*tu* as opposed to *vous*. You'll give her airs above her station. Not that she doesn't already suffer from them—I don't actually think it's appropriate for her to be using the pool during her time off. But Jean-Luc said it was all right, so now there's no getting rid of her."

I sit there gaping at her some more, completely unable to believe the words that have just come out of Dominique's mouth. Shari, for her part, is actually covering her face with her book, she's trying so hard not to let it show how much she's laughing.

As if Dominique would even notice. Not when she's busy doing what she does next, which is say, "It's *so* hot . . ."

Which, actually, it is. It's broiling out. In fact, before Dominique started in on that *vous*-versus-*tu* thing, I'd been thinking about taking a plunge into that clear blue water shimmering so tantalizingly in front of us . . .

But then Dominique does me one better by suddenly sitting up, undoing her bikini top, flipping it over the back of her chaise longue, then stretching and saying, "Ah. That's better."

The year 1848 (aptly nicknamed the Year of Revolutions) saw many peasant uprisings throughout Europe and the fall of the monarchy in France, as well as the potato famine in Ireland, and fashion responded to the unrest by requiring women to look as covered up as possible, with "poke" bonnets and skirts that trailed filthily to the floor declared the season's "must-haves."

This was the age of Jane Eyre, whom we all remember refused to accept Mr. Rochester's generous offer to make over her wardrobe, preferring merino wool to the silk organzas he ordered for her. If only she'd had Melania Trump to set her straight on this wrongheaded attitude toward fashion.

History of Fashion
SENIOR THESIS BY ELIZABETH NICHOLS

14

Never to talk about ourselves is a very noble piece of hypocrisy.
—*Friedrich Nietzsche (1844–1900),*
German philosopher, classical scholar, and critic

and okay. I *know* this is Europe and people here are much more laid-back about their bodies and nudity than we are (except that Dominique isn't European. She's Canadian. Which I guess is sort of like European. But still).

It's just very hard to sit and talk to someone whose bare nipples are sort of . . . *pointing* at you.

And Shari's no help at all. She's keeping her gaze resolutely on the pages of the book she's reading. Though I notice she's not actually *turning* any of those pages.

I realize there's nothing I can do except try to act normal. I mean, it's not like I'm not used to seeing bare-chested women, considering the gang showers back in McCracken Hall.

Still. I *knew* all those girls.

Plus, Dominique's knockers are—how can I put this?—a bit more suspiciously perky than even Brianna Dunleavy's.

And Brianna worked part-time at Bare Assets Cocktail Lounge.

"So," I say, casually, "have you mentioned all these ideas you have for, um, improving Mirac to Luke?"

Because I can't help wondering what *he* thinks of Dominique's plans.

"Of course," Dominique says, lifting a hand to slick back her long blond hair. "And to his father as well. But the old man is only interested in one thing. His wine. So until he dies . . ." Dominique gives a metaphoric shrug.

"Luke's waiting for his father to die before turning this place into a Hyatt Regency?" I ask, my voice cracking a little in my astonishment. Because I simply can't believe the Luke I met yesterday would ever do such a thing.

"A Hyatt?" Dominique looks scandalized. "I told you, it will be five-star luxury accommodation, not part of a cheap American hotel chain. And no, Jean-Luc is not entirely enthusiastic about my plans. Yet. For one thing because he would have to move to France full-time to see them implemented, and he isn't interested in giving up his job at Lazard Frères. Although I've told him it would be a simple thing to transfer to their Paris offices. Then we could—"

"We?" I'm on the word like Grandma on a can of Bud. "You two are getting married?"

"Well, certainly," Dominique says. "Someday."

It's ridiculous that this statement sends a shaft of pain through my heart. I barely know him. I only met him yesterday.

But then I'm the same girl who traveled all the way to England to see a guy I had only spent twenty-four hours with three months earlier.

And look how *that* turned out.

"Oh," Shari finally pipes up, "you and Luke are engaged? That's funny, Chaz never mentioned that to me. I'd have thought Luke would have told him."

"Well, nothing so formal as an engagement," Dominique says with obvious reluctance. "Who even gets engaged anymore? It's so old-fashioned. Today's couples, they form partnerships, not marriages. It's all about combining incomes and investing in a shared future. And I knew, from the first moment I saw Mirac, that this is a future I wanted to invest in."

I blink at her. Today's couples form partnerships, not marriages? They combine incomes and invest in a shared future?

And what's this about *from the first moment I saw Mirac*? Doesn't she mean *from the first moment I saw Jean-Luc*?

"It *is* a beautiful place," Shari says, turning a page of her book that I know she hasn't read. "Why do you think it is that Luke doesn't want to move to Paris?"

"Because Jean-Luc doesn't know what he wants," Dominique says with a frustrated sigh.

"Does any man?" Shari asks mildly. And I can tell, from her tone, that she is highly amused by the conversation.

"Maybe he doesn't want to be that far away from you," I offer— very generously, in my opinion, considering my little crush on her boyfriend. Since that's all it is. Just a crush. Really.

Dominique turns her head to look at me. "I have offered to transfer to Paris with him," she says tonelessly.

"Oh," I say. "Well. His mom lives in Houston, right? Maybe he doesn't want to leave her."

"That's not it," Dominique says. "It's that if he puts in a request to transfer to Paris and it goes through, he'll have to go. And then he'll be stuck there. And there'll be no chance for him ever to pursue the career he really wants."

"What's the career he really wants?" I ask.

"He wants," Dominique says, picking up the bottle of water she has by her chaise longue and raising it to her lips, then swallowing, "to be a doctor."

"A doctor?" I'm thrilled. I can't believe Luke didn't mention this on the train when I said all those bad things about investment bankers. "Really? But that's so great. I mean, doctors . . . they heal people."

Dominique looks at me as if I've just said the most obvious thing in the world. Which, of course, I have.

But she obviously hasn't figured out that I routinely say the first thing that pops into my head. Seriously. It's like a disease.

"What I mean is," I hasten to add, "doctors are so important. You know. To society. Because without them, we'd all . . . be a lot sicker."

I look over at her to see what she thinks of this stroke of deductive brilliance on my part. Dominique has leaned up on her elbows—though the movement, mysteriously enough, did not cause her breasts to move at all—to look past me, over at Shari.

"Your friend," she says to Shari, "talks very much."

"Yes," Shari says. "Lizzie does have a tendency to do that."

"I'm sorry," I say, feeling myself blush. But it's not like I'm going to shut up. Because I physically *can't.* "But why doesn't Luke go to medical school? I mean, if that's what he wants to do? Because it can't be that doctors don't make enough money." The Luke I know—the one who let me, a total stranger, cry on his shoulder on that train yesterday—and shared his nuts with me—would never choose a career based on what kind of salary he might earn in said career.

I mean, would he?

No. No way. Hugo instead of Hugo Boss! Come on! That is the choice of a man who prefers personal comfort over style . . .

"Is it the cost of medical school?" I ask. "Because surely Luke's parents would support him while he was in school. Have you thought of talking about it to Luke's mom and dad?"

Dominique's expression changes from one of mild disgust—with me, apparently—to one of horror.

"Why would I do that?" Dominique looks completely perplexed. "I want Luke to transfer to Paris with me and work at Lazard Frères so that he and I can turn this place into a five-star hotel, turn over a considerable profit, and come here on weekends. I don't want to be a doctor's wife and continue to live in *Texas*. Is that so hard to understand?"

I blink at her. "Um," I say, "no."

But inwardly, I'm thinking, *Wow. This is one lady who knows what she wants. I bet SHE wouldn't have any reservations about moving to New York City with no degree, no job, and no place to stay already lined up.*

In fact, I bet she'd EAT New York City.

It's at this point Agnès returns from the kitchen, holding a plate of snacks.

"*Voilà*," she says to me, looking extremely pleased with herself as she hands me the creation she's prepared for me.

Which appears to be half a French baguette, sliced down the middle and stuffed with—

"Hershey bar!" Agnès cries, excited to be using the only English words she apparently knows.

I have just been handed a Hershey bar sandwich.

Agnès holds out the plate to Shari, who takes one look and says, "No thank you."

Shrugging, Agnès then offers the plate to Dominique. The teenager doesn't appear the least shocked that her boss's girlfriend is half naked, proving that French people of all ages are way cooler about nudity than I am.

Dominique takes one look at the sandwich on the platter in front of her, shudders, and says, "*Mon Dieu. Non.*"

Well, okay. Maybe she wouldn't eat New York City after all. Too fattening.

Agnès shrugs again, takes her own chocolate sandwich off the plate, sinks back down onto her chaise longue, and digs in. Crispy bits of crust fall all over the front of her bathing suit as she takes her first bite. Chewing, she gives me a chocolaty smile.

"*C'est bon, ça,*" she says, indicating the sandwich.

That much is obvious. The real question, of course, is how could it not be good?

Also, how can I say no to such a thoughtful and lovingly prepared snack? I don't want to hurt the girl's feelings.

There's really only one thing I can do, of course. And so I do it.

And it is, without a doubt, the best sandwich I have ever eaten.

But it's the kind of sandwich I can tell that Dominique—if she were to sink her business-oriented claws into this place—would outlaw immediately! Women recovering from lipo don't want to be offered Hershey bar and baguette sandwiches! People on a corporate retreat can't be served candy bars! I can practically see Dominique thinking this, even as she lifts a bottle of sunscreen and resolutely sprays her chest with it.

Agnès, and her Hershey bar sandwiches, will soon be a thing of the past if Dominique has her way with the running of Mirac.

Unless, of course, someone stops her.

"Ladies."

I nearly choke on the huge bite of chocolate bar sandwich I've just taken. That's because Luke and Chaz have just shown up at the far end of the pool, looking sweaty and dirt-smeared from their morning spent hacking at the underbrush along the driveway.

"*Salut,*" Dominique says, lifting a darkly tanned arm to wave at them. Her breasts, I notice, don't move at all as she does this. It is a miracle of gravity.

"Hello, boys," Shari says.

I don't say anything for once, because I'm still too busy trying to swallow.

"Are you girls having a nice time?" Chaz wants to know. He is grinning, and I know why: half-naked Dominique. It's hard to miss the amused glance he throws Shari, who only says, mildly, "Oh, we're having a *dandy* time. You?"

"Dandy," Chaz replied. "Thought we'd go for a swim to cool off a little." Even as he says it, he's peeling off his shirt.

One thing I'll say about Chaz. He may have a master's in philosophy, but he's got the body of a physical trainer.

But Luke—I'm able to note all too clearly when he, too, pulls off his shirt a second later—is an even more spectacular example of athletic masculinity than Chaz. There's not an ounce of body fat on his tanned, well-muscled body, and his dark chest hair, while not copious, still forms a very distinct arrow that seems to point directly down to his . . .

SPLASH! Both guys leap into the sparkling water, not bothering to drop their shorts first, robbing me of the pleasure of seeing just what that trail of hair from Luke's chest down into his waistband leads to.

"Christ, that feels good," Chaz says when he surfaces. "Shar, get in here."

"Your wish is my command, master," Shari says. She lays down her book, stands up, and jumps. Some of the spray from the splash she makes gets on Dominique, who flicks it off.

"Dominique," Luke calls from where he surfaces at the deep end. "Come on in. The water's great."

Dominique prattles something in French that I don't completely catch, although the word *cheveux* is mentioned several times. I try to remember if *cheveux* means hair or horses. Somehow I don't think Dominique is saying that she doesn't want to get her horses wet.

Shari swims to the side of the pool and, folding her arms on the edge, leans out to say to me, "Lizzie, you have to get in here. The water is fabulous."

"Let me finish my sandwich first," I say, since I'm still working on the messy—but sinfully delicious—concoction Agnès handed me.

"Better wait half an hour after eating," Luke says, teasingly, from the deep end. "You don't want to get a cramp."

Fortunately, I'm busy chewing, so my mouth is too full for me to ask, *If I get one, will you rescue me, Luke?* Flirting would be totally inappropriate, considering the fact that his girlfriend is sitting right next to me. Topless.

And looking way better that way than I could ever hope to.

"Ah, the new girl!"

I practically spit out the wad of bread and chocolate in my mouth, I'm so startled by the heavily French-accented male voice behind me. When I whip around on my chaise longue, I find myself staring at an older gentleman in a white shirt and khaki pants held up by a pair of stylishly embroidered suspenders.

"Um," I say after I've swallowed, "hello."

"This is the new girl?" the old man asks Dominique as he points at me.

Dominique turns around, looks at the old guy, and says, in a much pleasanter tone than I've ever heard her use before, "Why, yes, monsieur. This is Shari's friend Lizzie."

"*Enchanté,*" the old man says, lifting my hand—the one that isn't clutching the remains of my Hershey bar sandwich—and bringing it to the vicinity of—but not touching it with—his lips. "I am Guillaume de Villiers. Would you like to see my vineyard?"

"Dad," Luke says from the side of the pool he's hastily climbing out of, "Lizzie doesn't want to see your vineyard right now, okay? She's relaxing by the pool."

So this charming old man is Luke's father! I can't say I can really see a resemblance—Monsieur de Villiers's hair is wispy, not curly, like Luke's, and snow white, not dark.

But he does have Luke's same twinkling brown eyes.

"Oh, that's all right," I say, reaching for my sundress. "I want to see your vineyard, Monsieur de Villiers. I've heard so much about it. And last night I had some of your delicious champagne . . ."

"Ah." Monsieur de Villiers looks delighted. "But technically it is not correct to call it champagne, unless it was made in the region of Champagne. What I make can only be called sparkling wine."

"Well," I said, having polished off the remains of my sandwich so that I have both hands free to struggle into my dress, "whatever it was, it was lovely."

"*Merci, merci!*" Monsieur de Villiers exclaims. To Luke, who has come up to my chaise longue and is dripping on Dominique's legs—causing her to give him an annoyed look—he says, "I like this girl!"

"You don't have to go with him," Luke says to me. "Really. Don't let him bully you. He's notorious for it."

"I *want* to go," I assure Luke, laughing. "I've never been to a vineyard before. I'd love to see it, if Monsieur de Villiers has time to show it to me."

"I have all the time in the world!" Luke's father cries.

"You don't, actually," Dominique says, with a glance at her slim gold watch. "Bibi will be here in less than two hours. Don't you need to—"

"No, no, no," Monsieur de Villiers says. He takes hold of my elbow to help me balance while I slip on my sandals. Or maybe to keep me from running away. Because that's sort of what I feel like doing, considering that Luke's dad is having this conversation with Luke's girlfriend while the latter is completely TOPLESS!!!

I try to imagine a scenario in which I would ever have felt comfortable being topless in front of one of my ex-boyfriends' fathers, and fail.

"We will make it short," Monsieur de Villiers assures Dominique.

"I'll just go along to make sure you stick to that, Dad," Luke says, accepting a towel Agnès is handing him. "We don't want to bore Lizzie to death her first day here."

But now that I know Luke is coming along, I know that's one thing I definitely won't be: bored, I mean.

Especially since, as we move away from the pool and toward the vineyard behind the main house, I realize Luke has left his shirt behind.

Really, there's something to be said for this topless thing after all.

The Industrial Revolution did not just introduce the concepts of the steam engine and the rotation of nitrogen-fixing and cereal crops. No! The mid 1850s saw the invention of something much more crucial and useful to humankind: the crinoline, or hooped petticoat. By being able to step into a cage of steel hoops rather than having to don pounds and pounds of petticoats in order to give her skirts the mandatory width a fashionable woman of the day demanded, women everywhere were now at liberty to actually move their legs.

What seemed a brilliant stroke of genius, however, soon revealed itself to be the fatal undoing of many an unsuspecting country lass, for the crinoline not only attracted improper suitors, but was also responsible for hundreds upon hundreds of young picnicking ladies being torched by lightning.

History of Fashion
SENIOR THESIS BY ELIZABETH NICHOLS

15

Man, truly the animal that talks, is the only one that needs conversations to propagate its species... In love, conversations play an almost greater role than anything else. Love is the most talkative of all feelings and consists to a great extent completely of talkativeness.
—*Robert Musil (1880–1942), Austrian author*

Okay, so it's the middle of the afternoon and I'm drunk.

But it's not my fault! All I've had to eat today is a cappuccino, a Hershey bar sandwich, and a few dusty, not-very-ripe grapes Monsieur de Villiers picked for me when we were touring his vineyard.

Then, after we headed into the cask room, Luke's dad kept pouring me cups of wine from all the different oak barrels, making me taste each individual one. After a while, I tried saying no. But he looked so hurt!

And he's been so kind to me, taking me all around the vineyard—the farm behind it, too, waiting tolerantly while I patted the velvet nose of the enormous horse that stuck his head over the stone wall to greet us, and while I squealed over the source of those cowbells I knew I'd heard (actual cows, three of them, that supply the milk for the château).

Then there were the dogs that showed up, eager to greet their master, a basset hound named Patapouf and a dachshund called Minouche. They needed sticks thrown to them—even though the basset hound tripped over his own ears going after them—and their entire life histories told to me.

And there was the farmer to greet, and his gnarled hand to shake, and his incomprehensible French—after which Monsieur de Villiers asked how much I understood, and when I said none, caused him to laugh uproariously—to listen to.

And there was the tractor to ride on the back of, and the history of the area to learn—it's no wonder I'm tipsy. All that, and ten different kinds of wine, too? I mean, they were all totally delicious.

But I'm starting to feel a little light-headed.

Or maybe that's just because of Luke's proximity. Sadly, he went back to the house and changed into a clean shirt and pair of jeans before rejoining us.

But his hair was still wet and clung damply to the back of his tanned neck in a way that made me, out on the back of that tractor, long to throw my arms around him. Even now, in the relative cool of the cask room, I can't help glancing at the sun-kissed skin of his forearms and wondering what it would feel like beneath my fingertips . . .

Oh my God, what's WRONG with me? I really *must* be drunk. I mean, he's TAKEN. And by someone way prettier and more accomplished than I am.

Plus, there's the whole rebound factor. I mean, I'm barely over Andy.

But still. I can't help thinking Dominique isn't right for Luke. And I'm not talking about her shoes, either. Lots of totally otherwise nice people own totally overpriced shoes.

And I'm not talking about her whole turning-Mirac-into-a-hotel scheme, either. Or even her disdain for Luke's secret dream of being a doctor (not, of course, that he's shared this secret dream with me. I'll just have to take Dominique's word for it that Luke even *has* a secret dream).

No, it's the fact that Luke is *so* good with his father, showing endless patience with the old man's fixation on his winery and its history and the telling of it. How he made sure the old man didn't trip over any of the machinery he was climbing on top of in order to show me how it worked. The way he ordered Patapouf and Minouche to sit when he felt they'd jumped all over his father for long enough. The way he gently pried his father's shirtsleeve from the mouth of that enormous horse.

You just don't see that sort of kindness from a son toward his father every day. I mean, Chaz doesn't even *speak* to his dad. And okay, Charles Pendergast Sr. is, by all reports, sort of an ass.

But still.

A guy like that—so patient and tolerant and sweet—deserves better than a girl who doesn't support his secret dreams. . . .

"You are very old-fashioned," Monsieur de Villiers is saying, breaking in on my unkind thoughts about Luke's girlfriend. The three of us are leaning in companionable silence against a cask, sipping a cabernet sauvignon Luke's dad has told me is very young . . . too young to bottle yet. As if I'd even know the difference.

"Excuse me?" I know I'm drunk. But what on earth is he talking about? I'm not old-fashioned. I totally gave my last boyfriend a blow job.

"This dress." Monsieur de Villiers points at my sundress. "It is very old, no? You are very old-fashioned for a young American girl."

"Oh," I say, realizing at last what he means. "You mean I like vintage. Yes. Well, this dress *is* old. Older than me, probably."

"I have seen a dress like this before," Monsieur de Villiers says. It's clear from the way he waves a fly away from his face—none too steadily—that he, too, has had a few too many sips of his own wine. Well, it's a hot day. All that running—and riding—around makes a person thirsty. And the cask room isn't air-conditioned.

Still, it's a comfortably cool temperature inside. It has to be, Monsieur de Villiers told me, in order for the wine to ferment properly.

"Upstairs," he goes on. "In the . . ." He looks questioningly at Luke. "*Grenier?*"

"The attic," Luke says, and nods. "Right. There are a bunch of old clothes up there."

"In the attic?" I instantly forget how drunk I feel—and how hot Luke looks. I straighten up and stare at the two of them with my eyes narrowed. "*There are vintage Lilly Pulitzer dresses in your attic?*"

Monsieur de Villiers looks confused.

"I do not know that name," he says. "But I have seen dresses like this up there. My mother's, I think. I have been meaning to donate them to the poor—"

"Can I see them?" I ask. I don't mean to sound overeager.

But I guess I do, anyway, since Luke's dad chuckles and says, "Ah! You love the old clothes the same way I love my wine!"

I start to blush—how embarrassing! I didn't mean to sound so greedy.

But Monsieur de Villiers lays a comforting hand on my shoulder and says, "No, no. I do not mean to laugh at you. I am just very pleased. I like to see people show passion for something, because, you know, I have my own passion." He holds his glass of wine aloft to illustrate just what that passion is—in case I hadn't guessed.

"But it is especially nice to see a young person with a passion for something," he goes on. "Too many young people today—they care for nothing but making money!"

I glance nervously at Luke. Because of course if what Dominique said is true about Luke choosing a business degree over medicine, he is one of the "young people" his dad is talking about.

But Luke is showing no guilt that I can see.

"I'll take you up into the attic if you really want to see it," Luke volunteers. "But don't get your hopes up that any of it's in decent condition. We had a pretty bad leak last year and a lot of the stuff stored up there got ruined."

"It's not *ruined*," Monsieur de Villiers says. "Just a little moldy, perhaps."

But I'll take moldy Lilly Pulitzer over no Lilly Pulitzer any day.

Luke must sense my eagerness since he says, with a laugh, "Okay. Let's go." To his father, he adds, "Don't you think you'd better go inside and have some coffee? You might want to sober up before Mom gets here."

"Your mother." Monsieur de Villiers rolls his eyes. "Yes, I suppose you are right."

Which is how a few minutes later, after thanking the elder Monsieur de Villiers profusely for the lovely tour and dropping him off in the château's enormous—but, as Dominique mentioned, hardly high tech—kitchen, I find myself in the cobweb-filled attic with the younger Monsieur de Villiers, riffling through old trunks of clothes and trying unsuccessfully to contain my excitement.

"Oh my God!" I exclaim as I open the first trunk and find, beneath a bone china tea set, an Emilio Pucci slip skirt. "Whose stuff did your dad say this is? His mother's?"

"There's no telling, really," Luke says. He's examining the rafters above our heads, ostensibly for more leaks. "Some of these trunks have been here since well before I was born. The de Villiers, I'm sorry to say, are definite pack rats. Help yourself to whatever you like."

"I couldn't," I say—even as I'm holding the skirt to my hips to see if it might fit. "I mean, this skirt right here? You could get two hundred bucks for it on eBay, easy." Then I gasp and dive incredulously back into the trunk.

But it's true. I've found the rarest of rare—Lilly Pulitzer's elusive tiger-print housedress . . . *with matching kerchief.*

"Well, I'm not going to go to the trouble of selling it," Luke is saying. "So it might as well go to someone who can appreciate it. Which, from the way things look, is you."

"Seriously," I say, bending down and finding what appears to be a wadded-up—but genuine—John Frederics blue velvet hat, "you have some great stuff in here, Luke. All it needs is a little TLC."

"That's a pretty good description"—Luke spins a wooden chair around and straddles it, backward, leaning his elbows on its back while he watches me—"for Mirac in general."

"No," I say, "this place is gorgeous. You guys have done a fantastic job of keeping it up all these years."

"Well, it hasn't been easy," Luke says. "When the Crash came—in 1929—my grandfather lost nearly everything—including that year's crop, to a blight. We had to sell off a lot of the land just to afford to pay the taxes on the place that year."

"Really?" Suddenly the unopened trunks all around me aren't nearly as interesting anymore. At least, not as interesting as what Luke is saying. "That's amazing."

"Then came the Nazi occupation—my grandfather avoided having SS officers housed in the place by claiming my father had contagious yellow fever . . . which he didn't, but it tricked the Germans into going elsewhere. Still, the war years weren't the best for wine-making."

I sink down onto the top of a trunk next to the one I've just plundered. There's something lumpy beneath me, but I hardly notice.

"It must be so weird," I say, "to own something that has such a *history*. Especially if . . ."

"If?"

"Well," I say hesitantly, "if owning a château isn't exactly your dream job. Dominique was saying something about how you actually wanted to be a, um, doctor."

"*What?*" His back straightens and his gaze, in the golden light that flows in from the diamond-shaped panes on either end of the long, sloped ceiling, is impenetrably dark. "When did she say *that*?"

"Today," I say innocently. Because I *am* innocent. Dominique didn't say it was a secret. Not that, given my history, it would have made a difference if she had. "By the pool. Why? Is it not true?"

"No, it's not true," Luke says. "Well, I mean, sure, at one time— Jesus, what else did she say?"

That you're an attentive and thoughtful lover in bed, I want to say. *That a girl doesn't have to worry about taking care of her own needs when she's with you because you are totally willing to take care of them for her.*

"Nothing," is what I say instead. Because of course Dominique didn't say any of those things. That's just my totally dirty, filthy imagination talking. "Oh, except some stuff about how she wants to turn Mirac into a hotel or a spa for people to go to while they're recovering from plastic surgery."

Luke looks even more startled. *"Plastic surgery?"*

Oops.

"Nothing," I say, turning crimson. Oh. No. I. Did. Not. Just. Do. It. Again. I turn back to the trunks to hide my blush. "Gosh, Luke. This stuff is *amazing.*"

"Wait. *What* did Dominique say?"

I fling him a guilt-stricken look.

"Nothing," I say. "Really. I shouldn't have—I mean, it's between you and her. I . . . I know it's none of my business—"

But it all comes spilling out anyway.

"—but I don't think you ought to turn this place into a hotel," I say all in a rush. "Mirac just seems so special. Commercializing it like that would just ruin it, I think."

"Plastic surgery?" Luke repeats, still looking incredulous.

"I guess I can understand the appeal," I say. "Since you wanted to be a doctor and all, but—"

"I didn't—" Luke springs up from the chair and takes a few quick steps toward the far end of the attic, raking one hand through his thick, curly hair. "I told her I wanted to be a doctor when I was a *kid*. Then I grew up and realized I'd have to be in school for another *four* years after college . . . plus three more years as a resident. And I don't like school that much."

"Oh," I say, sinking back down onto the lumpy trunk-top. "Then it's not just because doctors don't make as much money as investment bankers these days?"

"Did she—" He spins around to face me. "Is that what she told you I said?"

I can see I am treading on rocky terrain here. I hop up and, eager to change the subject, say, "What is this lumpy thing I've been sitting on?"

"Because it's not true," Luke says, striding toward me as I bend to lift up the long white object. "It had nothing to do with the money. I mean, it's true that for the years I'd be in school, there'd be no money coming in. And, yeah, okay, that's a concern. I'm not going to lie. I like having my own money so I don't have to depend on my parents for support. A guy wants to be able to pay his own bills, you know?"

"Oh," I say, unwinding what appears to be a length of white satin from the long, hard object it's been wrapped around. "Totally."

"And, okay, I looked into the postbaccalaureate premedical programs at a few schools—because, you know, not having been premed in college, even if I wanted to try to get into med school now, I'd have to take some postgrad science classes."

"Sure," I say, still working at unraveling whatever's been wrapped inside what appears to be some kind of tablecloth.

"And, yeah, okay, maybe I applied to a few of them. And maybe I got into the ones at Columbia and New York University. But I mean even if I go full-time, with summers included, that's another year in school that doesn't even count toward whatever medical degree I eventually go for. Is that really what I want? To be in school for another *five* years? When I don't have to be?"

"Oh my God," I say. Because I have finally unraveled the long, hard thing. And gotten a good look at what was being used to wrap it.

"That," Luke says, looking alarmed, "is my dad's hunting rifle. Don't—Lizzie, don't hold it like that. Jesus Christ." He hastily takes the long thing from my hands, then opens it and looks down the barrel.

"It's still loaded," he says in a small voice.

Now that Luke's taken the gun from me, I have both hands free and can give the thing the gun was wrapped in a good shaking.

"Lizzie." Luke sounds kind of stressed. "In the future, when you're holding a hunting rifle—even an unloaded one—don't fling it around like that. And definitely don't point it at your own head. You nearly gave me a heart attack."

His voice seems far away. All my concentration is on the dress I'm holding. Even in its wrinkled, rust-stained state, I can see that it's a cream-colored full-length satin gown with slender spaghetti straps (complete with tiny snapped loops on the underside, for hiding the wearer's bra straps), fine gathers over the double-lined molded breast cups, and a row of buttons down the back that can only be real pearls.

"Luke, whose dress is this?" I ask, searching inside for a label.

"Did you hear me?" Luke says. "This thing is loaded. You could have taken the top of your head off."

Then I find them. The words that nearly cause my heart to stop, though they are discreetly stitched in black on a small white label: *Givenchy Couture.*

I feel as if someone has kicked me.

"Givenchy—" I stagger backward, to sink back down onto the top of the trunk, because my knees no longer appear to be working. "Givenchy Couture!"

"Jesus Christ," Luke says again. He's unloaded the rifle, and now he sets it down on the chair he'd abandoned and hurries across the room to bend over me solicitously. "Are you all right?"

"No, I'm not all right," I say, reaching up and grabbing a handful of his shirt, pulling him down until he's kneeling by my chair, his face just inches from mine.

He doesn't understand. He just doesn't understand. I have to *make* him understand.

"This is a Hubert de Givenchy evening gown. A priceless, one-of-a-kind couture evening gown from one of the most innovative and classic fashion designers in the world. And someone used it to wrap up an old gun that . . . that . . ."

Luke gazes down at me, concern in his dark eyes. "Yes?"

"That RUSTED on it!"

Something causes Luke's lips to twist upward a little. He's smiling. How can he be *smiling*? I can tell he still doesn't get it.

"RUST, Luke," I say desperately. "RUST. Do you have any idea how hard it is to get rust out of fine fabrics like silk? And look, look here . . . one of the straps is broken. And the hem—there's a tear here. And here. Luke, how could someone have done something like this? How could someone have . . . MURDERED a beautiful vintage gown like this?"

"I don't know," Luke says. He's still smiling, which means he still isn't getting it.

But he's also laid a hand over mine, where I'm still clutching his shirt. His fingers are warm and reassuring.

"But I have a feeling if there's anyone in the world who can resuscitate the victim," he goes on in his deep, quiet voice—which sounds even deeper and quieter in the stillness of the long attic—"it's you."

His eyes, as I gaze into them, look very dark, and very friendly . . . just as his lips, as always, look eminently kissable.

HOW CAN HE HAVE A GIRLFRIEND? It's not fair. It's just not.

I do the only thing I can, under the circumstances. I gently release his shirt and drop my hand—and my gaze—away from his.

"I guess . . ." I say, looking down at the yards of stained fabric in my lap, hoping he doesn't notice my blush—or the sudden speeding up of my heartbeat, which I can feel slamming against my ribs. "I guess I could try. I mean . . . if it's okay with you, I'd *like* to try."

"Lizzie," Luke says, "that dress has been up in this attic for God knows how long, and, as you mentioned, wasn't exactly treated very nicely. I think it deserves to belong to someone who will give it the care and attention it needs."

Just like you, Luke! I want to cry. *You deserve to belong to someone who will give YOU the care and attention YOU need . . . someone who will support your dream of being a doctor, and not nag you to move to Paris, who will stick by you for those five more years of school, and who will promise never to turn your ancestral home into a spa for people recovering from plastic surgery, even if it would bring in more money than weddings.*

But of course I can't say this.

Instead I say, "You know, Chaz is going to New York University in the fall. Maybe if you do decide to go to that postbacca-whatever-it-is thingie, you two could find a place to live together."

That is, I add silently, *if Dominique doesn't insist on coming with you . . .*

"Yeah," Luke says, still smiling. "It'd be just like old times."

"Because," I go on, keeping my hands strictly away from him, and on the silky smoothness of the dress in my lap, "I think, if there's something you really want to do—like being a doctor—you should go for it. I mean, because otherwise you'll never know. And you might regret it your whole life."

Luke, I can't help noticing, is still kneeling beside my chair, his face still way too close to mine for comfort. I'm trying not to think about how my advice—about how he should go for it—could also apply to my kissing him. Because, you know, I might never get another chance to see what it would be like.

But kissing a guy who has a girlfriend is just wrong. Even a girlfriend who doesn't necessarily have his best interests in mind, like I do. It's the kind of thing Brianna Dunleavy, back at McCracken Hall, would do.

And no one liked Brianna.

"I don't know," Luke says. Is it my imagination, or is his gaze on my mouth? Do I have something stuck to my lip gloss? Or—oh God—are my teeth purple from all that red wine? "It's a really big step. A life-changing one. A risky one."

"Sometimes," I say, my gaze on his own lips—his teeth, I note, are not purple at all, "we need to take big risks if we want to find out who we are, and what we were put on this planet for. Like me, jumping on that train and coming to France, instead of staying in England."

Okay, he is definitely leaning in. He's *leaning in toward me.* What does this mean? Does he want to kiss me? How can he want to kiss *me* when he has the world's most gorgeous girlfriend lying half naked out there by the pool?

I can't let him kiss me. Even if he wants to. Because that would be wrong. He is taken.

And besides, I'm sure I still have stinky wine breath.

"Was the risk worth it?" he wants to know.

I can't seem to tear my gaze from his lips, which are coming closer and closer toward mine.

"Totally," I say. And close my eyes.

He's going to kiss me. He's going to kiss me! Oh no!

Oh. Yes.

It was an American woman named Amelia Bloomer who first spoke out against the dangers of the crinoline (and also the unhygienic practice of wearing skirts that swept the earth and floor). She encouraged women to adopt the "bloomer," a baggy-legged pant worn beneath a knee-length skirt that would not in any way be considered immodest today. The Victorians, however, objected strongly to women wearing the pants in the family, and "bloomers" went the way of Members Only jackets and Hall & Oates.

History of Fashion
SENIOR THESIS BY ELIZABETH NICHOLS

A lover without indiscretion is no lover at all. Circumspection and devotion are a contradiction in terms.
—*Thomas Hardy (1840–1928), British author and poet*

*J*ean-Luc?"

Wait. Who said that?

"Jean-Luc?"

My eyes fly open. Luke is already on his feet and rushing for the attic door.

"I'm up here," he calls down the narrow staircase to the third floor. "In the attic!"

Okay. What just happened? One minute he was about to kiss me—I'm almost sure of it—and the next—

"Well, you had better come down now." Dominique's voice sounds prim. "Your mother's just arrived."

"Shit," Luke says. But not to Dominique. To Dominique, he calls, "Right. I'll be down in a second."

He turns around to look at me. I'm sitting there, the Givenchy evening gown still spilling off my lap, feeling as if something was just ripped from me. My heart, maybe?

But that's ridiculous. I didn't want him to kiss me. I *didn't*. Even if he was going to.

Which he wasn't.

"We should go," Luke says. "Unless you want to stay up here. You're welcome to anything you want to take—"

Except the one thing I'm starting to realize I want most.

"Oh," I say, standing up. I'm mildly surprised to find that my knees can still support me. "No. I couldn't."

But I haven't let go of the evening dress, a fact Luke notices, and which causes one corner of his mouth to go up in a knowing way.

"I mean," I say, looking down guiltily at the armful of silk I'm holding, "if I could just take this and maybe try to restore it—"

"By all means," Luke says, still trying to hide his smile.

He's laughing at me. But I don't care, because now we have another secret together. Soon I'll have more secrets with Luke de Villiers than I do with anyone else.

Although, thanks to the Lizzie Broadcasting System, I don't have secrets with *anyone* else. This is definitely something I need to work on.

I follow Luke down the stairs. Dominique is waiting at the bottom. She's changed from her bathing suit into a cream-colored, very contemporary linen dress that leaves her shoulders bare and makes her waist look tiny. On her feet, I'm quick to note, are a pair of slides with wickedly pointy toes.

"Well," she says when she sees me trailing behind Luke, "you certainly got the full tour, didn't you, Lizzie?"

"Luke and his father were very thorough," I say, trying to hide my guilt. Why should I feel guilty, though? Nothing happened. And nothing was *going* to happen.

Probably.

"I'm sure they were," Dominique says in a bored voice. Then she casts a critical eye over Luke. "Look at you. You're all dusty. You cannot greet your mother like this. Go and change."

If Luke doesn't like being bossed around like this, he doesn't show it. Instead he heads off down the hall, calling, "Tell Mom I'll be there in a minute," over his shoulder.

I start for my own room, where I intend to stash the evening gown until I can find some lemons or, even better, cream of tartar to soak it in. I've had luck in the past getting rust stains out of silk with both.

But Dominique stops me before I can take a single step.

"What is it that you have there?" Dominique asks.

"Oh," I say. I unfold the dress and hold it up for her to see. "It's just an old dress I found up there. It's such a shame, it's covered in rust stains now. I'm going to see if I can get them out."

Dominique casts a critical eye up and down the garment. If she recognizes its significance as a piece of fashion history, she doesn't let on.

"It is very old, I think," she says.

"Not that old," I say. "Sixties. Maybe early seventies."

She wrinkles her nose. "It smells."

"Well," I say, "it's been sitting in a moldy attic. I'm going to soak it for a while to see if I can get the stains out. That will help with the smell as well."

Dominique reaches out to finger the smooth silk. A second later she's reaching for the label.

Uh-oh. She's seen it.

She doesn't squeal, though, the way I did. That's because Dominique can actually control herself.

"You are good at sewing?" she asks very calmly. "I thought I heard your friend Shari say so . . ."

"Oh, I'm just okay," I say modestly.

"If you cut off the skirt here," Dominique says, indicating a place where, if I were to cut off the skirt, the hem would hit her just above the knee, "it would be a cute cocktail dress. I would have to dye it black, of course. Otherwise it looks too much like an evening gown, I think."

Whoa. Wait a minute.

"Because it *is* an evening gown," I say. "And I'm sure it belongs to someone. I'm just going to try to restore it. I'm sure whoever it belongs to would love to have it back."

"But that could be anyone," Dominique says. "And if whoever it belongs to really cared for it, she would not have left it here. If it is a matter of cost, I will gladly pay you—"

I snatch the dress from her fingers. I can't help it. It's like she's turned into Cruella De Vil, and the gown is a dalmatian puppy. I can't believe anyone would be so vicious as to suggest cutting—not to mention dyeing—a Givenchy original.

"Why don't we see if I can get the stains out first," I say as calmly as I'm able to, seeing as how I am practically hyperventilating in shock.

Dominique shrugs in her French Canadian way. At least, I suppose it's French Canadian, since I've never met one before.

"Fine," she says. "I suppose we can just let Jean-Luc decide what to do with it since it's his house . . ."

She doesn't add, . . . *and I'm his girlfriend, and therefore all couture spoils in his house should rightfully go to me.*

Because she doesn't have to.

"I'll just go put it away," I say, "and then come down to meet Mrs. de Villiers."

Mention of the name seems to remind Dominique that she's wanted elsewhere.

"Yes, of course," she says, and hurries to the stairs.

Hideously relieved, I dart into my room and close the door behind me, then lean against it as if I have to catch my breath. Cut a Givenchy! Dye a Givenchy! What kind of sick, twisted . . .

But I don't have time to worry about that now. I want to go see what Luke's mother is like. I gently hang the evening gown from a peg in the wall (my room not having a closet), then strip off the swimsuit and dress I've been wearing all day. Then I throw on my robe and zip into the bathroom for a quick wash, makeup reapplication, and hair combing before coming back into my room to throw on my Suzy Perette party dress (I finally got the paint out).

Then, following the sounds of conversation drifting up from downstairs, I hurry to meet Bibi de Villiers.

Who turns out to be nothing like what I expected. Having met Luke's father, I had built up a picture in my head of the kind of woman he would marry—diminutive, dark, and soft-spoken, to go with his dreamy absentmindedness.

But none of the women I see from the second-floor landing when I reach it fit this description. There are three women standing in the foyer—not including Shari, Dominique, and Agnès—and none of them is dark or diminutive.

And they're DEFINITELY not soft-spoken.

"But then where are Lauren and Nicole going to stay?" a girl about my own age, only considerably blonder, is demanding in a heavy Southern accent.

"Vicky darlin', I told you." Another blonde, who has to be the girl's mother, since the resemblance between the two is uncanny (except that Mom has about twenty pounds on her daughter), is speaking in long-suffering, but still distinctly Texan, tones. "They're just going to have to stay in Sarlat. Aunt Bibi told you she could only fit so many people here in Mirac—"

"But why do Blaine's friends get to stay here," Vicky is whining, "and my friends have to go to a hotel? And what about Craig? Where are *his* friends going to stay?"

A sullen-looking young man lurking in the corner by a marble pillar says, "I didn't know Craig *had* any friends."

"Shut up, you retard," Vicky hurls at him.

"Well," declares the other blond middle-aged woman, "I know I could sure use a drink. Anybody with me on that one?"

"Here, Bibi." Monsieur de Villiers is quick to move in with a tray of champagne flutes he's had standing by, apparently in case of an emergency just like this one.

"Oh, thank the Lord," says Luke's mother, quickly taking hold of a glass. Nearly a head taller than her French soon-to-be-ex-husband (although maybe that's just because her hair is so big), she is a striking woman in a brightly patterned Diane von Furstenberg wrap dress that shows off her still-trim figure to advantage.

"Here, Ginny," she says, taking another glass of champagne and handing it to her sister. "You need one of these even more than I do, I'll bet."

Vicky's mother doesn't even wait until everyone else is served before downing the contents of her glass. She looks like a woman on the verge of . . . well, something not very good.

Dominique, I see, has already made her way back downstairs and is standing at Mrs. de Villiers's elbow, supervising the handing out of the champagne. When Monsieur de Villiers gets to Agnès, Dominique says something rather sharp in French and Luke's dad looks startled.

"Oh, surely just a taste," he says. "It's my new demi-sec . . ."

Dominique looks disapproving.

But this apparently doesn't bother Luke, who steps forward, plucks a champagne glass off the tray his father is holding, and hands it to Agnès, who looks surprised and thrilled.

"It's a special occasion," Luke says, seemingly to everyone in general. But I can't help thinking his remark is directed at Dominique. "My cousin is here for her wedding. Everyone needs to be in on the celebration."

I see Shari—changed out of her swimsuit into a neat white blouse and olive capris—exchange glances with Chaz, who's also changed—into khakis and a clean polo shirt—since I last saw him. Her look seems to say, *See? I told you so.*

Told you so about what, though? What's going on?

"Well," Mrs. de Villiers says, holding up her glass, "let's toast, then. To the bride and groom. Who isn't here yet. The lucky bastard." She throws back her head and laughs. "Just kidding."

Then, having spied me when she threw her head back, Mrs. de Villiers adds, "Oops, Guillaume, one more. There's one more comin'." And Monsieur de Villiers turns, spots me coming down the stairs, and breaks into a wide grin.

"Ah, there she is," he says, holding the last glass of champagne out to me. "Better late than never. And definitely worth waiting for."

Blushing, I take the glass and say, speaking to the room in general, the way Luke had, "Hello. I'm Lizzie Nichols. Thank you so much for having me here," as if I'd actually been an invited guest and not the complete party crasher that I am.

Then I stand there wishing something heavy would fall on my head and knock me unconscious.

"Lizzie, how do you do?" Mrs. de Villiers steps forward to shake my hand. "You must be the friend of Chaz's I've been hearing about. So nice to meet you. Any friend of Chaz's is a friend of ours. He was just so sweet to our Luke when he was at school. Always helping him get into trouble."

I glance at Chaz, who is grinning. "I'm sure," I say, "knowing Chaz."

"Not true," Chaz is saying. "Not true. Luke got into plenty of trouble on his own with no help from me."

"This is my sister, Ginny Thibodaux, and her daughter Vicky," Bibi de Villiers is saying as she steers me around the foyer to meet her family. Mrs. Thibodaux's handshake, compared to her sister's hearty one, is like holding a wet sponge, and Vicky's is only a little better. "And this is Blaine, Vicky's not-so-little-anymore brother—" Blaine's handshake is a little better than his sister's, but his face seems to be molded into a permanent sneer and he has a letter of the alphabet tattooed on each of his fingers. I can't tell what they spell when seen in a row, though.

"Well," Bibi says when she's done introducing me, "here's to the lovely couple."

Then she polishes off her champagne. Fortunately, her husband is standing nearby with a new bottle, ready to freshen everybody's glass.

"It's good, no?" he's asking eagerly of anyone who will reply. "The demi-sec? They don't make many demi-secs anymore. Everyone is always clamoring for the bruts. But I think to myself, why not?"

"Way to think outside the box, Guillaume," Chaz says amiably. I sidle over toward him and Shari and lean over to ask, "Do you have any idea what a demi-sec is?"

"Oh, hell, no," Chaz says, just as amiably, and drains his glass. "Hey, I'll take some more," he says, hurrying after Luke's father.

Shari looks up at me—she's never gotten over being only five four, whereas I've never gotten over having a butt that's twice as big as hers (until recently)—and says, "Where did you disappear to all afternoon? And how come you're so dressed up?"

"Luke and his dad gave me a tour of the vineyard," I say. "And I'm not dressed up. This dress got downgraded to everyday wear after Maggie got paint on it. Remember?"

"There's no paint on it now," Shari observes.

"Well, it was water-soluble. Nobody gives a four-year-old non-water-soluble paint. Not even my sister."

"Whatever," Shari says. She's never understood my complicated wardrobe rules, though I've offered to explain them multiple times. "We're invited to dinner tonight. It'll just be the bride's family, which is why. Groom's family and the rest of the guests get here tomorrow. You up for helping out in the kitchen?"

"Totally," I say, picturing me with a cute apron on, preparing spaghetti due for everyone.

"Great," Shari says. "Agnès's mother is making it. She's supposed to be a fantastic cook. We'll be on dish patrol. Let's get nice and toasted to make it go faster."

"Sounds like a plan to me," I say, and follow her over to where Luke is standing, having taken over champagne-pouring duties from his dad, for refills.

"Ah," Luke says when he notices me. "There she is. Nice dress."

"Thanks," I say. "You don't clean up so badly yourself. Do you know if you have any cream of tartar in your kitchen?"

Shari chokes on the sip of champagne she's just taken. Luke, however, calmly replies, "I have no idea. Tell me what cream of tartar would be called in French and I'll ask."

"I don't know," I say. "You're the Frenchman."

"Half," Luke says, casting a glance at his mother, who is throwing her head back and laughing at something else Chaz has said.

Crème de tartre?" Shari suggests.

"I'll ask," Luke says, and goes to refill his aunt's glass.

"What was that all about?" Shari wants to know when he's out of earshot.

"Oh, nothing," I say innocently. It's kind of fun, I'm discovering, keeping secrets from her. It's something I've never done before in my life.

But there are quite a few things I've never done before in my life that I've been trying lately. Some without success, but some . . . well, time would tell.

"Lizzie." Shari narrows her eyes at me. "Is there something going on between you and Luke?"

"No! God, no."

But I can't help blushing, thinking about that near-kiss in the attic. And what about last night at the train station? Had Luke been about to kiss me then? Somehow I had sort of thought he might . . . if Dominique hadn't showed up. Both times.

"He has a girlfriend," I remind Shari, hoping saying it out loud will also help me remind myself. "Like I would ever make a move on a guy who has a girlfriend. Who do you think I am, anyway? Brianna Dunleavy?"

"No need to get huffy," Shari says. "I was just asking."

"I'm not huffy," I say, trying to sound very unhuffy. "Did I seem huffy? Because I didn't mean to."

"Whatever you say, psycho." Shari shoots me an amused glance. "I'm gonna get another refill. Care to join me?"

I look in the direction she's nodding toward. Luke is just opening a new bottle of his dad's champagne. He happens to lift his head and see us looking at him from across the room. He smiles.

"Um," I say. "Well, okay. Maybe one more."

The mid-1870s saw something of a fashion revolution, thanks to the invention of the sewing machine and the introduction of synthetic dyes. While mass manufacturing meant inexpensive, stylish clothes were available to everyone, it also meant that, for the first time in recorded history, you could be walking down the street and actually see someone wearing your exact same outfit. The hoop skirt disappeared, transformed into the "bustle," the last time it was stylish to look as if one had a big butt until the birth of J.Lo.

History of Fashion
SENIOR THESIS BY ELIZABETH NICHOLS

Talk is a pure art. Its only limits are the patience of listeners who, when they get tired, can always pay for their coffee or change it with a friendly waiter and walk out.

—*John Dos Passos (1896–1970),*
U.S. novelist, poet, playwright, and painter

Dinner isn't so much a meal as it is a war council.

That's because Vicky and her mother want to make sure everything is ready for when the guests—and Vicky's future husband and in-laws—start arriving tomorrow.

I guess I can understand their concern. I mean, you only have one wedding (hopefully). So you want to make sure you do it right.

Still, it would be nice if we could concentrate more on the food Agnès's mother, Madame Laurent, has prepared for us than on Mrs. Thibodaux's complaints about the bumpiness of the driveway.

Because this is possibly one of the most delicious meals I've ever had, starting with a creamy fish *cassoulet* (which means stew) with slices of apple in it as a starter; then duck caramelized in some kind of delicious sweet sauce; a salad of baby lettuce in a garlicky dressing; and an enormous cheese platter, all of it accompanied by huge chunks of perfectly baked bread—crunchy and golden on the outside, soft and warm in the middle—and a wine to go with each course, poured by Monsieur de Villiers, who tries to tell us about each glass we're sampling but who keeps getting interrupted by Luke's aunt Ginny, who says things like "Speaking of bouquet, has anyone talked to that florist over in Sarlat? She knows we changed to the white roses from the white lilies, right? What's the French word for rose again?"

To which Luke replies dryly, "*Rose*," causing some of the water I've just sipped to go up my nose, I start laughing so hard.

Fortunately he doesn't notice—Luke, I mean—because he's sitting all the way down at the opposite end of the enormous dining table—which Dominique informed me (on our way into the impressively high-ceilinged and dramatically decorated dining room) seats twenty-six—with his mother on one side and Dominique at the other. I'm at the other end, by Luke's father, with the surly Blaine on my other side.

Not that I mind. Especially since I don't even like Luke that way. Or so I am telling myself, now that Shari is on to me.

At least I got the opportunity to observe up close what the letters tattooed on Blaine's fingers spell: F-U-C-K Y-O-U!

I think the exclamation mark is a nice touch. I imagine his mother must be very proud of him.

If she thinks anything about him at all, which seems unlikely given the amount of gushing she is doing over her daughter, who isn't, to put it mildly, a very happy bride. Nothing, apparently, has been done right so far, and Vicky doesn't seem to have much faith that anything is going to be done right in the future, despite protestations to the contrary from her mother, Luke, and even Monsieur de Villiers.

"Darlin', I already called the hotel and the concierge assures me there's plenty of space there for your sorority sisters. Or there will be tomorrow after some German tourists check out. At least"—Mrs. Thibodaux shoots her sister a look—"I think that's what he said. It was hard to tell with that accent . . ."

"But why can't Blaine's friends stay in the hotel?" Vicky wants to know. "Why do mine have to? I'm the bride!"

"Blaine's friends are in the wedding party," her mother reminds her. "You're the one who wanted them to play at the reception."

"Huh," Blaine, beside me, grunts as he stabs a piece of Camembert over and over with his butter knife. "Yeah, only *after* we landed that recording contract."

"You guys aren't celebrity recording artists yet," Vicky hurls at him from the far end of the table. "I don't see where you get off acting like one. Your stupid friends could stay in their VAN and not know the difference."

"My stupid friends," Blaine hurls back, "are the only remotely cool thing about your wedding, and you know it."

"Um, excuse me. I think getting married at a *French château* is plenty cool enough," Vicky snaps.

"Oh, right," Blaine says, rolling his eyes. "Like having the hottest band on the Houston music scene right now play at your wedding isn't something you've been bragging about to every publicist in town."

"Would you two kindly *shut the hell up*?" their aunt Bibi asks in a voice I suspect is even more slurry than usual, thanks to all the champagne she put back earlier, while stonily ignoring her estranged husband, who continues to make every effort possible to sit or stand near her and include her in the conversation. It is kind of sad, actually, to watch how excited Monsieur de Villiers is to have his wife back—even if only temporarily and even if only for her niece's wedding—and how totally unexcited she is to *be* back.

"Really, you two," Mrs. Thibodaux says, looking close to tears, "now is not a time for bickering. It's a time for pulling together, to try to weather this crisis as best we can."

"Crisis?" Monsieur de Villiers looks confused. "What crisis? Victoria is getting married! How is this a crisis? It is a joyous occasion, no?"

Both Bibi and her sister look at him and say at the same time, "No."

Vicky, after looking from one woman to the other, suddenly pushes her chair back, leaps to her feet, and runs from the dining room, a hand flung dramatically over her face.

Which is when Shari stands up and says, "On that note . . . thank you so much. We've had a lovely evening. And I'm pretty sure we're all clear on what we'll be needed to do tomorrow when the rest of your guests start arriving. But right now I think Lizzie and I will just get a head start on the dishes."

"I'll help you," Chaz says, springing to his feet, obviously eager to get away from the fighting and talk of floral arrangements.

"Me, too," Luke says.

But the minute he starts to get up, his mother lays a restraining hand upon his wrist and says, not slurring the word at all now, "Sit."

Luke sinks slowly back into his chair, a pained expression on his face.

I start clearing the empty plates around my end of the table. I don't think I can get out of that tense silence fast enough.

As I come into the high-ceilinged—but still old-fashioned—kitchen, I smile at Agnès and her mother when they look up from the supper they're sharing at the massive butcher-block table.

"*Ne pas se lever,*" I say to them, not sure if this is the right way of saying "Don't get up." But I guess it is, since it has the desired effect—they both sit back down to finish their meal.

"Oh my God," Shari says to me after smiling at the Laurents. "Oh my God. Oh my God. What *was* that out there?"

Chaz looks visibly shaken. "I feel violated," he says.

"Oh, whatever," I say, grabbing a trash can and beginning to scrape the remains on the plates off into it. "My own family is way more embarrassing."

"Well," Shari says, "I hadn't thought of it quite like that. But that is a good point."

"Weddings are just stressful, you guys," I say, reaching for the plates Chaz has carried in and scraping them as well. "I mean, the expectations are so high, and then if things don't go perfectly, people melt down."

"Sure," Shari says. "Melt down. But not spontaneously combust. You know what her problem is, don't you? Vicky's, I mean?"

"She's a Bridezilla?" Chaz asks.

"No," Shari says. "She's marrying beneath her."

"Shut up," I say, laughing.

"I'm serious," Shari says. "Dominique was telling us all about it at the pool today after you left for your little vineyard tour, Lizzie. Vicky's marrying some computer software programmer whose family all comes from Minnesota or something, instead of the rich Texas oil baron her mom had all picked out for her. Mrs. Thibodaux is fit to be tied about it, but there's nothing she can do to change Vicky's mind. It's *lurve*."

"Where's *Mr.* Thibodaux in all this?" Chaz wants to know. "Vicky's dad?"

"Oh, he has some big important meeting to go to in New York for his investment company or something. He'll be here just in time to walk her down the aisle, and not a minute before, if he's smart." Shari hands Chaz a dish towel. "Here. I'll rinse. You dry."

"Oh, I love it when you talk dirty dishes to me," Chaz says.

I gaze at the two of them as they bicker at each other over the sink, thinking how lucky they are to have found each other. It hasn't all been funny one-liners and trips to France for them, of course. There was the time Shari had to kill and dissect Mr. Jingles, her university-assigned lab rat, in order to pass advanced behavioral neuroscience, and Chaz urged her to spare Mr. Jingles by surreptitiously replacing him with a look-alike rat he found at PetSmart in the mall.

But Shari wouldn't swap rats because she said as a scientist she needed to learn how to distance herself from her subjects . . . after which Chaz wouldn't speak to her for two weeks.

Still. Overall, they are the cutest couple I know. Besides my mom and dad.

And I would give anything to have a relationship like that of my own.

Except, of course, I wouldn't resort to busting up someone else's to get it. Even if I could. Which I can't.

So I don't even know why I'm standing here thinking about a certain person I met on a train just the day before.

Agnès and her mother, once they finish their meal, refuse to leave without helping us with the rest of the dishes, and the job is done sooner than I would have thought, given the number of courses we had and the number of utensils we'd ended up using to eat them.

But even better than being done with our chores sooner than I thought we would be is the fact that Madame Laurent actually understands me when I ask her if she knows whether there's any *crème de tartre* in the kitchen. Even better yet—she manages to produce a container of it for me. She looks a little confused at my joy over securing a common acidic compound but seems pleased to have been able to help. She and her daughter both wish us a *bonne nuit*—which we enthusiastically return—before returning to the millhouse for the night.

Chaz announces he's going to see if he can't rescue Luke from the clutches of his mother and Mrs. Thibodaux and cajole him into having a nightcap. He and Shari invite me along, but I tell them I'm tired and am going to bed.

Which is a lie, but I'm embarrassed to admit that I have other plans . . . and that they involve needing to find a basin big enough to soak the Givenchy dress in—with the cream of tartar—overnight.

I'm on my hands and knees with my head in the cabinet under

the kitchen sink examining something I think might work—a plastic bucket that must have been placed there during some ancient leak—when I hear a door open behind me. Worried it might be Luke, and that if so he'll be seeing me from my least flattering angle, I start to get up, misjudge the distance between the sink and my scalp, and bang my head on the inside of the cabinet.

"Ouch," says a male voice from behind me. "That had to hurt."

Clutching my head with one hand, I look over my shoulder and see Blaine, in his baggy black jeans, dyed-black hair, and Marilyn Manson T-shirt, which I believe he is wearing to be ironic.

"You okay?" he asks, eyebrows raised.

"Yeah," I say. Letting go of my head, I reach for the bucket and climb to my feet.

"Whatcha doing down there, anyway?" Blaine wants to know.

"Just getting something," I say, trying to hide the bucket behind my voluminous skirt. Don't even ask me why. I just don't feel like getting into an explanation of why I have it.

"Oh," Blaine says. That's when I notice the unlit, apparently hand-rolled cigarette dangling from his lips. "Okay. Well, listen. You got a light, by any chance?"

"Sorry," I say. "No."

He sags in the doorway. Really. He looks genuinely crushed. "Shit."

I don't approve of smoking, of course, but considering what this guy has had to sit through all night, I don't blame him for needing a little stimulant.

"You could use one of the burners," I suggest, pointing at the massive—and ancient—stove in the corner.

"Oh," Blaine says. "Sweet."

He slouches toward the stove, switches on the flame, bends down, and inhales.

"Ahhhh," he says after he's straightened again and exhaled. "Now that's what I'm talkin' about."

And I recognize a sweet, pungent scent that immediately reminds me of McCracken Hall. That's when I realize what's rolled into his cigarette is not tobacco.

"How," I ask, truly stunned, "did you get that onto a transatlantic flight?"

"They're called tighty-whities, baby," Blaine says, dropping down into the kitchen chair Madame Laurent only recently vacated and swinging his combat-booted feet up onto the butcher-block table.

"You smuggled marijuana into France in your *underwear*?" I am stunned.

He looks at me and chuckles. "Marijuana," he echoes. "You're cute, you know that?"

"They have those sniffy dogs at airports now," I remind him.

"Sure they do," he says. "They're trained to sniff for bombs, though, not ganja. Here." He takes a deep toke on the joint, then holds it out to me. "Have some."

"Oh," I say, wrapping both arms around my bucket, then realizing, belatedly, that I must look very prim. "No thank you."

He eyes me incredulously. "What? You don't smoke weed?"

"Oh no," I say, "I can't afford to lose any more brain cells. I didn't have that many to start with."

He chuckles some more. "Good one," he says. "So what's a nice girl like you doing in a dump like this?"

I assume he's joking, since Château Mirac is hardly a dump.

"Oh," I say, "I'm just visiting with my friends."

"That tall dude," Blaine says, "and the dyke?"

I take umbrage at this. "Shari isn't a lesbian! Not that there's anything wrong with being a lesbian. But Shari isn't one."

He looks surprised. "She isn't? Whoa. Coulda fooled me. Sorry."

"She and Chaz have been dating for two years!" I'm still shocked.

"Okay, okay. Jeez, no need to jump all over me. I said I was sorry. She just seems kinda dykey to me."

"She hardly said two words to you!"

"Right."

"What, any woman who doesn't fall all over you is a lesbian?"

"Relax," Blaine says, "would you? God, you're worse than my sister, for Christ's sake."

"Well, I can see why your sister might be upset with you," I say, "if you go around accusing her friends of being lesbians when they're not. Again, not that there's anything wrong with that."

"Jesus," Blaine says, "chill out. What, are you a lesbian or something?"

"No," I say, feeling my cheeks start to heat up, "I'm not a lesbian. Not that—"

"—there's anything wrong with it. I know, I know. Sorry. It's just, you know, you're here by yourself, and you got so upset when I asked about your friend . . ."

"For your information," I say, "I'm here by myself because I just got out of a very bad relationship with a British guy. Yesterday. That's why I'm here, as a matter of fact."

"Yeah? What'd he do? Cheat on you?"

"Worse. He cheated on the British government. Welfare fraud."

"Oh." Blaine looks impressed. "Hey, that's bad. My last girlfriend turned out to be a disappointment as well. Only *she* dumped *me*."

"Really? What for? Did you accuse her of being a lesbian, too?"

He smiles. "Funny. No. *She* accused *me* of being a sellout when my band signed with Atlantic Records. Dating a musician with a trust fund is one thing. Dating a musician with an actual recording contract turns out to be something else completely."

"Oh," I say. And he looks so sad that for a moment I really do feel sorry for him. "Well, I'm sure you'll meet someone else. There must be lots of girls out there who'd enjoy dating someone with a recording contract *and* a trust fund."

"I don't know," Blaine says, looking depressed. "If so, I haven't met any."

"Well," I say, "give it time. You don't want to rush into anything right away. You need to give yourself a chance to heal emotionally." This sounds like such good advice. I should give serious consideration to taking it myself.

"Yeah," Blaine says, sucking on his joint, "I hear ya. That's what I told my sister about Craig. But did she listen? No."

"Oh? Craig is your sister's fiancé? Is he a rebound?"

"Oh, hell, yeah. I mean, he's better than the last guy she almost married—least this one's not part of Houston 'society'"—he makes quotes around the word with the fingers that aren't holding the joint—"but talk about boring. I mean, the guy practically makes Bill Gates look like freaking Jam Master Jay, if you get my drift."

"Right," I say.

"Still," Blaine says with a shrug. "He makes her happy. Or as happy as any guy can. Still, Mom'd much rather have her marrying some guy like ol' Jean-Luc."

I am disgusted with myself for the way my heart turns over even at the mention of Luke's name.

"Oh really?" I say in an attempt to appear only casually interested in the topic.

"Shit," Blaine says, "are you serious? If Mom could get Vicks to hook up with some guy who went to one of those fruity boarding schools, like Luke did, and has a castle in France, she'd frigging cream herself. Instead," he says with a sigh, "she got stuck with Craig." He holds out a hand and examines the fingers that say F-U-C-K. "And me."

"Oh yes," I say, "I noticed your tattoos at dinner. That must have . . . hurt."

"Truthfully," Blaine says, "I don't remember if it did or not, I was so wasted. Soon as I get back home, I'm having 'em lasered off. I mean, it was funny for a while, but I'm makin' serious business deals now and shit. It's embarrassing to walk into those corporate meetings with 'Fuck You!' tattooed on your hands, you know? We just sold one of our songs to Lexus, for a commercial. Six figures, dawg. It's unbelievable."

"Wow," I say. "I'll be sure to look out for it. What's the name of your band, anyway?"

He blows a blue plume of marijuana smoke toward the ceiling.

"Satan's Shadow," he says reverently.

I cough. And not because of the smoke.

"Well," I say, "that's an . . . unusual name."

"Vicky thinks it's dumb," Blaine says. "But I notice she still wants us to play her gig."

"Well," I say, "weddings are a big deal to girls. You should probably go apologize to your sister, don't you think? I mean, she's really stressed. I'm sure she didn't mean to take it out on you."

"Yeah," Blaine says, lumbering, with an effort, from his chair, "you're probably right. Hey, you wouldn't be interested, would you?"

I blink, confused. "Interested? In what?"

"You know," Blaine says. "*Me*. I'd never cheat the government. I've got a CPA for that."

"Oh." I smile at him, startled but flattered. "Thank you very much for the offer. Ordinarily, of course, I'd jump at the chance. But like I said, I'm just coming out of a relationship and I probably shouldn't rush into anything new too soon."

"Yeah," Blaine says with a sigh, "it's all about the timing. Well, g'night."

"Night," I say. "And, um, good luck. With Satan's Shadow and all."

He waves and shuffles from the kitchen. And I hurry out as well, clutching my bucket.

The late 1800s saw the prominence of the "puffed sleeve" on women's gowns for which Anne Shirley so longed in the classic children's book series *Anne of Green Gables*. Dresses were longer than ever, requiring skirts to be lifted while crossing the street, thus revealing lace-trimmed petticoats available now not only to the rich, thanks to mass production.

Amelia Bloomer's trousers, meanwhile, finally found eager supporters in young female enthusiasts of the newly invented bicycle, and no amount of chastising from their parents, priests, or the press could induce girls to give up their "bloomers," or their bicycles.

History of Fashion
SENIOR THESIS BY ELIZABETH NICHOLS

His talk was like a spring, which runs
With rapid change from rocks to roses
—*Winthrop Mackworth Praed (1802–1839), British poet*

I got the rust stains out.

I know. I can barely believe it myself. I'm standing in the kitchen of Château Mirac early the next morning, having soaked the gown overnight in my room, then hurried downstairs—seemingly at the crack of dawn, but a glance at my cell phone tells me it's only eight—to rinse it in the kitchen sink, which is much wider than the one in the bathroom across the hall from my room.

I swear that's the only reason. It has nothing to do with my fearing Dominique might find me there and demand I hand the dress over to her now that it's saved.

Really. Nothing to do with that.

Saved, but still not perfect. I have to mend the torn strap and the jaggedy parts along the hem, plus give the thing a supergood ironing when it finally dries.

But I did it. I got the rust stains out.

It's a French miracle.

I'm gazing at the dress with rapturous self-satisfaction when I hear someone behind me say, "You did it!"

And I nearly have a heart attack, I'm so startled.

"GOD!" I cry, spinning around to find a smiling Luke in the doorway, looking excited. "What are you trying to do, kill me?"

"Sorry," Luke says, "I didn't mean to scare you. But . . . you did it! The stains are gone!"

My heart is hammering a mile a minute—but I have to admit it's not just because he startled me. It's also because he looks so gorgeous in the morning light. His freshly shaved face is still glowing a little pinkly from whatever he uses as aftershave (I suspect plain alcohol, since he doesn't smell like anything in particular, except clean), and the ends of his dark hair are curling damply against the collar of his blue polo shirt. He's got on those jeans again—the ones he was wearing the first time I met him, the Levi's that fit his butt so perfectly, not too snug, but not too loose, either. He looks like something dropped from a helicopter—you know, the perfect guy, for a needy girl trapped on a desert island.

That girl being me, and the desert island being my life.

Except, of course, he isn't mine.

A fact about which he is undoubtedly vastly relieved, I realize, when I see his gaze going from the gown I'm holding to the clothes I'm wearing—which happen to be my Sears jeans and Run Katie Run T-shirt.

Well, Mrs. Thibodaux had been pretty explicit about what we'd be doing all day—setting up tables and chairs in preparation for tomorrow's wedding. I don't want to get one of my nice dresses dirty.

Plus I couldn't be bothered with my hair this morning, so it's piled into a ponytail coming out of the top of my head. At least I have makeup on. Some, anyway. Enough to keep my eyes from looking piglike.

"Cream of tartar works, huh?" is all Luke says, though, as his gaze goes from me back to the dress. Which is something of a relief. I get positively jumpy when those dark brown eyes turn in my direction.

"It sure does," I say, giving the gown a satisfied flick. "Of course, it doesn't always work this fast. Sometimes you have to go through multiple soakings. I don't think that gun could have been there that long. The grease and rust didn't really set in that deeply. Now I just need to mend and iron it, and it'll be as good as new. Whoever it belongs to is going to be stoked to get it back good as new."

Luke grins. "I think tracing its ownership is going to be a tad difficult. We've had a lot of guests here over the past few centuries."

"Well, this one probably stayed here sometime in the past few decades," I say. "I'm thinking late sixties, early seventies. Though, I grant you, with Givenchy it's hard to tell. His lines are so classic . . . he really isn't influenced by the vagaries of popular trends."

Luke's grin broadens. "The vagaries of popular trends?"

I blush. "I thought that sounded good."

"Oh, it did. You've got me convinced. So. Want to come with me to get the croissants?"

I stare at him. "Croissants?"

"Yeah. For breakfast. I'm going into town to the bakery now, to get them before everybody wakes up and comes downstairs, whining for breakfast. I know you haven't seen Sarlat and I think you'll like it. Want to come with me?"

If he'd asked me if I wanted to go to Family Day at the local Gap, where all Gap employees give their friends and relatives thirty-five percent off all Gap products—which is basically my idea of hell on earth—I would have wanted to come with him. That's how far gone I am about him.

Except, of course, for that one trifling detail.

"Um," I say, "where's Dominique?"

I feel like that's a nice, neutral way to ask if his girlfriend is going along, too. Without coming right out and asking it that way. Because "Is your girlfriend coming?" might sound as if I don't like her, or that I only want to go if I can get him alone, or something like that. Which isn't true. At all.

Although if she is coming along, I might find something else I have to do instead. Just because having to sit and watch the two of them together isn't really high on my list of fun things to do while on vacation in the south of France.

"She's still sleeping," Luke says. "Little too much champagne with Mom last night."

"Oh," I say, keeping my expression carefully neutral. "Well, just let me hang this to dry. And I'll be right back."

"I'll be out in the car," Luke says, indicating the back door to the kitchen, in front of which the butter-colored convertible is parked.

I run like the wind. I hang the dress from the peg (what servants used for their uniforms in the olden days?) on my wall, with the bucket underneath to catch the drips.

Then I grab my purse and tear back downstairs.

Luke is sitting behind the wheel. There is no one else in the car. Around us, the morning air smells as fresh as newly folded laundry, and the sun, already getting hot, feels delicious on my skin. It's completely quiet except for birdsong and the huffing of Patapouf, the basset hound, who has come sniffing around the back kitchen door in hopes of getting some handouts.

"Ready?" Luke asks me with a smile.

And, despite all my best efforts, my heart bursts right out of my chest and flies around my head on little cherub wings. Just like in a cartoon.

"Yes," I say to him in what I think sounds like a perfectly normal voice—considering the fact that my heart is twittering around and around my head—and hurry to slide into the front passenger seat.

I am so, so dead.

But so what? I'm on vacation! It's okay to have a little crush. In fact, it's better to have a crush on Luke, who is safely taken, than it would be to have one on, say, Blaine. Because I might actually end up hooking up with Blaine, who is available, and that would be very emotionally risky, considering my fragile state of rebound.

No, it's fine that I have a crush on Luke. He's safe. Because nothing will come of it. Nothing at all.

The ride down the same driveway it took us so long to climb up the night before last is hilariously bouncy. I have to hang on to keep from being thrown around the massive front seat. But Luke and Chaz really did do a good job cutting the tree branches back—none of them whip at us.

And then suddenly we're bursting out of the trees onto the same road along the river that we'd traveled from the train station the other night ... but that had been in the dark. Seeing the river up close for the first time in daylight, I can't help gasping.

"It's so beautiful!" I cry. Because it is. A sun-dappled, gently flowing river, with wide, grassy banks, over which tall oak trees tower, their leafy branches providing bathers and rafters with welcome shade.

"The Dordogne," Luke explains. "I used to go rafting on it when I was a kid. Although that makes it sounds like there are rapids, which there aren't, really. We'd go down it on inflatable tires. It's a nice, lazy ride."

Impressed by so much natural beauty, I shake my head. "Luke, I don't get how you can go back to Houston when you have all this."

Luke laughs and says, "Well, much as I love my dad, I don't exactly want to live with him."

"No," I say mournfully. "Neither does your mom, I guess."

"He drives her crazy," Luke agrees. "She thinks all he cares about is his wine. When he's here, all he does is fuss over his vines, and when he's back in Texas, with her, all he ever did was worry about them."

"But he loves her so much," I say. "I mean, can't she tell that? He can barely take his eyes off her."

"I guess she needs more than that," Luke says. "Some kind of proof that when she's not around, he thinks about her, too. And not just his grapes."

I'm mulling this over when we turn a corner and I see the Laurents' millhouse—with Madame Laurent outside, watering the explosion of blossoms in her arbored garden.

"Oh!" I cry. "It's Agnès's mom!" I wave. *"Bonjour! Bonjour, madame!"*

Madame Laurent looks up from her flowers and waves back, smiling, as we whiz past.

"Well," Luke says, glancing at me with a grin, "you're certainly in a good mood this morning."

"Oh," I say, sinking back into my seat in embarrassment over my excitement at seeing the Château Mirac cook in her own habitat. "This place is so beautiful. And I'm just. So happy. To be here."

With you, I almost add. But for once, I manage to shut my mouth before it runs away with me.

"I suspect," Luke says, making a turn toward the high-walled city I'd seen perched up on a cliff the night I'd arrived, "that you're the kind of person who's in a good mood wherever you are. Except when you've just discovered your boyfriend is a welfare cheat," he adds with a wink.

I smile a little queasily back at him, still feeling mortified. Of all the people I had to open my big mouth to about my romantic problems, why did it have to be *him*?

But a second later, as we enter the city of Sarlat, I forget my chagrin at the sight of all the red geraniums spilling down from window boxes above my head; the narrow cobblestoned streets; the villagers, hurrying along to the open-air market with their baskets filled with baguettes and vegetables. It's like a movie-set version of a French medieval village—only it isn't a movie set. It's a real medieval village!

And I'm right in the middle of it!

Luke pulls up in front of a quaint old shop with the word *boulangerie* written in gold on the large front window and from which the smell of freshly baked bread wafts, causing my stomach to growl hungrily.

"Do you mind waiting in the car?" Luke asks. "That way I don't have to find a parking space. It'll just take a second, I already phoned in the order. I just have to pick it up."

"Pas un problème," I say, which I think means "Not a problem." I guess I'm right since Luke smiles and hurries inside.

Still, my grasp of French is put to the test a second later when a carefully dressed old woman approaches the car and begins babbling to me a mile a minute. The name "Jean-Luc" is the only word I recognize.

"Je suis désolée, madame," I begin to say, which means "I'm sorry." I think. *"Mais je ne parle pas français—"*

Before the words are all the way out of my mouth, the old woman is saying, in French-accented English, looking scandalized, "But I understood Jean-Luc's *petite amie* was French!"

At least I know what the words *petite amie* mean.

"Oh, I'm not Jean-Luc's girlfriend," I say hastily. "I'm just a friend. I'm staying at Mirac for a little while. He's inside picking up some croissants—"

The old woman looks infinitely relieved. "Oh!" she says, laughing. "I recognized the car, you see, and I just assumed . . . you must forgive me. That was quite a shock. For Jean-Luc not to marry a Frenchwoman . . . it would be quite a scandal!"

I take in the woman's carefully knotted scarf—obviously Hermès—and light wool suit (she must be broiling in this heat) and say, "You must be a friend of Monsieur de Villiers, then?"

"Oh, I have known Guillaume for years. It was very shocking to all of us when *he* married that woman from Texas. Tell me"—the old woman narrows her perfectly made-up eyes—"is she there now? Madame de Villiers? At Château Mirac? I heard a rumor she was . . ."

"Um," I say. "Well, yes. Her niece is getting married there tomorrow, and—"

"Madame Castille," Luke says as he comes out of the bakery with two large paper bags in his arms. "What a pleasure." His smile, though, doesn't reach his eyes.

"Oh, Jean-Luc," the old woman says, beaming with pleasure at the sight of him (well, who wouldn't?).

And then she launches into a torrent of French against which Luke, I can tell, feels defenseless. Which is why I say, when Madame Castille pauses for breath, "Uh, Luke? Hadn't we better get back? People are going to be waking up and wanting their breakfast."

"Right," Luke says quickly. "We have to go, madame. It was lovely seeing you. I'll give my father your best, don't worry."

It isn't until we've pulled away that Luke gives a mighty exhalation and says, "Thanks for that. I thought she was going to talk all day."

"She's a big fan of yours," I say with cautious nonchalance. "She thought I was your girlfriend and she about had a heart attack that I wasn't French. She said it will be a big scandal if you don't marry a French girl. It was a big scandal when your dad married your mom, apparently."

Luke throws the car into gear with more force than is strictly necessary. "The only person who was scandalized was her. She's been after my dad since they were kids. Now that he and my mom are on the rocks, she can't wait for the chance to sink her claws into him."

"But it won't work," I say, "because your dad still loves your mom. Right?"

"Right," Luke says. "Although I could see the old guy marrying that witch just to get her off his back. Oh, here. I got you something." He pokes the bag of heavenly scented croissants that sits between us.

"A croissant?" I ask, opening up the bag. A wave of yeasty steam hits me. They're still warm from the oven. "Thanks!" I decide not to mention anything about my carb-free diet. I've pretty much given up on that since those rolls on the train down here, anyway.

"Not that bag," Luke says, looking at me like I'm crazy. "The other one."

I notice a smaller bag behind the one containing the croissants and open it.

And my eyes nearly pop out of my head.

"Wha—" I gasp. I am, for only the second time in my life, speechless. "How—how did you know?"

"Chaz said something about it," Luke says.

I pull the six-pack—glistening with moisture—from the bag and stare at it.

"They're . . . they're still cold," I say wonderingly.

"Well," Luke says a little dryly, "yes. I know Sarlat looks old, but they do have refrigeration."

I know it's ridiculous. But my eyes have actually filled with tears. I do my best to blink them away. I don't want him to know that I'm crying with joy over the fact that he's given me a six-pack of diet Coke. Because I'm not. It's the gesture, not the beverage.

"Th-thank you," I say. I know I need to keep the conversation short, or he'll hear the tremor in my voice. "D-do you want one?"

"You're welcome," Luke says. "And no, thank you. I prefer to get my caffeine the old-fashioned way, with a Colombian drip. So. What have you decided?"

I've taken one of the cans from the plastic holder and am about to crack it open. "Decided?"

"About what you're going to do," Luke says. "When you get back to the States. Are you going to stay in Ann Arbor? Or move to New York?"

"Oh." I crack open the can. The sharp hiss of carbonation is every bit as musical to my ears as the burble of the river to my left.

"I don't know. I want to move to New York. You know, with Shari. But what would I do there?"

"In New York?"

"Right. I mean, let's face it. It turns out there's not a whole lot you can do with an individualized major in history of fashion. I don't know what I was thinking."

"Oh," Luke says with a mysterious smile, "I'm pretty sure you'll figure something out."

"Right," I say—very sarcastically. I mean, for me, anyway. "And then there's the small fact that I haven't exactly graduated yet. How can I find a job if I don't even have my B.A. yet?"

"Well," Luke says, "I think that depends on the job."

"I don't know," I say. And take a sip of my diet Coke. The bubbles from the carbonation tickle my tongue. God, I've missed this. "It might just be simpler to stay in Ann Arbor for one last semester."

"Right," Luke says. "And see if you can patch things up with what's-his-name."

I am so shocked by this I nearly spit out the diet Coke I've just swallowed. Yes! Nearly one of sixteenth of one my six precious cans!

"WHAT?" I cry after I swallow. "Patch things up with—what are you TALKING about?"

"Just checking," Luke says. "I mean, you say you want to stay in Ann Arbor . . . and he'll be in Ann Arbor. Right?"

"Well, yeah," I say. "But that's not why. I mean, at least in Ann Arbor I still have my job at the shop. I could live at home and save up my money, then join Shari in January." If she hasn't already found another roommate.

"That," Luke says as he turns the car up the driveway to Mirac, "doesn't sound much like the girl I met on the train the other day, the one who took off for France without even knowing if she'd have a place to stay when she got there."

"I knew I'd have a place to stay," I say. "I mean, I knew Shari was here *somewhere*. I knew I wouldn't be alone."

"Just like you wouldn't be alone in New York," Luke says.

I laugh. "Oh, you're one to talk," I say. "Why aren't *you* moving to New York? You told me you got into NYU."

"Yeah," Luke says as we bounce along the steep driveway. "But I don't know if that's really what I want to do. I mean, give up my six-figure salary for five more years of school?"

"Oh, you'd rather help rich people figure out how to make more money than save lives?"

"Ouch," Luke says with a grin.

I shrug. Or as best I can when I'm being jounced around so much and am also trying to protect the precious elixir in the can I'm holding. "I'm just saying. I mean, managing stock portfolios is important. But if it turns out what you're actually good at is healing sick people, isn't it kind of a waste not to do that instead?"

"But that's just it," Luke says. "I don't know if I am. Good at healing sick people, I mean."

"Just like I don't know if there's anything I'm good at that someone in New York will actually pay me to do."

"But," he says, "as a certain person keeps telling me, you'll never know if you don't even give it a try."

Then we're bursting out of the trees again and onto the circular drive that leads to the house. It's even more impressive, it turns out, in daylight than it is at nighttime.

Not that Luke seems to notice. I guess because he's seen it so many times already.

"That's different," I say. "I mean, you already know there's something you can do. Someone's paying you a six-figure salary to do it. You know how much I get paid? I get eight bucks an hour at Vintage to Vavoom. You know how far eight bucks an hour goes in New York City? Well, I don't, either. But I'm guessing not very far."

Luke, I notice when I glance nervously his way to see what he thinks of my admission, is grinning more broadly than ever.

"Is this how you are with everybody?" he wants to know. "Or am I just lucky because, in a moment of weakness, you revealed all your deepest secrets to me?"

"You promised not to tell anyone about those," I remind him. "Especially Shari, about the thesis—"

"Hey," Luke says, pulling up in front of the château. His gaze is steady on mine. He's not smiling anymore. "I said I wouldn't tell. Remember? And I'm not going to. You can trust me."

And for a second—while we sit there looking at each other across the bag of croissants—I can swear that something . . . *happens* . . . between us.

I don't know what. But it's different from all the times I thought he was going to kiss me. There's nothing sexual about what happens there in the car. It's more like some sort of . . . mutual understanding. Some sort of acknowledgment that we are spiritual kin. Some sort of magnetic pull—

Or maybe it's just the smell of the croissants. It's been a really long time since I've had any kind of pastry.

Whatever it is that's going on between Luke and me—if anything—it's over a second later when the door to the château is thrown open and Vicky, standing there in a pale blue kimono, says, "God, what took you so long? We're all *starving*. You know I get hypoglycemic if I don't eat first thing in the morning."

And the moment between Luke and me—whatever it was—is gone.

"Got your cure for hypoglycemia right here," Luke says cheerfully, grabbing the bag of croissants.

Then, when Vicky stomps back into the house, Luke turns to me and winks.

"Look at that," he says. "I'm healing people already."

The dawn of the twentieth century is often referred to as "la Belle Époque," or "the beautiful age." Certainly the fashions of the age were beautiful, featuring, as they did, big hair, low décolletage, and tons and tons of lace (see: Winslet, Kate, *Titanic,* and Kidman, Nicole, *Moulin Rouge*). Achieving the look of a Gibson girl (created by a popular artist of the same name) became the rage, with even President Roosevelt's vivacious daughter, "Princess" Alice, wearing her hair in the Gibson girl's pompadour style—a look very hard to maintain while "motoring," Alice's favorite hobby.

History of Fashion
SENIOR THESIS BY ELIZABETH NICHOLS

Keep silence for the most part,
and speak only when you must,
and then briefly.

—*Epictetus (c. ACE 55–135), Greek Stoic philosopher*

The rest of the morning is a blur of deliveries. The first truck to arrive is the one carrying the dance-floor, stage, and sound equipment for the wedding's band—in this case, not the string quartet Luke tells me plays most weddings at Mirac, but Blaine's band, Satan's Shadow. As workers from the company in charge of setting this up begin their work, another truck—this one filled with folding tables and chairs for the rehearsal dinner and wedding reception (both of which are to be held on the lawn)—rumbles up the driveway (knocking down everything Luke and Chaz couldn't reach, and forcing the two of them to have to scramble back down the driveway to clear it of all the newly fallen branches) and needs help unloading.

Just as Shari, Chaz, Blaine—who, his band not having arrived yet, declares, "I'm bored," and begins pitching in—and I get the last of the folding chairs off the truck, another one arrives, this one carrying all the food the chef and staff from a local restaurant will be preparing for the festivities. This food needs to be unloaded and carried to the kitchen, where Madame Laurent supervises its storage, and the restaurant chef begins preparing canapés for the cocktail hour, which begins in the late afternoon . . .

Which is when the out-of-town guests begin showing up, either in their own rented vehicles or ferried from the train station by Dominique, who has managed to avoid having to do any hard labor by volunteering to do this instead. The groom arrives first, with his dazed-looking parents. I am very curious to see this computer programmer Vicky is marrying instead of the rich Texas oil baron her mother wanted for her, and I have to say, when I finally see Craig, I can understand the attraction. Not that he's good-looking—because he's not.

But when Vicky comes flying at him from inside the house, blathering about everything that's going wrong, from her friends still not having hotel rooms to Blaine having told her that she looks fat in her rehearsal-dinner dress, Craig's reply is as phlegmatic as his parents' reaction to Mirac.

"Vic. It's all right," he says.

And Vicky actually stops crying.

At least until half a dozen of Vicky's friends—as pretty and blond as she is—pile out of minivans and stumble across the gravel driveway in their wobbly high heels to hug her. Then she starts bawling all over again, and Craig, not looking in the least bothered by this, gently leads his parents to the vineyard, where Monsieur de Villiers happily shows them around the cavernous cask room.

Soon it seems the entire château is under attack by what appears to be the upper crust of Houston society, stylishly clad matrons with their navy-blue-blazer-wearing husbands in tow, with whom Dominique mingles and laughs.

These Houstonians, in turn, raise their eyebrows at the arrival of the remaining members of Satan's Shadow, who show up in an extremely disreputable-looking van and are greeted by Blaine with their signature Satanic cry, which involves tipping back the head and ululating (which causes Vicky to run inside, screaming, "Mo-o-o-om!" and Shari, as she helps me spread a tablecloth over the last of the twenty-five or so tables on the lawn, to shake her head and go, "God, am I glad I'm an only child").

I'm happy when the staff from the restaurant takes over and begins setting the tables. This leaves us free to run inside to change before the cocktails are served—a necessity since we're going to be manning the bar for the event, opening the bottles of wine and champagne Monsieur de Villiers will be supplying, and I personally don't want to gross anyone out with my sweat stains. I don't exactly have the most experience opening wine bottles, either, so I'm suspecting the evening should be pretty interesting, on the whole.

I'm just coming back down the stairs, feeling refreshed and semi-presentable in a black sleeveless Anne Fogarty linen dress, when I nearly collide with a group of people coming *up* the stairs, led by Luke, who is hauling a couple of really heavy-looking suitcases.

"I'm telling you, son," a portly bald gentleman in khaki pants and a black polo shirt is saying to Luke. "It's an opportunity you can't afford to miss. You were the first person I thought of when I heard."

Behind the balding man hovers Ginny Thibodaux, looking flustered.

"Gerald," she says, "did you hear me? I said I think Blaine's smoking again. I could swear I smelled cigarettes on him just now. That funny foreign kind he and all his friends like so much . . ."

Behind Mrs. Thibodaux, Vicky is saying, "Mom, you have got to talk to him. Now he's saying his stupid band won't play covers. Mom, he swore they'd play covers. Now he's saying they're only doing their songs. How am I supposed to have my father-daughter dance to some song called 'Cheetah Whip'?"

"I don't know, dear," Mrs. Thibodaux says. "Your brother just hasn't been the same since that Nancy left him. I wish he'd meet a nice girl. Wouldn't any of your friends—"

"Jesus, Mom. Would you worry about something that actually

matters for a change? What are we going to do about the fact that he won't play any covers? Craig and I are not having our first dance as a married couple to a song called 'I Wanna Bang Your Box' . . ."

"Well, hello," Luke says with a grin as I make room for him and the Thibodauxes to pass me. "Don't you look nice."

"Thanks," I say, looking carefully at the bald man. This, I assume, is Vicky's long-awaited dad.

"Think about it, son," Mr. Thibodaux is saying eagerly to Luke. "It's a tremendous opportunity."

Luke says, "Thanks, Uncle Gerald," with a wink at me, and continues up the stairs, with the Thibodauxes trailing along after him, still talking a mile a minute, and none of them listening to the other. Hurrying the rest of the way down the stairs, I find Mrs. de Villiers and Dominique in the foyer having a little tête-à-tête of their own . . .

But not in voices low enough for me not to overhear what they're saying.

"—opening a branch in Paris," Dominique is going on excitedly. "Gerald says he thought of Jean-Luc immediately. It's an incredible offer. Far more responsibility—and money—than Jean-Luc is getting at Lazard Frères. Thibodaux, Davies, and Stern is one of the most exclusive private-client investment companies in the world!"

"I'm familiar with my brother-in-law's company," Mrs. de Villiers says with a hint of irony in her voice. "What I'm not so sure of is just when Luke decided he wanted to move to Paris."

"Are you joking?" Dominique asks. "It's always been our dream!"

I am rooted to the spot by the words. *Our dream.*

And then Dominique is racing excitedly up the stairs after Luke, barely acknowledging me as she hurries past, except to give me a tight little smile.

So Luke's uncle has offered him a job. An investment banking job. In Paris. For a lot more money than he's making now.

It's ridiculous that I should feel so physically affected by the news. I mean, I only met Luke two days ago. All I have is a tiny crush on him. Just a crush. That thing in the car this morning—that thing I thought I felt pass between us . . . that was probably just my undying gratitude to him for buying me that six-pack of diet Coke. That's all.

But there's no denying that a lump has formed in my throat. Paris! He can't move to Paris! It's bad enough that he lives in Houston! But a whole *ocean* away from me? No.

What am I thinking? What's wrong with me? It's none of my business. *None* of my business.

I tell myself that firmly as I come the rest of the way down the stairs . . .

. . . and find that Mrs. de Villiers has sunk onto one of the velvet couches in the foyer and is looking perturbed. She smiles briefly when she sees me, then continues to look troubled, lost in her own thoughts.

I start to walk by. I know I'm probably wanted outside. I can hear the murmur of all the guests gathering on the lawn for aperitifs. I'm sure there are champagne bottles that need uncorking. And I did, after all, promise to help.

But suddenly I'm wondering if there's someone else I need to help first. Maybe this *is* my business. I mean, why else was it that Luke and I ended up sitting next to each other on that train? Granted, there were no other seats available. But *why* were there no other seats available?

Maybe because I was *supposed* to sit by him. So that I can do what I'm doing now.

Which is save him.

And so, before I can change my mind, I turn around and come back to where Mrs. de Villiers is sitting.

Seeing me standing in front of her, Luke's mother looks up.

"Yes, dear?" she says with a hesitant smile. "I'm sorry, I've forgotten your name . . ."

"Lizzie," I say. My heart has begun beating very hard within my chest. I can't believe I'm doing what I'm about to do. But on the other hand, I feel it's my duty, as lead anchor of the Lizzie Broadcasting System. "Lizzie Nichols. I couldn't help overhearing what Dominique told you just now"—I nod my head toward the stairs Dominique has just taken—"and I just wanted to say, strictly between you and me, that I'm not sure it's *entirely* true."

Mrs. de Villiers blinks. She really is a very attractive woman. I can totally see why Monsieur de Villiers fell so much in love with her and is so depressed about her not feeling the same way about him.

"What's not entirely true, honey?" she asks me.

"About Luke, wanting to move to Paris," I say in a rush, to get it all out before someone interrupts us. Or I come to my senses. "I know Dominique wants to move there, but I'm not so sure Luke does. In fact, he's playing with the idea of going to medical school. He's already applied to a program at NYU and gotten in. He hasn't told anyone, I guess—anyone but me—because he's not sure it's what he wants to do. But I personally think if he doesn't go, he'll always regret it. He told me he used to dream of being a doctor, but that he couldn't imagine going to school for four more years—well, five, counting the program he'd have to take to get all the science credits he'd need before he can even start . . ."

My voice trails off as I realize, from her stunned expression, how stupid what I'm saying must sound to her.

"Medical school?" Mrs. de Villiers's eyes are lined in pale blue. It brings out the green in her hazel eyes. The green is even more noticeable when she widens her eyes at me, which she does now.

"Luke always did want to be a doctor when he was a little boy," she says in a breathy, excited way. "He was forever bringing home sick and injured animals to try to cure, both here and back in Houston . . ."

"I think medicine is really what he would have preferred to go into," I say, nodding eagerly. "But I don't think converting Mirac into a place for plastic surgery patients to recover from their liposuction is necessarily a substitute for—"

"*What?*" A look of horror crosses Luke's mother's face.

Oh. No. Please don't tell me I've done it again.

But it's clear from the look on Mrs. de Villiers's face that I have. She looks as shocked as if I'd just told her that Jimmy Choo doesn't design the shoes with his name on them anymore. Which he doesn't.

Okay. So the lipo thing isn't something Dominique has run by Luke's parents yet.

"Um," I say. This is definitely *not* what I'd intended when I approached Luke's mom. I had never meant to rat out Dominique. All I'd wanted to do was let Mrs. de Villiers know that her son had a secret dream . . . a dream that, now that I think about it, he'd probably meant to *stay* secret. But, of course, I'd blown that.

"I'm just . . . I mean—if the vineyard really isn't doing all that well," I stammer, trying to change the subject, "I was thinking that a better alternative might be to rent Mirac out to people—rich people, obviously—who want a nice château to vacation in for a month, or maybe for a family or college reunion or something . . ."

"*Plastic surgery?*" Mrs. de Villiers repeats, in a stunned tone not unlike the one Luke had employed when I'd mentioned Dominique's idea to him. I can see that my attempt to change the subject hadn't gone over too well. "Who on earth ever suggested—"

"No one," I assure her quickly. "It was just an idea I heard being kicked around—"

"By *whom?*" Mrs. de Villiers wants to know, still looking horrified.

"You know what," I say, wanting to die. "I think I hear my friend Shari calling. I have to go—"

And then I do just that, jumping up and darting out of the house just as quickly as I can.

I'm dead. I'm so dead. I can't believe I did that. *Why* did I do that? Why did I open my big mouth? Especially about something that has nothing whatsoever to do with me. NOTHING. God, I'm such an *idiot*.

My cheeks flaming scarlet, I hurry across the lawn to where Chaz is already manning the bar (a long folding table covered with a white cloth). There is a long line of thirsty Houstonians, eager for their first cocktail of the day, in front of him.

"There you are," Chaz says when he sees me. He seems to notice neither my flaming cheeks nor my advanced state of nervous paranoia. "Thank God. Start cracking open some of those champagne bottles. Where's Shari?"

"I thought she was out here with you," I say, reaching for a bottle with trembling fingers.

"What, she's still inside changing?" Chaz shakes his head, then looks at the frat-boy type standing in front of him. "What can I get for you?"

"Stoli on the rocks," Frat Boy says.

"Sorry," Chaz says. "Beer and wine only, man."

"What the fuck?" cries Frat Boy.

Chaz levels him with a look. "You're on a vineyard, pal. What did you expect?"

"Fine." Frat Boy is sulking. "Beer, then."

Chaz all but throws a bottle at him, then looks at me. I've gotten the little metal cage off the champagne bottle, but the cork is eluding me. I don't want it to pop off and hit anyone.

Why did I tell Mrs. de Villiers that Luke wants to be a doctor? Why did I let slip that thing about the lipo? Why am I physically incapable of keeping my mouth *shut*?

"Use a napkin," Chaz says, throwing me one.

I give him a blank look. I have no idea what he's talking about. Am I drooling now, on top of everything else?

"To pull the cork," Chaz says impatiently.

Oh! Looking down, I wrap the napkin around the cork and pull—and it comes out easily, with a gentle pop, and no bodily harm to anyone.

Sweet. Okay. So there's one thing I can do right, anyway.

I am totally getting the hang of this. Chaz and I have a nice little rhythm going . . . that is, until Shari suddenly appears.

"Where have you been?" Chaz wants to know.

Shari ignores him. It's only then that I notice her eyes are blazing. And that she's staring straight at me.

"So just when," Shari demands, "were you going to tell me you didn't actually graduate yet, huh, Lizzie?"

The dawning of World War I found women's fashion going through a change almost as hot as the political climate. Corsets were abandoned as waistlines dropped and hemlines rose, sometimes to ankle length. For the first time in modern history, it became stylish not to have a bustline. Small-breasted women everywhere rejoiced as their more endowed sisters were forced to purchase chest "flatteners" in order to fit into the most popular fashions.

History of Fashion
SENIOR THESIS BY ELIZABETH NICHOLS

I can't believe he told. I trusted him and he completely betrayed me!

"I . . . I was going to tell you," I say to Shari.

"Kir royale, please," says a woman who looks as if she might be regretting her decision to wear long sleeves in such warm weather.

"When?" Shari demands.

"You know," I say, pouring a glass of champagne for the woman, then adding a splash of cassis. "Soon. I mean, I only just found out myself! How was I supposed to know I had to write a thesis?"

"If you paid a little more attention," Shari says, "to your studies, and a little less to clothes and a certain Englishman, you might have realized it."

"That's not fair," I say, passing the woman her kir royale and only splashing a little of it down on her hand. "My field of study *is* clothes."

"You're impossible," Shari spits. "How are you going to move to New York City with Chaz and me if you don't even have a degree?"

"I never said I was going to move to New York with you and Chaz!"

"Well, you're definitely not *now*," Shari declares.

"Hey," Chaz says, looking annoyed, "would you two cool it? We have a lot of Texans here who want their liquor and you're holding up the line."

Shari steps in front of me and says, "May I help you?" to the large woman I'd just been about to wait on.

"Hey," I say, hurt. "That's where I was standing."

"Why don't you go do something useful," Shari says, "and go finish your thesis."

"Shari, that's not fair. I *am* finishing it. I've been working on it all—"

It's right then that a shriek rends the stillness of the evening. It seems to be coming from the second floor of the house. It is followed by the words "No, no, no," uttered at the unmistakably high decibel achieved by one person, and only one person, staying at Mirac:

Vicky Thibodaux.

Craig, who is standing in front of the table where we're serving, glances at the house. Blaine, behind him in line, says, "Don't do it, man. Don't go. Whatever it is, you do not want to know."

But Craig looks resigned.

"I'll be right back," he says, and starts toward the house.

"You'll regret it," Blaine calls after him. Then, to me, he says, "There's a sucker born every minute."

"Did it ever occur to you that there might be something seriously wrong?" Shari, who is clearly in no joking mood, asks him. It's clear she's not sharing Blaine's unconcern—though she's one of the few. Everyone else on the lawn, seemingly used to Vicky's outbursts, is steadfastly ignoring what they've just heard.

"With my sister?" Blaine nods. "There's been something seriously wrong with her since the day she was born. It's called being a spoiled brat."

It's right then that Agnès comes running up to me, out of breath and panting, and says, "Mademoiselle. Mademoiselle. They want you to come. You must come now."

"Who wants me to come?" I ask in wonder.

"Madame Thibodaux," Agnès replies. "And her daughter. In the house. They say it is an emergency . . ."

"All right," I say, putting down my napkin. "I'll come. But—" Then, stunned, I gasp. "Wait. Agnès, you spoke English!"

Agnès blanches, then realizes she's been caught.

"Don't tell Mademoiselle Desautels," Agnès begs.

Chaz, amused, grins at her. "But if you speak English, why did you pretend you didn't?"

Now Agnès, instead of being pale, is blushing.

"Because I do not like her," she says with a shrug. "And my not understanding English annoys her very much. And I like to annoy her."

Whoa.

"Um," I say, "okay." To Chaz and Shari, I say, "I'll be back in a minute. Is that okay?"

Shari, her lips pressed into a thin line, refuses to comment. But Chaz, rapidly filling glasses, looks at me and says, "Go on. Agnès can take over for you. Can't you, Agnès?"

"Oh yes," Agnès says, and begins opening champagne bottles with the ease of someone who happens to be an old hand at it.

I don't hesitate a moment longer. I race around the table and head for the house, relieved to be out from under Shari's glare . . . but also furious that Luke told her. Why? Why did he say anything when only just this morning he promised he wouldn't?

And okay, I may not exactly have kept *his* secret . . .

But his secret isn't guaranteed to make anyone mad at him, the way mine was.

I should have known, of course. Men can't be trusted to keep a secret. Well, okay, I can't be trusted to keep one, either. But I thought

Luke was different from other guys. I thought I could tell him anything . . .

Oh my God! What *else* did he tell Shari? Did he tell her about the you-know-what? No, surely not. If he had, she'd have said something. She wouldn't have cared about shocking all those Daughters of the American Revolution. She'd have been like, "YOU GAVE ANDY A PITY BLOW JOB? ARE YOU INSANE?"

At least, I think she would have . . .

This is what I'm thinking to myself as I race into the house and up the stairs. I don't see anyone on my way to the second floor, where I find Craig, tapping on the door to Vicky's room and saying, "Vic. Let me in. Now."

"NO!" Vicky cries in an anguished voice from behind the door. "You can't see me! Go away!"

I approach, a little out of breath.

"What's wrong?" I ask Craig.

"I don't know," the groom-to-be says with a shrug. "Something to do with her dress. I'm not allowed to see it, or it's bad luck. She won't let me in."

Something to do with her dress?

I tap on the door.

"Vicky?" I say. "It's Lizzie. Can I come in?"

"No!" Vicky cries.

But the next thing I know, the door has been flung open.

Only not by Vicky. By her mother. Who snakes out an arm, grabs me by the shoulder, and pulls me into the room with a terse "Please go away, Craig" to her future son-in-law before slamming the door shut behind us.

As I stand in the large corner room, with its pink-papered walls and enormous canopy bed, my gaze is instantly drawn to the girl sobbing on a pink stuffed chair in the corner. Mrs. de Villiers is stroking her niece's hair in an attempt to calm her down. Dominique, looking darkly malevolent for some reason, glares daggers at me.

"Dominique says you know how to sew," Mrs. Thibodaux says, still not having let go of my shoulders. "Is that true?"

"Um," I say, completely confused, "yes. I mean, I *can* sew—"

"Can you do anything about this?" Mrs. Thibodaux demands, and spins me around so that I can get a look at her daughter, who has climbed to her feet and is now standing . . .

. . . in the most hideous wedding dress I have ever seen in my life.

It looks as if a lace factory threw up on her. There is lace everywhere . . . the poufed sleeves . . . the insert above the neckline . . . dripping from the bodice and skirt, then looped up in bunches all around the hem. It's the kind of wedding dress some girls dream of . . .

When they're nine.

"What *happened*?" I ask.

This just makes Vicky cry harder.

"You see?" she wails to her mother. "I knew it!"

Mrs. Thibodaux is chewing her lower lip. "I told her it wasn't that bad. She's so upset . . ."

I walk around the stricken bride to get a look at the back of the dress. Just as I suspected. There is an enormous lace butt bow in the back.

A butt bow.

Things could not be worse.

I exchange glances with Luke's mother. She looks, very briefly, to the ceiling.

I have no choice but to admit the truth.

"It's bad," I say.

Vicky lets out a hiccupy sob. "How c-could you let this happen, Mother?"

"What?" Mrs. Thibodaux looks indignant. "I'm the one who warned you! I'm the one who kept saying not to overdo it! She designed it herself," Mrs. Thibodaux explains to me, "and had a Parisian dressmaker hand-sew it, based on Vicky's sketch."

Oh. Well, that explains everything. Amateurs should never design their own dresses. And certainly not their own *wedding dress*.

"But I didn't mean it to look like *this*," Vicky wails. "It didn't even look like this at the last fitting!"

"I told you," Mrs. Thibodaux says to her daughter. "I told you not to wait until twelve hours before your wedding to try your dress on! And I told you not to add all that lace! But you wouldn't listen. You kept saying it would be fine. You kept saying you wanted more."

"I wanted something *original*," Vicky cries.

"Well, it's original all right," Mrs. de Villiers says wryly.

"The question is," Dominique says, speaking for the first time since I've entered the room, "can you fix it?"

"Me?" I fling a panicky glance at the gown. "Fix it? How?"

"Get rid of all this," Vicky says with a sniffle, lifting up a limp layer of lace that hangs, inexplicably, from the gown's bodice.

I stoop to examine the gown. It is, just as she asserted, hand-sewn. The stitching is superb.

And is going to be nearly impossible to rip out without damaging the material underneath.

"I don't know," I say. "I mean, it's sewn on there really well. Removing it might leave holes. It could end up looking really weird."

"Weirder than this?" Vicky demands, lifting her arms and revealing what appear to be wings of lace coming down from the sleeves.

"Good God in heaven!" Luke's mother exclaims, seeing the wings.

The wings seem to have clinched the matter for Mrs. Thibodaux.

"Can't you sew up the holes?" she asks me.

"In time for her to wear it tomorrow afternoon?" Luke's mother's tone is still wry. "Ginny, be reasonable. Even a professional seam-stress—if we could find someone this late in the day—couldn't do it."

"Oh, Lizzie is quite accomplished," Dominique chimes in. "Jean-Luc can't stop raving about her many talents."

Luke can't stop raving about me? Many talents? What talents? What is Dominique talking about?

"Really?" Mrs. de Villiers is looking at me with pointed interest. I can't tell if it's because of what Dominique just said, or if it's re-sidual curiosity concerning what I told her earlier in the evening, about her son's medical aspirations.

"Jean-Luc says she makes all her own clothes," Dominique says. "She even made that dress she's got on right now."

"What?" I'm so startled I jump. "No I didn't. This is by Anne Fogarty from, like, the 1960s. I didn't *make* it."

"Oh, don't be modest, Lizzie," Dominique says with a laugh. "Jean-Luc told me everything."

What is she *talking* about? What is going on? What did Luke say to her about me? What did Luke say to *Shari* about me? What is Luke doing, going around talking about me all over the place?

"It won't take Lizzie any time at all," Dominique is saying, "to whip Victoria's dress into shape."

"Oh!" Mrs. Thibodaux claps her hands together, tears—actual tears—glistening at the corners of her eyes. "Is that really true, Lizzie? Can you really do it?"

I look from Mrs. Thibodaux to Mrs. de Villiers to Dominique, then back again. Something is going on here. Something that, I'm starting to suspect, has more to do with Dominique than it does anything else.

"Do you think you can salvage it, Lizzie?" Mrs. de Villiers asks me, looking worried.

Did Luke really say I have many talents? That I'm accomplished?

I can't let him down. Even if he did rat me out to Shari.

"I'll see what I can do," I say hesitantly. "I mean, I can't promise anything—"

"I don't care," Vicky says. "I just don't want to look like Stevie Nicks on my wedding day."

I can see her point. Still—

"Take off your dress and give it to Lizzie," Mrs. Thibodaux tells her daughter. "And change into your rehearsal-dinner dress. There are a lot of people waiting to see us down there. God knows what they think is happening up here."

I didn't point out that it seemed as if most people hadn't been too alarmed by Vicky's screams, since she seems to let them out so often.

A minute later I find myself standing there clutching an armful of satin and lace.

"Do what you can," Mrs. Thibodaux says to me as Vicky, having changed into a demure pink sundress and repaired her tear-stained makeup, opens the door and goes out to greet Craig, who has been calmly waiting for her all this time.

"You can't possibly make it look any worse," is what Luke's mother says as she sails past me.

It's Dominique who adds, as she follows the sisters, "Good luck," with such malicious glee in her eye that I realize—belatedly—that I've just dug myself a grave I'll never be able to climb out of.

And that Dominique is the one who handed me the shovel.

Part Three

World War I was responsible for millions of deaths, but perhaps none more noticeable than the death of prewar conventions. A generation of women who had been doing "war work" in the absence of men, who were away fighting, realized that with the world about to end, they might as well start smoking, drinking, and in general doing everything else they had been forbidden from doing for so many years.

Girls who engaged in these activities soon earned themselves a special name—flappers—so-called because they were like baby birds, "flapping" the wings of their independence for the first time. In defiance of their parents and, in some cases, lawmakers, these girls bobbed their hair, hiked their skirts to knee length, and began paving the way for the fashion trendsetters of today's youth (see: Stefani, Gwen, L.A.M.B designs, and Spears, Britney, banana snake halter top).

History of Fashion
SENIOR THESIS BY ELIZABETH NICHOLS

21

It is vain to keep a secret from one who has a right to know it.
It will tell itself.
—*Ralph Waldo Emerson (1803–1882),*
U.S. essayist, poet, and philosopher

Okay. It's all right. I can do this. I can totally do this.

I'll just rip out the stitches. I have my sewing kit with me, with its seam ripper and stitch scissors. It'll be a snap. I'll just rip off all the lace and see what I've got to work with when I'm done. It'll be fine. Just fine. It has to be fine, because if it isn't, I'll have ruined a bride's big day. Not only that, but I'll have let down all these people who've been so kind to me.

Okay. I have to do a good job. I have to.

Rip.

Oh. Oh, okay, that looks really bad. Maybe I'll start with the butt bow. Rip. Yes, that looks better already. Good. Rip.

The thing is, one person, I know, wants me to fail. It's so obvious that's why Dominique said the things she did. Luke probably didn't say any of those things—rip—about me having many talents, or being so accomplished. I can't believe I fell for that. She only said those things because she knew if I heard them, it would be harder for me to say no.

And she wanted me to say yes so I could screw up.

It's just—rip—why would she want me to screw up? What did I ever do to her? I mean, I have been nothing but nice to her.

Well, okay, there was that thing about telling Luke's mom that he wants to be a doctor. She might be a *little* peeved about that, seeing as how she wants to move to Paris.

And then there's the fact that I let her little plan about converting Mirac to a lipo-recovery hotel slip.

But I never told Mrs. de Villiers that Dominique was the one who came up with it.

So why would she do something so incredibly bitchy? She knows as well as I do this dress is a lost cause. *Vera Wang* couldn't salvage this thing. Nobody could. What was Vicky thinking? How could she possibly ever have thought—

"Lizzie?"

Chaz. Chaz is at my bedroom door.

"Come in," I call.

He opens the door and pokes his head inside.

"Hey, what are you doing in here? We need you out—"

His voice trails off as he takes in the mess my room has become. Snowy fields of lace lay . . . well, everywhere.

"Sweet mother of God," Chaz says. "Did the Sugar Plum Fairy explode in here?"

"Bridal gown emergency," I say, holding up Vicky's gown.

"Who's getting married?" Chaz wants to know. "Björk?"

"Very funny," I say. "Anyway, don't expect me back at the bar anytime soon. I've got my hands full up here."

"That's kinda obvious. But not for nothing, Lizzie . . . do you even know anything about fixing wedding dresses?"

I am trying hard not to let him see me cry.

"I guess we'll find out, won't we?" I say brightly.

"Yeah. I guess we will. Well, don't worry, you're not missing much down there. Just a lot of windbags going on about their yachts. Oh, hey, listen, what's going on between you and Shar?"

I sniffle, and rub my nose with a shoulder as if it just tickles and isn't running.

"She found out I didn't actually graduate," I say.

Chaz looks relieved. "Is that all? Jesus, the way she's carrying on, I thought you said something about Mr. Jingles. You know she still feels guilty about that—"

"No," I say. "I just neglected to inform her that I haven't finished my thesis. And she found out. Somehow."

You know, it serves me right. Luke telling Shari about me not graduating, I mean. Since I told his mom about the doctor thing.

It's just that I physically *can't* keep a secret. What's his excuse?

"Didn't finish your thesis? Jesus, that's nothing," Chaz says dismissively. "You can crank that puppy out in no time. I'll tell Shar to cool it."

"Right," I say, sniffling. When he throws me a questioning look, I say, "Allergies. Really. And thanks, Chaz."

"Okay. Well. Good luck." Chaz looks around the room speculatively. "Looks like you're going to need it."

Then he leaves.

I let out a little sob but quickly pull myself together. I can do this. I can do this. I've done this hundreds of times to dresses at Vintage to Vavoom, dresses no one wanted to buy because they were too ugly. A few swipes of my scissors and a velvet rose here and there, and . . . *voilà! Parfait!*

And we were generally able to sell them at a fifty percent markup.

I've just managed to get the wings dripping from the sleeves off when there's another knock at the door. I have no idea how long I've been working, or what time it is, but I can see outside the tiny diamond-shaped window at the end of my bed that the sun is setting, turning the sky a brilliant ruby color. I can hear laughter drifting up from the lawn and the clink of silverware. The guests are eating.

And, having helped to carry in the food from the delivery truck it arrived in, I'm pretty sure, based on what I've seen, that what they're eating is delicious. I'm pretty sure, in fact, that truffles and foie gras are involved.

"Come in," I say in response to the knock, thinking maybe it's Chaz again.

I am totally shocked to see that it's not Chaz at all, but Luke.

"Hey," he says, letting himself into the tiny room, then looking around, clearly concerned.

And why shouldn't he be concerned? The place looks like a confetti factory.

"Chaz just told me what's up," he says. "I had no idea they'd roped you into this. This is completely insane."

"Yeah," I say stiffly. I am determined not to cry. At least, not in front of him. "It's insane all right."

Hold it together, Lizzie. You can do it.

"How did they talk you into this?" he wants to know. "I mean, Lizzie, no one can possibly make a wedding dress in one night. Why didn't you say no?"

"Why didn't I say no?" Oh no. Here come the tears. I can feel them, hot and wet, behind my eyelids. "Gosh, Luke, I don't know. Maybe because your girlfriend was standing there telling them how talented you said I was."

Luke looks taken aback. "What? I didn't—"

"I realize that," I cut him off. "*Now*. But at the time, I don't know, a part of me was hoping it was true or something. You know, that you had said something nice about me. I should have realized, of course, that it was all just a trick."

"What are you talking about?" Luke asks. "Lizzie—are you crying?"

"No," I insist, lifting a wrist to wipe my streaming eyes. "I'm not crying. I'm just really tired. It's been a really long day. And I really don't appreciate your doing what you did."

"What *I* did?" Luke looks totally confused.

He also, in the light from the little lamp by my bed, looks totally hot. He's changed into his party clothes, a collared white linen shirt and black trousers with a razor-sharp crease down the front of each leg. The white shirt brings out the deep tan of his neck and arms.

But I will not be swayed by masculine hotness. Not this time.

"Oh, right," I say. "Like you don't know."

"I *don't* know," Luke says. "I don't know what Dominique said that I said, Lizzie, but I swear—"

"I'm not talking about what you said to Dominique," I interrupt. "I already know that was a lie. But why . . ." My voice catches. So much for refusing to cry in front of him. Oh well. It's not like he's never seen my tears before. ". . . why did you tell Shari about my thesis?"

"*What?*" His expression, in the lamplight, is a mixture of incredulity and confusion. "Lizzie. I swear. I never said a word."

Wow. I really hadn't expected that. You know, denial. I'd fully expected him simply to come clean . . . to admit he'd done it and ask for an apology.

Which I'd been willing to accept, of course, on account of my own guilt for having spilled the beans about him to his mom. It's true things would never be the same between us, of course. But maybe, with time, we might have been able to build up some modicum of mutual trust . . .

But to stand there and deny it? To my *face*?

"Luke," I say, my disappointment causing my voice to throb a little, "it had to be you. No one else knew."

"It *wasn't*," Luke says. A glance at his face shows he's no longer feeling incredulous or confused. Now he's mad. At least if his frown is any indication. "Look, I don't know how Shari found out about your not graduating. But I didn't tell her. Unlike *some* people in this room, I can keep a secret. Or are you not the one who told my mother that I want to go to medical school?"

Oops. In the silence before I reply, I can hear more rattling of silverware from below, along with the chirp of crickets, and Vicky's voice, crying out very distinctly, "Lauren! Nicole! You made it!"

I swallow.

I. Am. So. Dead.

"Well," I say, "yes. Yes, I did. But I can explain—"

"Do you really think," Luke interrupts, "that it's okay for you to go around accusing people of failing to keep a secret when you obviously can't keep one yourself?"

"But—" I say, feeling all the blood drain from my face. Because he's right. Of course. I'm the biggest hypocrite in the world.

"But," I say again, "you don't understand. Your girlfriend—your uncle—everyone was going around saying you were going to take that job, and I just thought—"

"You just thought you'd get involved in something that was none of your business?" Luke demands.

I. Am. So. Stupid.

"I was trying to help," I say in a small voice.

"I never asked for your help, Lizzie," Luke says. "Help was never what I wanted from you. What I wanted from you was . . . what I thought we might have—"

Wait. Luke wanted something from me? Luke thought we might have—*what*?

Suddenly my heart starts pounding a mile a minute. Oh my God. Oh my God.

"You know what?" Luke says suddenly. "Never mind."

And he turns around and stalks from the room, closing the door very firmly behind him.

Some argue that the rise of Hitler—and Fascism—can be blamed for the return, in the 1930s, to longer skirt lengths and the restrictively tight waistline, sending women into corsets once again. The onset of the Depression made it nearly impossible for ordinary women actually to own the expensive Parisian fashions they saw sultry stars wearing in the movies—but talented seamstresses who could imitate the designs with less costly fabrics found plenty of business, and the "knockoff" was born at last . . . long may it live (see: Vuitton, Louis).

History of Fashion
SENIOR THESIS BY ELIZABETH NICHOLS

Gossip is charming! History is merely gossip.
But scandal is gossip made tedious by morality.
—*Oscar Wilde (1854–1900), Anglo-Irish playwright, novelist, and poet*

Can I just say it's really hard to snip straight when you're crying so hard you can't see?

Well, whatever. Who needs him, anyway? I mean, okay, sure, he seems really nice. And he's definitely good-looking. And smart and funny, too.

But he's a liar. I mean, obviously he told Shari about my thesis. How else could she have found out? I don't know why he couldn't have just admitted it, the way I did, about having told his mom about his secret dream of being a doctor.

At least I did that for a good cause. Because I suspect Bibi de Villiers is the kind of woman who, upon learning her child has a secret dream, will do everything in her power to see that that dream is achieved. Should a mother like that really be kept in the dark about her son's most heartfelt ambition?

I was actually doing Luke a *service* in telling his mother. How can he fail to see that?

Oh, all right. I'm a busybody and a loudmouth and a big stupid jerk.

And because of it, I've lost him . . . though the truth is, I never really had him. Oh, sure, there was that moment this morning, when he bought me the diet Coke—

But no. That was clearly all in my head. There's no doubt about it now. I am destined to live and die alone. Romance and Lizzie Nichols simply do not mix.

And that's just fine. I mean, there have been plenty of people who have had perfectly happy, fulfilled lives without a significant other. I can't think of any right now. But I'm sure there have been. I'll just be like one of them. I'll just be Lizzie . . . alone.

I'm trying to angle my scissors beneath a particularly tight row of stitches when there's yet another knock on my door.

Seriously. I don't know how much more of this I can take.

The door opens before I even have a chance to say "Come in."

And, much to my surprise, Dominique is standing there, looking tall and cool in high-heeled Manolo slides and a low-cut slinky green dress.

I shake my head.

"Look," I say, "I know it looks bad, but it's always worse before the storm. I'll get the dress done if people would just leave me alone so I can work."

Dominique steps into the room, looking around carefully, as if afraid there might be trip wires across the floor, instead of just mounds and mounds of lace.

"I didn't come here about the dress," Dominique says. She stops by my open suitcase and looks down at the jumble of vintage dresses and Sears jeans that are lying there. Then she smirks.

"Look," I say. I have really taken about all I can mentally stand. "If you want me to finish this thing by morning, you're going to have to leave me alone, okay? Tell Vicky I'm doing the best I can."

"I told you," Dominique says. "I'm not here about Victoria or her dress. I'm here about Luke."

Luke? That causes me to lay down my scissors. What could Dominique have to say to me about *Luke*?

"I know you're in love with him," she says, lifting my family-size pack of Tums from the top of the dresser and examining it closely.

I stare at her openmouthed. "Wh-what?"

"It's quite obvious," Dominique says, putting the Tums back where she found them. "At first I was not alarmed because . . . well, look at you."

Like the total jerk that I am, I actually do look down at myself. There are now approximately eighty-five thousand bits of white lace stuck to my black dress. I've pulled my hair into a haphazard ponytail and lost my shoes somewhere under all the folds of material lining my floor.

"But I know he's . . . *fond* of you," Dominique says, lifting her pointed chin.

Yeah. Well. Maybe at one time. Now? Not so much, I suspect.

"He thinks of you, I think, like a big brother thinks of a funny little sister," Dominique goes on.

Great. The way Blaine thinks of Vicky. Just great.

Although it's better than hating me, I guess.

"He tells you things, I think." She's found one of my many book lights and lifts it up to examine it. "I'm wondering if he has said anything to you about his uncle's offer."

I feign ignorance. What else can I do? I can't let on that I was eavesdropping. Even though of course I was.

"Offer?"

"Surely you heard? A job in Paris with Monsieur Thibodaux's very exclusive firm. Making a great deal more than he is making even now. Hasn't he mentioned it to you?"

"No," I say. And for once, I'm not even lying.

"How odd," Dominique says. "He's acting so strangely."

"Well," I say conversationally, "that can happen. You know, when a lot of money suddenly gets thrown your way. People freak. Look at what happened to Blaine."

"Blaine?" Dominique looks blank.

"Right. Blaine Thibodaux." When Dominique continues to look blank, I explain, "His band got signed by a record company, and Blaine's girlfriend left him. Because she says he's too rich now. Like I said. When it comes to large amounts of money, some people just . . . freak."

Dominique looks startled. My book light sits forgotten in her hand.

"Record companies pay that much?"

"Well, sure," I say. "Plus, you know, Blaine just sold the rights to one of his songs to Lexus. For a commercial."

Dominique's eyes narrow. "Really." She puts down the book light. "How interesting." Her tone suggests she finds it anything but. "Then you don't know why Luke is acting so strangely?"

"I have no idea," I say. Because I really don't. At least, not why he'd be acting strangely toward *Dominique*. Unless she, like me, accused him of being a liar. Then, of course, I'd understand.

"Well," she says. And starts for the door. "Thank you. Good luck with the dress." Her mouth twists at one end into something like a smile. "It looks as if you'll need it."

Then she's gone, before I can even say "Thanks."

Oh well. If that's the kind of woman Luke prefers—tall, naturally skinny, artificially inflated in the chest area (I'd stake Grandma's life on it), and obsessed with money, more power to him.

Although, you know. I can sort of understand why he might prefer that kind of woman to one who accuses him of being a liar. Even if he is one.

And that doesn't seem like something Dominique would do. She's way too crafty.

Crafty enough to have gotten me to commit to a project there's no way I'll ever complete on time. At least, not to anyone's satisfaction. By the time the toasts start downstairs—I can hear the clink of spoons on crystal, then a lull, then appreciative laughter—I've denuded Vicky's gown of lace.

And found that what the lace was covering is actually worse-looking than the lace.

I'm standing there asking myself if I should just put the lace back on and admit defeat, or possibly pack up all my things and just make a run for it, when the door to my room opens and Shari comes in, without knocking. In her hands is a plate of food.

"Before you open your mouth and make things even worse than they actually are," she says angrily as she sets the plate on top of my dresser, by the book lights, "I want you to know that I got my period today, and like a fool, I forgot to bring any tampons. So I came in here to look for some, because I know you always pack like you're going to Mount Everest and won't see civilization for weeks, even for an overnighter. And that's how I found the notebook you're writing your thesis in. I mean, you left it open, right on your bed. There's no way I could avoid looking at it. I thought it was your diary. And I had PMS. I *had* to read it, obviously."

I stare at her openmouthed.

"I know it was wrong," she goes on. "But I read it anyway. And that's how I knew you hadn't actually graduated. Luke didn't tell me. Although may I just take this moment to say I can't believe you told Luke, a man you only met a few days ago, and not me, who has been your best friend since kindergarten?"

I feel something rumble beneath me. At first I think it's the floor. Then I realize it's my entrails, clenching.

"Luke didn't tell you?" I ask in a weak voice.

"No," Shari says. She flops down onto my bed, heedless of the piles of lace there. "So it was really nice of you to accuse him of it. He seems to really appreciate it. And you."

"Oh God." Clutching my stomach, I sink down on the bed beside her. "What have I done?"

"Fucked up," Shari says. "Big time. I mean, considering you're in love with him and all."

I glance at her miserably. "Does it show that much?"

"To those of us who have known you for eighteen years? Yes. To him? Probably not."

I collapse back against the bed and stare with tear-filled eyes at the raftered ceiling.

"I'm such an idiot," I say.

"Yes," Shari replies. "You are. Why didn't you just tell me about your thesis in the first place?"

"Because," I say, "I knew you'd be mad at me."

"I *am* mad at you."

"See? I knew it."

"Well, come on, Lizzie," Shari says. "Just because your education was free doesn't mean it's all right for you to squander it. *History of fashion*? As a major?"

"Well, at least I didn't have to kill any rats!"

The minute the words are out of my mouth, I regret them. Because now Shari's eyes have filled with tears.

"I told you," she says. "I had to kill Mr. Jingles. A scientist has to be able to distance herself."

"I know," I say, sitting up and wrapping my arms around her. "I know, and I'm sorry I said that. I don't know what's wrong with me. I'm just . . . I'm just a mess."

Shari doesn't hug me back. Instead she looks across my room and says, "You *are* a mess, and you've gotten yourself *into* a mess. Lizzie, what are you going to do about that girl's dress?"

"I don't know," I say sadly, surveying the damage. "It actually looks worse than before."

"Well," Shari says, "I didn't see it before. But I don't see how it could look worse than it does now."

I take a deep breath.

"I'm going to fix it," I say. And I'm not just talking about Vicky's dress, either. "I don't know how. But I'm going to fix it. If I have to stay up all night."

"Well," Shari says. And she gets up off the bed and goes to retrieve the plate from the dresser. "Here. Peace offering."

She puts the plate in my lap. On it is an assortment of some of the food from the rehearsal dinner—what appears to be Cornish game hen, some kind of vegetable gratin, a salad in a vinaigrette, assorted chunks of cheese, and . . .

"That's foie gras," Shari says, pointing at a blob of brown on the edge of the plate. "I know you wanted to try some. I didn't get you any bread, because I trust you're still doing the low-carb thing— croissants and Hershey bar sandwiches aside. Here's a fork. Oh, and here—"

She goes to the door to my room, opens it, stoops down, and retrieves something from the floor outside.

It's an ice bucket. She lifts the lid to reveal—

"My diet Cokes," I say, fighting back a new wave of tears.

"Yeah," Shari says. "I found them wedged way back in the fridge, behind the Nutella. I figured you could use some if you were going to pull an all-nighter up here. Which"—she glances at the remains of Vicky's wedding dress—"is what it looks like you'll be doing."

"Thanks, Shar," I say, starting to sniffle. "And . . . I'm sorry. I don't know why I didn't stay more on top of things with school. I was just too wrapped up in Andy toward the end there, I guess, to really pay attention to what was going on."

"That's not it," Shari says. "I mean, that's probably part of it, but let's face it, Lizzie. School was never your thing." She nods at my sewing basket. "*This* is. And if anybody can fix that ugly dress, well, I guess it's you."

My eyes well up again. "Thanks. Only . . . I mean, what am I going to do about Luke? Does he . . . does he really hate me?"

"Hate might be a strong word for it," Shari says. "I'd say he's more . . . bitter."

"Bitter?" I wipe my eyes with my hands. "Bitter's better. I can deal with bitter. Not," I add quickly, seeing the curious look Shari darts at me, "that it matters. Since he's already got a girlfriend, and he lives in Houston, and I'm just coming out of a dead-end relationship, and I'm not interested in starting something new and all."

"Right," Shari says with one eyebrow raised. "Okay, then. Well, get to it, Coco. We'll all be eagerly awaiting your creation in the morning."

I try to laugh, but all that comes out is a hiccupy sob.

"And Lizzie?" she asks as she pauses on her way out the door.

Uh-oh. "Yeah?"

"Is there anything else I need to know?" Shari asks. "Any other secrets you might be harboring from me?"

I swallow. "Absolutely not," I say.

"Good," Shari says. "Let's keep it that way."

And then she stomps out of my room.

The thing is, I don't feel at all bad about not telling her about the blow job. There are some things even your best friend doesn't need to know.

When the Germans invaded Paris in 1940, fashion as the world knew it came to a standstill. The war put an end to the export of couture, and rationing to save resources for the war effort meant that items like silk, which was needed to make parachutes, were impossible to come by. Die-hard lovers of fashion, however, would not give up their stockings, and so stained their legs and drew seams down them to imitate the look of their favorite hosiery. Women who were not so artistically inclined opted instead to wear trousers, a look finally acceptable to a society becoming used to things like air raids and bebop.

History of Fashion
SENIOR THESIS BY ELIZABETH NICHOLS

Gossip is news running ahead of itself in a red satin dress.
—*Liz Smith (1923–), U.S. journalist and author*

$\mathcal{I}$ wake to find a strip of lace stuck to my face. Also to an urgent knocking on my door.

I look around blearily. A wan gray light fills my room. I realize I forgot to close my drapes the night before. I realize I forgot to do a lot of things the night before. Such as change into pajamas. Wash my makeup off. Or brush my teeth.

The banging on my door continues.

"Coming," I say, rolling out of bed—then staggering a little as a wicked head rush seizes my temples in a vise. This is what comes, I know, of pulling a diet-Coke-fueled all-nighter.

I make my way to the door and pull it open a few cautious inches.

Vicky Thibodaux, in a pale blue peignoir, stands in the hallway.

"Well?" she demands anxiously. "Are you finished? Did you do it? Could you save it?"

"What time is it?" I ask, rubbing my gritty eyes.

"Eight," she says. "I'm getting married in four hours. FOUR HOURS. *Did you finish?*"

"Vicky," I say, slowly forming the words that I have been going over and over in my head since around two in the morning. "Here's the thing—"

"Oh, fuck it," Vicky says, and throws her full body weight against the door, shoving it open, and me aside.

Three steps into the room, she freezes when she sees what's hanging from the hook on my wall.

"Th-that . . ." she stammers, her eyes wide. "Th-that's—"

"Vicky," I say. "Let me explain. The gown that your dressmaker used to sew all that lace onto didn't have enough structural integrity in and of itself to exist on its own without—"

"I love it," Vicky breathes.

"—all the lace that covered it. In essence, your bridal gown *was* lace . . . and that's it. So I—wait. You what?"

"I love it," Vicky says. She reaches excitedly for my hand and squeezes it. She hasn't once taken her eyes off the gown on the wall. "It's the most beautiful gown I've ever seen."

"Um," I say, relief coursing through me. "Thanks. I think so, too. I found it in the attic upstairs the other day. It was kind of stained, but I got those out, and fixed a few tears along the hem, and reattached one strap. Last night I adjusted the fit according to the measurements on your old dress. It should fit, so long as you haven't shrunk—or grown—in the night. Then I spent about an hour pressing it . . . thank God I found an iron down in the kitchen . . ."

Vicky, I realize, is barely listening to me. She still hasn't unglued her gaze from the glistening Givenchy.

"Um," I say, "do you want to try it on?"

Vicky nods, apparently unable to speak, and begins stripping off her peignoir without another word.

I gently pluck the gown from its hanger. Vicky's original dress— the lace disaster—hangs on another hook nearby. I'd put the two side by side in order to let her choose. Her original gown doesn't look *that* bad—if I do say so myself. I managed to tone down the lace, though there was no way I could remove it all and still have a dress left. Instead of looking like something Stevie Nicks might wear, it now resembled something Oksana Baiul might sport at *Barbie on Ice*.

But next to the Givenchy, it hadn't stood a chance.

Which was just what I was hoping.

I find myself holding my own breath as I drop the yards and yards of creamy white silk over Vicky's head. Then, as she slips her arms through the straps, I step behind her to begin fastening the pearl buttons. One by one, they easily close. And she isn't, I know, holding her breath, because I can hear her excited panting as she looks down at herself.

"It fits," she cries excitedly as I get to the top buttons. "It fits *perfectly*."

"Well," I say, "it should. I moved the darts—"

Vicky whirls away from me. "I want to see," she cries. "Where's a mirror?"

"Um," I say. "There's one in the bathroom across the hall—"

She runs from my room, noisily banging the door, then just as noisily barges into the bathroom.

From which I hear, "Oh my God! It's *perfect*!"

I find myself sagging against my bedroom wall in relief. She likes it.

I finally did *something* right, anyway.

Vicky barges back into my room.

"I love it," she says. For the first time since I've met her, she's all smiles.

And, smiling, Vicky transforms into an entirely different girl. She's no longer the spoiled socialite who hates her brother and just about everyone else in the world.

Instead I get a glimpse of the sweet, engaging girl who chose to marry a phlegmatic computer programmer from Minnesota instead of the rich heir to a Texas oil fortune her mom had picked out for her.

It's true, I guess, what they say about brides on their wedding day. They're all beautiful. Even this early in the morning, with no makeup on, Vicky looks stunning.

"I love it, and I love *you*," she gushes. "I'm going to go show my mom." She leans over to plant a kiss on my cheek and pulls me into a surprisingly hard bear hug. "Thank you. Thank you so much. I will never forget this. You're a genius. An absolute genius."

Then, in a whirl of white silk, she's gone.

And, completely exhausted, I fall back into bed, desperate for a few more minutes of sleep.

I'm able to snatch one, maybe two, more hours before I'm rudely awakened again, this time by someone hurling herself bodily against me. Someone who sounds very much like Shari as she says, "Oh my God, oh my God, Lizzie, wake up! You'll never believe this—WAKE UP!"

I wedge a pillow over my head, keeping my eyes tightly closed.

"Whatever it is," I say, "I don't want to know. Seriously. I'm exhausted. Go away."

"You'll want to know this," Shari assures me, prying the pillow out of my hands.

When she's successfully lifted my only protection from the bright sunlight spilling into my bedroom, I peer at her through my puffy eyelids and say, in tones of great hostility, "This better be good, Shar. I was up till five in the morning working on that stupid dress."

"Oh, this is good," Shari says. "Luke dumped her."

I just stare at her. "Who?"

"What do you mean who?" Shari hits me in the head with the pillow she's taken from me. "Dominique, you idiot. He just told Chaz, who told me. And I rushed up here to tell you."

"Wait." I raise up to my elbows. "Luke broke up with Dominique?"

"Last night, apparently, after we all went to bed. I thought I heard them fighting, but the walls in this place are so thick—"

"Wait." This is seriously too much for me to handle on a diet-Coke-buzz hangover. "They broke up last night?"

"They didn't break up," Shari says gleefully. "He *dumped* her. He told Chaz he finally realized they wanted totally different things in life. Also that her tits were fake."

"*What?*"

"Well, that's not one of the reasons why he broke up with her, of course. It's just something he said in passing."

"Oh my God." I lay there, trying to figure out how I feel. Mostly I feel bad. But maybe that's because I've only had, like, three hours of sleep, total.

"It's my fault," I say finally.

Shari looks at me as if I'm insane. "Your fault? How is it your fault?"

"I told Luke's mom what Dominique told us . . . about him wanting to be a doctor. And I also let slip that stuff about turning this place into a lipo-recovery hotel. I bet she said something about it to Luke. His mom, I mean."

Shari gives me a very sarcastic look.

"Lizzie," she says, "guys don't break up with their girlfriends because their mom doesn't like them."

"Still," I say. I feel terrible. "If I had kept my mouth shut—"

"Lizzie," Shari says, "Luke and his girlfriend were having problems way before you ever came along."

"But—"

"I know, because Chaz told me. I mean, the woman has six-hundred-dollar flip-flops. Come on. Get over yourself. It had nothing to do with you or anything you may or may not have said to Luke's mom."

I digest this. Shari's right, of course. It would be way conceited of me to think that what had happened between Luke and his girlfriend had anything to do with me.

"I knew they were fake," I say at last.

"I know," Shari says. "I mean, they never moved. Like when she was waving."

"I know!" I cry. "Whose boobs don't jiggle when they move? When they're that big, I mean."

"So you know what this means," Shari says. "You've totally got a chance with him after all."

"Shari," I say, feeling alarmed. Because I know I'm only going to get my hopes up for nothing. "He hates me. Remember?"

Shari frowns. "He doesn't hate you."

"You said he was bitter."

"Well. Yeah. He did sound kind of bitter about you last night."

"See," I say.

"But that was before he dumped his girlfriend!"

I flop back against the pillows. "Nothing's changed between him and me since last night, though," I say to the ceiling. "I still accused him of telling you about my thesis. When he totally didn't."

"Well, here's a brilliant idea. Why don't you try apologizing to him?"

"It won't change anything," I say, still speaking to the ceiling. "Not if he's still bitter. And he probably is. I know I would be, if it were me."

"Actually, you wouldn't. But that's another issue. Look, there's no doubt in my mind you're going to have to do some groveling," Shari says. "But come on. Don't you think he might be worth it?"

"Yes," I say. "Of course." I think about that day on the train, how kind and patient and funny he was. How long his eyelashes had looked against the setting sun. How sweet he was to me that day in the attic. The diet Coke he bought me.

The way he'd insisted I'm brave, in spite of all the evidence to the contrary.

And my heart lurches with longing.

"But, Shari," I say, "there's no point. I mean, look at—"

The door to my room thumps open and Chaz sticks his head in, looking annoyed.

"Excuse me, ladies," he said. "I know it's fun sitting around gossiping about my friend Luke. But has it occurred to either of you that we have a WEDDING WE PROMISED TO HELP SET UP?"

Which is how, an hour later, I find myself carrying around a tray of mimosas, offering welcome libations to the thirsty—and cranky—hordes gathered on the lawn for the wedding of Victoria Rose Thibodaux and Craig Peter Parkinson. It's much hotter than anyone anticipated it would be, and the men are all sweating in their suit jackets and ties while the women are using the wedding programs to fan themselves. The wedding is supposed to start at noon, and by all indications it actually will. The minister—imported all the way from the bride's own church in Houston—has arrived, as has the florist, the wedding cake, and even the string quartet that will march in the bride (Satan's Shadow still refusing to play covers, including *Lohengrin*).

Even the bride, to everyone's surprise, is actually ready, and is rumored to be waiting coolly in the house for the strike of twelve.

I wish I could be doing anything coolly, but I'm basically a mess. That's because I still haven't seen Luke yet. Well, I mean, I've *seen* him—he's running around all over the place, greeting guests, fielding problems, looking stunning in a dark suit, and, unlike so many of the men at Mirac, not at all uncomfortable in it in this heat.

But never once has he come anywhere close to me, much less even glanced my way.

I can totally understand why he's angry—I mean, bitter—with me. But the least he could do is give me a chance to explain.

"Is there alcohol in that?" Baz, Satan's Shadow's drummer, asks me as he points at the glasses I'm carrying.

"Yes," I say. "Champagne."

"Thank God," Baz says, and grabs two glasses, downs both of them, and puts them back on my tray empty. "It's frigging hot out here, huh?"

"Well," I observe politely, "at least you're dressed for it." Vicky's brother's band has, as far as I can tell, opted to eschew the dress code by wearing shorts, flip-flops, and, in the case of Kurt, the keyboardist, no shirt.

"Man," Baz says, "have you seen Blaine?"

"I have not," I say, my attention wandering. That's because I see Luke nearby, helping an elderly woman in one of the folding chairs Chaz and he were apparently up at seven in the morning setting in rows to form an aisle down which they're about to unroll a white carpet.

Baz follows my gaze and, spying Luke, raises an arm. "Luke!" he yells. "Yo, over here."

No! Oh God, no! I want to have a word with Luke, of course, but not like this . . . a *private* word. I do not want our first meeting since that unpleasant scene the night before to be in front of anyone—particularly not a drummer named Baz.

"Yes?" Luke asks politely as he comes over.

As usual, the sight of him causes my pulse to flutter like a tween at a sale at Claire's. He just looks so gorgeous standing there in the sunlight with his broad shoulders and freshly shaved face and, oh God, wingtips. Shiny, newly polished WINGTIPS!

It's all I can do to keep from dropping my tray.

Why did I have to do something as stupid as accuse him of telling Shari about my thesis? Why, just because *I* can't keep a secret, do I go around assuming no one else can, either?

"Dude, have you seen your cousin Blaine?" Baz asks Luke. "Nobody can find him anywhere."

"I haven't seen him," Luke says. His gaze, I can't help noting, is on mine. Though I can't for the life of me read what's going on behind those dark eyes. Does he hate me? Does he like me? Or does he ever even think about me at all? "Has anyone tried his room? Blaine's a late sleeper, if I remember correctly."

"Oh yeah," Baz says. "Good idea."

And he shuffles off, leaving Luke and me standing awkwardly alone together—an opportunity I seize before Luke has a chance to slip away.

"Luke," I say, my voice sounding very soft compared to the drum of my heartbeat in my ears, "I just wanted to say . . . about last night . . . Shari told me—"

"Let's forget about it, okay?" Luke says tersely.

Tears spring to my eyes.

Shari had said he was bitter. And he has a right to be.

But won't he even let me *apologize*?

But before I have a chance to say another word, Monsieur de Villiers, looking spry in a cream-colored suit and tie, comes up to me, holding a bottle of champagne.

"Lizzie, Lizzie," he chastises me merrily, "I see empty glasses on this tray. I think you need to go back to Madame Laurent for a refill."

"Here." Luke tries to take the tray from me. "I'll do it."

"*I'll* do it," I say, snatching the tray back. Only the fact that there are three glasses sitting on it, including Baz's two empty ones, keeps disaster from ensuing.

"I said," Luke says, reaching out again, "*I'll* do it."

"And I said, *I will*—"

"Lizzie!"

Luke, his father, and I all turn at the sound of Bibi de Villiers's excited voice. Looking stunning in butter yellow, with a picture hat framing her face, she exclaims, "Lizzie, where did you find that dress?"

I look down at myself. I have on the mandarin dress I last wore at Heathrow, when I'd been hoping to impress Andy ... a million years ago. It's the only thing I brought with me that seems remotely appropriate for a wedding. Well, the fact that I can't wear panties with it aside. Besides, no one has to know about that but me.

"Um," I say, "at this shop where I work back in Michigan called Vin—"

"Not *that* dress," Luke's mother says. Her expression is a strange combination of excited and anxious. Not that that seems to matter to Luke's dad, who's staring at her as if she were something Santa had just dropped down the chimney.

"I mean the dress Vicky is wearing," Mrs. de Villiers says. "The one she says you fitted for her overnight."

Beside me, Luke grows very still. His father, on the other hand, is still staring at his wife in a thoroughly besotted manner.

Alerted by Luke's stiffness that something is up, I answer his mother's question very carefully.

"I found it here at Mirac," I say. "In the attic."

"The attic?" Mrs. de Villiers looks stunned. "*Where* in the attic?"

I don't have the slightest idea what's going on. But I do know that Mrs. de Villiers's interest in the Givenchy isn't casual. Was the dress hers? The size is right ... it fit Vicky, and Vicky is Bibi's niece, so ...

I'm not taking any chances. No way am I telling her the horrifying condition in which I found her dress. That's one secret I'll take with me to the grave.

Unlike all the rest I know.

"I found it in a special box," I say, fabricating rapidly. "It was wrapped in tissue. I would almost say *lovingly* wrapped—"

I know I've said the right thing when Mrs. de Villiers turns toward her husband and cries, "You saved it! After all these years!"

And suddenly she's thrown her arms around the neck of Luke's father, who is glowing with pleasure.

"Why, yes," Monsieur de Villiers is saying, "of course I saved it! What do you think, Bibi?"

Though it's clear—to me, anyway—he has no idea what his wife is talking about. He's just happy to be holding her in his arms again.

Beside me, I hear Luke swear beneath his breath.

But when I look up at him, alarmed that I've done the wrong thing—again—I see that he's smiling.

"What's this all about?" I ask him out of the corner of my mouth.

"I knew that dress looked familiar," Luke says in a low voice so his parents—who are nuzzling each other—won't overhear. "But I've only seen it in black-and-white pictures, so I never . . . That dress you found? The one you took to get the rust out of? That was her wedding gown."

I gasp. I can't help it. "But—"

"I know," Luke says, taking me by the arm and steering me away from his parents, "I know."

"But . . . a gun! It was wrapped around—"

"I know," Luke says again as he guides me across the lawn, toward the table where Madame Laurent has the orange juice pitcher. "That dress has been a bone of contention between them for years. She thought he threw it out along with everything else after the attic leaked—"

"But he didn't. He—"

"I know," Luke says again. He stops walking and—much to my disappointment—drops his hand from my elbow. "Look, he really loves her. But he's not exactly the sentimental type. Mom means a lot to him. But so does his hunting rifle. I doubt he even realized what that dress was. He just saw that it was the perfect size to wrap his gun in and . . . well, there you go."

"Oh my God," I say, horror clutching my heart, "and I moved the darts to make it fit Vicky!"

"Somehow," Luke says, turning around to gaze at his parents, who are still practically making out in front of everybody across the lawn, "I don't think my mom minds."

We stand there watching his parents for almost a full thirty seconds before I remember I'm supposed to be apologizing to him. Even though last time I tried, I didn't exactly have the best results.

I open my mouth, wondering how I'm going to say this—will a simple sorry suffice? Shari had said something about groveling. Do I need to drop to my knees?

But before I can say anything, he asks, in a voice that's very different from the terse one in which, a few minutes earlier, he suggested we just forget about it, "How did you know? Not to mention the way you *really* found it? That dress, I mean?"

"Oh," I say, suddenly unable to meet his eye. I keep my gaze on my retro kitten heels, which are slowly sinking deeper and deeper into the grass the longer I stand still. "Well, you know. I could tell that dress meant something to your mom, so I just tried to imagine how I'd want a Givenchy of mine to be treated . . ."

It's then that Luke takes the tray of glasses from my hands, puts it down at the table Madame Laurent and Agnès have commandeered, and grabs my fingers in his own.

"Lizzie," he says in a deep voice.

And I have to look up from my French pedicure. I *have* to.

This is it, I realize. This is when he forgives me.

Or not.

"Luke," I say, "I'm so—"

But then, before I can say another word, the string quartet, seated in the shade of a nearby oak tree, suddenly breaks into those four familiar notes:

Dum dum da-dum.

The end of World War II brought about a new beginning in fashion. The hourglass silhouette was back, and suddenly even top designers were producing ready-to-wear styles—particularly for teenagers, who, in the economic boom following the war, had enough disposable allowance finally to afford to buy their own clothes. How else to explain the rise of the "poodle skirt"? Like today's "low-rise jeans," the appeal seemed known only to the wearers themselves.

History of Fashion
SENIOR THESIS BY ELIZABETH NICHOLS

Love is only chatter,
Friends are all that matter.
—*Gelett Burgess (1866–1951), U.S. artist, critic, and poet*

Vicky's wedding to Craig is lovely.

And I'm not just saying that because I'm one of the people who helped make it that way, by ensuring that the bride wore a gown of such stunning beauty. It would have been lovely even if Vicky had worn her original dress.

Just, you know. More lacy.

Shari and Chaz and Madame Laurent and Agnès and I sit in the back, watching the exchange of vows, while Madame Laurent and I dab at our eyes and Chaz smirks (what is it with guys and weddings?).

And the whole time, I keep a surreptitious eye on Luke, sitting near the front row of chairs, on the bride's side (they're actually both the bride's side, given that, with the exception of his parents, his sister, and three former college buddies, the groom's side was pretty much empty until the bride's guests were urged to fill in the seats). Luke, I can see, glances often in the direction of his parents, who are still giggling with each other and smooching like high school sweethearts.

There is no sign, that I can see, of Dominique. Either she's refusing to come down from her room or she's left the château altogether.

Then, suddenly, the minister is saying, "Craig, you may kiss the bride," and Mrs. Thibodaux lets out a huge happy sob, and it's over.

"Come on," Shari says, plucking my arm. "We're in charge of the bar again."

I look longingly after Luke. Am I *ever* going to get to tell him I'm sorry? Even if I can get him alone—will he actually listen?

We hurry to beat the rush of hot, thirsty wedding guests and immediately start popping (or, in my case, carefully pulling off) champagne corks. Everyone seems to be in a much better mood now that the ceremony is over. Men are loosening their ties and removing their jackets, and women, fearful of getting grass stains on their fabric shoes, are going barefoot. Patapouf and Minouche, the farm dogs, are hanging around, directly in the path of the caterers with their trays of canapés. Everything seems to be going exactly as planned . . .

. . . until Luke comes by and asks us, in a low voice, "Have any of you seen Blaine?"

I look across the yard and see the stage that had been set up yesterday for the band. Baz and Kurt are at the drums and keyboard, respectively. The bass player is there (I've forgotten his name), tuning up. Even a group of Vicky's friends are standing on the wooden dance floor, eagerly awaiting the concert.

But there's no one standing in front of the microphone in the middle of the stage.

"Satan's Shadow seems to have lost its lead singer," Shari observes.

It's right then that Agnès comes running up, looking angelic in what has to be her best party dress, a pink organza number better suited to the prom than a wedding.

But that's what makes it so cute.

She says something in breathless, rapid French to Luke, whose eyebrows go up.

"Oh no," he says. And hurries off in the direction of his aunt and uncle.

"Agnès," I say, hurrying to fill the glasses that are being handed to me, "what is it? What'd you just say to Luke?"

"Oh," Agnès says, brushing some of her hair from her face, "only that the room of Blaine is empty. His suitcase, everything, is gone. And so is the room of Dominique. The van of the Satan's Shadow is gone as well."

I feel something cold and wet on my hand, and look down to see that I've poured champagne all over my arm.

"Shit," Chaz is saying, having overheard. He can't seem to stop laughing. "Oh, shit!"

"What?" Shari looks annoyed. She's never coped well in food service situations. "What's so funny?"

"Blaine and Dominique," I say, through lips that have gone suddenly numb. Because I'm remembering the conversation I had in the kitchen that night with Blaine—assuring him that somewhere out there, there was a girl who wouldn't mind his newfound wealth.

And my conversation with Dominique last night, about Blaine and his new recording contract . . . not to mention his Lexus commercial.

It looks as if Blaine's found his new girlfriend, and Dominique a man who might actually listen to her get-even-richer schemes.

"Yes," Shari says impatiently. "Blaine and Dominique, what?"

"It looks like they've run off together," I say.

And it's all my fault.

Again.

It's Shari's turn to spill champagne. She's so startled she jerks the bottle she's holding, pouring sparkling wine all over Chaz's high-tops.

"Hey, watch it!" he cries.

"Blaine and Dominique?" Shari echoes. "Are you sure?"

"He's not here, and neither is she," I say. I glance in the direction of the stage. "Things are not looking good for Satan's Shadow."

Vicky's friends have been joined by Vicky, who, resplendent in her bridal gown and veil, seems to be noticing for the first time that her brother has skipped out on her nuptials.

"Hope Blaine wasn't the only one who knows how to sing," Chaz says.

"Can we get the string quartet back?" Shari wonders.

"You can't have a father-daughter dance to Tchaikovsky," I say.

I can't believe this is happening. I can't believe Blaine would do this to his own sister!

Well, actually, considering the fact that Dominique is involved, I sort of can.

But that doesn't make it any less my fault. *Why* did I tell her about Blaine? He was clearly in a vulnerable state, romantically. Of course he'd have no resistance to her wiles!

And after Luke dumped her, she must have been smarting . . . of course she'd need the kind of therapeutic balm only a guy with a trust fund can provide a girl like Dominique.

And no matter what Shari might think, it's my fault Luke and Dominique broke up. Not because he secretly loves me or anything. But because of my encouraging Luke to pursue his medical school dream, instead of Dominique's living-in-Paris dream . . .

It really is all my fault.

There's only one thing, I realize, that I can do. If I want to make things right again for everyone, that is.

The only question is, am I brave enough to do it?

I guess I have to be.

"I'll be right back," I say, throwing down my cork-unscrewing napkin.

And I begin marching toward the stage.

"Hey," Shari calls after me, "where ya going?"

I keep moving. I don't *want* to do this. But it's not like I have a choice. Vicky, I see, is crying now. Craig is attempting to comfort her, as are her parents. The wedding guests are milling around, more concerned about the fact that Vicky seems so upset than about the fact that there's no music.

"How could he do this to me?" Vicky is wailing. *"How?"*

"Darling," Mrs. Thibodaux says comfortingly, "it's all right. The boys will find something to play. Won't you, boys?"

Baz, Kurt, and the bass player exchange glances. Baz is the only one with the guts to go, "Um. None of us can sing."

"But you can still *play,*" Mrs. Thibodaux snaps. "Your fingers aren't broken, are they?"

Baz actually looks down at his fingers. "No. But, like . . . what should we play? Blaine took the playlist."

"Play something appropriate for the couple's first dance," Mrs. Thibodaux hisses.

Baz and Kurt look at each other. "'Cheetah Whip'?" Baz asks.

"I don't know, man," Kurt says, looking alarmed. Or as alarmed as a twenty-year-old who is aggressively stoned *can* look. "We say 'fuck' a lot in that one."

"Yeah," Baz says, "but if no one is singing—"

I glance at Luke. He is gazing with concern at his sobbing cousin.

That's it. I know what I have to do.

Before I can talk myself out of it, I step up onto the stage. Baz and Kurt look at me. The bass player—what's his name again?—says, "Hey," and grins at my bare legs.

"Is this on?" I ask, and grab the microphone from its stand.

Is this on Is this on Is this on? My voice seems to reverberate across the valley.

"Oh," I say. "I guess it is."

is is is is is.

Everyone on the lawn before me turns to stare up at me ... including, I see, an openmouthed Vicky.

And Luke.

Who looks like someone just kicked him.

Great.

"Hi," I say into the microphone. What am I doing? And why am I doing it again?

Oh yeah. It's all my fault.

I wonder if they can see that my knees are shaking.

"I'm Lizzie Nichols. Blaine Thibodaux was supposed to be up here—not me—but he had, ahem, an emergency—" I glance behind me for support. Baz nods energetically. "Right. An emergency crisis and he had to leave. But we still have the rest of Satan's Shadow," I say, flinging out an arm to introduce the band. "Guys?"

The band members shuffle their feet. The crowd, confused but polite, applauds a little.

I seriously cannot believe these guys just signed a multimillion-dollar recording deal.

"So, uh," I say as I notice Shari, a look of abject shock on her face, weaving her way through the guests toward me, "I just want to say congratulations to Vicky and Craig. You two make a really beautiful couple."

More applause, this time heartfelt. Vicky hasn't stopped crying, but she isn't crying as much. She looks more stunned than anything else.

Sort of like her cousin Luke.

"And, uh," I say into the microphone. *And uh And uh And uh And uh.* "Since we're missing a singer, I thought, in honor of your special day—"

I see Shari, out on the dance floor, shake her head at me, her eyes wide with alarm. *No,* she mouths. *No, don't do it.*

"—my friend Miss Shari Dennis and I will sing a song traditionally played during the newly wedded couple's first dance where we come from—"

Shari's shaking her head so fast her bushy hair is whacking her in the face. "No," she says. "Lizzie. *No.*"

"—the great state of Michigan," I go on. "It's a song I'm sure you all know. Feel free to sing along if you want to. Guys." I turn around to face Satan's Shadow. "I know you know it, too. Don't act like you don't."

Baz and Kurt raise their eyebrows at each other. The bass player still hasn't torn his gaze from my legs.

"Vicky and Craig," I say, "this one is for you."

you you you you.

Then I clear my throat.

"'Now, I,'" I sing, just as I have a hundred times before, at family gatherings, grade-school talent shows, dorm competitions, karaoke nights, and anytime I've had one too many beers.

Only this time my voice is so magnified I can hear it carrying all across the lawn . . . across the vineyard . . . down the cliff and into the valley below. The German tourists floating on rubber inner tubes along the Dordogne can hear me. The tourists arriving by the busload to look at the cave paintings at Lascaux can hear me. Even Dominique and Blaine, wherever they are, can probably hear me.

But no one joins in.

Well, maybe they need more of a lead-in.

"'—had—'"

Hmm. Still no one joining in. Not even the band. I turn around to look at them. They're staring at me blankly. What is wrong with them?

"'—the time of my life—'"

It can't be that they don't know this song. Okay, sure, they're guys. But what, they didn't have sisters?

"'And I never—'"

What is going on? I *can't* be the only person here who knows this song. *Shari* knows it.

But she's still standing down there on the dance floor, shaking her head, mouthing *No, no, no.*

"Come on, guys," I say encouragingly to the band. "I know you know this one. '—felt this way before.'"

At least Vicky is smiling. And swaying a little. *She* knows this song. Although Craig looks a little confused.

Oh my God. What am I doing? *What am I doing?* I'm standing up here in front of all these people, singing my favorite song of all time—the perfect wedding song—and they're all just standing there, staring up at me.

Even Luke is staring up at me like I was just beamed down from the starship *Enterprise.*

And now Shari's disappeared. Where did she go? She was there a second ago. How can she let me down this way? We've been doing this song together since kindergarten. She always plays the girl part. *Always.*

How could she leave me hanging like this? I know I screwed up with the thesis thing, but how long can you stay mad at someone you've been friends with your whole life? Plus, I apologized for that.

Then I hear it. The snap of a snare drum.

Baz. Baz is joining in.

I *knew* he knew this song. *Everyone* knows this song.

"'Oh, I—'" I sing, turning around to grin at him gratefully. Now Kurt's playing an experimental chord. Yes, Kurt. You got it, Kurt.

"'—had the time of my life—'"

Oh, thank you, guys. Thank you for not leaving me hanging.

Then a voice not my own booms out, "'—It's the truth—'"

And Shari climbs up onstage and comes to stand beside me, singing into the microphone.

And the bass player, whatever his name is, begins plucking out the familiar notes, while below us Craig gives Vicky a twirl . . .

And everyone applauds. And starts singing along.

"'And,'" Shari and I sing, "'I owe it all to you—'"

Oh my God. It's working. It's working! People are having a good time! They're forgetting about the heat, and the fact that the brother of the bride has run off with the girlfriend of their host's son. They're starting to dance. They're singing along!

"'You're the one thing,'" Shari and I sing—along with Satan's Shadow, the Thibodauxes, and the rest of the wedding guests, "'that I can't get enough of, baby—'"

I look down and see Luke's parents dancing along with everyone else.

"'So I'll tell you something—'" I sing, not quite believing what I'm seeing below me. "'This must be love!'"

People are having a good time. People are clapping their hands and dancing. Satan's Shadow has given the song a kind of Latin beat. Which it's not supposed to have, but whatever. Now it sounds kind of like *Vamos a la playa*.

But oddly, this isn't turning out to be a bad thing.

And then, just as we're getting to our big crescendo, Shari elbows me, hard—which is not actually part of our choreography. I glance at her and see that her face has gone as white as Vicky's dress. She points.

And I see Andy Marshall making his way toward the stage.

The Swinging Sixties brought about more than just a sexual revolution. Fashion underwent a revolution as well. Suddenly the feeling was "anything goes," from miniskirts to tie-dye. A return to natural fabrics—made from the same materials with which our ancient ancestors wove their loincloths—in the seventies brought fashion full circle, when hippies revealed other uses for hemp than those popularized by the beatniks of the decade before . . . although the most popular use for it is still very much in style on college campuses.

History of Fashion
SENIOR THESIS BY ELIZABETH NICHOLS

25

Fortunately we've just warbled our last "And I owe it all to
you." Because if he'd shown up at any other part, I'd have
choked on my own saliva.

The crowd bursts into enthusiastic applause, and Shari and I
take our bow. While our heads are down by our knees (and I see the
bass player duck to see if he can catch a glimpse of what's going on
under our skirts—which, in my case, is going to be quite a lot, if he
can actually see up there), Shari says, "Jesus Christ, Lizzie. What's *he*
doing here?"

"I don't know," I say back, wanting to cry. "What do I do?"

"What do you mean, what do you do? You have to go talk to him."

"I don't want to talk to him! I've already said everything I have
to say to him."

"Well, you obviously didn't say it forcefully enough," Shari says.
"So go say it again."

We both straighten just as one of Vicky's friends, to hoots of "Go,
Lauren!" and "You can do it, girl!" runs up onto the stage and grabs
the microphone from us.

"Hi," she says to us. "You guys were great." Then she spins around
to the band and cries, "D'you guys know 'Lady Marmalade'?"

Baz glances at Kurt. Kurt shrugs.

"We can probably figure it out," the bass player says.

And Kurt starts tapping out the beat.

"Lizzie," Andy says, standing at the bottom of the stage. He's got his leather jacket with him, strung over one arm.

What is he *doing* here? How did he find me? Why did he come? He doesn't love me. I know he doesn't love me.

So then why go to all this trouble?

My God. It must have been the blow job. Seriously!

I had no idea a blow job was such a powerful thing. If I had, I'd never have given him one, I swear.

I start climbing from the stage, Shari behind me, whispering, "Tell him to leave. Tell him you don't want anything to do with him. Tell him you're going to take out a restraining order. I'm sure they have those in France. Don't they?"

Andy is waiting for me at the bottom of the steps. His face is white and filled with anxiety.

"Liz," he says when I reach him, "there you are. I've been looking all over this place—"

"Andy," I say, "what are you doing here?"

"I'm sorry, Lizzie," he says, reaching for my hand. "But you just ran off! I couldn't leave things that way—"

"Excuse me," a woman with a heavy Texas accent interrupts us, "but are you the girl who designed the bride's gown?"

"Um," I say, "I didn't design it. It's vintage. I just rehabbed it."

"Well, I just wanted to tell you," the woman says, "you did a fantastic job. That dress is lovely. Just lovely. You'd never know it was vintage. Never in a million years."

"Well," I say, "thank you."

The woman goes away.

And I turn back to the man in front of me.

"Andy," I say. I can't believe this. I've never had a guy follow me across Europe before. Well, across a channel, anyway. "We broke up."

"No we didn't," Andy says. "I mean, you broke up with me. But you never even gave me a chance to explain—"

"Pardon me, miss." Another woman has come up to us. "But did you really make that wedding dress li'l Vicky's got on?"

"No, I didn't make it," I say. "I rehabbed it. It's a vintage gown. I just cleaned and fitted it for her."

"Well, it's beautiful," the woman says. "Just beautiful. And I liked your little song up there."

"Oh," I say, beginning to blush, "thanks." When she goes away, I say, to Andy, "Look, things just didn't work out between us. I'm really sorry about it. But you're just not the person I thought you were. And you know what? It turns out I'm not the person I thought I was, either."

It sort of surprises me to hear myself say that. But it's really true. I am not the same girl who got off that plane at Heathrow, even if I do happen to be wearing the same dress. I'm someone totally different now. I don't know who, exactly, but—

Someone else.

"Really," I say to Andy, giving his hand a squeeze. "I don't have any hard feelings toward you. We just made a mistake."

"I don't think we were a mistake," Andy says, his grip on my hand tightening. Not in a friendly squeeze like mine was, either. His is more like he isn't going to let go of me. "I think I *made* a mistake—plenty of mistakes. But, Lizzie, you never even gave me a chance to really apologize. That's why I'm here. I want to apologize properly, and then maybe take you out for a nice meal, and then take you home—"

"Andy," I say gently. Our conversation, already bizarre enough, has taken on an even weirder note, thanks to the musical accompaniment. Behind me, Lauren is shrieking, "'Gitchy gitchy ya ya da da!'" and doing some choreography that is making the bass player, at least, smile happily.

"How—how did you even know where to find me, anyway?" I ask wonderingly.

"You told me a million times in your e-mails that your friend Shari was staying the month in a château in the Dordogne called Mirac. It wasn't that hard to find. Now say you'll come home with me, Liz. We can start over. I promise it will be different this time . . . *I'll* be different."

"I'm not going back to England with you, Andy," I explain as kindly as I can. "I just don't feel that way about you anymore. It was very nice knowing you, but really. I think this is where we have to say good-bye."

Andy's jaw is slack.

"Excuse me," a woman says. I turn and find a middle-aged woman looking apologetic. "I'm sorry, I really don't mean to interrupt, but I heard you rehabbed the bride's gown. Which I assume means you took an old gown and fixed it up?"

"Yes," I say. What is going on here? "I did."

"Well—I really am sorry to interrupt—but my daughter would like to wear my grandmother's wedding dress for her wedding next June, but we just haven't been able to find anyone willing to, um, rehab it. Everyone we've seen about it says the fabric is too old and fragile, and they don't want to risk ruining it."

"Well," I say, "that is a concern with old fabric. I mean, it's much better quality than the materials used in bridal gowns today. But I've found if you use all-natural cleansers—no chemicals—you can get quite good results."

"All-natural cleansers," the woman repeats. "I see. Honey, do you have a business card? Because I would love to be in touch with you about this again"—she glances up at Andy's face—"but I can see that you're busy right now."

"Um." I pat myself, then remember my mandarin dress has no pockets. And that even if it did, I have no business cards, anyway. "No. But I'll find you and give you my contact information in a little while. Would that be all right?"

"That'd be just fine," the woman says with another nervous glance at Andy. "I'll just . . . I'll see you in a bit."

She slinks off and Andy, as if he can hold it in no longer, bursts out with, "Lizzie, you can't mean that. I understand that maybe you feel we need some time apart. Maybe after a bit of time has passed you'll realize that what we've got, you and I, is really special. I'll show you. I'll treat you the way you want to be treated. I'll make it up to you, Lizzie, I swear. When you get back to Ann Arbor in the fall, I'll call you—"

The strangest feeling comes over me when he says that. I can't really explain it, except that it's as if suddenly he's given me a glimpse into the future . . .

A future I can now see quite clearly, as if it were in high definition.

"I'm not going back to Ann Arbor in the fall, Andy," I say. "Well, I mean, except to get my stuff. I'm moving to New York City."

Behind me, I hear Shari go, "Ye-esss."

But when I turn to look at her, she's stonily watching Lauren implore the wedding guests to *coucher avec* her tonight.

"New York City?" Andy looks confused. "*You?*"

I stick out my chin. "Yes, me," I say in a voice that sounds completely unlike my own. "Why? You don't think I can do it?"

Andy's shaking his head. "Lizzie, I love you. I think you can do anything. Anything you set your mind to. I think you're amazing."

It comes out more like, *I fink you're amazing.*

But that's okay. Because right then I forgive him. I forgive him for all of it.

"Thank you, Andy," I say to him, a big grin bursting out across my face. Maybe I was wrong about him. Oh, not about the two of us not being right for each other. But, you know. Maybe he's not so bad after all. Maybe, even though we can't be lovers, we can still be friends . . .

"Excuse me," someone says.

Only this time it's not a Houston society matron who's come up to ask me how to get stains out of fifty-year-old lace.

It's Luke.

And he doesn't seem too happy.

"Luke," I say. "Hi. I—"

"Is it true?" Luke asks me. "Is this him?"

He's jerked a thumb in Andy's direction.

I can't imagine what's come over him—Luke, so unfailingly polite to everyone.

Everyone but me, I mean. But then I guess I deserve it.

"Um," I say, shifting uncomfortably, "yes. Luke, this is Andy Marshall. Andy, this is—"

But I never get to finish my sentence. Because before I can, Luke pulls back his arm and sends his fist crashing straight into Andy's face.

Anarchy! That was the cry of members of the punk movement in the 1980s. But there was nothing anarchic about their postapocalyptic style. Punk, coupled with a fitness phase that began in the eighties and has been going steady ever since, went on to influence both high fashion and street style for many years to come, giving us such wardrobe staples as motorcycle boots and yoga pants.

History of Fashion
SENIOR THESIS BY ELIZABETH NICHOLS

26

Silence is the most intolerable of answers.
—*Mason Cooley (1927–2002), U.S. aphorist*

He tried to kill me," Andy keeps saying. Although his words are somewhat indistinct behind the ice-filled dish towel Madame Laurent is pressing to his lip.

"He didn't try to kill you," Chaz says in a tired voice. "Stop being such a fucking baby."

"Hey," Andy says from his perch on the butcher-block kitchen table, "fuck you! I'd like to see how you'd react if someone sucker-punched you in the mouth!"

Only with his swollen lip and accent, the words come out sounding more like, *Oi'd loik to see how you'd weact if someone sucker-punched you in the mouf.*

"Chaz," I ask worriedly, ignoring their squabbling, "where's Luke?"

"I don't know," Chaz says. He was the one who'd jumped in and broken up the fight. Well, not that there'd been much of one. It had been more like a one-man assassination attempt. Luke had landed his punch, then backed off, waving his hand, apparently having injured it on Andy's teeth.

Which Andy is now complaining feel loose.

Chaz, who'd come over to congratulate Shari for so thoroughly embarrassing herself onstage, was able to keep Andy from returning Luke's punch merely by placing a hand on his shoulder. Andy is much more of a lover than a fighter, it turns out.

Though he doesn't seem to know it.

"It was a completely unprovoked attack!" Andy insists. "I wasn't doing *anything* to Liz! I was just talking to her!"

"Lizzie," Shari corrects him, in a bored voice, from where she's leaning against the kitchen sink, trying to keep out of the way of the caterers, who are streaming in and out of the kitchen with the first course—salmon—and glaring angrily at us as the chef tries to make progress at the stove with the second course—foie gras. "Her name's Lizzie. Not Liz."

"Whatever," Andy says into the dish towel. "When I find that bastard, I'm going to show him a thing or two."

"You're not going to be showing anybody anything," Chaz says to Andy in a firm voice. "Because you're leaving. There's a three o'clock train back to Paris, and I'm going to make sure you're on it. You, my friend, have caused quite enough trouble for one day."

"I didn't do anything!" Andy cries. "It was that French git!"

"He's not French," Shari says, still bored, as she examines her cuticles.

"Lizzie," Andy says from behind the dish towel, "listen. I'm sorry to bring it up. And now may not be the greatest time, but I was wondering about the money."

I blink at him.

"Money?"

"Right. The money you said you'd loan me for my matriculation fees? Because I really do need it, Liz."

"Oh no!" Shari bursts out. "Oh no, he did not just—"

"Shari," I say to her sharply, "I can handle this."

Because I can.

And, okay, it's not like I ever really thought he came all this way to patch things up with me because he loves me.

But it honestly never occurred to me that he did it because of the money.

"Andy," I say, "you came all this way to ask if I'd still lend you five hundred dollars?"

"Actually," Andy points out, his words muffled by the dish towel, "you said you'd give it to me. But a loan's all right, too. I feel terrible about asking, but in a way, you do sort of owe me the money. I mean, I did open up my home to you, and there was the gas money, you know, Dad spent picking you up from the airport, and—"

"Can I hit him now?" Chaz wants to know. "*Please,* Lizzie?"

"No, you can't," I say to Chaz.

Although it must be obvious from my stunned expression that I'm not about to pony up the money, since Andy's hangdog expression has completely disappeared. In fact, his eyes have squeezed shut above the dish towel.

Shari gasps.

"Oh my God," she says. "Andy, are you *crying*?"

It's clear when he speaks that he is.

"Are you telling me," he says, weeping, "that I hitched all the way here and you're not going to give me the money after all?"

I'm shocked. Crying? He's crying?

Luke must have hit him harder than any of us thought.

"You said on the phone that you couldn't talk about it!" Andy sobs. "That's all! You never said—"

"Andy." I shake my head. Can this really be happening? "I mean, Andy, we broke up. What did you think was going to happen?"

"You don't understand," Andy cries. "If I don't pay these blokes the money I owe them, they're . . . they're going to break my legs."

I exchange confused looks with Shari and Chaz. "The bursar's office is going to break your legs if you don't pay your matriculation fees?"

"No." Andy takes a shuddering breath from behind the dish

towel. "I . . . I wasn't quite truthful about that bit. It's the blokes that run the poker ring that I owe the money to, actually. They're . . . well, they're quite serious about getting it back. I can't go to Mum and Dad for it—they'll throw me out. And my mates are all tapped out as well. Really, Lizzie . . . you were my last hope."

I stare at him as his words sink in. Then I glance at Chaz and Shari, to see that both of them are looking at me, Chaz with a little grin on his face, Shari with a glower that clearly says, *Don't you back down. Don't you do it, Nichols. Not this time.*

I turn back to Andy and say, "Oh, Andy. I'm so sorry!" I reach up and give him a sympathetic pat on the shoulder. I can't believe I once loved that shoulder.

And I can't believe he really thinks I'm such a sap I'll actually give him a dime. Who does he think I am, anyway? Some kind of pushover?

"At least," I say, "have some wedding cake before you go. Goodbye."

Then I slip out the back door, where Patapouf and Minouche are waiting, eager for scraps dropped by the caterers. Behind me, I hear Chaz saying in a hearty voice, "Andy, my boy. I'm open-minded, man. And I happen to be loaded. So let's talk business. What've you got in the way of collateral? Is that jacket you've got there worth anything, by any chance?"

Agnès is outside, leaning against the butter-yellow Mercedes. She perks up when she sees me, eager for more gossip. I realize Luke's fight with Andy is the most exciting thing that's happened at Mirac in a long time. She's going to have a lot to tell her girlfriends when school starts again in the fall.

"Does the Englishman need to go to hospital?" she asks me brightly. "Because I can call my father, and he can come to take your friend to hospital."

"He's not my friend," I say. "And he doesn't need to go to hospital. I mean, to the hospital. Chaz is going to take him to the train station, and that will be the last we'll see of him."

Agnès looks disappointed. "Oh," she says, "I was hoping for more of the fighting."

"I think there's been enough fighting for one day," I say. "Speaking of which, did you see where Luke went after the fight?"

Agnès brightens again. "Oh yes! I see him go to the vineyard. I think he is in the cask room."

"Thanks, Agnès," I say, and start around the side of the house, to the lawn.

The wedding reception is in full swing and going well now that Satan's Shadow has gotten the hang of playing covers. One of Vicky's sorority sisters is onstage, shrieking lines from Alanis Morissette's "You Oughta Know." Not exactly wedding fare, but everyone appears far too drunk to notice. Most of them, thanks to the mimosas, had been too drunk even to realize there'd been a fight. Only a few people who happened to be standing nearby noticed, and Chaz's quick intervention had put a damper on any hopes for a continuation of the dramatic scene, and so they had all turned their attention back to what was happening onstage.

Still, even though no one seems aware of the fight, they all seem to know who I am. Well, I guess that's what happens when you make a complete and utter ass of yourself onstage in front of two hundred total strangers. They all feel like you're their best friend.

Or maybe it's just that word of my prowess with cream of tartar has spread. Because every woman there seems to have some question for me about an antique wedding dress—how they can get out a stain or insert a gusset; how they can update it without damaging the fine material; even how they can find a vintage wedding gown of their own.

I wrestle with these as best I can and finally manage to cross the lawn and reach the cask room—a thick-walled, cavernous structure, as centuries-old as the house itself—and pull open the heavy oak and iron door.

Inside, it's still as a mausoleum—although unlike in a mausoleum, golden light filters in through mullion-paned windows high up along the walls. You can't hear the sound of the band outside—which you can probably hear clear across the valley—or the chatter of the wedding guests. The walls are lined with waist-high oak wine casks, the contents of many of which Luke's father had insisted I try during my tour two days before. The glasses we—and then all the wedding guests Monsieur de Villiers had brought through for subsequent tours—used are piled up beside a stone sink at the far end of the room.

The stone sink at which Luke is running water over his hand.

He doesn't hear me come in. Or, at least, if he did, he doesn't react. He is standing with his back to me, his dark head ducked, letting the water run over his hand. He must, I realize, have really hurt himself on Andy's teeth.

Which is when I forget that my heart is in my throat at the prospect of talking to him after all the nasty things I accused him of last night, and hurry forward.

"Let me see," I say when I reach his side.

He jumps.

"Jesus," he says, looking down at me in surprise. "Sneak up on a guy, why don't you?"

I pull his hand from the stream of water gurgling out of the old-fashioned faucet. His knuckle, I see, is red and swollen. But the skin's not broken.

"You're lucky," I say, looking down at his hand. "He says his teeth are loose. You could have cut yourself on them."

"I know," Luke says, reaching out with his left hand to turn off the water. "I should have known better than to aim for the mouth. I should have gone for his nose."

"You shouldn't have 'gone for' anything," I say. I let go of his hand. "I had the situation totally under control, you know."

Luke doesn't even try to argue. He dries his hand on a nearby dish towel.

"I know," he says sheepishly. "I don't know what came over me. I just couldn't believe he'd have the nerve to show up here. Unless . . ."

I stare at him. I can't help noticing how thick and dark his hair looks in the bright shafts of sunlight coming down from the windows so close to the ceiling.

"Unless what?"

"Unless you *asked* him to come here," Luke says, not meeting my gaze.

"What?" I have to start laughing at that one. "Are you serious? Do you honestly think—"

"Well," Luke says. He lays the dish towel aside. "I didn't know."

"I thought I made myself pretty clear on the train," I say. "Andy and I broke up. He only came after me because he thought I could bail him out of a financial situation he got himself into."

"And . . . did you?" Luke asks. His dark-eyed gaze is steady on my face.

"No," I say. "Although Chaz seems to be working on it."

"That sounds like Chaz," Luke says with a grin.

I have to look away, flustered by how handsome the grin makes him.

Then I remember that there's something I'm supposed to be saying to him, so, feeling incredibly shy, I say it, fast. To my French pedicure.

"Luke. I'm sorry about what I said last night. I should have known you didn't tell her," I say. "Shari, I mean. About my thesis. I don't know what I was thinking."

Luke doesn't say anything. I look up, just once, to see if he's heard me.

He is looking down at me with the most inscrutable expression I have ever seen—halfway between a smile and a frown. Does he hate me? Or can he possibly, in spite of my big, fat, stupid mouth—in spite of everything—like me?

With my heart hammering so hard I'm sure he must be able to see it through the silk of my dress, I look down again and say, keeping my gaze on his feet now, instead of my own—then regretting it when I notice the wingtips again—WINGTIPS! So hot! "And the thing with telling your mom about you getting into NYU. And about Dominique's plans for the château. I mean, I was really only trying to suggest alternatives to turning this place into a spa. Like maybe renting it out to wealthy families who just want a nice château to vacation in for a month, or maybe for a reunion, or whatever. Honestly, I was only trying to help—"

"Well, actually, I've managed to get along without your help pretty well for the past twenty-five years," Luke says.

Ouch!

Stung, I can't help looking up and saying, "And that's why you're so happy with your career and your life and your girlfriend? And why Vicky looked so great in her dress and your parents seem to be getting back together and everyone out there is having . . . such a . . . fun time . . ."

My voice trails off as I realize he's smiling down at me.

"Joke," he says. "That was a joke. I told you I'm no good at them."

That's when he reaches out, pulls me toward him, and starts kissing me.

I'm in complete and utter shock. I can't understand what's happening. I mean, I *can* . . . but it makes no sense. Luke de Villiers is kissing me. Luke de Villiers's arms are going around me, holding me so tightly to him I can feel his heart slamming as hard against his ribs as mine is slamming against mine. Luke de Villiers's lips are raining thousands of tiny featherlight kisses on my lips.

And now my lips are falling open, surrendering to the onslaught of his. And he's kissing me hard and long and sweet, and I'm clinging to him because my knees have given out entirely and his arms are the only thing holding me up. And his tongue is in my mouth, like he can't taste me enough, and I can feel something hard pressing against me through the fabric of his trousers. And his hand, the hand he hit Andy with, is cupping my breast through the silk of my mandarin dress, and I want him to cup more of me, and I make a sound . . .

"Christ, Lizzie," he says in a voice that doesn't sound anything like the way it usually does.

And the next thing I know, he's lifting me up and putting me down again on top of the closest wine cask, and somehow my legs have fallen open and he's standing between them. The front of my dress is open, too. I don't even know how he did that because those snaps are supposed to be hidden. And I can feel his fingers—and the hot sunlight streaming in through the high windows—on my bare breasts.

And I can't stop kissing him, or running my fingers through his thick dark hair when his mouth starts traveling down my throat, then dips below to scorch the skin on my breasts. All the places where the sun is touching me, his lips are touching me, too.

Until suddenly he mutters, "Christ, Lizzie, you haven't got on any underwear," and I say, "I know, I didn't want visible panty lines," and he puts his lips there, too.

And on top of the cask I feel as if the sunlight is piercing me all over—but piercing me in a good way—and I look down through half-lidded eyes and think how bizarre it is that Luke de Villiers's dark head is between my legs—but bizarre in a *very* good way—and then I don't think about anything at all for a while except the sun, which seems to have turned into a supernova, right there inside Monsieur de Villiers's cask room.

And then Luke straightens and wraps an arm around my waist and pulls me close against him and my legs wrap around him and I feel his naked chest beneath my fingers and wonder how. And then he's inside me, thick and hard, and it feels even better than when his mouth was there, and we're moving against each other in just the right rhythm, with him burying himself more and more deeply in me, and me trying to get closer and closer to him, and he's kissing my neck and shoulders where the sun is hitting me, and suddenly there's sun all *over* me, like I'm being showered in golden sun drops, and I cry out at how good it feels, and Luke does, too.

And then as he stands there, holding me slickly to him and panting in my hair, I realize that we just had sex on a wine cask.

And that it was fantastic. I didn't even have to worry about taking care of my own good time! Luke totally made sure I had one. Or two, actually.

"Have I mentioned," Luke wants to know when he's caught his breath, "that I think I'm in love with you?"

I laugh. I can't help it.

"Have I mentioned," I ask, "that the feeling is mutual?"

"Well," he says, "that's a relief." He doesn't move, and neither do I. It feels good to stand like that. Or, in my case, sit.

"I should also probably tell you," Luke says, "that I decided to go ahead and enter that program I got into at NYU."

I wonder if he can see my heart leap inside my chest. Although I try to sound casual.

"Really?" I say. "That's funny. I'm moving to New York, too."

"Well," Luke says, leaning his forehead against mine and smiling, "isn't that a coincidence."

"Isn't it, though?" I say, smiling back.

A little while later, we slip hand in hand from the cask room just in time to see the bride and groom cutting the multitiered cake. Agnès, spotting us first, rushes over with a tray of champagne glasses, and we each take one and stand, side by side, as Vicky and Craig feed each other the first piece.

"I hope they don't cram it into each other's faces," I say. "I hate when they do that."

"Plus," Luke says, "then you'll have chocolate stains to get out."

"Don't even say that," I say, shuddering, and hug his arm.

"Why, hello," Shari says, appearing, with Chaz in tow, a minute later. "Where did you two disappear to?"

"Nowhere," I say quickly, blushing to my hairline.

"Oh, right," Shari says with a knowing smile. "I've been there."

"What are you talking about?" Chaz, clueless, wants to know. "You've been here the whole time. *I'm* the one who had to take that freak to the train station. I've decided that from now on, Lizzie, I'll be screening all your boyfriends. You can't be trusted to choose your own."

"Is that so?" I say, exchanging an amused glance with Luke, who puts his arm around me.

"I'll give you a hand with that, Chaz," Luke volunteers. "I think Lizzie is more than you can handle on your own."

Chaz, spying Luke's arm around my shoulders, narrows his eyes at us.

"Hey," he says, "what's going on?"

"I'll explain it to you someday, baby," Shari says, patting him on the arm.

"Nobody ever tells me anything." Chaz pouts.

"That's because you've got to go straight to the source," Shari says.

"Which is?"

"The LBS. Who else?" Shari says, tipping her head in my direction.

Which is right when an extremely tipsy Ginny Thibodaux spies me and hurries over to plant a kiss on my cheek.

"Lizzie!" she exclaims. "I've been looking everywhere for you. I wanted to thank you for what you did for my Vicky. That dress—it's beautiful! You know you're a lifesaver, don't you? I've never seen anything like it. Why, you ought to open your own business!"

"Maybe," I say with a smile, "I will."

In conclusion, we have seen the important role fashion has played in the development of world culture and history. Starting from strips of fur worn for warmth and protection by cavemen gathered round a fire, to Prada shoes worn for their beauty and cachet by the modern working woman at a cocktail party, fashion has, over the centuries, come to be one of man's—and woman's—greatest and most interesting accomplishments.

This author in particular looks forward to seeing what surprises and innovations await her in the world of fashion—and beyond—in the coming years.

History of Fashion
SENIOR THESIS BY ELIZABETH NICHOLS

QUEEN of BABBLE
IN THE BIG CITY

For Benjamin

Acknowledgments

Many thanks to Beth Ader, Jennifer Brown, Babara Cabot, Carrie Feron, Michele Jaffe, Laura Langlie, Sophia Travis and especially Benjamin Egnatz

Lizzie Nichols's Wedding Gown Guide

Finding the right wedding gown for your special day isn't easy, but it shouldn't drive you to tears, either!

Even if you are planning a formal ceremony with a traditional long dress, there are many different styles of gowns to choose from.

The trick is to match the right gown to the right bride before she becomes a Bridezilla . . . and that's where a wedding-gown specialist like myself comes in!

Lizzie Nichols Designs™

• Chapter 1 •

I open my eyes to see the morning sunlight slanting across the Renoir hanging above my bed, and for a few seconds, I don't know where I am.

Then I remember.

And my heart swells with giddy excitement. No, really. *Giddy.* Like, first-day-of-school-and-I've-got-a-brand-new-designer-outfit-from-TJ Maxx giddy.

And not just because that Renoir hanging over my head? It's real. Although it *is*, and not a print, like I had in my dorm room. An actual original work, by the Impressionist master himself.

Which I couldn't actually believe at first. I mean, how often do you walk into someone's bedroom and see an original Renoir hanging over the bed? Um, never. At least if you're me.

When Luke left the room, I stayed behind, pretending like I had to use the bathroom. But really I slipped off my espadrilles, climbed onto the bed, and gave that canvas a closer look.

And I was right. I could see the globs of paint Renoir used to build up the lace he so carefully detailed on the cuff of the little girl's sleeve. And the stripes on the fur of the cat the little girl is holding? Raised blobby bits. It's a REAL Renoir, all right.

And it's hanging over the bed I'm waking up in . . . the same bed that's currently bathed in sunlight from the tall windows to my left . . . sunlight that's bouncing off the building across the street . . . that building being the METROPOLITAN MUSEUM OF ART. The one in front of Central Park. On Fifth Avenue. In NEW YORK CITY.

Yes! I am waking up in NEW YORK CITY!!!! The Big Apple! The city that never sleeps (although I try to get at least eight hours a night, or my eyelids will get puffy, and Shari says I get cranky)!

But none of that is what's making me so giddy. The sunlight, the Renoir, the Met, Fifth Avenue, New York. *None* of that can compare to what's really got me excited . . . something better than all of those things, and a new back-to-school outfit from TJ Maxx put together.

And it's in the bed right next to me.

Just look how cute he is when he's sleeping! Manly cute, not kitten cute. Luke doesn't lie there with his mouth gaping wide with spit leaking out the side, like I do (I know I do this because my sisters told me. Also because I always wake up to a wet spot on my pillow). He manages to keep his lips together very nicely.

And his eyelashes look so long and curly. Why can't my eyelashes look like that? It's not fair. I'm the girl, after all. *I'm* the one who is supposed to have long curly eyelashes, not stubby short ones I have to use an eyelash curler I've heated with a hair dryer and about seven layers of mascara on if I want to look like I have any eyelashes at all.

Okay, I've got to stop. Stop obsessing over my boyfriend's eyelashes. I need to get up. I can't lounge around in bed all day. I'm in NEW YORK CITY!

And okay, I don't have a job. Or a place to live.

Because that Renoir? Yeah, it belongs to Luke's mother. As does the bed. Oh, and the apartment.

But she only bought it when she thought she and Luke's dad

were splitting up. Which they're not now. Thanks to me. So she said Luke could use it as long as necessary.

Lucky Luke. I wish MY mom had been planning on divorcing MY dad and bought a totally gorgeous apartment in New York City, right across the street from the Metropolitan Museum of Art, that she now only planned on using a few times a year for shopping trips in the city, or to attend the occasional ballet.

Okay, seriously. I have to get up now. How can I stay in bed—a king-sized bed, by the way, totally comfortable, with a big white fluffy goose-down-stuffed duvet over it—when I have all of NEW YORK CITY right outside the door (well, down the elevator and outside the ornate marble lobby), just waiting to be explored by me?

And my boyfriend, of course.

It seems so weird to say that . . . to even think it. Me and my boyfriend. My *boyfriend*.

Because for the first time in my life, it's real! I have an honest-to-God boyfriend. One who actually considers me his girlfriend. He isn't gay and just using me as a cover so his Christian parents don't find out he's really going out with a guy named Antonio. He isn't just trying to get me to fall so deeply in love with him that when he springs the idea of doing a threesome with his ex, I'll say yes because I'm so afraid he'll break up with me otherwise. He isn't a compulsive gambler who knows I have a lot of money saved up and can bail him out if he gets too deeply in debt.

Not that any of those things have happened to me. More than once.

And I'm not just imagining it, either. Luke and I are *together*. I can't say I wasn't a little scared—you know, when I left France to go back to Ann Arbor—that I might never hear from him again. If he hadn't really been that into me, and wanted to get rid of me, he had the perfect opportunity.

But he kept calling. First from France, and then from Houston, where he went to pack up all his stuff and get rid of his apartment and his car, and then from New York, when he arrived. He kept saying he couldn't wait to see me again. He kept telling me all the stuff he was planning on doing to me when he *did* see me again.

And then when I finally got here last week, he *did* them—all those things he'd said he'd been going to.

I can barely believe it. I mean, that a guy I like as much as I like Luke actually likes me *back*, for a change. That what we have isn't just a summer fling. Because summer's over, and it's fall now (well, okay, almost), and we're still together. Together in New York City, where he'll be going to medical school, and I'm going to get a job in the fashion industry, doing something—well, fashion-related—and together, we're going to make a go of it in the city that never sleeps!

Just as soon as I find a job. Oh, and an apartment.

But I'm sure Shari and I will find a charming pied-à-terre to call home soon. And until we do, I have Luke's place to crash, and Shari can stay in the walk-up her boyfriend Chaz found last week in the East Village (he rightfully refused his parents' invitation to move back into the house in which he grew up—when he wasn't being shipped off to boarding school—in Westchester, from which his father continues to commute to the city to work every morning).

And even though it's not on the best block exactly, it's not the worst place in the world, having the advantage of being close to NYU, where Chaz is getting his Ph.D., and cheap (a rent-controlled two-bedroom for only two grand a month. And okay, one of the bedrooms is an alcove. But still).

And okay, Shari's already witnessed a triple stabbing through the living room window. But whatever. It was a domestic dispute. The guy in the building across the courtyard stabbed his pregnant wife and mother-in-law. It's not like people in Manhattan go around getting stabbed by strangers every day.

And everyone turned out to be fine. Even the baby, who was delivered by the cops on the building's front stoop when the wife went into early labor. Eight pounds, six ounces! And okay, his dad is locked up in a prison cell on Rikers Island. But still. Welcome to New York, little Julio!

In fact, if you ask me, Chaz is sort of secretly hoping we won't find a place, and Shari will *have* to move in with him. Because Chaz is romantic that way.

And seriously, how fun would that be? Then Luke and I could come over, and the four of us could hang out just like we did back at Luke's place in France, with Chaz mixing kir royales and Shari bossing everyone around and me making baguette-and-Hershey-bar sandwiches for everyone, and Luke in charge of the music, or something?

And it could really happen, because Shari and I have had no luck on the apartment front. I mean, we've answered about a thousand ads, and so far the places are either snapped up before one of us can get there to look at them (if they're at all decent), or they're so hideous no one in their right mind would want to live there (I saw a toilet that was balanced on wooden blocks over an OPEN HOLE in the floor. And that was in a studio apartment in Hell's Kitchen for *twenty-two hundred dollars a month*).

But it will be all right. We'll find a place eventually. Just like I'll find a job eventually. I'm not going to freak out.

Yet.

Oh! It's eight o'clock! I'd better wake up Luke. Today is his first day of orientation at New York University. He'll be attending the postbaccalaureate premedical program there, so he can study to be a doctor. He wouldn't want to be late.

But he looks so sweet lying there. With no shirt on. And his tan so dark against his mother's cream-colored, thousand-thread-count Egyptian cotton sheets (I read the tag). How can I—

Ack! Oh, my goodness!

Um, I guess he's already awake. Considering that he's now lying on top of me.

"Good morning," he says. He hasn't even opened his eyes. His lips are nuzzling my neck. And other parts of him are nuzzling other parts of me.

"It's eight o'clock," I cry. Even though of course I don't want to. What could be more heavenly than just lying here all morning making sweet sweet love to my man? Especially in a bed under a real Renoir, in an apartment across from the Metropolitan Museum of Art in NEW YORK CITY!

But he's going to be a doctor. He's going to cure children of cancer someday! I can't let him be late for his first day of orientation. Think of the children!

"Luke," I say, as his mouth moves toward mine. Oh! He doesn't even have morning breath! How does he *do* that? And why didn't I jump up first thing and hurry into the bathroom to brush my teeth?

"What?" he asks, lazily touching his tongue to my lips. Which I'm not opening, because I don't want him to smell what's going on inside my mouth. Which appears to be a small party given by the aftertaste of the chicken tikka masala and shrimp curry from Baluchi's that we had delivered last night, which was apparently impervious to both the Listerine and Crest with which I attempted to combat them eight hours ago.

"You have orientation this morning," I say. Which isn't an easy thing to say when you don't want to open your lips. Also when there are a hundred and eighty pounds of delicious naked man lying on top of you. "You're going to be late!"

"I don't care," he says, and presses his lips to mine.

But it's no good. I'm not opening my mouth.

Except to say, "Well, what about me? I have to get up and go look for a job and a place to live. I have fifteen boxes of stuff sitting in my parents' garage that they're waiting to send me as soon as I can give them an address. If I don't get it all out of there soon, I just know Mom's going to have a garage sale, and I'll never see any of it again."

"It would be more expedient," Luke says, as he plucks at the straps to my vintage teddy, "if you would just sleep naked, like I do."

Only I couldn't even get mad at him for not listening to a word I've said, because he manages to get the teddy off with an alacrity that really is breathtaking, and the next thing I know, his being late for orientation—my job and apartment search—and even those boxes sitting in my parents' garage are the last things on my mind.

A little while later he lifts his head to look at the clock and says, in some surprise, "Oh. I'm going to be late."

I am lying in a damp puddle of sweat in the middle of the bed. I feel like I've been flattened by a steamroller.

And I love it.

"I told you so," I say, mostly to the girl in the Renoir above my head.

"Hey," Luke says, getting up to head to the bathroom. "I have an idea."

"You're going to hire a helicopter to pick you up here and take you downtown?" I ask. "Because that's the only way you're going to make it to your orientation on time."

"No," Luke says. Now he's in the bathroom. I hear the shower turn on. "Why don't you just move in here with me? Then all you'll have to do today is look for a job."

He pops his head—his thick dark hair adorably mussed from our recent activities—around the bathroom door and looks at me inquisitively. "What do you think about that?"

Only I can't reply, because I'm pretty sure my heart has just exploded with happiness.

There are many different styles and cuts of gowns for brides who choose a traditional long dress, but the five most common are:

The Ballgown

The Empire Waist

The Column or Sheath

The A-line

The Fishtail

But which shape gown is right for you?

That is the universal question, asked by every bride in the history of time.

• Chapter 2 •

A gossip goes about telling secrets, but one who
is trustworthy in spirit keeps a confidence.

—Bible: Hebrew, Proverbs 11:13

One Week Earlier

Well, at least you're not moving in with him," my older sister Rose says, as ten shrieking five-year-old girls take turns whacking a pony-shaped piñata hanging from a tree limb behind us.

This stings. Rose's remark, I mean. The five-year-olds I can't do anything about.

"You know," I say, irritated, "maybe if you had lived with Angelo for a while before you got married, you'd have figured out he wasn't your perfect soul mate after all."

Rose glares at me from across the picnic table.

"I was *pregnant*," she says. "It's not like I had much of a choice."

"Uh," I say, eyeing the five-year-old who is shrieking the loudest, the birthday girl, my niece Maggie. "It's called birth control."

"You know, some of us actually take pleasure in the moment," Rose says, "instead of obsessing over the future all the time. So birth control is not the first thing that springs to mind when a handsome man begins making love to us."

I think of lots of ways to reply to this, as I sit there watching Maggie decide that whacking the piñata with her stick is less interesting than whacking her father with it. But for once, I keep my mouth shut.

"I mean, God, Lizzie," Rose goes on. "You go off to Europe for a couple of months and come back thinking you know everything. Well, you don't. Especially about men. He won't buy the cow if he can get the milk for free."

I blink at her. "Wow," I say. "Could you be getting more like Mom every day?"

My other sister, Sarah, can't keep from snorting into her plastic margarita glass at that one. Rose glares at her.

"Oh," she says. "You're one to talk, Sarah."

Sarah looks shocked. "Me? I'm nothing like Mom."

"Not Mom," Rose says. "But don't tell me that wasn't Kahlúa you were pouring into your coffee this morning. At *nine-fifteen.*"

Sarah shrugs. "I don't like the taste of coffee straight."

"Oh, whatever, *Gran.*" Then, narrowing her eyelids at me, Rose continues, "For your information, Angelo *is* my perfect soul mate. I didn't *have* to live with him before we got married to know that."

"Uh, Rose," Sarah says. "Your perfect soul mate is currently getting racked by your eldest."

Rose looks over and sees Angelo crumpled to the ground with his hands pressed between his thighs. Maggie, meanwhile, is now whacking the side of her parents' minivan, to the enthusiastic support of her birthday-party posse.

"Maggie!" Rose shrieks, leaping up from the picnic bench. "Not Mommy's car! Not Mommy's car!"

"Don't listen to Rose, Lizzie," Sarah says, as soon as Rose is out of earshot. "Living with a guy before you marry him is the perfect way to find out if you two are compatible in the ways that really count."

"Like what?" I ask.

"Oh, you know," Sarah says vaguely. "If you both like watching TV in the morning, or whatever. Because if one person wants to watch *Live with Regis and Kelly* in the morning, and the other person needs absolute silence in order to face the day, there can be fights."

Wow. I remember how mad Sarah used to get if any of us turned on the TV in the morning. Also, I had no idea Sarah's husband, Chuck, was a *Regis and Kelly* fan. No wonder she needed that Kahlúa in her coffee.

"Besides," Sarah says, running a finger along the side of what's left of Maggie's horse-shaped birthday cake, then sucking off the vanilla icing, "he hasn't asked you, right? To move in with him?"

"No," I say. "He knows Shari and I are getting a place."

"I just don't understand," Mom says, coming up to the picnic table with a new pitcher of lemonade for the kids, "why you have to move to New York City at all. Why can't you stay in Ann Arbor, and open a bridal gown refurbishment boutique here?"

"Because," I say, explaining for what has to be the thirtieth time alone since I got back from France a few days before. "If I really want to make a go of this, I need to do it in a place where I can have the broadest customer base possible."

"Well, I think it's just silly," Mom says, plunking down onto the picnic bench beside me. "The competition for affordable apartments and things like appointments to get cable installed in Manhattan are cutthroat. I know. Suzanne Pennebaker's oldest daughter—you remember her, Sarah, she was in your class. What was her name? Oh, right, Kathy—went to New York to try her hand at acting, and she was back in three months, it was so hard just to find a place to live. What do you think opening your own business is going to be like?"

I refrain from pointing out to Mom that Kathy Pennebaker also has a narcissistic personality disorder (at least according to Shari, based on the many, many boyfriends Kathy stole from girls we knew around Ann Arbor, then dumped as soon as the thrill of the chase was over). That kind of thing might not have made her too popular in a place like New York, where I understand heterosexual males are in somewhat short supply, and the womenfolk not opposed to using violence to make sure their man stays that way.

Instead, I say, "I'm going to start out small. I'm going to get a job in a vintage clothes shop, or something, and get to know my way around the New York City vintage clothing scene, save my money . . . and then open my own shop, maybe on the Lower East Side, where rents are cheap."

Well, cheaper.

Mom says, "What money? You aren't going to have any money left, once you've paid your eleven hundred dollars a month just for your apartment."

I say, "My rent isn't going to be that much, because I'll be splitting it with Shari."

"A studio—that is an apartment with no bedroom, just a single open space—costs two grand a month in Manhattan," Mom goes on. "You have to share it with multiple roommates. That's what Suzanne Pennebaker says."

Sarah nods. She knows about Kathy's boyfriend-stealing habit, too, which would have made getting along with roommates, at least of the female variety, difficult. "That's what they said on *The View*, too."

But I don't care what anyone in my family says. I am going to find a way to open my own shop somehow. Even if I have to live in Brooklyn. I hear it's very avant-garde there. All the really artistic people live there or in Queens, on account of being priced out of Manhattan by all the investment bankers.

"Remind me," Rose says, as she comes back to the picnic table, "never to let Angelo be in charge of the birthday-party planning again."

We look over and see that her husband is back on his feet, but limping painfully toward Mom and Dad's back deck.

"Never mind me," he calls to Rose, sarcastically. "Don't offer to help, or anything. I'll be fine!"

Rose looks heavenward, then reaches for the margarita pitcher.

"Perfect soul mate," Sarah says, chuckling to herself.

Rose glares at her. "Shut up." Then she plops the pitcher down. "Empty." There's growing panic in her voice. "We're out of margaritas."

"Oh, dear," Mom says, looking concerned. "Your father just mixed that batch—"

"I'll go in and make more," I say, hopping up. Anything to avoid having to hear more about how much of a failure I'm destined to be in New York.

"Make it stronger than Dad did," Rose advises, as a papier-mâché leg belonging to the piñata pony goes sailing past her head. "Please."

I nod and, seizing the pitcher, head toward the back door. I make it about halfway before I run into Grandma, who is just coming out of the house.

"Hey, Gran," I say. "How was *Dr. Quinn*?"

"I don't know." I can tell Gran's drunk, even though it's only one in the afternoon, because her housecoat is on backward again. "I fell asleep. Sully wasn't even in it. I don't know why they bother making episodes that don't have him in it. What's the point? No one wants to watch that Dr. Quinn run around in her gauchos. It's all about Sully. I heard them trying to talk you out of moving to New York."

I glance over my shoulder at my mother and sisters. They're all three of them running their fingers along the edge of the leftover cake, then sucking the frosting off the tips.

"Oh," I say. "Yeah. Well, you know. They're just worried I'm going to end up like Kathy Pennebaker."

Grandma looks surprised. "You mean a man-stealing whore?"

"Gran. She's not a whore. She just—" I shake my head, smiling. "How do you even know about that, anyway?"

"I keep my ear to the ground," Grandma says mysteriously. "People think because I'm an old drunk, I don't know what's happening. But I keep it real. Here. This is for you."

She shoves something into my hand. I look down.

"Grandma," I say, not smiling anymore. "Where did you get this?"

"Never you mind," Gran says. "I want you to have it. You're going to need it, moving to the city. What if you need to get out, and you need cash, fast? You never know."

"But, Grandma," I protest. "I can't—"

"For fuck's sake," Grandma yells at me. "Just take it!"

"Fine, I will," I say, and shove the neatly folded ten-dollar bill into the pocket of my black-and-white vintage Suzy Perette sleeveless day dress. "There. Are you happy now?"

"Yes," Grandma says, and pats me on the cheek. Her breath is pleasantly beery. It reminds me of all those times in grade school she helped me with my homework. Most of the answers were wrong, but I always got bonus points for imagination. "Good-bye, you rotten stinker."

"Grandma," I say, "I'm not leaving for three more days."

"Don't sleep with any sailors," Grandma says, ignoring me. "You'll get the clap."

"You know," I say with a smile. "I think I'm going to miss you most of all, Scarecrow."

"I don't know what you're talking about," Grandma huffs. "Scarecrow who?"

But before I can explain, Maggie, wearing the decapitated piñata pony's carcass on her head, marches silently past us, followed by her suddenly mute party guests, each wearing a piece of piñata—a hoofed foot here, a segment of the tail there—on their heads, and stepping in perfect formation.

"Wow," Gran says, when the last member of the macabre piñata-part parade has passed by. "I need a drink."

A sentiment I readily second.

Lizzie Nichols's Wedding Gown Guide

Which type of wedding gown best suits you?

If you are lucky enough to be tall and slender, you can pretty much get away with any type or shape of gown. That is why models are tall and slender—anything looks good on them!

But supposing you are one of the millions of women who aren't tall and slender? Which gown best suits you?

Well, if you are short, with a fuller figure, why not try a gown with an empire waist? The flowing silhouette will make your body look longer and more slender. That's why this style of gown was favored by both the ancient Greeks and the very fashion-conscious Josephine Bonaparte, Empress of France!

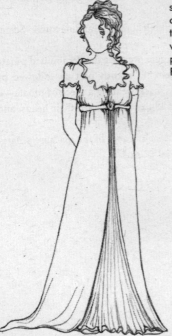

LIZZIE NICHOLS DESIGNS™

• Chapter 3 •

Great people talk about ideas, average people talk about things, and small people talk about wine.

—Fran Lebowitz (b. 1950), American humorist

t's my own fault, really. For believing in fairy tales.

Not that I ever mistook them for actual historical fact, or anything.

But I did grow up believing that for every girl, there's a prince out there somewhere. All she has to do is find him. Then it's on with the happily ever after.

So you can only imagine what happened when I found out. That my prince really IS one. A prince.

No, I really mean it. He's an actual PRINCE.

And okay, he isn't exactly recognized, really, by his native land, since the French did a pretty thorough job of killing off most of their aristocracy over two hundred years ago.

But in the case of my particular prince someone in his family managed to escape Madame Guillotine by hotfooting it to England, and years later, even managed to get the family castle back, probably through intense and prolonged litigation. If they were anything like the rest of his family, I mean.

And okay, today owning your own château in the South of France means about a hundred grand a year in taxes to the French government, and nonstop headaches over roof tiles and renters.

But hey, how many guys do you know who actually own one? A château, I mean.

But I swear to you, that's not why I fell in love with him. I didn't know about the title or the château when I met him. He never bragged about it. If he had, I would never have liked him in the first place. I mean, what woman would? That you'd want to be friends with, anyway.

No, Luke acted exactly the way you'd expect a disenfranchised prince to act about his title—as if he were embarrassed by it.

And he IS embarrassed by it, a little. That he's a prince—an ACTUAL prince—and the only heir to a sprawling château (on a thousand-acre, sadly not very productive vineyard) a six-hour train ride from Paris. I only found out about it by accident, when I noticed this portrait of a very ugly man in the main hall at Château Mirac, and I noticed that on the nameplate, it said he was a prince, and he had the same last name as Luke.

Luke didn't want to admit it, but I finally pried it out of his dad. He says it's a lot of responsibility, being a prince, and running a château and all. Well, not the prince thing, so much, but the château part. The only way he can do it all—and turn enough of a profit to pay off their taxes every year—is by renting the place out to rich American families, and the occasional film studio, to shoot period movies in. God knows his vineyard doesn't turn much of a profit.

But by the time I found out about it—the prince stuff—I was already head over heels for Luke. I knew right away he was the guy for me, the minute I sat down next to him on that train. Not that I thought he'd ever, in a million years, feel the same way about me and all. He just had such a nice smile—not to mention really long eyelashes, the kind that Shu Uemura try so hard to emulate—I couldn't help falling for him.

So the fact that he has a title and an estate are really just frosting on what's already the most delicious cake I've ever tasted. Luke isn't like any of the guys I knew in college. He isn't the least bit interested in poker or sports. All he cares about is medicine—it's his passion—and, well, me.

Which suits me just fine.

So I guess it's only natural that I started planning my wedding immediately. Not that Luke's proposed—at least, not yet.

But, you know, I can still start PLANNING it. I know we'll be getting married SOMEDAY. I mean, a guy doesn't ask a girl he doesn't intend to marry to move in with him, right?

So, you know, WHEN we get married, it will be at Château Mirac, on the big grassy terrace there, overlooking the entire valley—over which the de Villiers at one time practiced their feudal lording. It will be in the summer, of course, preferably the summer right after my vintage bridal gown refurbishment shop—Lizzie Nichols Designs—is bought out by Vera Wang (another thing that hasn't happened yet. But it's bound to, right?). Shari can be my maid of honor, and my sisters can be my bridesmaids.

And unlike what they did for their bridesmaids (namely, me), I will actually choose tasteful gowns for them to wear. I won't force them to cram into any mint-green taffeta hoop skirts, the way they made me. Because unlike them, I am kind and thoughtful.

I suppose my whole family will insist on coming, even though none of them has ever been to Europe before. I'm a little worried my relatives won't be quite sophisticated enough for the cosmopolitan de Villiers.

But I'm sure they'll end up actually getting along like a house on fire, my father insisting on manning the firepit, Midwest-barbecue style, and my mother offering Luke's mother tips on how to get the yellow out of her nineteenth-century linen sheets. Gran might be a little bit trying, seeing as how they don't have *Dr. Quinn, Medicine Woman* in France. But after a kir royale or two, I'm sure she'll calm down.

I just know my wedding day will be the happiest day of my life. I can totally picture us standing in the dappled sunlight on the grassy terrace, me in a long white sheath, and Luke looking so handsome and debonair in an open-collared white shirt and black tuxedo pants. Like a prince is how he'll look, really . . .

I just have to figure out how I'm going to handle this next part, and I'm home free.

"Okay," Shari says, opening up the copy of the *Village Voice* she's just snagged, and turning it to the classifieds. "Basically, there's nothing out there that's worth looking at that isn't listed by a broker."

The thing is, this is going to take finesse. Not to mention subtlety.

"Which means we're just going to have to bite the bullet and pay one. It sucks," Shari goes on, "but in the long run, I think it's going to be worth it."

I can't just blurt it out. I have to lead up to it, slowly.

"I know you're short on cash," Shari says. "So Chaz says he can loan us what we need to pay the broker. We can pay him back when we get on our feet. Well, when *you* get on *your* feet." Because Shari has already landed a job at a small nonprofit, based on an interview she had last summer, before she left for France. She starts work tomorrow. "I mean, unless Luke is willing to front you. Is he? I know you probably hate to ask, but come on, the guy is loaded."

I can't just spring it on her out of nowhere.

"Lizzie? Are you even listening to me?"

"Luke asked me to move in with him," I blurt out before I can stop myself.

Shari stares at me across the booth's sticky tabletop. "And you were going to tell me this . . . when?" she asks.

Great. I've already blown it. She's mad. I knew she was going to get mad. Why can't I ever keep my big mouth closed. *Why?*

"Shari, he just asked me this morning," I say. "Just now, before I left to come meet you. I didn't say yes. I said I had to talk to you about it."

Shari blinks at me. "Which means you want to," she says. There's a definite edge to her voice. "You want to move in with him, or you'd have said no right away."

"Shari! No! I mean, well . . . yes. But think about it. I mean, face it, you're always going to be over at Chaz's place anyway—"

"Spending the night at Chaz's," Shari says acidly, "isn't the same as *living* with him."

"But you know he'd love you to," I say. "Think about it, Shari. If I move in with Luke, and you move in with Chaz, then we don't have to waste time looking for apartments anymore . . . or waste money on a broker and first and last month's rent. It will save us about five grand. Each!"

"Don't do that," Shari says sharply.

I blink at her. "Do what?"

"Make it about money," she says. "It's not about money. You know if you needed money, you could get money. Your parents would send you money."

I feel a spurt of irritation with Shari. I love her to death. I really do. But my parents have three kids, all of whom need money all the time. Supervisors at the cyclotron, which is what my dad is, make a comfortable living. But not enough to support their adult children in perpetuity.

Shari, on the other hand, is the only child of a prominent Ann Arbor surgeon. All she ever has to do when she needs money is ask her parents for some, and they fork over however much she wants, no questions asked. *I'm* the one who's been working in retail—and before that, babysitting every Friday and Saturday night throughout my teens, thus denying me anything resembling a proper social life—for the past seven years, scraping by on minimum wage, and denying myself life's more expensive pleasures (movies, eating out, shampoo other than Suave, a car, et cetera) in order to save enough to one day escape to New York, and pursue my dream.

I'm not complaining. I know my parents did the best they could by me. But it's annoying how Shari doesn't understand that not everyone's parents are as forthcoming with cash as hers are. Even though I've tried to explain it to her.

"We can't let ourselves become slaves of New York," Shari goes on. "We can't make major life decisions—like moving in with a boy-friend—be about the cost of rent. If we start doing that, we're lost."

I just look at her. Seriously, I don't know where she gets this stuff.

"If it's just about money," she says, "and you don't want to go to your parents, Chaz will float you a loan. You know that."

Chaz, who comes from a long line of fiscally thrifty lawyers, is loaded. Not just because his relatives keep dropping dead and leaving their financial assets to him, but because in addition to their cash, he's also inherited their frugality, and invests conservatively while living quite modestly—at least in comparison to his net worth, which is allegedly even more than Luke's. Not that Chaz has a château in France to show for it.

"Shari," I say. "Chaz is YOUR boyfriend. I'm not taking money from YOUR boyfriend. How is that any different than moving in with Luke?"

"Because you aren't having sex with Chaz," Shari points out with her usual asperity. "It would be a business arrangement, strictly impersonal."

But for some reason, the idea of asking Chaz for a loan—even though I know he'd think nothing of it, and say yes in an instant—isn't working for me.

Besides, it's not really about the money. It never was.

"The thing is," I say slowly. "It's not just about the money, Share."

Shari lets out a moan, and drops her face into her hands.

"Oh, God," she says to her lap. "I knew this was going to happen."

"What?" I don't understand what she's so upset about. I mean, I know Chaz is no prince and all, with his turned-around Michigan baseball hats and perpetual razor stubble. But he's really funny and sweet. When he isn't going on about Kierkegaard or Roth IRAs. "I'm sorry. But can't we make this work? I mean, what's the problem, exactly? Is it the triple stabbing? You don't want to live in Chaz's place because of the neighborhood? But the police told you, it was a domestic dispute. That will never happen again. I mean, unless they let Julio's dad out of Rikers—"

"It has nothing to do with that," Shari snaps. In the glow from the neon Pabst Blue Ribbon sign on the wall beside our booth, her wildly curling black hair has a bluish sheen. "Lizzie, you've known Luke a month. And you're going *to move in with him*?"

"*Two* months," I correct her, hurt. "And he's Chaz's best friend. And we've known Chaz for *years*. *Lived with* Chaz for years. Well, in the dorm, anyway. So it's not like Luke's this complete stranger, like Andrew was—"

"Exactly. What *about* Andrew?" Shari demands. "Lizzie, you just got out of a relationship. A completely fucked one, but a relationship, nonetheless. And look at Luke. Two months ago, he was living with someone else! And now he's just going to rush right in to live with someone new? Don't you think maybe you guys need to take it a little more slowly?"

"We're not getting *married*, Share," I say to her. "We're just talking about living together."

"Luke might be," Shari says. "But Lizzie, I know you. You're already secretly fantasizing about marrying Luke. Don't deny it."

"I am not!" I cry, wondering how she could possibly know the truth. And okay, she's known me for my whole life, practically. But come on. That's spooky.

She narrows her eyes at me. "Lizzie," she says, in a warning voice.

"Oh, all right," I say, slumping back against the bloodred vinyl booth. We're at Honey's, a seedy Midtown karaoke bar halfway between Chaz's apartment, where Shari is staying on East Thirteenth between First and Second Avenues, and Luke's mom's place, on East Eighty-first and Fifth Avenue, so it's equally difficult (or easy, depending on how you want to look at it) for us to get to.

Honey's may be a dive, but at least it's usually empty—at least before nine at night, when the serious karaoke practitioners show up—so we can talk, and the diet Cokes are only a dollar. Plus, the bartender—a punky Korean-American in her early twenties—doesn't seem to care if we order something or not. She's too busy fighting with her boyfriend over her cell phone.

"So I want to marry him," I say dejectedly, as the bartender yells, "*You know what? You know what? You suck,*" into her pink Razor. "I love him."

"It's fine that you love him, Lizzie," Shari says. "It's perfectly natural. But I'm still not convinced moving in with him is the best idea." Oh, great. Now she's chewing her lower lip. "I just . . ."

I look up from my diet Coke. "What?"

"Look, Lizzie." Her dark eyes seem fathomless in the dim light of the bar. Even though outside it's sunny, only being noon. "Luke's great and all. And I think what you did—getting his parents back together, and convincing Luke to go after his dream of pursuing a medical career—was really cool of you. But as far as you two long-term—"

I blink at her, totally stunned. "What about it?"

"I just," Shari says, "don't see it."

I can't believe she's saying this. My best friend—ALLEGEDLY.

"Why?" I demand, horrified to feel tears stinging my eyes. "Because he's a prince—sort of? And I'm just a girl from Michigan who talks too much?"

"Well," Shari says. "More or less. I mean, Lizzie . . . you like to watch *The Real World* marathons in bed with a pint of Coffee Heath Bar Crunch and the latest issue of *Sewing Today*. You like to listen to Aerosmith at full volume while you hem fifties cocktail dresses on your Singer 5050. Can you imagine ever doing either of those things in front of Luke? I mean, do you really act like yourself around him? Or do you act like the kind of girl you think a guy like Luke would want?"

I glare at her. "I can't believe you're even asking me that." I'm practically crying, but I'm trying to hide it. "Of *course* I act like myself around Luke."

Although it's true I've been wearing my control-top Spanx every day since I got to New York. And that they leave angry red lines along my waistline that I have to wait to fade before I let Luke see me naked after I've peeled them off.

But that's only because I started eating bread again when I was in France, and I gained back a little of the weight I lost over the summer! Just a little. Like fifteen pounds or so.

Oh, God. Shari's right!

"Look," Shari says, apparently noticing my stricken expression. "I'm not saying you shouldn't move in with him, Lizzie. I'm just saying you might want to cool it on the wedding-planning thing. Your wedding, anyway. With Luke."

I reach up to wipe the tears from my eyes. "If the next words out of your mouth are that he won't buy the cow if he can get the milk for free," I say bitterly, "I will seriously vomit."

"Of course I'm not going to say that," Shari says. "Just take things one day at a time, okay? And don't be afraid to be yourself in front of him. Because if he doesn't love the real you, he's not Prince Charming after all."

I can't help gaping at her a little. Because, really. It's like she's a mind reader.

"How," I ask tearfully, "did you get so smart?"

"I majored in psych," Shari said. "Remember?"

I nod. Her new job is counseling women at a nonprofit program that helps victims of domestic abuse find alternative housing, obtain orders of protection, and secure public benefits such as food stamps and child support. It's not a high-paying job, salarywise. But what Shari doesn't receive in financial compensation, she'll make up for in the knowledge that she is saving lives, and helping people—especially women—to attain better existences for themselves and their children.

Although if you think about it, those of us in the fashion industry do the same thing. We don't save lives, necessarily. But we help make lives better, in our own small way. It's like the song says . . . young girls, they do get weary, wearing that same old shaggy dress.

It's our job to get them into a new one (or a refurbished old one), so they can feel a little bit better about themselves.

"Look," Shari says. "The truth is . . . I don't know. I'm kind of bummed. I was really looking forward to us getting a place together. I even thought about how much fun it was going to be thrifting for old furniture and then fixing it up. Or borrowing a car and going to IKEA in New Jersey to buy a bunch of stuff. Now I'm going to have to live with Chaz's hand-me-down furniture from his family's law offices here in town."

I have to laugh. I've seen the elaborate gold-trimmed couches in Chaz's living room—the one with the wood floor that gently slopes south, and the windows with the folding gates over them because they look out over a fire escape . . . the same windows from which Shari saw Julio's dad go on his stabbing spree.

"I'll come over and see what I can do about the couches," I say. "I have a bunch of bolts of material I got when So-Fro Fabrics closed down. When my mom ships my boxes to me, I can make a slipcover for you. And some curtains," I add. "So you won't have to see any more stabbings."

"That'd be nice," Shari says, with a sigh. "Well. Here." She slides her copy of the *Village Voice* toward me. "You're going to need this."

I look down at it blankly. "Why? If Luke and I already have a place?"

"To *find a job,* dufus," Shari says. "Or is Luke going to support your thrifting habit as well as provide your housing?"

"Oh." I let out a tiny laugh. "Yeah. Thanks."

And I flip to the jobs section of the classifieds . . .

. . . just as a dwarf with a long, Gandalf-like staff opens the door to Honey's, ambles up to our table, looks at us, then turns around and leaves, all without uttering a word.

Both Shari and I glance at the bartender. She doesn't appear to have noticed the dwarf. Shari and I look back each other.

"This town," I say, "is very weird."

"Tell me about it," Shari says.

~ Lizzie Nichols's Wedding Gown Guide ~

Know your . . .
Wedding-gown sleeve lengths!

Strapless—no sleeves at all, of course!

Spaghetti strap—very thin straps

Sleeveless—wider straps

Cap—very, very short sleeves, usually just an extension of the shoulder. Not attractive in brides over forty (unless they work out. With weights).

Short—lower edge of the sleeve usually falls straight across the middle of the upper arm.

This length is generally considered too casual for a formal wedding.

Above the elbow—this length works best on brides who are concerned about "chicken skin" beneath their arms.

Three-quarter—this sleeve ends three fourths of the way down the arm, midway between the elbow and the wrist. Flattering on nearly everyone.

Seven-eighth—ends two inches above the wrist. This is an awkward length for bridal gowns.

Wrist length—this length works nicely for more conservative brides, or those trying to hide unsightly eczema on their arms.

Full length—falls one inch below the wrist bone. This is the preferred length for brides favoring a "medieval" or "Renaissance" look to their gown.

• Chapter 4 •

Gossip is the tool of the poet, the shop-talk of the scientist, and the consolation of the housewife, wit, tycoon and intellectual. It begins in the nursery and ends when speech is past.

—*Phyllis McGinley (1905–1978), American poet and author*

aybe Shari's right. Maybe I do need to take things with Luke a little slower. There's no need to start planning our wedding now. After all, I only just got my degree . . . or not even, actually, since I just turned in my thesis, and my advisor says I won't technically graduate until January. Not that I'm changing my graduation date on my résumé, because, you know, who even checks that?

Besides, Mom and Dad would FLIP if they found out I took off for Europe—let alone accepted all those book lights as graduation gifts—without actually having finished my degree.

The same way they would FLIP if they found out I was moving in with a guy I met there. In Europe, I mean. I'm going to have to keep my living situation on the DL. Maybe I'll just tell them Shari and I are sharing a place . . . except what if they talk to Dr. Dennis? Dang . . .

Okay, I'll worry about that later.

Obviously, I need to use this time to concentrate on my career. I mean, how am I ever going to get interviewed by *Vogue* if I never actually *do* anything interview-worthy?

Although Shari would look really cute in a cap-sleeved dupioni silk bustier bridesmaid top, with a tea-length skirt in a sort
of antique-rose color, like that skirt on the mannequin in the
window . . .

Okay, stop it. Just stop. I'm not going to think about that now.
There'll be plenty of time to design a bridesmaid gown that will look
lovely on Shari and hideous on Rose and Sarah. Right now I need
to concentrate on getting a job. Because that's the most important
thing at the moment. What am I going to do with my life? I can't
just be someone's wife. Anybody can do that.

And okay, sure, I bet *Vogue* would interview me just for being
the wife of a prince. Well, a pseudoprince. They do interviews with
wives of pseudoprinces all the time. They call them "hostesses."

I don't want to be a "hostess." I don't even *like* parties.

No, I have to figure out a way to leave my mark on the world.
Something only I can do. Which appears to be refurbish vintage
wedding dresses.

Which you would think there'd be a huge demand for. Doesn't
everyone have an old wedding dress in the attic they'd like to have
fixed up? The trick is, how to reach all the women out there who
need my services, while at the same time being able to support
myself? Of course there's always the Internet, but—

Ooooh, that is the cutest Jonathan Logan red Spanish lace
dress . . . shame about the rip in the lace. Still, that's an easy fix. How
much—oh my God. Four hundred and fifty dollars? Are they insane?
We sold one just like this at Vintage to Vavoom in Ann Arbor for
one fifty. And this one is like a size two. Who can even fit into something this small?

"May I help you?"

Oh. Right. I'm not here to shop.

"Hi," I say, flashing what I hope is a dazzling smile in the direction of the clerk in the plaid pants (she's being ironic), with the multiple facial piercings. "I was wondering if the manager was around?"

"Why do you want to see the manager?"

Hmmm. Multiple Facial Piercings has a bit of an attitude, I see. Then again, seeing as how her shop is on a busy avenue in the Village, she probably sees all kinds. She probably has to be suspicious. Who knows what kind of crazy creepolas come in here? If they get a lot like that guy I just saw on the corner, with his pants down around his ankles, pawing through the trash can and muttering about Stalin, I can see why she might be a little standoffish with strangers.

"Actually," I say brightly, "I'm wondering if the store might be hiring. I've got years of experience in vintage retail, in addition to—"

"Leave your résumé at the counter," Multiple Facial Piercings says. "If she's interested, she'll call you."

But something tells me that the manager will never call. Just like the human resources representative from the costume department at the Metropolitan Museum of Art never called. Just like the head of the Museum of the City of New York's Costume and Textile Collection never called. Just like Vera Wang never called. Just like any of the gazillion places at which I've dropped off résumés haven't called.

Only in this case, I know the manager's not going to call because she's seen my résumé and she thinks I'm underqualified for the position, or because there aren't any openings, or because I don't have any local references, like all those other places. I know the manager's not going to call because she's never even going to *see* my résumé. Because Multiple Facial Piercings has already decided she doesn't like me, and is going to throw my résumé into the trash the minute I step out of her store.

"My hours are superflexible," I say, in a last-ditch effort. "And I have a lot of seamstressing experience. I'm great at alterations—"

"We don't do in-store alterations," Multiple Facial Piercings says with a sneer. "If people want something altered these days, they just take it to their dry cleaner."

I swallow. "Right. Well, I notice this Jonathan Logan you have here has some damage. I could easily repair this—"

"People who buy our clothes want to make repairs themselves,"

Multiple Facial Piercings says. "Leave your résumé at the counter, and we'll call you . . ."

Her heavily made-up eyes flick from the top of my head—my hair is pulled back in a wide, Jackie O–style scarf—to my dress, a rare 1950s Gigi Young blue and white polka dot with an accordion-pleated skirt—to my shoes—white ballet-style flats (because you can't wear heels when you're tromping around Manhattan). It is clear from her expression that Multiple Facial Piercings doesn't like what she's seeing.

". . . or not." Multiple Facial Piercings tosses her Mohawk, then lifts a hand to wave at me. I see that what I'd taken for festively col-ored sleeves is actually her bare arm, the skin of which is completely covered in tattoos. "Buh-bye."

"Um." I can't stop staring at the tattoos. "Bye."

Okay. Okay, so maybe the New York employment scene is a little . . . different from the one back in Ann Arbor.

Or maybe I just hit the wrong store on the wrong day.

Yeah, that's it. They can't all be like that one. Maybe heading to the Village first thing was a mistake.

Or maybe I shouldn't even be thinking retail. Maybe I should try hitting some bridal shops—not Vera Wang, obviously, since I already crashed and burned there (the woman who answered the phone at Vera Wang corporate, when I called to see if they'd received my résumé, made it more than clear that they would definitely be calling me—in ten years, when they managed to wade through all the other résumés aspiring wedding-gown designers had dropped off)—and leaving my résumé and some photos of some of the gowns I've worked on. Maybe that would make more sense. Maybe . . .

Oh God, what am I going to say to Luke? Shari's right, moving in with someone *is* a big deal, and not something you should just do because it's cheaper than paying a broker's fee.

Although of course that isn't why I'm doing it. I love Luke, and I think living with him would be totally dreamy.

So long as, you know, I enter into it without any expectations—

like Shari said—of marriage. Just take things one day at a time. Because we're both in transitional stages of our lives right now, Luke in school, and me . . . well, doing whatever it is I'm going to do. We can't be thinking of marriage. That's years away.

Although not too many years, I hope. Because I'd really like to go sleeveless on my wedding day and God only knows how long it's going to be before I lose all the elasticity in my arms and get that jiggle thing which can be so unattractive in a bride. Or anyone.

Okay, this isn't working. This traipsing around, dropping my résumé off at vintage clothing stores. I need to regroup. I need to get out the phone book or go online and really concentrate my efforts on places that fit my style. I need to—

Ooooh, look at those steaks. Maybe that's what I need to do. Pick up something for dinner. I mean, Luke isn't going to feel like going out after a long day of orientation.

And okay, I'm not the world's best cook. But anyone can grill a steak. Well, I guess broil it, since we have no grill.

That's what I'll do. I'll get some steaks, and a bottle of wine, and I'll make dinner. Then Luke and I can have a discussion about our living together, and what it means. And then I'll go back to job hunting tomorrow after we've got it all straightened out.

Perfect. Okay.

Only maybe I'll shop in Luke's neighborhood, instead of down here, since I don't want to have to carry a lot of stuff uptown on the subway. Where *is* the subway, anyway?

"Um, excuse me. Can you tell me how to get to the six train?"

Oh! How rude!

And I'm *not* an asshole. How can someone be an asshole just for asking where the subway is? God, is it really true what they say about New Yorkers? So far they *do* seem kind of rude. Is this why Kathy Pennebaker came back home? I mean, besides the whole other-people's-boyfriend addiction thing?

Or was she driven to steal even *more* boyfriends by the uncaring attitude of her New York neighbors?

Okay, where am I? Second Avenue and Ninth Street. East Ninth Street, because the east and west sides are divided by Fifth Avenue (where Luke's mother's apartment is. Overlooking Central Park . . . and the Met). Luke told me that to get to Fifth Avenue, if you're heading west from the East River, you have to cross First, Second, and Third avenues, and then Lexington, Park, and finally Madison (to remember the order in which these nonnumbered avenues go, Luke told me to "Look Past My Face"— or *L*exington, *P*ark, *M*adison, *F*ifth).

The streets—East Fifty-ninth Street, home to Bloomingdale's, and East Fiftieth Street, where Saks is, for instance—run perpendicular to the avenues. So Bloomingdale's is on Fifty-ninth and Lexington Avenue, Saks on Fiftieth and Fifth Avenue. Luke's mother's place is on Eighty-first and Fifth . . . around the corner from the Betsey Johnson on Madison between Eighty-first and Eighty-second.

Then of course there's the West Side. But I'll have to learn that later because right now I'm having a hard enough time figuring out the side I'm actually living on.

Okay, so the subway up and down the East Side runs along Lexington Avenue. So all you have to do when you're lost, Luke said, is find Lexington, and you'll eventually find the subway.

Unless of course you're in the Village, like I am, where Lexington suddenly turns into something called Fourth Avenue, then Lafayette, and finally Centre Street.

Again, not something I'm going to worry about right now. I'm just going to head west from Second Avenue, hoping to find Lexington in one of its many forms, and a subway stop home, somewhere around here . . .

Home. Wow. I'm already calling it home.

Well, isn't that what any place is? Any place that you share with someone you love, I mean?

Maybe that's why Kathy left New York. Not the rude people or the incomprehensible street layout or the whole boyfriend-stealing thing, but because there just wasn't anybody here that she loved.

Who loved her back, anyway.

Poor Kathy. Chewed up by the big city, then spat out again.

Well, that's *not* going to be me. I'm not going to be the next Kathy Pennebaker of Ann Arbor. I am *not* going back home with my tail between my legs. I am going to make it in New York City if it kills me. Because if I can make it here, I can make it any—

Oooh, a cab! And it's vacant!

And okay, cabs are expensive. But maybe just this once. Because I'm so tired, and it's so far to the subway, and I want to get back in time to start making Luke dinner, and—

"Eighty-first and Fifth, please."

—oh, look, there's the Astor Place subway stop right there. If I had just walked one more block, I could have saved myself fifteen bucks . . .

Well, that's okay. No more cabs this week. And this is so nice, sitting in this clean air-conditioned cab, instead of fighting my way down the stairs to the smelly platform to wait for a supercrowded train where I won't even be able to get a seat. And then there are the panhandlers in every car, asking for money. I can never seem to say no. I don't want to turn into one of those hardened, jaded New Yorkers, like Multiple Facial Piercings, who seemed to find my Gigi Young dress so amusing. When you can't empathize with another's hardship—or realize how hard it is to even FIND a Gigi Young dress in wearable condition—what's the point of even being alive?

So I end up getting off the subway five dollars poorer every time I ride it, not even counting the fare. It's practically cheaper to take a cab. Sort of.

Oh God. Shari's right. I have to get a job—and a life.

And fast.

Lizzie Nichols's Wedding Gown Guide

If you are on the petite side, why not try an A-line gown? Full skirts can make a short bride look as if she is being swallowed up by material—unless she opts for a ballgown or fishtail cut . . . but this does not flatter every petite bride universally, so tread with caution when trying on "princess" or "mermaid" gowns!

Off-the-shoulder and scoop necklines—even thin straps—are recommended for the petite bride. Column or sheath skirts are not. Remember, you are getting married, not working behind the counter at Ann Taylor Loft!

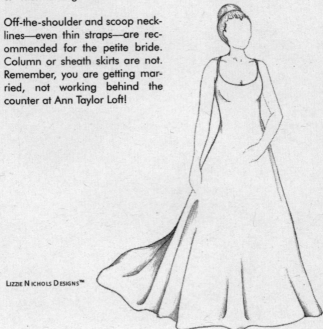

LIZZIE NICHOLS DESIGNS™

• Chapter 5 •

Show me someone who never gossips, and I'll
show you someone who isn't interested in people.

—*Barbara Walters (b. 1929), American television journalist*

I'm marinating the steaks when the phone rings. Not my
cell, but the apartment phone—Luke's mother's phone.

I don't answer it because I know it's not for me.
Besides, I'm busy. It's no joke trying to prepare a semigourmet meal
in a New York–style galley kitchen, which is basically about as big
as the inside of the cab I took to get back uptown this afternoon.
Luke's mom's apartment is really nice, as one-bedroom Manhattan
apartments go. It's still got its original prewar crown molding and
gold fixtures and parquet floors, and all.

But the kitchen seems to have been built more for unpacking
take-out than preparing eat-in.

Mrs. de Villiers's answering machine kicks on after about five
rings. I hear her voice—her Southern accent exaggerated for dramatic effect—drawl, "Hello, you've reached Bibi de Villiers. I'm
either on the other line or nappin' at the moment. Please leave a
message, and I'll get right back to y'all."

I giggle. Napping. *Vogue* should do a spread on Bibi. Talk about
professional hostesses. Plus, she's married to a prince. Well, a pseudo-

prince. And she's got great—if slightly conservative—taste in clothes. I've never seen her in anything but Chanel or Ralph Lauren.

"Bibi." A man's voice fills the apartment . . . which is also filled with the smell of freshly chopped garlic, which I'm using in the marinade, along with soy sauce, honey, and olive oil, all of which I picked up at Eli's over on Third Avenue . . . which is quite a hike from Fifth. "I haven't heard from you in quite a while. Where have you been?"

Clearly, this friend of Bibi's does not know she reconciled with her husband during her niece's wedding in the South of France, and that the two of them—Luke's parents—were still in Dordogne, tripping the light *fantastique* . . . as the French would say. Or not, actually.

"I will be waiting for you in the usual place," the man goes on, "this weekend. I only hope I do not wait in vain."

Wait a minute. The usual place? Waiting for her? Who the heck is this guy? And how come, if he and Bibi are so close, he doesn't even know which country she's in?

"Good-bye for now, *chérie*," the man says. And then he hangs up.

Chérie? Was this guy for real? Who goes around leaving messages on people's machines, calling them *chérie*? Except maybe gigolos.

Oh God. Did Luke's mother employ a gigolo?

No, of course not. She wouldn't have to. She's a vital, beautiful woman—and obviously loaded, as one can tell merely by glancing at the art on the walls of her Manhattan pied-à-terre. The Renoir is the crown jewel of her collection, of course. But she has no shortage of Mirós and Chagalls and even a tiny Picasso sketch that hangs in the bathroom.

And I'm not even going to mention her shoe collection, which crowds the entire top shelf of the bedroom closet . . . box after box marked Jimmy Choo, Christian Louboutin, and Manolo Blahnik.

What would a woman like that be doing with a gigolo?

Unless . . . unless he's not a gigolo, but a lover! It would make sense for Bibi de Villiers to have taken a lover. She was, after all, in divorce proceedings with Luke's father . . . until I came along, that is.

Why wouldn't a sophisticated woman of the world like Luke's mom have a boyfriend . . . a boyfriend she's forgotten all about since getting back together with Luke's dad?

At least, I assume she's forgotten about him. Obviously she has, if he doesn't even know where she is . . .

Oh God. This is so . . . awkward. Why did he have to call now, tonight, when Luke and I have to have our Moving in Together talk? I can't say to Luke, "Hey, this random guy left a message for your mom, calling her *chérie* . . . and we need to figure out how I can move in with you without losing my identity as an individual."

Maybe if I check the caller ID I can figure out where this guy called from. That, at least, might give me a clue as to—

Oh. Oh, great. I erased the message. At least if that flashing Delete sign is any indication.

Okay. Well, that solves that.

Besides, it's probably better this way. It's not like the guy left his name. I can't be all, "Um, hi, Mrs. de Villiers? Yeah, a random dude with a French accent who isn't your husband called and asked if you're going to meet him at the usual place, at which he will be waiting." Because that could embarrass her.

And I'm all about trying not to embarrass my future in-laws.

Dang. I just did it again, didn't I? I have to get marriage off my brain. I think I'll go set the dining table. With the beautiful silver that one day might be mine if—

Ack! Okay, maybe I need to turn on the TV. The news should be on. That will distract me.

"Police made a gruesome discovery in the backyard of a house the media is now calling the Harlem House of Horror. Human remains— six complete skeletons so far, with more expected to be uncovered—"

Oh my God, what kind of place is this? A backyard filled with human skeletons? No. Just no. Changing the channel.

"—seventh hit-and-run at that corner in the past month alone. This time it was a young mother killed as she was attempting to walk her small children to school—"

Good Lord! Maybe I'll try reading the want ads instead. Oooh, Page Six, the gossip section! I'll just take a quick look before I get to the job listings—

—*New York high society is all abuzz about the impending nuptials of John MacDowell, sole heir to the MacDowell real estate fortune. The bride, Jill Higgins, is an employee at the Central Park Zoo. The couple met at the Roosevelt Hospital emergency room, where Miss Higgins was being treated for a back injury she received while lifting a seal that had escaped its enclosure, and where John MacDowell was having an ankle wrapped after twisting it during a polo match—*

Oh! How romantic! And what a fun job, working with seals! If only I could—

Luke's key is turning in the lock! He's home!

Thank God I peeled off my Spanx two hours ago. The red marks must have faded by now.

And I'm not wearing them anymore. Luke is going to have to love me for me—the real me—or it's over.

Except . . . look how adorable he is, in those faded jeans and that nice button-down shirt I picked out for him to wear! Maybe it's all right to wear my Spanx just a little longer . . . until I've lost those fifteen extra pounds I brought home from France. Which I'm sure to do soon, given all the walking you have to do in this town. Plus, I completely ignored the baguettes at Eli's . . .

"Hey," he says. There's a big smile on his face. "How's it going?"

Hey, how's it going. This is what my boyfriend says to me, ten hours after asking me to move in with him. It's clear he hasn't exactly been agonizing over my answer.

Or maybe he has and is trying to play it casual.

"What's that smell?" he asks.

"Garlic," I say. "I'm marinating a couple of steaks."

"Great," he says, putting down his keys on the little marble-topped console table by the door. "I'm starved. How was your day?"

Wow. How was your day? This is what it's like to live with some-one. I mean, a guy. It's a lot like living with a girl, really.

Except that instead of waiting around for my answer, the way Shari used to when we were roommates, Luke comes over, puts his arms around my waist, and gives me a kiss.

Okay. Not so much like living with a girl. At all.

"So," Luke says, grinning down at me. "When are you going to break the news to your parents?"

Oh, okay. The reason he hasn't been agonizing over my answer to his question is that he already knew what my answer was going to be.

I drop my arms from around his neck, stunned.

"How did you know?"

"Are you kidding me?" He's laughing now. "The Lizzie Broadcasting System has been hard at work all day."

I glare at him. "That's impossible. I haven't told anyone! Anyone except—" I break off, flushing.

"Right," Luke says, playfully flicking the tip of my nose with one long index finger. "Shari told Chaz, who called to demand my intentions."

"Your—" Now I'm not just flushing. I'm blushing. "He had no right to do that!"

But Luke is still laughing. "He thinks he does. Oh, don't look so mad. Chaz thinks of you as the little sister he never had. I think it's sweet."

I didn't. In fact, I was going to give Chaz a very unsisterly piece of my mind next time I saw him.

"What did you say?" I can't help asking, curiosity overcoming my anger.

"About what?" Luke's found the bottle of wine I'd bought and opened to let breathe, and is pouring us each a glass.

"Your, um, intentions."

I'm trying to keep it casual. And light. Guys don't like it when you get too heavy, I've noticed. They especially don't like it when you try to talk too much about the future. They're like little woodland animals. Everything's well and good when you're just doling out the nuts and everything's cool.

But the minute you bring out the net to try to catch them—even if it's for their own good, like to help them escape a forest fire—all hell breaks loose. No WAY was I bringing up the C word with Luke. Two months into a relationship might be early enough to consider moving in together. But it was WAY too early to start bandying about the word "commitment."

Even if one of us did have wedding dresses permanently on the brain.

"I told him not to worry," Luke says, handing one of the wine-glasses to me. "That I would do everything in my power not to sully your reputation." Luke clinks the edge of his glass to mine. "Also that he should be thanking me," he adds with a wink.

"Thanking you?" I echo. "Why?"

"Well, because now Shari can move in with him. He'd asked her to before, but she said she couldn't abandon you."

"Oh." I blink a few times. I hadn't known that. Shari had never said a word.

But if she'd only been moving in with me out of pity, why had she reacted the way she did when I'd told her about Luke's offer?

"Anyway, I was thinking we could go out to celebrate," Luke was going on. "The four of us. Not tonight, obviously, because you picked up steaks. But maybe tomorrow night. There's this fantastic Thai place downtown I know you're going to love—"

"We need to talk," I hear myself saying. Whoa. Where did that come from?

Luke looks surprised, but not offended or anything. He sinks down onto his mother's white couch—I am so not sitting there with food or drink in my hands—and looks up at me with a grin.

"Sure," he says. "Of course. I mean, there's a lot of stuff we need to figure out. Like where you're going to put all your clothes." His grin gets broader. "I gather from Chaz that your collection of vin-tage wear is somewhat impressive."

Except it isn't my clothes I'm worried about. It's my heart.

"If I'm going to live with you," I say, moving to sit on the arm of the couch . . . there's less chance of catastrophic results if a spill occurs there. Plus, I'm far enough away from him that he can't distract me with his manliness. "I want to split the cost—utilities, groceries, all of that—fifty-fifty. You know. So it's fair. To both of us."

Luke isn't grinning now. He's sipping his wine and shrugging. "Sure," he says. "Whatever you want."

"And," I say, "I want to pay rent."

He looks at me oddly. "Lizzie. There's no rent to pay. My mother owns this place."

"I know," I say. "I mean I want to pay something toward the mortgage."

Luke's grinning again. "Lizzie. There's no mortgage. She paid cash for the place."

Wow. This is way harder than I thought it would be.

"Well," I say. "I have to pay *something*. I mean, I can't just sponge off you for free. That's not fair. And if I'm paying to live here, then I get some say in what goes on with the place. Right?"

Now one of his dark eyebrows has slid up. "I see what you mean," he says. "And are you planning on doing some redecorating?"

Oh God. This is not going at all the way I'd hoped it would. Why did Chaz have to call him? I get accused all the time of having a big mouth. But if you ask me, guys gossip way more than girls do.

"Not at all," I say. "I love what your mother's done to the place. But I'm going to have to move some stuff to make room." I clear my throat. "For my sewing machine. And things like that."

Now both of Luke's eyebrows are up. "Your *sewing* machine?"

"Yes," I say, a little defensively. "If I'm going to start my own business, I'm going to need my own space in here to do that. And I want to pay for that space. It's only fair. What about . . . is there a monthly maintenance fee? You know, that the building charges for upkeep?"

"Sure," Luke says. "It's thirty-five hundred dollars."

I nearly choke. It's a good thing I've sat on the arm of the couch, or I'd have spat all over it, and not the parquet floor, which is the recipient of a mouthful of red wine.

"*Thirty-five hundred dollars?*" I cry, jumping up and hastening to the kitchen for a dish towel. "A *month*? Just for *maintenance*? I can't afford that!"

Luke is laughing now. "How about a portion of it, then," he says, as he watches me clean up my mess. "A thousand a month?"

"Deal," I say, relieved. Although only slightly, since I have no idea how I'm even going to come up with a thousand dollars a month.

"Fine," Luke says. "Now that we've got that settled—"

"We don't," I say. "Have it settled, I mean."

"We don't?" He doesn't look alarmed, though. He looks more amused. "We've covered groceries, utilities, your need for space for your sewing machine, and rent. What more is there?"

"Well," I say. "Us."

"Us." He isn't running like a frightened woodland creature. Yet. He simply looks mildly curious. "What about us?"

"If I move in," I say, summoning all my courage, "it would only be on a trial basis. To see how it works out. Because, you know, we've only known each other for two months. What if it turns out, I don't know. In the winter I become a real crab or something?"

Both of Luke's eyebrows go up again. "Do you?"

"I don't know," I say. "I mean, I don't think so. But there was this girl, Brianna, from our floor in McCracken Hall? And she used to turn into a total psychopath when it got cold outside. Not that she was particularly stable when it was warm out. But she got way worse when it was cold. So, you know. I think we should reserve the right to call off the whole living-together thing if one or the other of us feels like it isn't working out. And since it's your mother's apartment, I'll be the one who moves out. But you have to give me thirty days to find a new place before you change the locks. That's only fair."

Luke is still grinning. But now the grin is slightly whimsical.

"You're very concerned," he says, "about fairness, aren't you?"

"Well," I say, feeling slightly deflated that this is his only response to my long speech. "I guess I am. I mean, there's so little justice in the world. Young mothers get killed by hit-and-run drivers, and people's skeletons turn up in backyards, and—"

Now Luke's frowning. And reaching for me.

"I have no idea what you're talking about," he says, pulling me down onto his lap. Fortunately, I've put down my wineglass. "But I'm awfully glad we've had this little chat. Is it over?"

I quickly run through all the things I'd hoped to cover with him. Splitting the rent and utilities, making room for my sewing machine, and a Get Out of Jail Free card in case either of us (him more than me, since I didn't plan on going anywhere) needed it. Yes. Done.

I nod. "It's over."

"Good," Luke says, and bends me back against the couch. "Now how do you get this thing off?"

Lizzie Nichols's Wedding Gown Guide

Pear-shaped girls, don't despair! True, according to the band Queen, fat-bottomed girls make the rockin' world go round. But often, we can't find a thing to wear!

Pear-shaped girls are in luck when it comes to wedding gowns, however. The A-line cut flatters by drawing attention away from the lower half of the body, and up toward the bustline.

This can be emphasized even more by going with an off-the-shoulder or deeply V'ed neckline, but stay away from halter-neck gowns and full or pleated skirts, as these looks can add bulk to the hips. The bias or straight-cut look is deadly to any pear-shaped bride . . . they cling to exactly what you're trying to draw attention away from!

Lizzie Nichols Designs™

• Chapter 6 •

Three may keep a secret, if two of them are dead.

—Benjamin Franklin (1706–1790), American inventor

edding Gown Restoration Specialists.

That's what the sign on the door says.

Well, that's certainly me. I mean, that's what I *do*. Not just wedding gowns, of course. I can restore—or refurbish—just about any garment. But wedding gowns are where the real challenges lie. And where the money is, too, of course.

Only I'm trying not to obsess about money. Even though it's really hard not to obsess about something that you seem to need so much of just to *exist* in this town. I mean, I have seen what some of the other tenants of Luke's mom's building are wearing when they come down the elevator. I never saw so much Gucci and Louis Vuitton in my life.

Not that you need Gucci and Louis to exist. But you need money—a lot of it—to lead anything like a normal life in Manhattan. If by normal you mean no splurges on cabs, movies, or lattes, and that you make your own breakfast, lunches, and dinners.

And okay, I can easily live without the latest monogram-canvas Louis Vuitton tote.

But it seems kind of harsh that I can't even pop into the nearby falafel place for a quick bite. Not that I am eating carbs, thanks to the size of my butt, or that there is a falafel place anywhere near the vicinity of the Met, which there most definitely is not, residences on Fifth Avenue being almost literally MILES from any affordable eateries and/or grocery stores. In fact, Fifth Avenue is like a wasteland, nothing but million-dollar apartments, museums, and the park.

I actually envy Shari her walk-up with Chaz. Sure, there are no Renoirs in it, and the floors slope toward the windows, and there's only a portable stand-up shower that leaks and the enamel on the claw-foot tub is so stained it looks as if someone might have been murdered in it.

But there's a totally cheap sushi place right across the street! And a bar with dollar Bud Lights at happy hour like two steps from their stoop! And a grocery store half a block away that delivers . . . for FREE!

I know I shouldn't complain. I mean, I have a doorman. AND a guy who runs the elevator. And a view of the Metropolitan Museum of Art, and Luke's mother's windows are all double-paned, so you can't even hear all the horns and sirens on Fifth Avenue.

And I'm only paying a thousand dollars a month for it. Plus utilities.

But I'd give it all up in a minute if I could just have a freaking *caffè misto* every now and then and not feel racked with guilt about it.

Which is what brings me to Monsieur Henri's, not four blocks from Mrs. de Villiers's pied-à-terre. It's one of Manhattan's premier wedding-gown restoration and preservation hot spots. Anybody who is anybody has Monsieur Henri restore, refurbish, and preserve her wedding gown. At least according to Mrs. Erickson from 5B, whom I met in the laundry room last night (the plumbing in Mrs. de Villiers's building is too old to allow each apartment to have its own individual washer and dryer, and the cost of renovating would raise the maintenance fees even higher). Anyway, she told me that adding half a cup of vinegar to the rinse cycle saves you from having to spend extra money on fabric softener. And she should know. I mean, she had on a cocktail ring with a diamond about as big as a golf ball. She said she was only doing her own laundry because she'd had to fire her maid due to drunkenness, and the service hadn't found her a new one yet.

So when I ring the bell to Monsieur Henri's place, I am fairly confident that for once, I won't be completely wasting my time. Mrs. Erickson had looked to me as if she'd know about wedding-gown restorers—the angle I am now pursuing, since the whole costume-restoration and vintage thing wasn't working out. I have, in the past two weeks, been to every vintage clothing store in the five boroughs . . . none of which was hiring.

Or so the managers claimed. Several saw my college degree on my résumé, and said I was overqualified. Only one of them was interested in looking at my portfolio of refurbished vintage clothes, and when he was through, he said, "This might impress people back in Minnesota, but around here our customers are a little more sophisticated. Suzy Perette just doesn't cut it."

"Michigan," I corrected him. "I'm from Michigan."

"Whatever," the manager said, rolling his eyes.

Seriously? I had no idea people could be so mean. Especially people in the vintage-clothing community. I mean, back home, thrifters are very supportive of and caring for one another, and it's about quality and originality—not the label. Here, in the words of one of the store managers I met, "If it's not Chanel, no one cares."

Wrong! So wrong!

And, in the words of Mrs. Erickson, "What do you want to work in one of those filthy shops for, anyway? Believe me, I know. My friend Esther volunteers at a thrift shop for Sloan-Kettering. She says the catfights over a simple Pucci scarf are not to be believed. Go see Monsieur Henri. He'll set you straight."

Luke suggested that taking career advice from a woman I met in a basement laundry room wasn't the soundest thing he'd ever heard of.

But Luke has no idea just how desperate things have gotten. Because I haven't told him. I am trying to appear sophisticated and full of savoir-faire where Luke is concerned. It's true he was kind of shocked when all my boxes from home arrived, and we realized there was nowhere to put them. Fortunately, Luke's mom's apartment comes with its own lockable storage unit in the basement garage, where I've stashed all my bolts of material and most of my sewing supplies.

The clothes, however, went straight to a portable hanging rack I bought at Bed Bath & Beyond and installed in the bedroom, under the Renoir girl's disapproving gaze. Luke seemed kind of shocked when he saw it—"I had no idea anyone owned more clothes than my mother," he said—but he recovered himself and even asked me to model some of the slinkier ensembles (as well as, for some reason, my Heidi outfit, which he seemed to get an enormous kick out of).

But what Luke doesn't know is that if something doesn't give soon, that outfit, as well as the rest of the collection, are going up onto eBay. Because I am down to my last few hundred dollars.

And though it will break my heart to have to sell the clothes I've been collecting for so many years, it would break my heart more to have to admit to Luke that I don't have the money for next month's rent.

And while I know he'll only laugh and say it's all right and not to worry about it, I can't *help* worrying about it. I don't want to be his live-in mistress or whatever. I mean for one thing that is hardly an effective career path, as we know from Evita Perón. But also, I want to go *shopping*! I want to add new things to my collection so badly!

Only I can't. Because I'm broke.

So Monsieur Henri is my only hope. Because if he doesn't work out, I'm totally selling off the Suzy Perettes for sure, and maybe even the Gigi Youngs.

Either that, or I'm signing up for a temp agency. I will fax and file for the rest of my life, so long as SOMEONE will hire me.

But as soon as Monsieur Henri (or whoever the guy is who buzzes me in when I press on the bell to Monsieur Henri's shop) ushers me into the waiting area of his shop, all smiles and graciousness—until I tell him I'm not getting married (yet), I'm there to ask about employment opportunities—I have a pretty good idea it's going to be the temp agency for me.

Because the middle-aged, mustached man's face falls, and he demands, in a suspicious, heavily French-accented voice, "Who sent you? Was it Maurice?"

I blink at him. "I have no idea who Maurice is," I say, just as a tiny, birdlike Frenchwoman comes out of the back with a big smile plastered on her face . . . until I say the word "Maurice."

"You think she is a spy from Maurice?" the woman asks the man, in rapid French (which I now understand—well, mostly—on account of having spent a summer in that country, and a semester before that learning it in class).

"She has to be," the man replies in equally rapid French. "What else would she be doing here?"

"No, honestly," I cry. I know enough French to understand it, but not enough actually to speak it myself. "I don't know anybody named Maurice. I'm here because I understand you're the best wedding-gown restorer in town. And I want to be a wedding-gown restorer. Well, I mean, I *am* one. Here, look at my portfolio—"

"What is she talking about?" Madame Henri (because that's who she has to be, right?) asks her husband.

"I have no idea," he replies. But he takes my book, and begins thumbing through it.

"That's a Hubert de Givenchy gown I found in an attic," I tell them, when they get to the page showing Bibi de Villiers's wedding gown. "It had been used to wrap a hunting rifle, which had rusted all over it. I was able to get the rust stains out by soaking it overnight in cream of tartar. Then I handstitched repairs to the straps and hem—"

"Why are you showing this to us?" Monsieur Henri demands, shoving my book back at me. Behind his head is a wall full of framed photographs of before-and-after shots of wedding gowns he's restored. It's pretty impressive. Some of them were so yellowed with age, they looked as if they'd fall apart at the merest touch.

But Monsieur Henri had managed to get them back to their original snowy-whiteness. He either had a way with fabrics, or some kind of wicked chemicals in his back room.

"Because," I say slowly. "I just moved here to New York from Michigan, and I'm looking for a job——"

"Maurice didn't send you?" Monsieur Henri's eyes are still narrowed suspiciously.

"No," I say. Really, what is going on here? "I don't even know what you're talking about."

Madame Henri—who has stood at her much taller husband's side, peeking around his arm at my portfolio—gives me the once-over, her gaze taking in everything from my perky ponytail (Mrs. Erickson advised me to keep my hair out of my eyes), to the Joseph Ribkoff sheath dress I'm wearing beneath a vintage beaded cardigan (it's gotten chillier outside since I arrived in New York. Summer isn't quite gone, but fall is definitely in the air).

"Jean, I believe her," she says to her husband in French. "Look at her. Maurice would not send someone as stupid as she is to trick us."

I want to yell "Hey!" in an enraged voice and stomp out of their shop in a huff, since I perfectly understood that she'd just called me stupid.

But on the other hand, I can see that Monsieur Henri has turned the page and is looking at the before-and-after shots I took of Luke's cousin Vicky's hideous self-designed wedding gown, which I managed to salvage into something semidecent (though in the end she chose the Givenchy I repaired instead). He actually seems interested.

So instead I say, "I had to do all that by hand," referring to the stitching on Vicky's dress. "Because I was traveling at the time, and didn't have my Singer."

"This is hand-done?" he asks, squinting at the photo, then reaching for a pair of bifocals tucked away in his shirt pocket.

"Yes," I say, trying hard not to look at his wife. Stupid! Well, what does *she* know? She obviously can't read. Because it says right on my résumé that I'm a University of Michigan grad. Or I will be in January, anyway. The University of Michigan doesn't accept stupid people . . . even if their fathers *are* supervisors at the cyclotron.

"You took out the rust stains," Monsieur Henri says, "without chemicals?"

"Just cream of tartar," I say. "I soaked it overnight."

Monsieur Henri says, somewhat proudly, "Here we too do not use chemicals. That is how we received our endorsement from the Association of Bridal Consultants and became Certified Wedding-Gown Specialists."

I don't know how to reply to that. I didn't even know there was such a thing as certified wedding-gown specialists. So I just say, "Sweet."

Madame Henri elbows her husband.

"Tell her," she says in French. "Tell her the other thing."

Monsieur Henri peers down at me through the lenses of his eyeglasses. "The National Bridal Service gave us their highest recommendation."

"That is more than they have ever given that *cochon* Maurice!" Madame Henri cries.

I think calling this poor Maurice guy—whoever he is—a pig might be a bit much.

Especially since I've never heard of the National Bridal Service, either.

But again I manage, for once in my life, to keep my mouth shut. There are two wedding gowns on dressmaker's dummies in the window of the tiny shop. They're restoration refurbishments, according to the placard in front of them . . . and they're exquisite. One is covered in seed pearls that dangle like raindrops, glistening in the sun. And the other is a complicated confection of lacy ruffles that my fingers itch to touch, in order to figure out how they were created.

Mrs. Erickson was right. Monsieur Henri knows his stuff. I could learn a lot from him—not just about sewing, either, but about running a successful business.

Too bad Madame Henri is such a—

"This is a very stressful job," Monsieur Henri goes on. "The women who come to us . . . to them, this is the most important day of their lives. Their gown must be absolutely perfect, and yet delivered on time."

"I'm a total perfectionist myself," I say. "I've stayed up all night to finish gowns when I didn't even *have* to."

Monsieur Henri doesn't even appear to be listening. "Our clients can be very demanding. One day they want one thing. The next day, something else—"

"I'm completely flexible," I say. "And I'm also very good with people. You might even say I'm a people person." Oh, God. Did I just say that? "But I would never let a client pick something that isn't flattering."

"This is a family-run business," Monsieur Henri says with sudden—and alarming—finality, closing my portfolio with a loud snap. "I am not looking to hire outsiders."

"But—" No. He is *not* turning me away. I *have* to know how he made those ruffles. "I know I'm not family. But I'm good. And what I don't know—I'm a very quick learner."

"*Non*," Monsieur Henri says. "It is no use. I built this business for my sons—"

"Who want nothing to do with it," his wife says bitterly in French. "You know that, Jean. All those lazy pigs want to do is go to the discotheque."

Hmmm. Her own sons are pigs, too? Also . . . discotheque?

"—and I do all my own work," Monsieur Henri continues loftily.

"Right," Madame Henri snorts. "That's why you have no time for me anymore. Or your sons. They run so wild because you are always here at the shop. And what about your heart? The doctor said you've got to reduce your stress levels, or you'll have a stroke. You keep saying you want to work less, leave the shop to someone else to run sometimes, so we can spend more time in Provence. But do you do anything about this? Of course not."

"I live right around the corner," I say, trying not to let them catch on that I understand every word they're saying. "I can be here whenever you want me. If, you know, you want to spend more time with your family."

Madame Henri's gaze locks onto mine. "Perhaps," she murmurs, in her native tongue, "she is not so stupid after all."

"Please," I say, fighting down an urge to yell, *If I'm so stupid, would I be living on Fifth Avenue?* Because, of course, people who judge you by what avenue you live on *are* stupid. "Your gowns are so beautiful. I want to open a shop of my own someday. So it only makes sense that I'd want to learn from the best. And I have references. You can call the manager of the last shop I worked in—"

"*Non,*" Monsieur Henri says. "*Non,* I am not interested."

And he shoves my résumé back at me.

"Who's stupid now?" his wife demands tartly.

But Monsieur Henri—perhaps because he's seen the tears that have suddenly sprung up in my eyes . . . which, I know. Crying! At a job interview!—seems to soften.

"Mademoiselle," he says, laying a hand on my shoulder. "It is not that I don't think you have talent. It is that we are a very small shop. And my sons, they are in college now. This is very expensive. I cannot afford to pay another person."

And then I hear four words come trickling out of my mouth—like spit does, while I sleep—that I never in a million years would have guessed I'd ever say. And immediately after I've spoken, I want to shoot myself. But it's too late. They're already out there.

"I'll work for free."

God! No! What am I saying?

Except that it's seemed to work. Monsieur Henri looks intrigued. And his wife is smiling as if she's just won the lottery or something.

"An internship, you mean?" Monsieur Henri lowers his bifocals to look at me more closely.

"I . . . I . . ." Oh God. How am I going to get out of this one? Especially since I'm not even sure I want to. "I guess so. And then when you see how hard I work, maybe you could consider promoting me to a paid position."

Okay. There, that sounds better. That's exactly what I'll do. I'll work like a dog for him, make myself indispensable. And then, when he can't do without me, I'll threaten to walk away unless he pays me.

I'm pretty sure this is not the most effective strategy for getting a job. But it's the only one I've got at the moment.

"Done," Monsieur Henri says. Then he whips off his bifocals and holds out his hand for me to shake. "Welcome."

"Um." I slip my hand in his, feeling all the calluses on his fingers and palm. "Thanks."

About which Madame Henri observes in smug French, "Ha! She really is stupid after all!"

— Lizzie Nichols's Wedding Gown Guide —

Know your . . .
Wedding-gown train lengths!

The three basic wedding-dress train lengths are:

The Sweep Length
Barely touches the floor

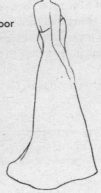

The Chapel Length
Trails on the floor about four feet
out from the dress

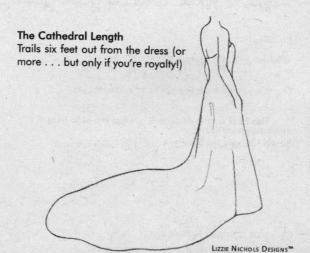

The Cathedral Length
Trails six feet out from the dress (or more . . . but only if you're royalty!)

LIZZIE NICHOLS DESIGNS™

• Chapter 7 •

The best way to keep one's word is not to give it.

—Napoleon I (1769–1821), French emperor

I'm crying as I measure.

I can't help it. I'm just so screwed.

And it's not like I know anyone is home.

So when Chaz comes out of his bedroom, holding a tattered paperback and looking sleepy, and goes, "Holy Christ, what are *you* doing here?" I let out this little shriek and fall over, sending the measuring tape flying.

"Are you all right?" Chaz reaches for my arm, but it's too late. I'm already flat on my butt on his living room floor.

I blame the sloping parquet. I really do.

"No," I sob. "No, I'm not all right."

"What's wrong?" Chaz isn't quite laughing. But there is a definite upward curl to the corners of his lips.

"It's not funny," I say. Life in Manhattan has completely robbed me of my sense of humor. Oh, sure, it's all fine and good when Luke and I are in bed together, or curled up on his mom's couch, watching *Pants Off/Dance Off* on her plasma screen (artfully hidden from view beneath a genuine sixteenth-century tapestry depicting a lovely pastoral scene when not in use).

But the minute he walks out the door to go to class—which is basically from nine to five every weekday—and I'm left on my own, all of my insecurities come rushing back, and I realize that I'm as close to striking out in Manhattan as Kathy Pennebaker did. The only difference between us, really, is that I don't have a personality disorder.

That's been clinically diagnosed, anyway.

"Sorry," Chaz says. He's trying not to smile as he looks down at me. "Do you want to tell me what you're doing sneaking into my apartment in the middle of the afternoon? Luke won't let you cry in his mom's place, or something?"

"No." I stay where I am on the floor. It feels good to cry. Also, Shari and Chaz keep the place pretty clean, so it's not like I'm worried about getting my dress dirty or anything. "Shari gave me your spare key so I could come in and measure for the slipcovers and curtains I'm making you."

"You're making us slipcovers and curtains?" Chaz looks pleased. "Cool." He stops looking pleased when I keep on crying. "Or maybe not cool. If it's making you cry."

"I'm not crying because of the slipcovers," I say, reaching to dab at my eyes with the backs of my wrist. "I'm crying because I'm such a loser."

"Okay. I'm going to need a drink for this one," Chaz says with a sigh. "You want one?"

"Alcohol won't solve anything," I wail.

"No," Chaz agrees. "But I've been reading Wittgenstein all afternoon, so it might make me feel less suicidal. You in or you out? I'm thinking gin and tonics."

"I'm i-in," I hiccup. Maybe a little gin is what I need to buck myself up. It always seems to work for Grandma.

Which is how, a little while later, I find myself sitting next to Chaz on his gold-trimmed couches (the cushions are gold, too. If I didn't know they came from a law office, I'd swear his couches came from a Chinese restaurant. An upscale one. But still), telling him the wretched truth about my finances.

"And now," I conclude, holding on to my tall, frosty drink glass, the contents of which are mostly consumed, "I have a job—I'm not going to say it's my dream job, or anything, but I think I could learn a lot—but it doesn't pay, and I have no idea how I'm going to get rent money for next month. I mean, I can't even temp now, because I don't have my days free, on account of having to be at Monsieur Henri's. And you know how much I suck at bartending and food service. Honestly, unless I sell off my vintage clothing collection, I don't think I'm going to make it. I don't even know how I'm going to get the subway fare to get back home from *here*. And I *can't* tell Luke, I just can't, he'll just think I'm stupid, like Madame Henri does, and it's not like I can ask my parents for money, they don't have any, and besides, I'm an adult, I should be supporting myself. So clearly I'm going to have to tell Monsieur Henri that I'm very sorry, but I made a mistake, and then head down to the closest temp agency and hope they have something—*anything*—for me."

I draw in a deep, shuddering breath. "It's either that, or go back to Ann Arbor and hope my old job at Vintage to Vavoom is still available. Except that if I do that, everyone will go around saying how Lizzie Nichols tried to make it in New York but struck out, just like Kathy Pennebaker."

"She the one who used to steal everyone's boyfriend?" Chaz asks.

"Yes," I say, thinking how nice it is that Shari's boyfriend already knows all the important people and references from our lives, so I don't have to explain them to him, the way I do Luke.

"Well," he says. "They won't compare you to her. She's got a personality disorder."

"Right. She has more of an excuse for striking out in New York than I do!"

Chaz considers this. "She's also a big whore. I'm just quoting Shari, here."

I think I'm getting a migraine. "Can we leave Kathy Pennebaker out of this?"

"You brought her up," Chaz points out.

What am I doing here? What am I doing, sitting on my best friend's boyfriend's couch, telling him all my problems? Worse, he's my boyfriend's best friend.

"If you tell Luke," I growl, "anything about what I said here today, I'll kill you. I really mean it. I'll—I'll kill you."

"I believe you," Chaz says gravely.

"Good." I climb to my feet—not very steadily. Chaz didn't skimp on the gin. "I've got to go. Luke'll be home soon."

"Hold on there, champ," Chaz says, and pulls me back down to the couch by the back of my beaded cardigan.

"Hey," I say. "That's cashmere, you know."

"Simmer down," Chaz says. "I'm going to do you a solid."

I hold up both hands, palms out, to ward him off. "Oh no," I say. "No way. I do not want a loan, Chaz. I'm going to do this on my own, or not at all. I'm not touching your money."

"That's good to know," Chaz says dryly. "Because I wasn't planning on offering you any of my money. What I'm wondering is if you could do the wedding-gown thing part-time. Like, afternoons only."

"Chaz," I say, putting my hands down. "I'm not getting *paid* to do the wedding-gown thing. When you aren't getting paid, you can pretty much make your own hours."

"Right," he says. "So you have your mornings free?"

"Regrettably," I say.

"Well, it just so happens," he says, "that Pendergast, Loughlin, and Flynn just lost their morning receptionist to a touring company of *Tarzan*, the musical."

I blink at him. "Your dad's law firm?"

"Correct," Chaz says. "The receptionist position there is apparently so demanding that it has to be split into two shifts, one from eight in the morning until two in the afternoon, and the other from two in the afternoon until eight in the evening. The afternoon shift is currently held by a young woman with modeling aspirations, who needs her mornings free for go-sees . . . or to recover from her hangover from partying the night before, whichever you care to believe. But they're looking for someone to fill in for the morning shift. So, if you're serious about wanting a job, it might not be a bad gig for you. You'd have your afternoons free for Monsieur Whatsisname, and you wouldn't have to sell off your Betty Boop collection, or whatever it is. It only pays twenty bucks an hour, but it comes with benefits like major medical and paid vaca—"

But he doesn't get to go on. Because I've already thrown myself at him when I hear the words "twenty bucks an hour."

"Chaz, are you serious?" I cry, grasping big handfuls of his T-shirt. "Will you really put in a good word for me?"

"Ow," Chaz says. "That's my chest hair you're pulling."

I let go of him. "Oh God. Chaz! If I could work all morning, then go to Monsieur Henri's in the afternoons . . . I might be able to make it. I might actually be able to make it in New York City after all! I won't have to sell my stuff! I won't have to go home!" More important, I won't have to admit to Luke how much of a failure I am.

"I'll call Roberta in human resources and set up an appointment for you," Chaz says. "But I'm warning you, Lizzie. It's not easy work. Sure, all you're doing is transferring phone calls. But my dad's law firm specializes in divorces and matrimonial planning—in other words, prenups. Their clients are pretty demanding, and the lawyers are pretty uptight. Things can get really tense. I know, my dad had me work in the mailroom one summer when I was just out of high school. And it sucked."

I'm barely listening. "Is there a dress code? Do I have to wear panty hose? I hate panty hose."

Chaz sighs. "Roberta can tell you all about that. Listen. Not to make it not all about you for a change, or anything, but do you know what's up with Shari?"

That gets my attention. "Shari? No. Why? What are you talking about?"

"I don't know." For a minute, Chaz looks younger than his twenty-six years—which is only three years older than Shari and I are, and yet in so many ways, light-years older than that, even. I personally think that's what comes of sending your kid off to boarding school during those integral tween and teen years. But maybe that's just me. I can't imagine having a kid and purposely sending him away, the way Chaz's parents did, just because he was a little ADD. "She just can't seem to stop talking about this new boss of hers."

"Pat?" I've heard the Pat stories ad nauseum myself. Every time I talk to Shari, it seems like she has another story about her intrepid new boss to share.

But it isn't a wonder, really, that Shari's impressed by the woman. She has, after all, been instrumental in saving hundreds, maybe even thousands of women's lives by getting them out of their abusive family situations and into new safe environments.

"Yeah," Chaz says, when I mention this. "I know all that. And I'm glad Shari likes her job, and all. It's just . . . I hardly ever see her anymore. She's always working. Not just nine to five, but evenings and some weekends, too."

"Well," I say. Regrettably, I'm beginning to sober up already. "I'm sure she's just trying to keep afloat. From what she says, the girl who had the job before her kind of left everything in a huge mess. She told me it would be months before she got it all straightened out."

"Yeah," Chaz says. "She told me that, too."

"So," I say. "You should be proud of her. She's helping to make a difference." Unlike me. And, I want to add, Chaz, who is only working on his Ph.D., after all. Although when he gets it, he intends to teach. Which is admirable. I mean, molding young minds, and all. Certainly more than I can say I'll ever be doing.

But young girls, they do get weary . . .

Okay, I totally have to stop thinking of that song all the time.

"I *am* proud of her," Chaz says. "I just wish she could help make a difference fewer hours of the day, is all."

"Aw." I smile at him. "You're sweet. You wuv your girlfriend."

He shoots a sarcastic look at me. "Maybe you *do* have a personality disorder," he says.

I laugh and take a swing at him, but he ducks.

"What about you and Luke?" he wants to know. "I mean, aside from the shameful secret you're keeping from him—about your abject poverty—how are you two getting along?"

"Great," I say. I think about asking him what I should do about Luke's mom. The guy who'd called—the one with the accent—had left another message, sounding wounded that Bibi hadn't shown up to their meeting. Again, he didn't leave a name, but again, he'd mentioned their standing appointment, and that he'd be waiting.

I'd erased the message before Luke got home from class. It just didn't seem to me like the kind of thing a guy would want to listen to. About his mother, that is.

Of course, I was considering the fact that I hadn't blabbed the whole thing out to Luke anyway the minute he walked through the door a sign of my newfound maturity and ability to keep my mouth shut.

The fact that I'm not blabbing it to Chaz now is even further proof of my incredible New York sangfroid.

Instead I say to Chaz conversationally, "I'm still doing the tiny woodland creature thing, and it seems to be working."

Chaz blinks at me. "The *what*?"

And I realize, belatedly, that I've been lulled into a false sense of comfort by his easygoing nature . . . so much so that I've started talking to him about stuff I normally reserve for Shari's ears only! What am I doing, talking about my woodland creature theory with another GUY? Worse than just another guy—my boyfriend's *best friend*?

"Uh, nothing," I say quickly. "Things are fine with Luke."

"What's the tiny woodland creature thing?" he wants to know.

"Nothing," I say again. "Just—nothing. It's a girl thing. It's not important."

But Chaz totally won't let it go. "Is it a sex thing?"

"Oh my God!" I cry. "No! It's not a sex thing! God!"

"Well, what is it then? Come on, you can tell me. I won't tell Luke."

"Oh, right," I say with a laugh. "I've heard that before—"

Chaz looks wounded. "What? Have I ever ratted you out to any of your boyfriends before?"

I glare at him. "I've never had a boyfriend before. At least, not one who wasn't gay or using me for my money. Back when I had some money, I mean."

"Come on, just tell me," Chaz says. "What's it mean to do the tiny woodland creature thing? I swear I won't tell anyone."

"Just . . ." I can see I have no choice but to tell him. Otherwise, he's never going to let it go. And with my luck, he'll bring it up in front of Luke. "It's just this theory I have, all right? That guys are like tiny woodland creatures. And to lure them in, you can't make any sudden moves. You have to be subtle. You have to be cool."

"Lure them in to do what?" Chaz asks, seeming genuinely not to know. "You've already got Luke. I mean, you're living together. Although I still don't understand why you can't tell your parents that's what you're doing. They're going to find out it isn't Shari you're sharing your place with eventually. Don't you think the fact that you have an address on Fifth Avenue is going to make them a *little* suspicious?"

I roll my eyes. "Chaz. My parents don't know from Fifth Avenue. They've never been to New York. And you know what I'm talking about."

"No, I really don't. Enlighten me?"

"You know," I say. Because he's clearly never going to let it go. "Get them to commit."

"Get them to . . ." Comprehension dawns across Chaz's face. Comprehension combined with what appears to be a healthy dose of horror. "You want to *marry* Luke?"

I have no choice but to lift up one of the gold cushions and hurl it at him in fury. "Don't say it like that!" I yell. "What's wrong with it? I love him!"

This time Chaz is too stunned to duck. The cushion bounces off him, nearly overturning his empty gin and tonic glass, already teetering precariously on the uneven floor.

"You've only known the guy like three months," he cries. "And you're already thinking about *marriage*?"

"Oh, what?" I can't believe this is happening. Again. Why did I open my big mouth? Why can't I ever keep *anything* to myself? "Like there's some kind of correct time frame in which you're supposed to decide these kinds of things? Sometimes you just *know*, Chaz."

"Yeah, but . . . *Luke*?" Chaz is shaking his head in disbelief. This is not a good sign. Considering Luke is his best friend. And he probably has insider information.

"What *about* Luke?" I demand. But I'll admit it, even though I sounded cool about it—to my own ears, anyway—my heart was beginning to race. What was he talking about? Why did he have that expression on his face? Like he'd just smelled something bad?

"Look, don't get me wrong," Chaz says. "I think Luke's a great guy to hang out with and all. But I wouldn't *marry* him."

"No one is asking you to," I point out. "In fact, in most states, that would be illegal."

"Ha, ha," Chaz says. Then he clams up. "Listen. Never mind. Forget I said anything. You go on forest-creaturing him, or whatever it is. Have fun."

"Woodland," I say. Now my heart isn't just racing. It feels like it's about to explode out of my chest. "Woodland creature. And tell me what you mean. Why wouldn't you want to marry Luke? I mean, aside from the fact that you're not gay." And that he hasn't asked. Me, I mean.

"I don't know." Chaz looks uncomfortable. "I mean, marriage is pretty final. You have to spend the rest of your life with the person."

"Not necessarily," I say. "I think your father's built himself a pretty lucrative career proving that this isn't always the case."

"That's what I mean, though," Chaz says. "If you pick the wrong person, it can end up costing you hundreds of thousands of dollars. If my dad's firm represents you, I mean."

"But I don't think Luke is the wrong person," I explain to him patiently. "For me. And I'm not saying I want to get married to him tomorrow. I'm not an *idiot*. I want to be established in my career before I start having kids and all of that. And I told him the whole moving-in-together thing was on a trial basis and all of that. I'm just saying that, if things work out, when I'm thirty or so, marrying Luke would be very nice."

"Well," Chaz says. "That's fine, I guess. But *I'm* just saying, a lot of stuff can happen in the six years before you turn thirty—"

"Seven," I correct him.

"—and that if you guys were horses, and I were a betting man, Luke's not the horse I would bet on to come in first. Or at all, for that matter."

I shake my head. My heart has slowed down. It's clear Chaz doesn't have the slightest idea what he's talking about. Not bet on Luke? What is he talking about? Luke is the most fantastic person I've ever met. What other guy does Chaz know who's memorized every song on the Rolling Stones' *Sticky Fingers* album by heart—and frequently sings them in the shower—on *key*? What other guy does Chaz know who can take oil, vinegar, some mustard, and an egg, and make the most delicious salad dressing I've ever tasted? What other guy does Chaz know who was willing to give up his lucrative salary as an investment banker to go back to school to become a doctor, and *help heal sick children*?

"That's not a very nice thing to say about your friend," I point out.

Chaz looks defensive. "I'm not saying he's a bad person. I'm just saying that I've known him a lot longer than you have, Lizzie, and he's always had a problem with—well, let's just say when the going gets tough, Luke has a habit of getting going. As in quitting."

I'm appalled. "Because he put off medical school to become an investment banker, then realized he made a mistake? People do that, you know, Chaz. People make mistakes."

"You don't," Chaz says. "I mean, you make mistakes. But not that kind. You've known what you've wanted to do since the day I met you. You've also known it was going to be hard, and that it would take a lot of sacrifice, and that you probably wouldn't make a lot of money at it right away. But that never stopped you. You never gave up on your dream when the going got tough."

I gape at him. "Chaz, have you even been in the same room with me for this entire conversation? I just got through telling you how I'm about to give up on my dream."

"You just got through telling me how you were going to move home and figure out some other way to pursue it that doesn't include New York City," Chaz corrects me. "That's different. Listen, Liz, don't get me wrong. I'm *not* saying Luke's a bad guy. I'm just saying I wouldn't—"

"Bet on him to finish first if he were a horse and you were a betting man," I finish for him impatiently. "Yes, I know, I heard you the first time. And I get what you're saying, I guess. But you're talking about the OLD Luke. Not the Luke he's turned into, now that he has me to support him. People change, Chaz."

"Not that much," Chaz says.

"Yes," I say. "They do. That much."

"Can you give me empirical data to support that statement?" Chaz asks.

"No," I say. Now I'm really getting impatient. I don't know how Shari puts up with Chaz sometimes. Oh, sure, he's cute, in a jockish kind of way. And he totally adores her, and is supposedly fantastic in bed (sometimes I think Shari shares a little too much). But what's with the turned-around baseball caps? And the *Can you give me the empirical data to support that statement?*

"Then that," Chaz goes on, "is a specious argument—"

What's that Shakespeare saying? *The first thing we do, let's kill all the lawyers?* It should be, *The first thing we do, let's kill all the graduate students getting a Ph.D. in philosophy.*

"Chaz!" I cut him off. "Do you want to help me measure your windows so I can go home and start on your curtains, or what?"

He glances at the windows. They are covered with hideous folding metal gates, in order to keep out the few remaining crackheads in the city, all of whom seem to live in his neighborhood, for some reason.

They are terrifically ugly. Even a guy should be able to see that.

"I guess," he says, looking deflated. "It's more fun arguing with you, though."

"Well, *I'm* not having any fun," I inform him.

He grins. "Okay. Curtains it is. And Lizzie."

I've scooped up the measuring tape and am slipping off my shoes so I can climb up onto the radiator to measure. "What?"

"About the job. In my dad's office. There's one more thing."

"What?"

"You're going to have to keep your mouth shut. I mean, about who you see and what you overhear in there. You're not supposed to talk about it. It's a law office. And they promise their clients total discretion—"

"God, Chaz," I say, irritated all over again. "I can keep my mouth shut, you know."

He just looks at me.

"If it's important, I *can*," I insist. "Like, if my paycheck depends on it."

"Maybe," Chaz says, almost as if to himself, "recommending you for the job isn't the best idea . . ."

I throw the measuring tape at him.

~ Lizzie Nichols's Wedding Gown Guide ~

Yes, I know. Everybody's doing it. Well, if everyone jumped off the Brooklyn Bridge, would you do it, too?

So stop letting your bra straps show!

I don't care how much you paid for your over-the-shoulder-boulder-holder, it's uncouth to force us to look at it (especially if the straps are graying or frayed—and ESPECIALLY on your wedding day)!

Keep your girls where they should be by having your wedding-gown specialist attach about an inch and a half of seam binding or a thread chain under the shoulder seam of your sleeve or strap. Then have her sew a ball snap to the free end of the guard, and a socket snap toward the neck edge.

Then snap your strap. It will be out of sight . . . and so will you!

LIZZIE NICHOLS DESIGNS™

The entrance with its banner proclaims dynasmooth, the
wooden plaque is gone, the façade is off. By a joke about the
banal looking women screwed on, in seemed-adventure telling
for many, half an hour in the bare, dusky, she'd opened from
and seemed couches to drop. Brown leather ones, which blurred
much with the dark wood paneling on the walls and rich green carpeting, less the one or two pleasant questions about how I knew

• Chapter 8 •

New York is a strange place. Things here can change in the blink of the eye. I guess that's what they mean when they say a New York minute. Everything just seems to go faster here.

Like, you can be walking down a street that seems perfectly tree-lined and pleasant, and not even one block later, you suddenly find yourself in a trash-filled, graffitied seedy underbelly of a neighborhood, resembling something out of a crime scene on one of the *Law and Order*s. And all you've done is crossed a street.

So I guess, considering all this, I shouldn't have been so amazed that in a forty-eight-hour period, I went from having no job in New York City to being the proud owner of *two* of them.

The interview with the human resources division of Chaz's dad's office is going well. *Really* well. It's like a joke, actually. The harried-looking woman whose office I'm escorted into after waiting for nearly half an hour in the fancy lobby (they'd upgraded from gold-trimmed couches to deep-brown leather ones, which blended nicely with the dark wood paneling on the walls and rich green carpeting) asks me one or two pleasant questions about how I know

Chaz—"From the dorm we all lived in in college," I say, not mentioning that Shari and I had met him at an outdoor movie night sponsored by the student government of McCracken Hall, at which Chaz had been the one who'd started passing around a joint, causing us to refer to him for days afterward as the Joint Man . . . until Shari spied him eating breakfast in the dining hall by himself one morning, plunked herself down beside him, asked him his name, and by that evening had slept with him in his single in McCracken's tower suites. Three times.

"Great," Roberta, my interviewer, says, apparently not realizing she's getting a less than complete relationship history from me. "We all love Charles. The summer he worked here in the mailroom, he had us all in stitches the whole time. He's so funny."

Yeah. Chaz is hilarious.

"It's just too bad," Roberta goes on wistfully, "that Charles didn't choose the law. He has his dad's same brilliant academic mind. When either of them starts arguing a point—well, get out of the way!"

Yeah. Chaz likes to argue a point, all right.

"So, Lizzie," Roberta says pleasantly. "When can you start?"

I gape at her. "You mean I got the job?"

"Of course." Roberta looks at me strangely, as if any other turn of events would be unthinkable. "Could you start tomorrow?"

Can I start tomorrow? Is there a grand total of three hundred and twenty-one dollars in my checking account? Are my credit cards maxed out to their limits? Am I fifteen hundred dollars in debt to MasterCard?

"I can *definitely* start tomorrow!"

Oh, Chaz, I take it all back. I love you. You can say whatever you want about Luke. You can be as pessimistic as you choose about the wisdom of my wanting to marry him. For this, Chaz, I owe you. Big time.

"I love your boyfriend." I call Shari on my cell to tell her as I come out of the skyscraper on Madison Avenue in which the offices of Pendergast, Loughlin, and Flynn take up the entire thirty-seventh floor.

"Really." Shari sounds, as always when I call her at her office these days, a little frantic. "You can have him."

"Taken," I say. I'm on Fifty-seventh Street between Madison and Fifth. It's such a nice fall day—just warm enough that you don't need a coat, and just cool enough that you don't feel sweaty—I decide to walk to Monsieur Henri's, just thirty blocks north, instead of taking the subway, saving myself a whopping two bucks. Hey, every little bit counts. "Chaz got me a job in his dad's office."

"A job?" I hear computer keys clacking. Shari is talking and e-mailing at the same time. But that's okay. I'll take whatever I can get, it's so hard to reach her these days. "I thought you already had a job. At that wedding-gown place."

"Yeah," I say, realizing I hadn't been quite as upfront with my friends about my deal with Monsieur Henri as I ought to have been. "That's not really a paying gig—"

"WHAT?" I realize by her tone—and the cessation of clacking keys—that I now have Shari's undivided attention. "You took a *non-paying* job?"

"Right," I say. It's kind of hard to walk down a busy sidewalk like the one I'm currently hurrying along and talk on your cell at the same time. There are so many businesspeople rushing back to their offices, street vendors hawking Prada knockoffs, tourists stopping to gawk at the tall buildings, and homeless people asking for spare change that it's as hard to navigate as the Indy 500 Speedway during the race. "Well, it's not easy to find a paying fashion gig in this city when you're just starting out."

"I can't believe that," Shari says, sounding incredulous. "What about *Project Runway*?"

"Shari," I say. "I'm not going on a *reality show*—"

"No, I just mean . . . they make it seem like it's all so easy—"

"Well," I say. "It's not. Anyway, I want us to get together to celebrate—you and me and Chaz and Luke. So what are you doing tonight?"

"Oh," Shari says. I hear the clacking start up again. Which isn't easy, considering the fact that there are cars honking and people talking loudly all around me. And yet, I can still hear the fact that my best friend is only half paying attention to me. "I can't. Not tonight. We're getting slammed here today—"

"Fine," I say. I understand that Shari's new job is the most important thing in the world to her right now. Which is as it should be. I mean, she is, after all, saving women's lives. "How about tomorrow night, then?"

"This week is really bad for me, Lizzie," Shari says. "I'm going to be working late just about every night."

"What about Saturday?" I inquire patiently. "You aren't working on Saturday night, are you?"

There's a pause. For a second or two, I think Shari's going to say that she does, indeed, plan on working through Saturday night.

But then she says, "No, of course not. Saturday it is."

"Great," I say. "We'll hit Chinatown. And then Honey's. On Saturday night the serious karaoke players come out. And, Shari?"

"What, Lizzie? I really have to go, Pat's waiting—"

"I know." There's always someone waiting for Shari these days. "But I wanted to ask you—are things okay between you and Chaz? Because he asked me about you."

I have her full attention again. "He asked you *what* about me?" Shari demands, somewhat sharply.

"Just if I thought you were all right," I say. "I said I thought you were. I guess he misses you as much as I do." I think about this as I wait for the light to change before crossing the street. "Actually, he probably misses you more . . ."

"I can't help it," Shari snaps, "if I'm too busy helping victims of domestic violence find safe places to live to worry about my boyfriend. This is part of the problem, you know. I mean, men think the entire world revolves around them. And so when the woman in his life finds herself thriving—excelling, even—in the workplace, a man naturally feels threatened, and eventually leaves her for someone who has more time to give to him."

I am, to put it bluntly, stunned by this speech. So stunned I actually stop walking for a second, and am bumped from behind by an irritated-looking businessman. "Excuse you," the businessman mutters before hurrying along.

"Shari," I say into the phone. "Chaz does *not* feel threatened by your new career. He loves that you love your job. He just wants to know when he's ever going to see you again. He isn't leaving you."

"I know," Shari says, after a pause. "I just—sorry. I didn't mean to lay all that on you. I'm just having a bad day. Forget I said anything."

"Shari." I shake my head. "This sounds like something more serious than just a bad day. Are you and Chaz—"

"I really have to go, Lizzie," Shari says. "I'll see you Saturday."

And then she hangs up.

Wow. What was *that* about? I wonder. Chaz and Shari have always had something of a stormy relationship, full of bickering and even some fights (the most serious of which was the one stemming from Shari's decision to kill and dissect her lab rat, Mr. Jingles, even after Chaz had found an identical replacement rat at PetSmart for whom none of us had developed the kind of affection we all felt for Mr. Jingles).

But they'd always made up quickly (except for the two weeks after Mr. Jingles's death that Chaz wouldn't speak to Shari). In fact, the fantastic makeup sex was one of the reasons Shari cited for picking so many fights with Chaz in the first place.

So is that what's going on now? Just an elaborate ploy on Shari's part to inject a little more excitement into their relationship?

Because, as I'm discovering myself, it's not easy to keep the flame alive when you're living together. Mundane everyday things can totally get in the way of blissful cohabitation. Like whose turn is it to do the dishes, and who gets control of the remote, and who unplugged whose cell phone charger to plug in the hair dryer instead then forgot to plug the cell phone charger back in.

Those kinds of things are real romance killers.

Not that I don't love every minute of living with Luke. I mean, from the moment I wake up to see the Renoir girl's smiling face above my head, to the moment I fall asleep, listening to Luke's gentle breathing beside me (he always falls asleep before I do. I don't know how he does it. The minute his head touches the pillow, he's out like a light. Maybe it's all that boring reading for his Principles of Biology and General Chemistry that he does before bed in order to keep up with his homework), I thank my lucky stars that I made the decision to leave England and go to France. Because otherwise I would never have met him, and I wouldn't be as happy as I am now (worries about finances aside).

Still, I guess I can understand it if Shari is trying to get a rise out of Chaz just to shake things up a little. Because I've watched television with Chaz before, and the way he flips up and down the channels instead of just leaving it on one semiinteresting program and then going to the onscreen guide to see what else is on can be almost as annoying as the way Luke, it turns out, considers really upsetting documentaries about things like the Holocaust suitable viewing for a fun Friday night at home.

But I don't have time to worry about Shari and Chaz—or even Luke's aversion to romantic comedies—because when I get to Monsieur Henri's that afternoon and ring the bell to be let in (he hasn't given me a key, and probably won't, I fear, until I've proved myself capable of doing something other than a cross-stitch), I find bedlam.

An older woman with big hair and the kind of brightly colored clothing that I've already learned pegs her as "bridge and tunnel" (someone who lives outside Manhattan, and has to take a bridge or tunnel to get to it) is holding this enormous white box and shouting, "Look! Just look!" while a girl who could only be her daughter (even though she's more stylishly attired in black and a blowout) stands nearby, looking sullen, and not a little rebellious.

Monsieur Henri, in the meantime, is saying, "Madame, I know. This is not the first time. I see this often."

I try to keep out of the way, and sidle up to Madame Henri, who is watching the drama unfold from the curtained doorway to the workroom at the back of the shop.

"What's happening?" I ask her.

She shakes her head. "They went to Maurice" is all she says in way of reply.

Which of course tells me nothing. I still don't have the slightest idea who Maurice is.

But then Monsieur Henri reaches into the box, and carefully pulls out a long-sleeved, virginal, fragile-as-gossamer-looking white gown.

At least, it used to be white. The lace has turned a sickening shade of yellow.

"He promised!" the woman is saying. "He promised the preservation box would keep it from yellowing!"

"Of course he did," Monsieur Henri says, in a dry tone. "And when you took it back to show him, he told you that the reason it turned this color was because you broke the preservation seal."

"Yes!" The woman's chin is trembling, she's so upset. "Yes, that's exactly what he said! He said it was my fault, for allowing air inside the box!"

I let out an involuntary sound of protest. Monsieur Henri glances in my direction. I immediately blush, and take a quick step backward.

But Monsieur Henri has fastened his blue-eyed gaze at me and isn't looking away.

"Mademoiselle?" he asks. "There is something you wish to say?"

"No," I say quickly, aware that Madame Henri is staring daggers at me. "I mean, not really."

"I think there is." Monsieur Henri's eyes are very bright. He can't see anything close up without his glasses. But his farsightedness is uncanny. "Go on. What is it that you wish to say?"

"Only," I begin reluctantly, fearing I might be saying something he won't like, "that storing textiles in a sealed container can actually harm them, especially if moisture gets in. It can cause the material to mildew."

Monsieur Henri, I see, looks pleased. This gives me the courage to continue. "Not one of the historic costumes at the Met is stored in an airtight room," I go on. "And they're doing just fine. It's important to keep old fabric out of direct sunlight—but there's no way breaking the seal on a preservation box caused the yellowing on that dress. That was caused by improper cleaning before storage . . . most likely the result of the gown not having been cleaned at all, and stains from champagne or perspiration being left untreated."

The smile Monsieur Henri bequeaths me upon my concluding this recitation is dazzling enough to cause his wife to suck in her breath . . .

. . . and throw me a look of surprise. It's clear she's reassessing her "stupid" remark from earlier in the week.

"But how can that be?" the woman asks, her brow furrowed. "If the gown was cleaned before it was put in storage—"

"God, Mom," the girl interrupts, sounding disgusted. "Don't you get it? That Maurice guy didn't clean it. He just stuck it in there, put the lid on, and gave it back, *saying* he'd cleaned it."

"And told you never to open the box," Monsieur Henri adds. "That breaking the seal would cause the material to yellow—and void your money-back guarantee." Making a tsk-tsking noise, Monsieur Henri looks down at the dress he's holding. Which, I have to say, is not the nicest gown I've ever seen. I mean, it's okay.

But if the reason the older woman broke the seal on the box in which the gown had been preserved was so that her daughter could wear it to *her* wedding, well, she was in for a surprise. Because I couldn't see Miss Blowout putting on that high-necked, Victorian-looking thing for all the Suzy Perettes in the world.

"I have seen this a thousand times," Monsieur Henri says sadly. "It is such a shame."

The older woman looks alarmed. "Is it ruined?" she wants to know. "Can it be saved?"

"I don't know," Monsieur Henri says dubiously. I can see that he's playing them. All the dress needs is a nice white-vinegar soak and maybe a cold-water wash with some OxiClean.

"Gee, that's too bad," Blowout says, before Monsieur Henri can say anything more. "I guess we'll just have to get a new dress."

"We are not getting you a new dress, Jennifer," Big Hair snaps. "This dress was good enough for me, and good enough for each of your sisters. It's good enough for you!"

Jennifer looks mutinous. Monsieur Henri doesn't need to put on his glasses to see this. He hesitates, and it's clear he's not certain how to proceed. Madame Henri clears her throat.

But I jump in, before she can say a word, with, "The stains can be removed. But that's not the real problem, is it?"

Jennifer is looking at me suspiciously. So, actually, is everyone in the shop.

"Elizabeth," Monsieur Henri says, using my first name for the first time in our acquaintance—and in a sugary-sweet voice I know is completely fake, too. He clearly wants to kill me. "There is no problem."

"Yes, there is," I say, in a voice just as fakey as his. "I mean, look at that dress, and then look at Jennifer here." Everyone in the shop glances at the dress, then at Jennifer, who preens a little, sweeping back the stick-straight ends of her blowout. "Do you see the problem now?"

"No," Jennifer's mother says bluntly.

"This dress was probably very flattering on you, Mrs.—" I pause and look questioningly at Jennifer's mom, who says, "Harris."

"Right," I say. "Mrs. Harris. Because you're a statuesque woman, with excellent carriage. But look at Jennifer. She's very petite. A dress with this much material will overwhelm her."

Jennifer narrows her eyes and scissors a glance in her mother's direction. "See?" she hisses. "I told you."

"Er, uh," Monsieur Henri blusters uncomfortably, still looking as if he wants to kill me. "In point of fact, Mademoiselle Elizabeth is not, er, technically speaking, an employee of—"

"But this gown could easily be altered to flatter someone of Jennifer's proportions," I say, pointing to the high neckline, "merely by opening up this area here, giving it more of a sweetheart neckline, and maybe getting rid of the sleeves—"

"Absolutely not," Mrs. Harris says. "It's a Catholic ceremony."

"Then tightening the sleeves," I go on smoothly, "so that they don't bell. A girl with a figure as good as Jennifer's shouldn't hide it. Especially on a day when she wants to look her best."

Jennifer has been listening to all of this intently. I can tell because she's stopped fiddling with her hair.

"Yeah," she says. "See, Mom? That's what I *told* you."

"I don't know," Mrs. Harris murmurs, chewing her lower lip. "Your sisters—"

"Are you the youngest?" I asked Jennifer, who nodded. "Yeah, I thought so. Me, too. It's hard being the youngest, always getting your big sisters' hand-me-downs. You get to a point where you'd just die to have something—*anything*—new, something all your own."

"*Exactly!*" Jennifer explodes.

"But in the case of your mother's wedding gown, you *can* have that," I say, "and still observe family tradition by wearing it . . . you just have to give it a few tweaks to make it uniquely your own. And we can easily do that here—"

"I want that," Jennifer says, turning to her mother. "What she said. That's what I want."

Mrs. Harris looks from the gown to her daughter and then back again. Then she lets out a little laugh and says, "Fine! Whatever you want! If it's cheaper than a new gown—"

"Oh," Madame Henri steps forward to say, "it will be, of course. If the young lady would like to come with me to change, we can begin measuring for the alterations right away . . ."

Jennifer flicks her blowout back and, without another word, follows Madame Henri to the dressing room.

"Oh," Mrs. Harris cries, after glancing at her watch. "I have to go put money in the meter if we're staying. Excuse me—"

She hurries out of the shop. As soon as the door eases shut behind her, Monsieur Henri turns to me and, indicating the yellowed dress he's still holding, says hesitantly, "You are quite adept with the, er, customer."

"Oh," I say modestly. "Well, that one was easy. I know exactly how she felt. I have older sisters myself."

"I see." Monsieur Henri's gaze is shrewd as he looks down at me. "Well, I will be interested to see if you can work a needle as well as you work your mouth."

"Watch me," I say, plucking the gown from his hands. "Just watch."

~ Lizzie Nichols's Wedding Gown Guide ~

If you are top-heavy, or have an hourglass figure, I have one word for you: strapless!

I know what you are thinking . . . strapless, at a wedding? But strapless is no longer considered immodest in most churches!

And with the right support in the bodice, this look can be extremely flattering on a top-heavy bride, especially when paired with an A-line skirt. V-necklines are also terrific on large-on-the-top women, as are off-the-shoulder and scoop-neck designs.

Just remember that the higher the neckline, the bigger the boobs look!

LIZZIE NICHOLS DESIGNS™

• Chapter 9 •

Nothing travels faster than light, with the possible exception of bad news, which follows its own rules.

—Douglas Adams (1952–2001), British author and radio dramatist

a receptionist?"

That's what Luke says when I tell him the news. For once, he's gotten home before I have, and is making dinner—coq au vin. One of the many advantages of having a boyfriend who is half French is that his culinary repertoire extends beyond mac and cheese. Plus, there's the kissing.

"Right," I say. I'm sitting on a velvet-cushioned stool in front of the granite-topped bar beneath the pass-through between the kitchen and dining/living room.

"But." Luke is pouring us each a glass of cabernet sauvignon, then hands me mine through the pass-through. "Aren't you . . . I don't know. A little overqualified to be a receptionist?"

"Sure," I say. "But this way I'll be able to pay the bills and still do what I love—for part of the day, anyway. Since I haven't had any luck finding a paying fashion gig."

"It's only been a month," Luke says. "Maybe you just need to give your job search a little more time."

"Um." How can I explain this to him without revealing the fact that I am flat busted broke? "Well, I am. If something better comes along, of course I can always quit."

Except I don't want to. Quit Monsieur Henri's, anyway. Because I'm starting to like it there. Especially now that I know who Maurice is: a rival "certified wedding-gown specialist" who owns not one but four shops throughout the city, and who has been stealing away Monsieur Henri's clientele with his promise of a new chemical treatment to combat cake and wine stains (no such treatment exists), and who overcharges his customers for even the simplest alterations, and underpays his vendors and employees (although I don't see how he could underpay them more than Monsieur Henri is underpaying me).

Worse, Maurice has been bad-mouthing Monsieur Henri, telling every bride in town that Jean Henri is retiring to Provence and could pick up and leave at any time, due to his business falling off—which is apparently true, judging from the Henris' private conversations, which they aren't aware I completely understand. Well, almost completely.

As if all of that were not bad enough, the Henris have heard a rumor that Maurice is planning on opening up another one of his shops . . . DOWN THE STREET FROM THEIRS! With his glitzy red awning and matching signature red carpet (yes!) outside the front door, the Henris don't have a chance of competing . . . not with their subtle yet tasteful front window display and modest brownstone.

No, even if the Costume Institute calls tomorrow, I plan on sticking around at Monsieur Henri's. I'm in too deep to get out now.

"Well," Luke says, sounding dubious, "if it makes you happy . . ."

"It does," I say. Then I clear my throat. "You know, Luke, not everyone is cut out for the traditional nine-to-five thing. There's nothing wrong with taking on a job you're maybe overqualified for if it pays the bills and allows you to do the thing you really love in your spare time. As long as you really do the thing you love, and don't spend all your free time watching television."

"Good point," Luke says. "Taste this and tell me what you think." He holds out a spoon containing some of the juice from the coq au vin. I lean over the bar to taste it.

"Delicious," I say, thinking my heart just might bubble over with joy. I have a boyfriend who loves me . . . and is a terrific cook. I have a job I love. And I have a way to pay the rent on the kick-ass apartment I'm living in.

New York isn't working out so badly after all. Maybe I won't be Ann Arbor's next Kathy Pennebaker.

"Oh, hey," I say. "We're going out Saturday night with Chaz and Shari. To celebrate my new job. And because we haven't seen them in forever. Is that okay?"

"That," Luke says, stirring, "sounds great."

"And you know?" I'm still leaning across the pass-through. "I think we should really try to make it a fun night. Because I think Chaz and Shari are going through a tough time."

"You get that feeling, too?" Luke shakes his head. "Chaz seems pretty miserable these days."

"Really?" I raise my eyebrows. I can't exactly say Chaz seemed miserable when I saw him. But then maybe I was too busy bawling my eyes out to notice. "Wow. Well, I'm sure it's just a transitional thing. Once Shari settles into her new job, they'll be fine."

"Maybe," Luke says.

"What do you mean, maybe?" I ask. "What do you know that I don't know?"

"Nothing," Luke says innocently. *Too* innocently. He's smiling, though, so I know whatever it is, it can't be that bad.

"What is it?" I'm laughing now. "Tell me."

"I can't tell you," Luke says. "Chaz made me swear not to tell. *You,* of all people, especially."

"That's not fair," I say, pouting. "I won't tell. I swear."

"Chaz said you'd say that." Luke is grinning, so I know whatever it is he's not supposed to tell me, it isn't something bad.

"Just tell me," I whine.

And then, just like that, I know. Or think I know, anyway.

"Oh my God," I cry. "He's going to propose!"

Luke stares at me over his bubbling chicken. "What?"

"Chaz! He's going to ask Shari to marry him, isn't he? Oh my gosh, that is so great!"

And I can't believe I didn't figure it out sooner. Of *course* that's what's going on. That's why Chaz asked me those searching questions about Shari in their place the other day. He was feeling me out to see if Shari had said anything about how living with him was going!

Because he wants to make it permanent!

"Oh, Luke!" I have to hold on to the counter to keep from falling off my stool, because I'm practically swooning, I'm so excited. "This is so fantastic! And I have the best idea for a dress for her . . . it's like a bustier, you know, but with off-the-shoulder capped sleeves, in dupioni silk, and with little pearl buttons down the back, totally fitted through the waist, and then pooching out into this totally elegant belled skirt—not a hoop skirt, she wouldn't like that . . . Oh, you know, she might not even want a belled skirt. Maybe I should make it more—well, here, this is what I mean."

I reach for a notepad that his mother has left lying around— Bibi de Villiers, it says on the top of each page, in cursive—and scribble out the design I'm thinking of with a pen from the bank we both use.

"See, something like this?" I hold up the sketch, and see that Luke is staring at me with a mingled expression of horror and amusement.

"What?" I ask, shocked by the look on his face. "You don't like it? I think it'll be cute. In ivory? With a detachable train?"

"Chaz isn't asking Shari to *marry* him," Luke says, half grinning and half frowning. It's clear he can't tell which to do, so he's doing both.

"He isn't?" I put down the notepad and stare at my sketch. "Are you sure?"

"I'm *positive*," Luke says. Now he's completely grinning. "I can't even believe you'd think that!"

"Well." I am so crestfallen, I can't hide it. "Why not? I mean, they've been going out forever—"

"Right," Luke says. "But he's only twenty-six. And he's still in school!"

"*Graduate* school," I point out. "And they *are* living together."

"So are we," Luke says with a laugh, "but we're not getting married anytime soon."

I force a laugh along with him, although the truth is, I don't see anything funny about the situation. No, we may not be getting married anytime soon. But the *possibility* is still there, isn't it?

Isn't it?

But of course I don't ask him this out loud. Because I'm still woodland-creaturing him.

"Chaz and Shari have known each other for a lot longer than we have," I settle for saying instead. "It wouldn't be the weirdest thing if they got engaged."

"I guess not," Luke admits—but grudgingly. "Still, I don't exactly see either of them as the marrying kind."

"What's the marrying kind?" I ask . . . sort of hating myself even as the words are coming out of my mouth. Because it's totally obvious from this conversation that marriage is the last thing on Luke's mind.

And it's ridiculous that it's on my mind. At all. I mean, I have so many other things to worry about besides getting married. Like making a name for myself in my chosen field. Or even getting a *paying job* in my chosen field.

Plus, I'm supposed to be playing it cool. We're living together on a trial basis. Like Shari said, Luke and I haven't known each other that long . . .

But I can't help it . . . maybe because my chosen field is all about helping women who have someone who is willing to make a commitment to them do so in the most perfect gown imaginable.

And I can't help thinking that if I could get my love life in order, I'd have more time to concentrate on the career thing.

So, really, the only reason I want to get married—or even just engaged—is so I can be better at my job.

Plus the fact that Luke is . . . well. Luke de Villiers, the hottest, coolest guy I've ever known. And he picked me—ME.

"You know what I mean," Luke is saying. "The marrying kind. People who don't have anything else going for themselves. So they just get married, because they don't know what else to do."

I blink at him. "I don't know anybody like that," I say. "I don't know anybody who just got married because they had nothing else going for them."

"Oh, yeah?" Luke eyes me. "What about your sisters? I mean, no offense or anything, because my cousin Vicky's no different. But from what you've said . . ."

"Oh," I say. I'd forgotten about Rose and Sarah. Who actually got married because they got pregnant. It's like no one in my house ever heard of birth control. Except for me. "Yeah."

"I actually know plenty of couples like that," Luke assures me. "You know, from school . . . people who just don't have a life, so they glom on to someone else's—be it for money, or stability, or just because they think that's what they're supposed to do straight out of college. And trust me . . . they're insufferable."

"Yeah," I say. "I'm sure they are. But . . . some of them must really be in love."

"They probably think they are," Luke says. "But when they're that young, how do they even know what love is?"

"Um," I say. "The way I know I love you?"

"Ah." He reaches out to cup my cheek in his hand, smiling tenderly down at me. "That's sweet. But I'm not talking about us. Hey, I almost forgot." He raises his glass. "To the new job."

"Oh," I say, a little surprised. My new job is the last thing on my mind at the moment. "Thanks."

We clink rims.

I'm not talking about us, he'd said. That's something, isn't it? That he believes we're different. Because we *are* different.

"Want to set the table?" Luke asks, as he checks the coq au vin—which is filling the apartment with such delicious aromas that I suspect Mrs. Erickson, from 5B, will be knocking soon, to ask if she can have a bite. "I think this is going to be ready in a minute or two."

"Sure," I say—then, with elaborate casualness as I hop down from the stool and walk over to the case on the sideboard where Mrs. de Villiers keeps her silver—not her silverWARE. Her silver. Which has to be hand-washed after use, and put back in its special antitarnish cloth-lined case—so I can set the table, "So if he isn't proposing, what is it?"

"What is what?" Luke wants to know.

"What Chaz told you not to tell me," I say.

"Oh." Luke laughs. "You promise not to say anything to Shari?"

I nod.

"He's thinking about surprising her with a cat. From the animal shelter. You know. For the two of them. Because Shari loves animals so much."

I blink at him. Because Shari doesn't love animals. Chaz does. Chaz must be thinking about getting a cat for himself. Which isn't a wonder. I mean, he's alone so much, with Shari working all the time, he probably just wants some company. I kind of know the feeling, with Luke in classes all day.

But I don't say this out loud. Instead I smile and say, "Oh."

"Remember, don't tell her," Luke warns me. "You'll ruin the surprise."

"Oh, don't worry," I lie. "I won't tell her."

Because you *have* to tell your best friend when her boyfriend is planning on surprising her with a pet. Any other course of action is unthinkable.

Jeez. Guys really *are* weird.

Know your . . .
Bridal-gown necklines!

Halter neck—This cut features straps of material that join at the back of the neck. While it looks great on women with nice shoulders, it is usually cut low in back, making finding a bra difficult.

Scoop or round neckline—U-shaped neckline, often cut similarly low in both front and back. Flattering on just about anyone!

Sweetheart neckline—A heart-shaped neckline that is low in front and high in back.

Queen Anne neckline—This is a more accentuated version of the sweetheart neckline.

Off-the-shoulder neckline—This style features small sleeves or straps which actually sit just below the shoulder, leaving the shoulders and collarbone bare. This is not an ideal look for brides with wide shoulders, but it works nicely for curvy brides with full or medium-sized bosoms.

Strapless—This figure-hugging bodice has no straps or sleeves. Fuller-figured or broad-shouldered brides often look best in this style.

V-neck—Just like it sounds! This neckline dips to a V shape in front, which deemphasizes a large bustline.

Square—Again, just like it sounds. A neckline shaped like a square, and one that looks good on nearly everyone!

Bateau—This wide-necked look follows the collarbone to the edge of the shoulders, where the front and back panels join.

Jewel—Round and high cut, this style is good for small-busted brides, or those who belong to churches that frown on showing the upper chest and collarbone area for reasons of modesty.

Asymmetrical—This neckline, different on one side than it is on the other, often precludes its wearer from being able to find a suitable bra. Unless your dressmaker can put in built-in support, you're going to have to wear a strapless bra or go braless if you choose this design . . . and is that really the first impression you want to give your future in-laws?

Lizzie Nichols Designs™

• Chapter 10 •

Officially, the office of Pendergast, Loughlin, and Flynn doesn't open for business until nine A.M.

Unofficially, the phones start ringing at eight sharp. Which is why they need the receptionist there early, ready to transfer calls.

I'm in the fancy black leather swivel chair (with wheels on it) behind the reception desk, trying to grasp what Tiffany, the afternoon receptionist (no, really. That's her name. I thought she was making it up, but when she got up to get us coffee from the high-tech kitchen in the back, I peeked in the drawers on either side of the desk, and I saw that, in addition to twenty different shades of fingernail polish and about thirty different samples of lipstick, she's crammed all her pay stubs in there, and I read one, and it said, right there, in pink and black, "Tiffany Dawn Sawyer"), is explaining to me.

"Okay," Tiffany says. She is supposed to be a model when she isn't working behind the reception desk at Pendergast, Loughlin, and Flynn, and I believe it, because her skin is as clear and as smooth as porcelain, her hair is a lustrous shoulder-length curtain of tawny gold, she's six feet tall, and she looks as if she weighs about a hundred and twenty pounds—especially after a big breakfast like the one she's enjoying at the moment, courtesy of Pendergast, Loughlin, and Flynn's kitchens, black coffee and a pack of cherry Twizzlers.

"So, like, when you get a call," Tiffany explains, her carefully made-up eyes heavy-lidded, because, as she's already explained to me, she drank "way too many mojitos" last night, and she's "still wasted," "you ask who's calling, and then you tell them to hold, and then you press the transfer button, and then you put in the person's extension, and then when that person picks up, you say who's calling, and if the person says he'll talk to whoever is calling, you press send, and if the person says he doesn't want to talk to whoever is calling, or if he doesn't pick up, you hit the line the caller is on, and you take a message."

Tiffany takes a deep breath, then adds gravely, "I know it's rilly complicated. That's why they asked me to come in early today so I could sit here with you and make sure you get the hang of it. So don't, like, panic, or anything."

I look at the two-sided typed list of extensions that Roberta from human resources has helpfully shrunk down to palm size, then sealed in clear contact paper, so I can't stain or tear it. There are over a hundred names on it.

"Transfer, extension, say who's calling, send or take a message," I say. "Right."

Tiffany's ocean-blue eyes widen in surprise. "Good. You got it. God. It took me like a week to get that."

"Well," I say, not wanting to hurt her feelings. Tiffany has already told me her life story—she left her home in North Dakota right after high school graduation to come to the big city to model; in the four years since, she's done a lot of print work, including the annual fall Nordstrom catalog; lives with a photographer she met in a bar, who's promised to get her more print work and is "like, married, but, like, she's a total bitch. Only he can't divorce her 'cause he's from, like, Argentina, and the INS is breathing down his neck, so he's got to, like, pretend the whole thing is for real for a while longer. As long as he keeps paying for her place in Chelsea she'll lie that they're still together, but really she's living with her personal trainer. But as soon as he gets his green card, it's over. Then he's going to marry me"; and dislikes the flavor grape—and I don't want to make her feel bad, on account of the fact that she only has a high school diploma, and I'm a college graduate (well, practically), and so naturally I'm going to catch on to things a little faster than she is. "It *is* hard."

"Ooooh, here's a call," Tiffany says, as the phone chirps softly. The ringers in the offices of Pendergast, Loughlin, and Flynn are kept at a very low volume, so as not to annoy the partners—who, according to Tiffany, are extremely high-strung, due to their demanding hours and jobs—or the clients, who are extremely high-strung due to the hourly rates they are paying for legal help from Pendergast, Loughlin, and Flynn. "So, answer it, just like I told you."

I pick up the receiver and say confidently, "Pendergast, Loughlin, and Flynn, how may I direct your call?"

"Who the hell is this?" the man on the other end of the line demands.

"This is Lizzie," I say, as pleasantly as I can, considering his tone.

"You the temp?"

"No, sir," I say. "I'm the new morning receptionist. How may I direct your call?"

"Get me Jack" is the terse reply.

"Certainly," I say, frantically scanning my little shrink-wrapped list. Jack? Which one is Jack? "Who may I say is calling?" I ask, stalling for time as I look for the name Jack.

"Jesus Christ," the man on the other end of the line yells. "This is Peter fucking Loughlin, for fuck's sake!"

"Of course, sir," I say. "Please hold."

"Don't you fucking—"

I press hold with trembling fingers, then turn toward Tiffany, who is dozing in her seat, her lusciously long black eyelashes perfectly curled against her high cheekbones.

"It's Peter Loughlin," I cry, waking her up. "He wants someone named Jack! He swore at me! I think he's mad I put him on hold . . ."

Tiffany is on it like a frat boy on a pizza, snatching the receiver from me and muttering, "Shit. Shit shit shit," beneath her breath before leaning over me to press the hold button, then saying smoothly, "Hi, Mr. Loughlin, it's me, Tiffany . . . Yes, I know. Well, she's new . . . Yes, I will . . . Of course. Here he is."

Then her long, manicured fingers fly over the keypad, and the call—and Peter fucking Loughlin—is gone.

"I'm sorry," I say tremulously, as Tiffany hangs up. "I just couldn't find anyone named Jack on the list!"

"Stupid bitch," Tiffany says, pulling out a ballpoint pen and scribbling something on the list Roberta gave me. Passing the list back to me, she sees my alarmed expression, and laughs. "Not you. That whore, Roberta. She thinks she's so great, because she went to an Ivy League college. Like, so what? All it got her was a job scheduling people's vacations. A monkey could do that. Big fuckin' whoop."

I blink down at the change Tiffany's made on my list. She's crossed out the first name "John" in front of the last name "Flynn" and written "Jack" over it. Because she'd used a ballpoint to write over clear contact paper, the change is barely legible.

"John Flynn's real name is Jack?" I ask.

"No. It's John. But he calls himself Jack, and so does everybody else," Tiffany assures me. "I don't know why Roberta put his real name instead of what people actually call him. Maybe because she wants to fuck with you. Roberta's totally jealous of girls who are better looking than she is. You know, since she looks like a horse-faced troll."

"Oh, there you are!" Roberta cries, as she pushes open the glass door from the elevator lobby and steps into the reception area. She's wearing a trench coat—from the lining, I can tell it's Burberry—and carrying a briefcase. For someone who only "schedules people's vacations," she looks superbusinesslike. "Everything all right? Tiffany showing you the ropes?"

"Yes," I say, throwing Tiffany a panicky look. What if Roberta overheard her calling her a horse-faced troll?

But Tiffany doesn't look the least bit worried. She's fished a nail file from one of the many drawers into which she's crammed her personal belongings, and is working on one of her gel tips.

"How are you this morning, Roberta?" Tiffany inquires sweetly as she files.

"I'm great, Tiffany." Roberta, now that I look at her, does sort of resemble a horse. She has a really long face, and superbig teeth. And she's kind of short and has terrible posture, making her, truth be told, a little bit troll-like. "Thanks so much for helping us out by pulling a double today in order to train Lizzie. We really appreciate it."

"I'm making time and a half after two o'clock, right?" Tiffany wants to know.

"Of course," Roberta says, her smile tightening perceptibly. "Just like we discussed."

Tiffany shrugs. "Then it's all good," she says in a syrupy-sweet voice.

Roberta's smile tightens even more. "Great," she says. "Lizzie, if you—"

The phone chirps. I leap upon it. "Pendergast, Loughlin, and Flynn," I say into the receiver. "How may I direct your call?"

"I have Leon Finkle for Marjorie Pierce," a woman's voice purrs.

"One moment please," I say, and press the transfer button. Then, highly aware that Roberta is watching my every move, I find Marjorie Pierce's extension on my cheat sheet, press the numbers, then say, when a voice on the other end picks up, "Leon Finkle for Marjorie Pierce?"

"I'll take the call," the voice says. And I press send and watch as the little red light by the transfer buttons disappears. Done. I hang up.

"Very nice," Roberta says, looking impressed. "It took Tiffany weeks to even learn that much."

The look Tiffany darts Roberta would have frozen the hottest mochaccino. "I didn't have as good an instructor as Lizzie does," she says coldly.

Roberta gives us another brittle smile and says, "Well, carry on. And, Lizzie, I'll need you to stop by my office before you leave so you can fill out those forms to get you on our insurance."

"I'll do that," I say, and since the phone is chirping again, leap to seize the receiver. "Pendergast, Loughlin, and Flynn," I say.

"Jack Flynn, please," a voice on the other end of the phone says. "Terry O'Malley calling."

"One moment, please," I say, and press transfer.

"Stupid fucking bitch," Tiffany is muttering beneath her breath, as she nibbles a Twizzler.

"Terry O'Malley for Mr. Flynn," I say, when a woman picks up Mr. Flynn's line.

"Her vagina has cobwebs from lack of use," Tiffany says.

"Send the call, please," the woman says. I press send.

"You know she had the nerve to tell me not to paint my nails at the desk?" Tiffany is rolling her eyes in the direction Roberta has just disappeared. "She said it wasn't *professional.*"

I refrain from pointing out that I don't think it's very professional to paint your nails at your job in a law office, either.

The phone chirps again. I answer it. "Pendergast, Loughlin, and Flynn," I say. "How may I direct your call?"

"To yourself," Luke says. "I just called to wish you luck on your first day."

"Oh." I feel my knees melt as they always do when I hear his voice. "Hi."

I've gotten over the thing from last night. The thing where he'd said people our age are too young to know what love really is. Because he said he didn't mean us. Obviously he was just making a generalization. Most people our own age probably don't know what love is. Tiffany, for instance, probably doesn't know what love really is.

Besides, after dinner, he illustrated *very* competently that he knows what love is. Well, making love, anyway.

"How's it going?" Luke wants to know.

"Great," I say. "Just great."

"You can't talk because there's someone sitting right next to you, right?" Which, of course, is one of the reasons that I love him so much. Because he's so perceptive. About most things, anyway.

"Right," I say.

"That's okay, my first class starts in a minute anyway," he says. "I just wanted to see how things were going."

As he's speaking, the glass door to the reception area opens and a blond, slightly stocky-looking young woman comes in. She's dressed in jeans and a white turtleneck sweater that does nothing to flatter her, along with a pair of Timberland boots. You don't really expect to see a lot of these kinds of boots in the Pendergast, Loughlin, and Flynn offices. The woman looks familiar for some reason, but I can't place her.

I do notice, however, that Tiffany has looked up from the nail she is repolishing and that her jaw has fallen.

"Uh, I gotta go," I say to Luke. "Bye."

I hang up. The young woman is approaching the reception desk. I see that she's pretty, in a healthy, all-American-girl kind of way, although she wears very little makeup and doesn't seem to mind that a layer of belly fat is resting gently across the waistband of her too-low low-rise jeans, instead of being safely tucked away inside the waistband of jeans with a slightly higher rise, as would be more flattering.

"Hi," the woman says to me. "I'm Jill Higgins. I have a nine o'clock appointment with Mr. Pendergast?"

"Of course," I say, quickly scanning my cheat sheet for Chaz's dad's extension. "Have a seat and I'll let him know you're here."

"Thank you," the woman says with a smile that reveals a lot of healthy-looking white teeth. While she goes to sit down on one of the leather couches, I punch in Mr. Pendergast's extension.

"Jill Higgins is here for her nine o'clock appointment with Mr. Pendergast," I say to Esther, Mr. Pendergast's attractive, fortyish assistant, who'd stopped by to introduce herself upon arriving at work.

"Shit," Esther says. "He's not in yet. I'll be right up."

I hang up just as Tiffany pokes me in the shoulder.

"Do you know who that is?" she whispers, nodding at the young woman on the couch.

"Yes," I whisper back. "She told us her name. It's Jill Higgins."

"Yeah, but, like, do you know who Jill Higgins is?" Tiffany wants to know.

I shrug. The woman's face looks familiar, but I'm pretty sure she isn't a television or movie star, because she's too normal-size.

"No," I whisper back.

"She's only marrying, like, the richest bachelor in New York," Tiffany hisses. "John MacDowell? His family owns more Manhattan real estate than the Catholic church. And the church *used* to own the most of anyone in the city . . ."

I swivel my head to look at Jill Higgins with renewed interest.

"The girl who works in the zoo?" I whisper, remembering the Page Six article I read about her. "The one who threw her back out lifting the stranded seal?"

"Exactly," Tiffany says. "The MacDowell family's trying to get her to sign a prenup. Basically, they're trying to make it so she doesn't see, like, a dime unless she pushes out an heir. But the groom wants to make sure her rights are protected, so he's hired Pendergast, Loughlin, and Flynn to represent her."

"Oh!" I am struck by the pathos of this. Jill Higgins looks so nice and normal! How could anyone be so mean as to think she might be a gold digger? "That's so sweet of him. I mean, John MacDowell, to hire lawyers for her."

Tiffany grunts. "Yeah, right. He's probably only doing it so that later on, when things go, like, south, she can't say she was swindled."

This seems like a very cynical take on it to me. But then what do I know? This is only my first day. Tiffany's been working here for two years, the longest any receptionist has stayed with Pendergast, Loughlin, and Flynn so far.

"Did you hear what they call her?" Tiffany whispers.

"Who?"

"The press. What they call Jill?"

I look at her blankly. "Don't they just call her Jill?"

"No. They're calling her 'Blubber.' Because she works with seals, and she's got that tummy."

I frown. "That's mean!"

"Also," Tiffany goes on, clearly enjoying herself, "because she cried when one of them asked her if it makes her insecure to know there are so many women out there who are way more attractive than she is, dying to get their hands on her fiancé."

"That's horrible!" I glance over at Jill. She looks remarkably calm for someone dealing with all of that. Lord knows how I'd react in the same situation. The press would probably call me Niagara—because I'd never *stop* crying.

"Miss Higgins!" Esther appears in the lobby, looking trim in a houndstooth skirt suit. "How are you? Won't you come on back? Mr. Pendergast is running a little late, but I've got coffee for you. Cream *and* sugar, right?"

Jill Higgins smiles and gets up. "That's right," she says, following Esther down the hall. "How nice of you to remember!"

After she's out of earshot, Tiffany snorts and goes back to painting her nails. "You know, that MacDowell guy may be rich and all," she says. "And yeah, okay, she gets to quit her job throwing fish to those nasty seals. But I wouldn't marry into that family for less than twenty mil. And she'll be lucky if she sees a few hundred thousand."

"Oh," I say, thinking Tiffany should be an actress *and* a model, she has so much flair for the dramatic. "They can't be *that* bad—"

"Are you kidding?" Tiffany rolls her eyes. "John MacDowell's mom is such a battle-axe, she isn't letting that girl plan one single part of her own wedding. Which I guess makes sense, since she's from Iowa or something, and her dad's, like, a mailman or some-thing. But still . . . Blubber doesn't even get to choose her own wed-ding gown! They're making her wear some old monstrosity they've had moldering around the mansion for a million years. They say it's 'tradition' that MacDowell brides wear it . . . but if you ask me, they're just trying to make her look bad so that John MacDowell has second thoughts and dumps her for some society bitch his mom's got all picked out for him."

My ears have perked up at this. Not the part about the society girl John MacDowell's mom wishes he were marrying instead of Jill, but the other part. "Really? Who is she using as her wedding-gown specialist? Do you know?"

Tiffany blinks at me. "Her what?"

"Her wedding-gown specialist," I say. "I mean, she *has* one . . . right?"

"I don't have the slightest idea what you're talking about," Tif-fany says. "What's a wedding-gown specialist?"

But at that moment the reception area doors open again and a man I recognize as Chaz's father—basically an older, grayer version of Chaz, only without the turned-around baseball cap—walks in . . . then stops when he sees me.

"Lizzie?" he asks.

"Hi, Mr. Pendergast," I say brightly. "How are you today?"

"Well, I'm just great," Mr. Pendergast says with a smile, "now that I've seen you. I'm really happy you've joined us here at the firm. Chaz couldn't seem to say enough good things about you when I spoke to him the other day."

This is high praise, considering the fact that Chaz, so far as I know, goes out of his way to avoid speaking to his parents when-ever possible. The fact that he called them on my behalf is enough to make my eyes fill with tears. He really is the greatest guy in the world. Aside from Luke, of course . . .

"Thank you so much, Mr. Pendergast," I say. "I'm so happy to be here. It's so nice of you to—"

But at that moment the phone chirps.

"Well, duty calls," Mr. Pendergast says with a twinkle. "See you later."

"Sure," I say. "And Miss Higgins is already here . . ."

"Great, great," Mr. Pendergast calls, as he hurries back to his office.

I pick up the phone. "Pendergast, Loughlin, and Flynn," I say. "How may I direct your call?"

After I send the caller successfully on his way, I hang up and look at Tiffany. "I'm starving," she says. "Want to order from Burger Heaven downstairs?"

"It's not even ten," I point out.

"Whatever, I'm so hungover I could die. I need some grease in my stomach or I'll york."

"You know what?" I say to Tiffany. "I really think I'm getting the hang of this. You can leave if you want."

But Tiffany doesn't take the hint. "And give up time and a half? No, thanks. I'm getting a double cheeseburger. You want one?"

I sigh . . . and give in. Because it looks like it's going to be a long day. And the truth is, I can tell I'm going to need the protein.

Lizzie Nichols's Wedding Gown Guide

Okay, big girls, don't think I've forgotten you! Designers may have—so many dressmakers seem scared to take on those of us who are size sixteen or higher.

But there's really no need, because large-size women CAN look great in a wedding gown . . . if they pick the right one! The best option is to go for a fitted bodice with an A-line skirt.

Full skirts are out on the plus-side bride, as they tend to make wide hips look even wider, as do column or sheath skirts. But an A-line skirt that gently skims the contours is a flattering look on a larger girl. Strapless gowns are not usually recommended for very large brides as they require a very fitted bodice that can be unflattering to someone with a sizable belly. But this varies from body shape to body shape.

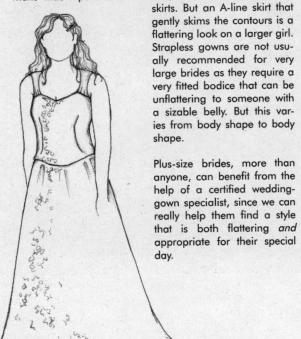

Plus-size brides, more than anyone, can benefit from the help of a certified wedding-gown specialist, since we can really help them find a style that is both flattering *and* appropriate for their special day.

LIZZIE NICHOLS DESIGNS™

• Chapter 11 •

To find out a girl's faults, praise her to her girlfriends.

—Benjamin Franklin (1706–1790), American inventor

The dwarf is singing "Don't Cry Out Loud."

"I don't know about anyone else," Chaz says, "but I find his performance exceptionally moving. I give it an eight."

"Seven," Luke says. "I find the fact that he's *actually* crying a little distracting."

"I give it a ten," I say, blinking back tears of my own. I don't know if it's that all Melissa Manchester songs make me a little nostalgic, or if it's the fact that this particular one is being sung so poignantly by a weeping dwarf dressed like Frodo from *Lord of the Rings*, complete with a Gandalf staff. Maybe it's the three Tsingtaos I had with dinner, and the two Amaretto sours I've downed since, here in the booth. But I'm gone.

The same can't be said of my best friend Shari, however. She's picking at the label of her Bud Light, looking distracted—pretty much how she's been all night.

"Hey," I say, nudging her with my elbow. "Come on. How do you rate his performance?"

"Uh." Shari sweeps some of her curly dark hair from her eyes and peers at the man on the little stage at the back of the bar. "I don't know. A six."

"Harsh," Chaz says, shaking his head. "Look at him. He's singing his guts out."

"That's just it," Shari says. "He's taking it too seriously. It's *karaoke*."

"Karaoke is an art form in many cultures," Chaz says. "And, as such, should be taken seriously."

"Not," Shari says, "at a dive bar called Honey's in Midtown."

The tenor of Shari's voice has changed. Chaz is just being playful, but she sounds genuinely annoyed.

Then again, she's seemed that way ever since she and Chaz arrived at the Thai place downtown where we met to have dinner. No matter what Chaz says, Shari either disagrees or ignores him. She even berated him for ordering too much food . . . as if there *is* such a thing.

"It's probably just stress," I had said to Luke, as the two of us walked slightly behind Chaz and Shari on our way toward Canal Street, dodging fish guts that had been tossed into the gutters by the Chinese markets on either side of the street. "You know how hard she's been working lately."

"You've been working pretty hard yourself," Luke had replied. "And *you* aren't acting like a grade-A—"

"Hey, now," I'd interrupted. "Come on. Her job is slightly more stressful than mine. She's dealing with women whose *lives* are at stake. The only thing the women I work with have at stake is whether or not their butt is going to look big on their wedding day."

"That can be stressful," Luke had insisted with touching loyalty. "You shouldn't put yourself down."

But the truth is, I don't actually believe what's bothering Shari is work stress. Because if it was just that, the delicious piles of pad thai and beef satay we'd just consumed—not to mention all that beer—would have helped. But it hadn't. She's as cranky now, after dinner, as she'd been before dinner. She hadn't even wanted to come to Honey's. She'd wanted to go straight home to bed. Chaz had practically forced her into the cab with us, instead of letting her find a separate one to take her back to their place.

"I just don't get it," Chaz had said to us after Shari excused herself to go to the bathroom between courses at dinner. "I know she's unhappy. But when I ask her what's wrong, she says everything's fine and that I should leave her alone."

"That's the same thing she says to me," I'd said with a sigh.

"Maybe it's hormonal," Luke had suggested. Which, considering all the bio he was taking, was a natural leap.

"For six weeks?" Chaz had shaken his head. "Because that's how long it's been. Ever since she started that job . . . and moved in with me."

I'd swallowed. It was all my fault. I just knew it. If I had just moved in with Shari like I'd promised, instead of ditching her to live with Luke, none of this would have happened . . .

"If you think you can do so much better," Chaz is saying now, shoving the songbook across the table of the booth we're sitting in, "why don't you give it a whirl?"

Shari looks down at the black binder in front of her. "I don't do karaoke," she says coldly.

"Um, that's not what I recall," Luke says, waggling his dark eyebrows. "At least, not from a certain wedding I remember . . ."

"That," Shari says dourly, "was a special occasion. I was just trying to help out Big Mouth over there."

I blink. *Big Mouth?* I mean, I know it's true and all . . . but I've been getting better. Really. I haven't told ANYONE about meeting Jill Higgins. And I've managed to keep from Luke the fact that his mother's lover (if that's who the guy even is . . . which, more and more, I'm starting to suspect) has called the *apartment yet again.* I'm a veritable vault of incendiary information!

But I decide to cut Shari some slack. Because I did leave her in the lurch and all.

"Come on, Shari," I say, reaching for the binder. "I'll find us something fun to sing. What do you say?"

"Count me out," Shari says. "I'm too tired."

"You can never be too tired for karaoke," Chaz says. "All you have to do is stand up there and read from a teleprompter."

"*I'm too tired,*" Shari says again, this time more adamantly.

"Look," Luke says, "somebody has to get up there and sing something. Otherwise, Frodo is going to perform another ballad. And then I'll have to slit my wrists."

I've started flipping through the binder. "I'll do it," I say. "I can't let my boyfriend commit suicide."

"Thanks, honey," Luke says, winking at me. "That's so nice of you."

I've found the song I want and am filling out the little slip of paper you're supposed to give to the waitress if you want to sing. "If I do this," I say, "you guys have to do one, too. Luke and Chaz, I mean."

Chaz looks solemnly at Luke. "'Wanted Dead or Alive'?"

"No," Luke says, shaking his head vehemently. "No way."

"Come on," I say. "If I'm doing it, you guys have to—"

"No." Luke is laughing now. "I do not do karaoke."

"You have to," I say gravely. "Because if you don't, we'll be subjected to more of that." I nod toward a group of giggly twentysomethings, each wearing the light-up penis necklaces and slackly drunken expressions that give away the fact that they are part of a bachelorette party—as if the fact that they're screeching "Summer Lovin'" from *Grease* into a single microphone is not evidence enough.

"They are making a mockery of the karaoke," Chaz agrees, pronouncing "karaoke" with the correct Japanese inflection.

"'Nother round?" the waitress, wearing an adorable red silk mandarin dress, with a not-so-adorable metal bar through her lower lip, wants to know.

"Four more," I say, sliding two song slips toward her. "And two songs, please."

"No more for me," Shari says. She holds up her mostly full beer bottle. "I'm good."

The waitress nods and takes my song slips. "Three more, then," she says, and goes away.

"What did you mean, *two* songs?" Luke asks me suspiciously. "You didn't—"

"I want to hear you sing that you're a cowboy," I say, my eyes wide with innocence. "And that on a steel horse you ride . . ."

Luke's mouth twists with suppressed mirth. "*You*—" He lunges at me, but I shrink against Shari, who goes, "Stop it."

"Save me," I say to Shari.

"Seriously," she says. "Cut it out."

"Oh, come on, Share," I say, laughing. What's wrong with her? She used to love goofing around in dive bars. "Sing with me."

"You're so annoying," she says.

"Sing with me," I beg. "For old times' sake."

"Get out," Shari says, giving me a shove toward the end of the bench we were sitting on. "I have to go pee."

"I won't get out," I say, "unless you sing with me."

Shari pours her beer over my head.

Later, in the ladies' room, she apologizes. Abjectly.

"Seriously," she says, sniffling as she watches me stick my head beneath the hand dryer. "I am so, so sorry. I don't know what came over me."

"It's okay." I can barely hear her above the roar of the hand dryer—not to mention the keening of the bachelorettes onstage. "Seriously."

"No," Shari says. "It's not okay. I'm a terrible person."

"You're not a terrible person," I say. "I was being a jerk."

"Well." Shari is leaning against the radiator. The ladies' room at Honey's is not what anyone would call the height of chic decor. There is one sink and one toilet, and the walls have been covered in vomit-beige paint that does little to hide the layers of graffiti beneath it. "You *were* being a jerk. But not any more than usual. I'm the one who's turned into such a massive bitch. I seriously don't know what's wrong with me."

"Is it your job?" I ask. The hand dryer is solving the problem of my wet hair. But it isn't doing much for the beery smell coming from my Vicky Vaughn Junior minidress. That's something I'm going to have to tackle with the Febreze bottle when I get home.

"It's not my job," Shari says mournfully. "I love my job."

"You do?" I can't hide my surprise. All Shari ever seems to do is complain about her hours and workload.

"I do," she says. "That's the problem . . . I'd rather be there than at home, any day."

I open my double-flap seventies Meyers handbag (in stunning lime-green vinyl, only thirty-five dollars with my Vintage to Vavoom employee discount) to look for something—anything—that I could spray on myself to get rid of the beery smell. "Is that because you love your job so much?" I ask carefully. "Or because you don't love Chaz anymore?"

Shari's face crumples. She puts her hands over it to hide her tears.

"Oh, Share." My heart twisting, I step away from the hand dryer to put my arms around her. Through the door, I can hear the thump-thump-thump of the bass as the bachelorettes shriek that it's up to you, New York, New York.

"I don't know what happened," Shari sobs. "I just feel like whenever I'm with him, I'm suffocating. And even when he's not around . . . it's like he's smothering me."

I am trying to be understanding. Because that's how best friends are with each other.

But I've known Chaz for a long time. And he has so never been the suffocating or smothering type. In fact, it would be hard to find a more happy-go-lucky guy. I mean, except when he's jabbering on about Kierkegaard.

"What do you mean?" I ask her. "How is he smothering you?"

"Well, like he calls me all the time at work," Shari says, furiously wiping away her tears. Shari hates it when she cries . . . and conse-quently doesn't do so very often. "Sometimes even twice a day!"

I blink down at her. "Calling someone twice a day at work isn't all that much," I say. "I mean, I call you that many times a day. A lot more than that, actually." I don't even mention how many times a day I've started e-mailing her, now that I spend so many hours at a workstation with an actual computer, on which I'm supposed to record any notes and messages for the lawyers I work for.

"That's different," Shari says. "Besides, it's not just that. I mean, there's the whole cat thing." My revealing to Shari that Chaz was thinking about adding a four-legged friend to their domicile had resulted in her being "diagnosed" with a previously unknown dander allergy, and the sad admittance that she would never, alas, be able to live in a house or apartment with anything furry. "There's also the fact that when I get home from work, he wants to know how my day went! After already having talked about it on the phone."

I drop my arms from her. "Shari," I say. "Luke and I talk to each other about a million times a day." This is a slight exaggeration. But whatever. "And we always ask each other how our day went when we get home."

"Yeah," Shari says. "But I bet Luke doesn't spend the whole day you're gone lying around the apartment reading Wittgenstein, then going grocery shopping, cleaning the apartment, and making oatmeal cookies."

My jaw drops. "Chaz goes grocery shopping, cleans, and makes oatmeal cookies while you're at work?"

"Yes," Shari says. "And does the laundry. Can you believe that? He does the laundry while I'm at work! And folds everything up into these perfect squares! Even my underwear!"

I am looking at Shari with suspicion now. Something is wrong. Very wrong.

"Share," I say. "Are you even listening to yourself? You're mad at your boyfriend because he calls you regularly, cleans your apartment, does the grocery shopping, makes you cookies, and does your laundry. Do you realize that you've basically just described the most perfect man in the world?"

Shari scowls at me. "That may sound like the perfect man to some people, but it isn't to me. You know what would be the perfect man to me? One who was around less. Oh, and get this: he wants sex. *Every day*. I mean, that was all right back when we were in France. But we were on *vacation*. Now we've got responsibilities—well, some of us do, anyway. Who has time for sex *every day*? Sometimes he even wants it twice a day, morning and then again at night. I can't take it, Lizzie. That's just . . . that's just too much. Oh my God . . . can you believe I just said that?"

I'm glad she asked that, because the answer is no, I can't. Shari's always been more sexually aggressive—and adventurous—than me. It looks like the tables have finally turned. I have to keep myself from blurting out that Luke and I often have sex twice a day—and that I quite enjoy it.

"But you and Chaz used to, um, do it that much all the time," I say. "I mean, when you first started going out. And you liked it then. What's changed?"

"That's just it," Shari says. She looks truly upset. "I don't know! God, what kind of counselor am I, when I can't even figure out my own problems? How can I help people with theirs?"

"Well, sometimes it's easier to help other people with their problems than deal with your own," I say in what I hope is a soothing voice. "Have you talked about all of this with Chaz? I mean, maybe if you told him what was bothering you—"

"Oh, right," Shari says sarcastically. "You want me to tell my boyfriend that he's too perfect?"

"Well," I say. "You don't have to put it quite like that. But maybe if you—"

"Lizzie, I am perfectly aware that I sound like a lunatic. There's something wrong with me. I know it."

"No," I cry. "Shari, it's just . . . it's hard. It's my fault, really. Maybe you guys weren't ready to move in together. I should never have bailed on you like I did and moved in with Luke. I deserved to have beer poured on me. I deserve to have a lot worse than that done to me—"

"Oh, Lizzie," Shari says, looking up at me with her dark eyes filled with tears again. "Don't you get it? It has nothing to do with you. It's me. There's something wrong with *me*. Or at least with the concept of Chaz and me. The truth is . . . I just don't know anymore, Lizzie."

I stare at her. "Know what?"

"I mean, I look at you and Luke, and how perfect you two are together—"

"We're not perfect," I interrupt quickly. I don't want to remind her about the woodland creature thing. Or the fact that I'm pretty sure Luke's mom is having—or was having, anyway—an affair, and I haven't told him. "Seriously, Shari. We—"

"But you seem so happy together," Shari says. "The way Chaz and I used to be . . . but for some reason, it's gone."

"Oh, Shari." I chew my lower lip, frantically trying to think of the right thing to say. "Maybe if you two got couples counseling . . ."

"I don't know," Shari says. She looks—and sounds—hopeless. "I don't know if it would even be worth it."

"Shari!" I can't believe she would say that. About Chaz, of all people!

"Lizzie?" Someone bangs on the door. A woman's voice calls my name again. "You're up!"

I realize it's the waitress and that my song's waiting to be played—and performed.

"Oh no," I say. "Shari, I . . . I don't know what to say. I really think maybe you and Chaz are just going through a weird phase right now. I mean, Chaz is a great guy, and I know he really loves you . . . I'm sure things will get better with time."

"They won't," Shari says. "But thanks for letting me unload on you. Literally. Sorry about the beer."

"It's okay," I say. "It was kind of refreshing, in a way. It was getting hot out there."

"Are you coming?" the waitress demands. "Or not?"

"Coming," I call. Then I appeal to Shari. "Will you sing with me?"

"Not a chance," she says with a smile.

Which is how I find myself all alone on the stage at Honey's, assuring the bachelorettes, who are drunkenly catcalling me, the dwarf, who is glaring at me angrily for robbing him of yet more time in the spotlight, and Chaz, Shari, and Luke that young girls do get weary of wearing that same old shaggy . . . and that when they get weary, it would behoove everyone to try a little tenderness.

A piece of advice that, sadly, Chaz seems to have already employed . . . with less than satisfying results.

Fittings

Ensuring that your gown fits properly is one of the many duties of your certified wedding-gown specialist. You can help by bringing with you to your fittings the shoes, the headdress, and the kind of support or undergarments you plan on wearing on your special day. Too often a bride has not tried on her gown with the bra or shoes she plans to wear at her wedding, only to discover her straps are showing or that her gown is too long or short!

It's important as well to be at or very close to whatever weight you want to be on your wedding day at your first fitting. Gowns can of course be taken in . . . but the less your seamstress has to do so, the better. And don't even talk about letting gowns out . . . that's a whole other story, and you don't want to go there.

Generally only two fittings are necessary, but of course more can be scheduled if necessary . . . so long as you don't wait too long! Not even the most brilliant certified wedding-gown specialist can work wonders overnight. Plan on having your last fitting about three weeks prior to your wedding day— and lay off the Krispy Kremes!

LIZZIE NICHOLS DESIGNS™

Chapter 12

A rumor without a leg to stand on will get
around some other way.

—John Tudor (b. 1954), American Major League baseball player

So what are you doing for Thanksgiving?" Tiffany wants
to know.

Even though her shift doesn't start until two, Tiffany
has been showing up every day at noon, and hanging out with me
at the reception desk until I go home . . . sometimes even bringing
lunch for both of us to nibble on surreptitiously beneath the desk-
top, since food is banned in the reception area ("Highly unprofes-
sional," is what Roberta called it the day she caught me innocently
nibbling on a bag of microwave popcorn I filched from the office
kitchen).

At first I just thought this was an odd habit of Tiffany's—showing
up two hours early to work every day, I mean. Until Daryl, the "fax
and copy supervisor" (he's in charge of making sure all the office fax
and copy machines are fully stocked and in working order, and the
faxes delivered promptly to their addressees), informed me that I had
only myself to thank for Tiffany's new and improved work ethic.

"She likes hanging out with you," he said. "She thinks you're
funny. And she doesn't have any friends except that nasty-ass boyfriend of hers."

I was touched but surprised when I heard this. The truth is that Tiffany and I have little in common (save the desk chair we sit in, and a love for fashion, of course), and her potty mouth can be a little alarming at times. And I have never, for instance, seen her outside of work . . . hardly surprising, since we work completely different shifts. But not exactly what I'd call a true bond.

On the other hand, we're both regularly screamed at by Peter fucking Loughlin. And that's something that scars someone for life and therefore cemented our friendship.

Still, when Tiffany asks the Thanksgiving question, I'm afraid. Afraid that she's about to follow it with an invitation to join her and the "nasty-ass boyfriend" (so called by Daryl for no other reason— that I can ascertain, anyway—than that he is keeping Tiffany from being available for Daryl to date) for their holiday meal.

Which I'm sure would be fun and all of that, but not something I think Luke is quite ready for—to be subjected to my coworkers, I mean. So far, I've managed to keep him a safe distance from both Monsieur and Madame Henri, and the fine folks of Pendergast, Loughlin, and Flynn.

Although, considering that I still haven't told my family he and I are living together, you might say I'm keeping him from my family, as well.

"Luke's parents are coming to town," I say truthfully.

"Rilly?" Tiffany looks up from the nail she's filing. "They're coming all the way from France?"

"Uh, no, Houston," I say, after a slight pause during which I pick up, answer, and transfer a call for Jack Flynn. "They only spend part of the year in France, and the rest in Houston, where Luke's from. They're coming here for Thanksgiving so his mom can do some holiday shopping and his dad can go to some Broadway shows."

"So they're taking you out for Thanksgiving dinner?" Tiffany looks impressed. "Sweet."

"Uh," I say. "Not exactly. I mean, I'm cooking the dinner. Luke and I are. For the two of them, and Shari and Chaz, too."

Tiffany stares at me. "Have you ever cooked a turkey before?" she wants to know.

"No," I say. "But I'm sure it won't be hard. Luke's a really good cook, and I printed out a bunch of recipes from the Food Network's Web site."

"Oh yeah," Tiffany says, her voice tinged with sarcasm. "That'll work out great, then."

But I don't let her negativity get me down. I'm convinced our Thanksgiving is going to work out great. Not only will Luke's parents—whom we'll be giving up our bed to, since it is, technically, his mom's bed—have a great time, but so will Chaz and Shari. In fact, if everything goes as planned, Chaz and Shari will be so moved by the example of loving bliss Luke and I (and his parents) make, that they'll start getting along again.

I'm sure of it. More than sure. I'm *positive.*

"Your own family must miss you," Tiffany says casually. "Are they mad you aren't coming home for Thanksgiving?"

"No," I say, glancing at the clock. Four more minutes before I can leave . . . and be rid of Tiffany for another day. Not that I mind her that much, she's just . . . well, wearing. "I'm going home for Christmas."

"Oh? Luke going with you?"

"No." I'm having to hide my annoyance now. Luke's parents spend Christmas and New Year's at their château in France. They'd asked him to join them this year.

And yeah, I was disappointed about this. Not that he hadn't asked me to come with him. He had. Although he'd preceded the invitation with the words, "I suspect you'll want to spend the holidays with your own family, but . . ."

Which he had actually suspected wrongly.

But not completely. I DID want to spend the holidays with my own family . . . *and* with Luke. I'd wanted him to come back to Ann

Arbor with me to meet my parents. This didn't seem like an unreasonable expectation to me, either. I'd met his family, after all. It
seemed to me that if Luke really wanted to make a long-term thing
out of our relationship, he'd want to meet my family.

But when I'd asked him if he wanted to fly home with me, he'd
winced and said, "Oh hey, I'd love to. But, you know, I already got
my ticket to France. I got a really excellent deal on it. And it's nontransferable and nonrefundable. I could check and see if they have
any left for you, though, if you want to come with me . . ."

But the truth is, I only get three days off work at Pendergast,
Loughlin, and Flynn (Monsieur Henri's is shutting down for the
entire week between Christmas and New Year's), not exactly enough
time to fly to France and back. But—lucky me—plenty of time
to visit Ann Arbor. When I get back, I'll be stuck working—and
living—alone until Luke gets back after New Year's.

That's right. *After* New Year's. I get to ring in the New Year solo
here in Manhattan while he's off whooping it up in the South of
France. Happy New Year to me!

Not that I shared any of this with Tiffany. It wasn't any of her
business. Besides, I knew what she'd say. *Her* boyfriend had come
out to meet *her* parents in North Dakota the first year they'd started
dating.

"Well." Tiffany is heaving a sigh. "I guess Raoul and I will just
hang out at home and have take-out or something. Since neither of
us cooks."

I am *not* going to ask Tiffany and her boyfriend to join us for our
Thanksgiving meal. It's just going to be me and Luke, his parents,
and Chaz and Shari. A nice, civilized meal, like the ones we all used
to have over the summer at Château Mirac.

One fifty-nine. I am so close to being out of here.

"The Chinese place near us does a kind of turkey dumpling on
Thanksgiving," Tiffany goes on. "It's pretty good. Though of course
I miss sweet potatoes. And pecan pie."

"Well, there are lots of restaurants in my neighborhood that are serving three- and even four-course Thanksgiving meals that day," I say cheerfully. "Maybe you guys could make a reservation at one of those."

"It's not the same as being in someone's home," Tiffany says. "Restaurants are so cold. For Thanksgiving, you want cozy. There's nothing cozy about a *restaurant*."

"Well," I say. Two o'clock. I'm done. I'm out.

I stand up. "I'm sure you can find a restaurant that delivers Thanksgiving dinner."

"Yeah," Tiffany says with a sigh, getting up to take my chair. "But it's not the same as home-cooked."

"That's true," I say. *Don't do it, Lizzie,* I'm telling myself. *Do not fall for it. No pity invitations.* "Well, I have to run—"

"Yeah," Tiffany says, not looking at me. "Good luck with the wedding dresses thing."

I am halfway out the door, my coat over my arm, when I feel myself pulled back, as if by some kind of tracking device.

"Tiffany," I hear my mouth saying, even though my brain is shrieking *Nooooo!*

She glances up from the computer screen, which she's using, I know, to check her horoscope. "Yeah?"

"Would you and Raoul like to come over for Thanksgiving dinner?" *Nooooo!*

Tiffany does a good job of dissembling indifference. She really would make a terrific actress.

"I don't know," she says with a shrug. "I'll have to check with Raoul. But, like . . . maybe."

"Well," I say. "Just let me know. Bye."

I curse myself in the elevator the whole ride down to the lobby. What is the *matter* with me? Why did I invite her? She can't cook so it's not like she's going to bring anything.

And she certainly isn't going to be able to add anything to the table conversation. All Tiffany Sawyer knows anything about is the latest pump from Prada and which Hollywood celebrity is sleeping with which Hollywood producer's son . . .

And I've never even met this Raoul character, her married— married!—lover. Who knows what *he's* like. From what Daryl says, nothing that great (though Daryl is admittedly biased).

Oh, why do I let my big mouth get me into these things?

I try to cheer myself up, however, with the thought that Raoul might balk at the idea of coming to Thanksgiving dinner at a perfect stranger's place.

Although considering that this perfect stranger has an apartment on Fifth Avenue, this seemed unlikely. Having a Fifth Avenue address, I'm finding out, is like living in Beverly Hills or something. New Yorkers—even transplanted ones—are insane about real estate . . . maybe because there's so little of it actually available, and what there is is prohibitively expensive.

So whenever I tell people where I live, their eyes bulge out a little. And without my even mentioning the Renoir.

Oh well. I'm doing a kind thing. It's not like Tiffany has anyone else, not being particularly close to her ultraconservative parents, who don't approve of her relationship with Raoul. And Lord knows Roberta isn't likely to have her over for dinner anytime soon. My doing so will score me some bonus karma points, which I really need, given the amount of trouble my big mouth is always getting me into . . .

. . . a fact driven home harder than ever when the elevator doors open on the lobby level and I step out to see a familiar face at the security desk. Jill Higgins, on her way up to another appointment with Chaz's dad. Today she's wearing her usual ensemble of jeans, sweater, and Timberlands—even though the *Post* did a whole makeover spread about her this weekend, where they had a paper-doll cutout of Jill with all these different outfits to put on her, including her zoo uniform and a tacky bridal gown.

I hesitate. I've been thinking about Jill a lot—every day, practically. Well, it's kind of hard not to, considering there always seems to be some story or other about "Blubber" in the local rags. It's like New Yorkers can't seem to believe that someone as rich as John Mac-Dowell could fall in love with a woman who isn't as stereotypically beautiful as . . . well, Tiffany.

And the fact that Jill's a working girl—and works with *seals*, no less—seems to have made her an even bigger target for acid-tongued New York society. Apparently, she'll be the first MacDowell wife ever to hold a job (aside from volunteer work for charity that is).

And the fact that Jill has said she intends to keep her job working with the seals even after she's married has the matrons of Fifth Avenue (I know. My own street!) cringing.

All of which has me worried. Seriously. And okay, not as worried as I am about Shari and Chaz (naturally). But still. I can't stop thinking about what Tiffany told me my first day of work—that John MacDowell's family is making that poor girl wear some ancestral bridal gown that's been in their family for a million years on her big day.

I'm willing to bet that ancestral gown's a size two, at the largest.

And Jill's a size fourteen or twelve, at the smallest.

How's she going to fit into a dress like that? And she has to—she *has* to wear it. That whole thing about the dress . . . that is a clear challenge by her fiancé's mother. It's like Mrs. MacDowell is saying, "Do this . . . or you'll never fit in with the rest of us. *Literally.*"

Jill has got to rise to the challenge, or she'll never have any peace from her in-laws. And the press'll certainly never stop calling her Blubber.

And okay. Maybe I'm projecting. But from what I've read—and what I know, from working at Pendergast, Loughlin, and Flynn—I'm not far off.

So what's Jill going to do? She has to be taking that dress to *some-one* for alterations . . . but who? Is it someone who understands the urgency of the situation? Is it someone who is going to tell her the truth—that there is no way you can squeeze a size-twelve body into a size-two gown without using a lot of hideous panels?

Oh God. Just the thought of panels is making me shudder.

And as I stand there, watching Jill show her driver's license so that the security guard can make her a pass, I realize that I want her to come to me. I know it sounds crazy. But I don't want anybody else working on Jill's dress. Not because I'm afraid of her falling prey to a huckster like Maurice . . . although I am. But because I want her to look beautiful on her wedding day. I want John's family to gasp as she comes down the aisle, because she looks so beautiful. I want that dress to be an in-your-face to her mother-in-law. I want the New York press to take back that "Blubber," and substitute it with "Beautiful."

And I know I can make that happen. I just know it. Doesn't Jennifer Harris *love* what I—under Monsieur Henri's watchful eye, of course—have done so far to her mother's bridal gown? Even her mother grudgingly admitted during her daughter's latest fitting that the gown looks "better" on Jennifer than it ever did on any of her other girls.

There's only one reason for that: my hard work.

I want to do the same for Jill. I mean, she threw out her back *lifting a seal*! A girl like that deserves the very best in certified weddinggown specialists.

And okay, I don't quite have my certification yet. But it's really only a matter of time . . .

Only how? How can I let Jill know I'm here for her if she needs me? I can't very well slip her my business card (oh yes. I'd had business cards made up, with Monsieur Henri's address and my cell number on them), while also maintaining the level of "discretion and professionalism" Roberta told me Pendergast, Loughlin, and Flynn expects from its employees. I'm pretty sure something like that could get me fired . . . and I still need this job.

But not as much, I realize all at once, as Jill moves toward the security gate, and I spot the most hideous of all fashion faux pas— VPLs, or visible panty lines—below her waist. Oh God! VPLs! Someone must help her!

And, by God, that someone is going to be me. Which is more important anyway, my making rent or this poor, put-upon girl looking the best she possibly can on her wedding day? That's a no-brainer. I'm just going to go up to her and offer my services. We're not in the office now, I'm on my own time. And maybe she won't even remember where she's seen me before. No one ever remembers receptionists . . .

"Excuse me—"

Oh! Too late! She's going through the security gate. Dammit! I've missed her.

Well, that's okay. No, really, it's fine. I'll get her next time. If there *is* a next time . . .

There *has* to be a next time.

"So." A lanky guy in gray cords that I'd noticed hanging around one of the magazine stands in the lobby is sidling up to me.

Great. This is all I need. To be hit on by yet another guy who thinks from my clothes that I'm some midwestern rube who is going to fall for his line about how he's a photographer for a modeling agency, and do I want to go back to his studio with him so he can take some pictures of me? Because he wants to make me a star. Yawn.

"Sorry," I say, turning around and heading toward the lobby doors. "Not interested."

This, of course, is why New Yorkers have a reputation for rudeness. But it's not our fault! It's guys like this who make New Yorkers so suspicious of any stranger who tries to speak to them on the street!

"Wait." Gray Cords is following me. Oh no! "Was that Jill Higgins you were waving to just then?"

I stop. I can't help myself. The words "Jill Higgins" have this magic effect on me. That's how much I want to get my hands on her wedding dress.

"Yes," I say. Who *is* this guy? He certainly doesn't look like a pervert . . . but then, how do I know what a pervert looks like?

"So, you're a friend of hers?" Gray Cords wants to know.

"No," I say. And suddenly—just like that—I know who he is. It's amazing how hardened you can become after just a few months in Manhattan. "What paper are you with?"

"The *New York Journal*," he says matter-of-factly, taking a PDA from one of his pockets and turning it on. "Do you know what she's doing here? Jill, I mean? There are a lot of law firms in this building. Was she headed up to one of them? Would you happen to know which one . . . and why?"

I can feel my face turning bright red. Not because I'm embarrassed for having said something indiscreet. Because for once I haven't. My face is getting red because I'm angry.

"You people—" I want to hit him. I really do. "You should be ashamed of yourself! Following that poor girl around, calling her 'Blubber'—what gives you the right to judge her? Huh? What makes you think you're so much better than she is?"

"Relax," Gray Cords says, looking bored. "Why do you feel so sorry for her, anyway? She's gonna be richer than Trump in a couple of months—"

"Get away from me!" I shout. "And get out of this building, before I notify security!"

"Okay, okay." Gray Cords slinks away, muttering the four-letter word for the female sex organ that I apparently remind him of.

But I don't care.

And just to ensure he stays away from Jill when she comes out, I march up to the security desk, point Gray Cords out to Mike and Raphael, and inform them that he just exposed himself to me. The last I see of Gray Cords, he is being chased out of the building by two men wielding billy clubs.

There are times when having a big mouth and no great reservations about telling outright lies really comes in handy.

Lizzie Nichols's Wedding Gown Guide

The last thing anyone wants on her wedding day is to end up on prime-time television—you know, with one of those moments where the bride slips and a dominolike effect causes everyone she comes into contact with to fall as well, until the last person lands with his face in the wedding cake, like something on *America's Funniest Home Videos* (although there is really nothing funny about wasted cake).

So be sure to break in your wedding shoes before the big day . . . not just to save yourself from blisters, but to keep yourself from slipping, as well. Women's shoes have notoriously slick soles. You can avoid having your feet slide out from under you at an inopportune moment by applying no-skid stickers to the bottom of your shoes (on the outside, not the inside, silly).

Forget to buy stickers? Never fear! By carefully (so as not to cut yourself) running a knife blade across the sole of your shoe in a hatchmark pattern, you can also prevent slipping on just about any surface (save ice. But if you're getting married on ice, you have a completely different set of problems).

LIZZIE NICHOLS DESIGNS™

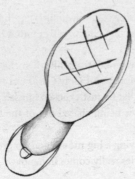

• Chapter 13 •

Gossip is dying out because fewer and fewer people care to talk about anything besides themselves.

—Mason Cooley (1927–2002), American aphorist

B y the time I finally get to Monsieur Henri's shop later that afternoon, I'm no longer freaking out about having invited Tiffany and her boyfriend to dinner. It was the right thing to do. Thanksgiving is about family, and Tiffany is certainly part of mine.

Well, my work family, anyway. Sure, she can be annoying—she's still only cleared one drawer in the reception desk for me, and she leaves sticky, half-gnawed Twizzlers *everywhere*. Plus, she's repeatedly erased my wedding-gown site bookmarks on our shared computer.

But she's been pretty nice to me, as well. I mean, she leaves all her fashion magazines behind for me to read (since I can't exactly afford to buy my own), and almost always has some little beauty tip to give me—like that Vaseline works just as well for dry skin as expensive moisturizers, or that putting deodorant on your bikini line after shaving prevents ingrown hairs.

Which is more than I can say for Madame Henri. Not about the deodorant (not that I've ever gone up to her and taken a big whiff) but about being nice to me. Oh, sure, she tolerates me.

But only because I take on a significant portion of her husband's workload, leaving him free to spend more time at home . . . a fact about which I'm not entirely sure he's that happy.

When I walk through the door that afternoon, in fact, Monsieur Henri and his wife are having a violent argument—only in French, of course, so that Jennifer Harris and her mother, who are there for Jennifer's final fitting, can't understand what they're saying.

"We've got to do it," Madame Henri is saying viciously. "I don't see how we're going to manage otherwise. Maurice has sucked away every last bit of our business with those newspaper ads of his. And when he opens up that new shop of his down the street—well, I don't need to tell you, that will be the nail in our coffin!"

"Let's wait," her husband says. "Things might pick up."

Then, noticing me, he says in English, "Ah, Mademoiselle Elizabeth! Well, what do you think?"

As if he has to ask. I'm standing there staring at Jennifer Harris, who has come out of the dressing room in her gown, and looks . . .

Well, like an angel.

"I love it," Jennifer says.

And anyone could see why. The gown—now with an open, Queen Anne–style neckline, and tight, over-the-wrist lace sleeves (with loops that go over the middle finger, to keep the lace in place)—looks fantastic.

But it's Jennifer herself who's the most beautiful of all. She's glowing.

Of course, she's glowing because I did a kick-ass job on her dress. But that's beside the point.

"Are you wearing the shoes you're going to have on for the ceremony?" I ask, Monsieur and Madame Henri's latest tiff forgotten as I hurry forward to fuss with her skirt. I've added a lace drape—to match the sleeves—at the waist, giving her more of a Renaissance-style look. Which, with her long neck and stick-straight hair, really works.

"Of course," Jennifer says. "You told me to, remember?"

The hem is the perfect length—just sweeping the floor. She looks like a princess. No, like a fairy princess.

"Her sisters are going to kill me when they see her," Mrs. Harris says—but not unpleasantly. "Because she looks so much better than any of them ever did."

"Mom!" Jennifer knows she looks fantastic, so she can afford to be gracious. "You know that's not true."

But the fact that she can't take her gaze off her own reflection illustrates that she knows it *is* true.

Pleased with the results of my labor—and Monsieur Henri's, as well. He did, after all, provide the lace—I help Jennifer remove the gown and am packing it up for her while her mother pays the not insignificant bill (although it's a lot less than if they'd bought a whole new dress, even if they'd gone to—shudder—Kleinfeld's).

I've given Jennifer her garment bag with instructions on how to steam any creases out (by hanging the gown in the bathroom with a hot shower going). Whatever happens, I inform her, DO NOT IRON it. Jennifer is so high on how pretty she looks in her dress that she just says "Okay" in a daze, and runs out to where her mother has parked the car without another word.

Her mother, however, is more circumspect, stopping beside me after paying Monsieur Henri to squeeze my hand and say, while looking into my eyes, "Lizzie. Thank you."

"Oh, no problem, Mrs. Harris." I'm a little embarrassed. It's weird to be thanked for doing something you love and would have done in any case, whether or not anyone was paying you (which, in this case, no one was).

But when Mrs. Harris takes her hand away from mine, I see that I'm wrong. Because she's surreptitiously pressed a bill into my hand.

Reminded immediately of Grandma and her emergency sawbuck (which I still have in my handbag), I look down and am surprised to see two zeroes after the number one on the bill Mrs. Harris has given me.

"Oh, I can't accept this," I start to say.

But Mrs. Harris has already swept out the door, with a promise that she's going to tell all her friends with daughters of marriageable age about Monsieur Henri. "And I'll make sure they stay away from that horrible Maurice!" is her parting cry.

The second she's gone, Madame Henri starts in again on her husband.

"And as if things were not bad enough, those boys of yours stayed in the apartment again last night!"

"They're your sons, too," Monsieur Henri points out.

"No," Madame Henri corrects him. "Not anymore. If all they are going to do is come into the city to go to the clubs, then dirty up my perfectly clean apartment—which they know they are not supposed to stay in—they are *your* boys. Because you will not discipline them."

"What do you want me to do?" he demands. "I want them to have the advantages I did not have growing up!"

"They have had enough advantages," says Madame Henri emphatically. "Now is the time to let them fend for themselves. Let them see what it is like in real life, to have to earn a paycheck."

"You know it's not that easy," Monsieur Henri says.

Has he got that right. I look down at the hundred-dollar bill in my hand. It's the first "found" money I've had since moving to this city. Everything here is so expensive! It seems like no sooner do I get a paycheck than it's gone again, first to rent, then to Con Ed, then to food, then to cable (because I can't live without the Style channel), and then, if there's anything left over, to my cell phone bill.

"Well," Madame Henri says with a sniff. "I am having the apartment locks changed. And I am keeping the key here in the shop. Hidden."

And what about FICA taxes? FICA—Federal Insurance Contributions Act (or as Tiffany insists the letters really stand for, Fucking Idiots taking my Cash Assets)—seems to eat up more of my paychecks than anything.

"How much is *that* going to cost me?" Monsieur Henri wants to know.

"However much it is, it will be worth it," Madame Henri declares. "If it means those pigs will be kept out of the place. You should see what I found in the bedroom wastebasket. A condom! Used!"

It's impossible to pretend I don't understand French when I hear this. I can't help making a face . . . especially when Madame Henri brandishes a plastic trash bag that apparently holds the evidence of her claim.

"Ew!" I cry.

When both Henris look at me curiously, I quickly wrinkle my nose and say, "That garbage smells." Because, truthfully, it totally does. "Do you want me to take it out for you?"

"Er, yes, thank you," Madame Henri says after a moment's hesitation. "It's the garbage from our flat upstairs."

I take the bag between two fingers. "You own the apartments upstairs?" This is news to me. I didn't know they owned the entire brownstone the shop is in. And I thought they lived in New Jersey. They certainly seemed to complain enough about the commute.

Monsieur Henri nods. "Yes. The second floor we use for storage. The top floor is a little flat. I sleep there sometimes when I have to work late on a gown—" Which hasn't happened, as far as I can tell, in a long, long time. Business hasn't been good enough for any of us to pull any all-nighters. "Otherwise, it sits empty. Our sons use it from time to time—"

"Without permission!" Madame Henri cries in English. "I would like to rent it out, help with some of the costs of the business—and to keep my pigs of sons from thinking they can sleep there whenever they miss the train home after a night of debauchery. But this oaf here does not like the idea!"

"I don't know," Monsieur Henri says, not looking as if his sons' alleged debauchery bothers him that much. "I don't want the responsibility of being a landlord. And supposing we get one of those crazy tenants, eh? Like we read about in the papers? The ones with all the cats, who won't move out? I don't want that."

Madame Henri responds by shaking a balled-up fist at her husband. I smile and slip outside to deposit the trash bag in the can by the stoop. With everyone in New York seemingly scrambling to find a better place to live, it's weird to hear about a place sitting empty . . . well, except for when it's used as an occasional flophouse by a couple of party boys.

"Mademoiselle Elizabeth," Madame Henri says when I come back inside. "Do you know, perhaps, of someone looking to rent a small efficiency?"

"No," I say. "But if I hear of someone, I'll let you know."

"It can't be just anyone," Monsieur Henri insists. "They must have references—"

"And be willing to pay two thousand dollars a month," Madame Henri adds.

"Two thousand?" Monsieur Henri cries in French. "That is robbery, woman! Are you mad?"

"Two thousand dollars a month for a beautiful one-bedroom is perfectly reasonable!" she fires back, also in French. "Do you know how much they are charging for studio apartments? Twice that!"

"In buildings that have a swimming pool on the roof!" Monsieur Henri scoffs. "Which ours most decidedly does not have!"

And the two of them are off and running, arguing back and forth. But I'm not alarmed. I've spent enough time with them by now to know that this is how they are. I mean, they argue all day long . . .

. . . but I've seen Madame Henri fuss over her husband's hair in an extremely loving way, while at the same time accusing him of purposely practicing unhealthy dietary habits in order to expire sooner and be rid of her.

And Monsieur Henri regularly ogles his wife's legs, while simultaneously telling her how much her nagging drives him crazy.

Once I caught them kissing in the back room.

Couples. They're all a little nuts, in their own way, I think.

I hope that when Luke and I are as old as Monsieur and Madame Henri, we can be just like them.

Minus the failing business and degenerate sons, I mean.

～ Lizzie Nichols's Wedding Gown Guide ～

It's in the bag!

Ever wonder what a bride should carry on her wedding day? Well, I'm here to let you in on the mystery:

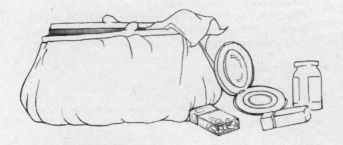

—Lipstick, pressed powder (to control shine), and concealer (in case of blemishes)—
Even if you have your makeup done by a professional, carry these items with you in a small pouch or clutch. You will need them—especially between toasts at the reception (brides, be subtle with makeup fixes at the table . . . excuse yourself for anything more than a quick check in the compact mirror).

—Breath mints—
Trust me, you're going to need them.

—Medications—
If you are prone to migraines, count on getting one on your wedding day. Migraines are often brought on by stress, and what's more stressful than committing yourself for all eternity to your lover in front of hundreds of friends and family members? Make sure you have your prescription migraine medication with you on your special day, or any other medications that might help you through the day, including aspirin, muscle relaxants (go easy on these), beta-blockers, and homeopathics like aromatherapy oils.

—Deodorant—

If you perspire more than average, especially when stressed or overheated, have a minitube of this in your bag for emergencies. You won't regret it.

—Feminine hygiene products—

It happens. Some of us will be having our period on our big day. If you're due for yours, wear protection just in case, and carry some extra for even more security.

And, of course,

—Tissues—

You know you're going to cry—or someone close to you will, anyway. So come prepared.

LIZZIE NICHOLS DESIGNS™

• Chapter 14 •

It is one of my sources of happiness never to desire a knowledge of other people's business.

—Dolley Madison (1768–1849), American First Lady

I completely regret agreeing to let Luke's parents stay with us over the Thanksgiving weekend.

And okay, I know it's his mom's apartment. And I know it's supernice of her to allow us to live in it, rent free (well, in Luke's case).

And I know we all got along great when we were staying at Château Mirac, the de Villiers ancestral home in France, over the summer.

But it is one thing to share a château with your boyfriend's parents.

It is quite another to share a one-bedroom apartment with them . . . while also having promised to prepare a traditional Thanksgiving dinner when, truth be told, you've really never cooked all that much before.

The gravity of the situation didn't really hit me until Carlos, the doorman, buzzed up to say Luke's parents had arrived. An hour before we were expecting them, and while I was in the middle of sorting through several bouquets of freesia and irises, to which I'd treated myself—as well as Mrs. Erickson from 5B—from the flower section at Eli's, and purchased with part of Mrs. Harris's hundred dollars. There's nothing more welcome than having a vase of fresh cut flowers sitting out when people come to visit—and there's no nicer gift for someone who has helped you, as Mrs. Erickson had by recommending Monsieur Henri's to me, either.

But when the flowers are purchased in bunches from a florist, and still have to be arranged, and are lying in messy piles on top of the stove while you look for vases, it's sort of hard to feel the welcoming effect. Especially when you're still in your sweats from doing the grocery shopping—which is still sitting in bags on the kitchen floor—and your boyfriend isn't home from school yet, and the doorman buzzes to inform you that your "guests" are here . . .

"Send them up," I tell Carlos through the intercom. What else could I say?

Then I run around like a crazy person, trying to clean up. The place isn't *that* bad—I'm something of a neat freak—but all of the lovely touches I'd been hoping to have when Luke's parents walked in—a tray of freshly mixed cocktails (kir royales, their favorite), party nuts in bowls, assorted cheeses on a platter—have to be abandoned as I cram the dirty laundry in a hamper, run a quick brush through my hair, slap on a bit of lip gloss, then fling open the door.

"Helloooo!" I cry, noticing that Mr. and Mrs. de Villiers look—well, *older* than when I'd last seen them. But then, who doesn't after a plane ride? "You're early!"

"There was *no* traffic coming into the city from the airport," Mrs. de Villiers drawls in her Texan accent, giving me a kiss on either cheek, as is her custom. "Leaving the city, yes. But coming in? No." Her gaze sweeps the apartment, taking in the grocery bags, the lack of cocktails, and my sweats. "Sorry we're early."

"Oh, it's no problem," I say breezily. "Really. It's just that Luke isn't home from class yet—"

"Well, we will just have to start celebrating without him," Monsieur de Villiers says, as he unveils a bottle of chilled champagne he's managed to procure somewhere along the way from the airport.

"Celebrating?" I blink. "Is there something to celebrate?"

"There is always something to celebrate," Monsieur de Villiers says. "But in this case the fact that the Beaujolais nouveau has been released."

His wife is pulling an Armani wheelie-suitcase. "Where can I park this?" she wants to know.

"Oh, your room, of course," I say as I hurry to produce champagne flutes. "Luke and I will be taking the couch."

Monsieur de Villiers winces as the cork from the bottle of champagne he is opening pops. "I told you we should have stayed in a hotel," he calls to his wife. "Now these poor children will have spinal injuries from sleeping on a pull-out couch."

"Oh no," I say. "The couch is fine! Luke and I are so grateful to you for—"

"It's a fine pull-out couch!" Mrs. de Villiers insists on her way to the bedroom. "I'll admit it's not the most comfortable in the world, but no one is going to suffer a spinal injury!"

I try to imagine how this conversation would go if it were my own parents, and fail. My parents are still in the dark about Luke and me living together, and I have every intention of keeping it that way . . . at least until we announce our engagement. I mean, if we ever get engaged, that is. It's not that they're morally against people living together before they get married. They're just against me living with someone I've only known for a few months.

Which actually says a lot about how much they trust my judgment about people.

Although, looking back on some of my exes, I think maybe they have a point.

"It's fine," I assure Monsieur de Villiers. "Really."

"Well." Mrs. de Villiers has dropped her bag off in the bedroom and returned. "I'm happy to see you've made yourself at home in there."

I realize she's referring to the standing rack from Bed Bath & Beyond—and my vintage-dress collection.

And that she sounds . . . well, *bemused* about it.

And not necessarily in a good way.

"Oh," I say. "Yes. I'm sorry. I know my clothes take up a lot of room. I hope you don't mind—"

"Of course not!" Mrs. de Villiers says—a little too heartily. "I'm glad you're making use of the space. Is that a *sewing machine* I saw on my dressing table?"

Oh. My. God.

"Um, yes . . . well, you see, I needed a table to put it on, and your dressing table is just the right height . . ." She hates me. I can tell. She totally hates me. "I can move it if you need me to. It's no problem . . ."

"Not at all," Mrs. de Villiers says with a smile that's, well, a trifle brittle. "Guillaume, I'll take a little of that champagne. Actually, make that a lot."

"I'll just go move it," I say. "The sewing machine. I'm sorry, I should have thought about it before. Of course you need a place to do your makeup—"

"Don't be silly," Mrs. de Villiers says. "You can do it later. Sit down right now and have some champagne with us. Guillaume and I want to hear all about your new job. Jean-Luc says you're working in a law office! That must be so exciting. I had no idea you were interested in the law."

"Uh," I say, taking the glass Monsieur de Villiers offers me. "I'm not—" Why didn't I move that sewing machine last night, when it occurred to me that Mrs. de Villiers might not appreciate having it sitting there smack in the middle of her dressing table? *Why*?

"Are you doing paralegal work?" Mrs. de Villiers wants to know.

"Um, no," I say. What about all my stuff in the bathroom? I have a ton of beauty products in there. I tried to consolidate it all in my plastic shower caddy from the dorm, but ever since I started working with a model, it's gotten a lot bigger, since Tiffany won't stop giving me samples, and some of them are pretty awesome. Like anything from Kiehl's, which I admit I never heard of until I moved here. But now I'm addicted to their lip balm.

But where would I put all that stuff, if not the bathroom? There's only the one bathroom . . . and that's the place where shower caddies *go* . . .

"Administrative work?" Mrs. de Villiers is asking.

"No," I say. "I'm the receptionist. Do you want me to move my stuff out of the bathroom? Because I totally can. I'm sorry if it seems like my stuff is everywhere, I know there's a lot, but I can really move it—"

"Don't worry about it," Mrs. de Villiers says. She's finished her first glass of champagne and holds out her glass toward her husband for a refill. "When does Jean-Luc get home?"

Oh, God. This is awful. She's already wondering when Luke's going to get here. I'm wondering the same thing. Someone needs to save us from this awkward silence—oh, wait. Monsieur de Villiers is turning on the TV. Thank God. We can watch the news or something—

"Oh, Guillaume, turn that off," his wife says. "We want to visit, not watch CNN."

"I just want to see the weather," Monsieur de Villiers insists.

"You can look outside to see the weather," his wife scoffs. "It's cold. It's November. What do you expect?"

Oh, God. This is excruciating. I'm going to die, I just know it. I saw her disappointed expression when I said I'm just a receptionist at Chaz's dad's firm. Why did she wince like that? Because she can't imagine her son dating a mere receptionist? It's true his last girlfriend was an investment banker. But she was older than me! Well, by a couple of years. But whatever, she had a business degree! I was a liberal arts major. What does anybody expect?

Oh, God. There's an awkward silence. Nooooo . . . Okay, think of something to say. Anything. These are bright, intellectual people. I should be able to chat with them about anything . . . anything at all . . .

Oh! I know . . .

"Mrs. de Villiers, I just love your Renoir," I say. "The one hanging over your bed?"

"Oh." Luke's mother looks pleased. "That little thing? Thank you. Yes, she's adorable, isn't she?"

"I love her," I say truthfully. "Where did you get her?"

"Oh." Mrs. de Villiers looks toward the windows overlooking Fifth Avenue, a faraway gleam in her eyes. "She was a gift from someone. A very long time ago."

I don't have to be a mind reader to know that the "someone" Mrs. de Villiers was referring to had been a lover. It *had* to have been. How else to explain the dewy look that came over her face?

Could it, I couldn't help wondering, have been the same man who keeps calling the apartment, asking for her?

"Um," I say. Because I don't know what else *to* say. Luke's father seems oblivious, switching the channels from New York 1 to CNN. "Nice gift."

The most expensive thing anybody has ever given me is an iPod. And that was from my parents.

"Yes," Mrs. de Villiers says with a catlike smile as she sips her champagne. "Wasn't it?"

"Look." Monsieur de Villiers points at the television. "You see? It's going to snow tomorrow."

"Well, we don't have to worry about it," his wife says. "We don't have to go anywhere. We'll be nice and snug in here."

Oh, God. It's true. We'll all be stuck inside the whole day, me cooking (with Luke's help, hopefully), and his parents . . . God. I don't even know. What are they going to do? Watch the Macy's Thanksgiving Day parade? The football games? Somehow they didn't strike me as parade or football people.

Which meant they were just going to be sitting here. All day. Slowly sucking out my soul with their well-meaning but ultimately barbed comments . . . *You really should consider becoming a paralegal, Lizzie. You'd make a lot more money than a mere receptionist.*

What? Certified wedding-gown specialist? I've never heard of that as a career path. Well, it's true you did do wonders with my wedding gown. But that's hardly a career for a college-educated person. I mean, aren't you a glorified seamstress? Don't you worry that you're wasting all the money your parents paid for your education?

No! Because my education was free! Because my dad works at the college I went to, and free tuition is one of his job benefits!

Oh, God. Why did we all get along so well in France, and yet we have nothing to say to one another here?

I know why. Because they thought I was just Luke's summer fling. Now it's clear I'm more than that, and they aren't happy about it. I know it. I just know it.

"You guys must be starving after your long plane ride," I say as I spring up, determined not to let myself sink into despair. "Let me fix you something to eat."

"No, no," Monsieur de Villiers says. "We are taking you and Jean-Luc out tonight. We have reservations. Don't we, Bibi?"

"Right," Mrs. de Villiers says. "At Nobu. You know how much Jean-Luc loves sushi. We figured it would be just the right pick-me-up for him, considering how hard he's been studying."

"Right," I say, in desperation. Desperation because I'm longing to get out of the same room with them. "I, uh, just got back from the store. I bought some cheese. Let me just put it out for you both. You can snack on it until Luke gets home and we can leave for the restaurant—"

"Don't go to any trouble on our account," Monsieur de Villiers says, waving a hand dismissively. "We can get our own snacks!"

Oh, God. They won't even let me act like a hostess. Which I guess is understandable, since this isn't even my apartment anyway.

Still. They don't have to rub it in so much.

The telephone rings, startling me from my sullen musings. Not my cell phone—the apartment phone, the one listed under Bibi de Villiers's name. The one only a single person has ever called on, since I'd moved in.

The man who leaves the disappointed messages for Bibi! The messages I've never mentioned to Luke.

Or his mother.

"Um, that's probably for you," I say to her. "Luke and I don't use your number. We have our cells."

Mrs. de Villiers looks startled but pleased. "I wonder who that can be," she asks, getting up and heading to the phone. "I didn't tell anyone I was coming to town. I wanted to be free to shop uninterrupted. You know how it is."

Actually, I did. There's nothing more irritating than friends who want to schedule lunch with you when you've blocked out the whole weekend for shopping.

"Hello?" Mrs. de Villiers says, after lifting the receiver and removing the clip-on earring from her right ear.

And I thought my mom was the only woman left without pierced ears.

I know instantly that it's the Guy Who's Been Leaving All Those Messages. I can tell by the surprised but pleased expression on Mrs. de Villiers's lovely face. Also the quick, wary look she darts at the back of her husband's head as she breathes, "Oh, darling, how sweet of you to call. You have? Well, no, I haven't been here. No, I've been in France and then back in Houston. Yes, of *course* with Guillaume, silly."

Hmmm. So Guy Who's Been Leaving All Those Messages knows she's married.

What am I thinking? Of *course* he does. That's why he only calls on her private line.

Wow. I can't believe Luke's mom is cheating on his dad. Or used to be, I guess. Which wasn't necessarily cheating then, either, because they were separated, and in the act of divorcing. They only got back together a few months ago, over the summer . . . because of me.

The question is, now that summer's over, and life's gotten back to normal—if you can call a life where you have three homes, including a château in France, a mansion in Houston, and a Fifth Avenue apartment in Manhattan, normal—will their renewed love be able to survive?

"Friday? Oh, darling, I'd love to, but you know I've blocked that day out for shopping. Yes, the whole day. Well, I suppose I could. Oh, you're so persistent. No, I do admire that in a man. Fine. Friday it is, then. Buh-bye."

Yeah. Maybe not.

Mrs. de Villiers hangs up and puts her earring back on. She's smiling in a pleased kind of way.

"Who was that, *chérie*?" Luke's father asks.

"Oh, no one," Mrs. de Villiers says casually. *Too* casually.

At that moment, I hear Luke's key in the lock. And I nearly crumple with relief.

"You're here!" he cries when he walks in and sees his parents. "You're early!"

"Eh!" Monsieur de Villiers looks pleased. "There he is!"

"Jean-Luc!" His mother throws open her arms. "Come give your mother a kiss!"

Luke crosses the living room to hug his mother, then gives his dad a kiss on both cheeks as well. Then he comes over to me and, giving me a kiss (on the lips, not the cheeks), he whispers, "Sorry I'm so late. I got stuck on the subway. What'd I miss? Anything going on I need to know about?"

"Oh," I say. "Not really."

Because what else am I going to say? *Your parents won't let me make them any snacks, they don't think I'm good enough for you, tomorrow's dinner is going to be a disaster, and by the way, I think your mom's having an affair?*

I may have a big mouth—but I'm learning.

But what about your crowning glory?

Brides have many different options when it comes to head-gear for their special day. While some brides opt to leave their head bare, others opt for a veil, floral wreath, or tiara—or sometimes all three!

There are as many different headdresses as there are brides. Some of my favorites include:

The Wreath: Nothing says "bride" like flowers . . . and a circlet of fresh white rosebuds and baby's breath never goes out of style.

The Tiara: Not just for royalty anymore! Many brides are opting to top their veil with a diamond (or diamante) sparkler.

The Band: Anything from a slim headband to a wider, highly decorated comb to hold both hair and veil in place.

The Bun: This circular band is attached to the bride's updo, from which the veil sweeps.

The Crown: Why cheat yourself? If a tiara works, why not go bigger and better?

The Snood: It worked for your grandmother. A snood is a decorative net fitted over the back of the head, generally holding back the hair in a net.

The Juliet Cap: Like Juliet wore in the famous play—a round skullcaplike hat that sits closely on top of the head, usually decorated in seed-pearls.

And, of course, the ever popular:

Cowgirl Hat: Western brides wouldn't be caught dead without one!

Which one looks best on you? Well, trying them on to find out is half the fun!

LIZZIE NICHOLS DESIGNS™

• Chapter 15 •

t's an hour until the turkey will be ready, and I think I
have things under control.

No, really.

For one thing, Mrs. Erickson turned me on to a little New York
secret—precooked turkeys from the local meat market. All you
have to do after it arrives is bang yours in the oven and baste it
every once in a while . . . and it looks (and smells) like you slaved
all day.

And it was completely easy to snow all the de Villiers—even
Luke—that this is what I'd done. All I had to do was make sure I
got up before any of them did—which was no problem, since they
all sleep like the dead—and sneak down to Mrs. Erickson's apartment. I'd had my turkey delivered to her place, where she'd promised to store it until I could pick it up.

Once I had it—and the little bag of giblets that came with it, for
the gravy—I hightailed it back up to Mrs. de Villiers's apartment,
and threw out all the telltale packaging. Perfect.

Luke got up a little while later and started whipping up his con-
tribution to the meal—garlic-roasted onions and Brussels sprouts—

and Mrs. de Villiers insisted on contributing a sweet potato side dish (thankfully minus the marshmallow fluff. Which I love, but Chaz and Shari were already bringing three different kinds of pie, because I like pumpkin, Chaz likes strawberry-rhubarb, and Shari likes pecan, and that's more than enough sweet stuff).

Monsieur de Villiers contributed by puttering around, assembling all his wines in the order in which he wants us to consume them.

So in all, everything is going pretty much according to plan. The guests are arriving. Tiffany—looking resplendent in the suede catsuit Roberta once sent her home for wearing to the office—has shown up with Raoul, who's turned out to be a surprisingly pleasant, fairly normal thirty-year-old, with very good manners—he's brought along a bottle of the Beaujolais that Monsieur de Villiers is so excited about. Apparently, he's something of a wine connoisseur—albeit of the Argentinean variety—himself.

So the two of them immediately start talking grapes and soil, while Mrs. de Villiers sets the table, carefully folding each of her cloth napkins into an upright fan pattern, and using all three forks from her silver set, placing them with extra care beside one another . . . perhaps thanks to the Bloody Marys Luke insisted on preparing for his parents—and has kept filled—since they've woken up. ("How else," he asked me, sotto voce, "are we all going to get along all day in such a small space?")

Not that his parents seem to mind. Once I moved the sewing machine, Luke's mother was all smiles. Although that might have something to do with the fact that Luke's been careful not to leave us alone together again.

Which is fine. I actually have work tomorrow (partners may get the Friday after Thanksgiving as a holiday in busy law firms, but receptionists certainly don't), so it will be up to Luke to keep his parents entertained. His mother, of course, has already made other plans (about which she's informed no one). Luke and his father plan on going to the museums . . .

... where I'll be joining them all day on Saturday, before we head off to the theater together for my first Broadway show—Mrs. de Villiers has four tickets to *Spamalot*. Thankfully they'll be leaving on Sunday, by which time I think my tolerance for sharing a one-bedroom with my boyfriend's parents will have been totally spent.

Tiffany, however, seems completely enthusiastic about the de Villiers ... fascinated by them, actually. She keeps sidling up to me in the kitchen as I pretend to be sweating over my turkey and whispering, "So ... that old guy? He's really a prince?"

I rue the day I ever mentioned the whole royalty thing to Tiffany. Seriously, I don't know what I was thinking. Telling something in confidence to Tiffany is like telling it to a parrot. Only a fool would expect it not to be repeated.

"Um, yeah," I say, basting. "But remember, I told you. France doesn't recognize its former monarchs—or whatever—anymore. And, you know. There are like a thousand princes. Or I guess counts is what they really are."

Tiffany, as is her custom, completely ignores my reply.

"So Luke is a prince, too." She is observing Luke across the pass-through, as he arranges a tray of appetizers—shrimp cocktail and crudités—on the coffee table in front of the sofa on which his father and Raoul are having their animated wine discussion. "Man. Did you score in the boyfriend department."

I'm annoyed now. Not just because it's nearly five o'clock and I asked Chaz and Shari to be here at four and there is no sign of them. Which isn't that unusual, especially since it's snowing out, and even the slightest snowfall seems to paralyze New York City ... but even more so when everyone is off work on a holiday.

Still, it isn't like Shari not to call. Or leave me stranded like this with my future (hopefully) in-laws and no comic relief in the form of my best friend.

Although Tiffany appears to be trying. Unconsciously (the comic part, I mean).

"That's not why I like him," I whisper to Tiffany. "You know that."

"Right," Tiffany says tiredly. "I know, I know. It's because of the doctor thing, he's going to be saving the lives of little children. Yada yada yada."

"Well," I say. "That's not totally why. But yeah, that's part of it. That and the whole part where he's like the best boyfriend who ever lived."

"Yeah," Tiffany says, reaching for a cheese stick from the basket of them I have on the counter, ready to go out to the table as soon as Chaz and Shari get here—whenever that is. "But, you know, doctors, they don't make, like, any money anymore. Because of the HMOs. I mean, unless they go into plastic surgery."

"Yeah," I say, slightly annoyed by this. "But Luke's not doing it to make money. He used to be an investment banker. But he gave it up because he realized saving lives is more important than making money."

Tiffany chews noisily on the cheese stick. "That depends on whose life it is," she says. "I mean, like, some lives are worth more than others. I'm just saying."

"Well." I don't know how to reply to this. "It doesn't matter whether or not he makes money, anyway. Because I plan on making enough money for both of us," I say.

Tiffany actually looks interested when I say this. "Rilly? Doing what?"

"Bridal-gown design," I say. "You know." It would help if she actually paid attention from time to time. "Or, I should say, refurbishment. And restoration."

Tiffany stares at me. "You mean like Vera Wang?"

"Something like that," I say. It doesn't seem worth it to try to explain.

"I didn't know you went to design school," Tiffany says.

"I didn't," I say. "But I majored in fashion history at the University of Michigan."

Tiffany snorts. "Oh, well. That explains a lot."

I glare at her. I only invited her to be nice. I don't need to be insulted in my own home. Or my boyfriend's mother's own home.

Before I can say anything, however, we're interrupted . . . and sadly, not by the arrival of Chaz and Shari.

"We are moving on from Bloody Marys," Monsieur de Villiers appears in the pass-through to announce. He is holding one of the bottles of red wine Raoul brought with him. "This is a bottle of the first Beaujolais of the season. You simply have to try a glass. I am sorry your friends are not here yet, but this is an emergency! A wine emergency! Everyone must have some!"

"Oh, that sounds great, Monsieur de Villiers," I say, and accept the glass he's just poured for me. "Thanks."

Tiffany takes a glass as well, then says with a laugh, as Luke's father moves away, "He's sweet."

"Yes," I say, looking after the older man, in his navy-blue sportscoat and spotted ascot. "Isn't he?" How can Bibi de Villiers be cheating on him? It just seems so . . . cold.

And completely unlike her in a way. Oh, she's very stylish, and seems to enjoy making people think that the only thing she's got on her mind is the latest Fendi bag and Marc Jacobs couture.

But I saw how her face melted a little when I mentioned the Renoir. She loves that painting—not just the person who gave it to her, but the painting itself. You have to be a little less than shallow to love a painting that much. At least in my opinion.

So what is a woman like that doing, agreeing to meet her lover (if that's what Phone Guy is) behind the back of the husband with whom she's been newly reunited?

Not that I'm about to say anything about it, though. When Luke got home the first night his parents arrived and his mother asked, after she'd kissed him hello, "Darling, did I get any messages here in the apartment? A friend said he'd left several . . ."

Luke had just shrugged and said, "I never got any messages for you. Lizzie? Did you ever come home to find any messages for my mom?"

I'd nearly swallowed my tongue, I'd been so embarrassed.

"Messages? You mean on the answering machine?" I'd been stall-ing for time, but all I ended up doing was making myself look like a bigger idiot than Luke's mother already thinks me.

"That is generally where people leave messages," she'd said, not altogether unkindly.

Great. Now she thinks I'm an even bigger idiot.

"Um," I'd said, still stalling for time. "Uh." Great. Because stam-mering always helped.

Then, as always, my tendency to babble kicked in . . . for once to my advantage.

"Well, you know," I'd said, "a few times I came home and the light was blinking, but when I pressed play there was never anything on the tape. Maybe the machine is broken or something."

To my everlasting relief, Mrs. de Villiers had nodded and said, "Oh, yes, of course, it might be. It's quite old. I suppose I should stop being such a technophobe and get voice mail, anyway. Well, another thing to put on the shopping list!"

Great. Now Luke's mom was going to enroll in a voice mail plan, because I'd made her think there was something wrong with her perfectly functional answering machine.

But what was I supposed to have said? *Oh yes, Mrs. de Villiers, this man with a sexy foreign accent left multiple messages, but I erased them because I assumed he was your lover and I want you and your husband to stay together?*

Yeah. That'd make me more popular than ever with Luke's parents.

"What do you think of the wine?" Raoul pops his head across the pass-through to ask Tiffany and me. He is darkly handsome—but not objectionably good-looking or what Shari would call a "pretty boy." He has an easy smile and lots of chest hair peeping from the open collar of his shirt . . . and he only has just the one button undone.

"It's great," I say.

"I love it." Tiffany leans across the pass-through to kiss him, practically putting her knee in my bowl of cranberry relish. "Just like I love you . . ."

The two of them are exchanging baby-talk and I'm doing my best not to vomit when the buzzer rings.

"Ah," I hear Luke say. "That must be them at last." He picks up the intercom phone and tells Carlos to send Chaz and Shari up.

Finally. And about time, too. My turkey was in danger of drying out. Just how long can you keep poultry warming, anyway? Especially poultry that's already been cooked once—or however they make precooked turkeys.

I pull it from the oven, relieved to see that the skin is dark golden in color, and not blackened as I'd started to fear it might become, and let it rest in its own juices, as the little handbook that came with it—and Mrs. Erickson, who, at seventy, knows from good turkey—advised.

The doorbell rings, and Luke goes to answer it. "Hey!" I hear him say cheerfully. "What took you so—hey, where's Shari?"

"I don't want to talk about it." Chaz is trying to keep his voice low, but I can still hear him. "Hey, Mr. and Mrs. de Villiers. Long time no see. You guys are lookin' good."

Tiffany has popped down from the kitchen counter and is now leaning her sinewy body (I'm positive she isn't wearing Spanx beneath all that leather) through the doorway to peer at Chaz.

"Hey," she says, sounding disappointed. "I thought he was bringing your girlfriend. That friend of yours you're always talking about, Shari. Where is she?"

I pop my head out the kitchen doorway and see Chaz handing over two pie boxes to Luke. The door to the hallway is closed. And Shari is nowhere in sight.

"Hey," I say, coming out of the kitchen with a smile. "Where's—"

"Don't ask," Luke mouths, coming toward me with the pie boxes. In a louder voice, he says, "Look, Chaz spent all day baking not one but two pies for dessert. Strawberry-rhubarb and your favorite, Lizzie—pumpkin. Shari's feeling under the weather, so she couldn't make it. But that just means there's more for the rest of us, right?"

Has he lost his mind? He tells me my best friend can't make Thanksgiving dinner because she's under the weather—and he expects me not to ask?

"What's wrong with her?" I demand of Chaz, who has headed directly to the bar Monsieur de Villiers has set up on his wife's antique rolling drink cart, and is helping himself to a whiskey—straight—that he quickly downs before pouring another. "Is it the flu? It's going around. Is it stomach or head? Does she want me to call her?"

"If you're gonna call her," Chaz says, his voice rough from the whiskey—and something else maybe, "you better do it on her cell. Because she's not home."

"Not home? When she's sick? She's—" I widen my eyes . . . then lower my voice, so the de Villierses and Tiffany and Raoul can't hear me. "Oh my God, she didn't go into the office, did she? She went to the office when she's not feeling well—and on a public holiday? Chaz, has she completely lost her mind?"

"It's entirely possible," Chaz replies. "But she's not at the office."

"Where is she, then? I don't understand . . ."

"Neither do I," Chaz says, going for his third whiskey. "Believe me."

"Charles!" Monsieur de Villiers has finally caught on that Chaz is helping himself at the bar—and not to the wine Raoul brought, either. "You must try the wine this young man brought with him. It's the new Beaujolais! I think you will like it better than whiskey, even!"

"I highly doubt that," Chaz says. But the liquor seems already to have improved his mood. "How you doing there, Guillaume? You're lookin' good in that cravat there. Is that what you call it? A cravat? Or is it an ascot?"

"Well, I don't know," Monsieur de Villiers confesses. "But it doesn't matter. You must come and try a glass of this—"

He leads Chaz away before I can ask him any more questions.

"So your friend's sick, huh?" Tiffany slinks over to thrust her concave stomach at me. "That's too bad. I was looking forward to meeting her. Hey, so what's the deal with all these paintings on the walls? Are they real or what?"

"Could you excuse me for a moment please?" I ask Tiffany. "I just have to, um, check the turkey."

She shrugs. "Whatever. Hey, Raoul. You should tell them about that racehorse you owned that one time—"

I hurry into the kitchen, where Luke is trying to find a place to put down the pies—no easy task, considering all the food the granite counters are practically sagging under.

"So what did he say to you?" I stand on tiptoe to hiss in his ear. "Chaz, I mean. About Shari. When he came in?"

Luke just shakes his head. "Not to ask. I think that means—not to ask."

"I have to ask," I sputter. "He can't just come in here without my best friend and say not to ask where she is. Of course I'm going to ask. I mean, what does he think?"

"Well, you asked," Luke says. "What did he say?"

"That she was sick. But that she wasn't at home or at the office. But that doesn't make any sense. Where else could she be? I'm calling her."

"Lizzie." Luke looks helplessly at all the food, some of which is still sizzling on the stove. Then he looks back at me. Something in my expression must have told him not to pursue it, though, since he just says with a shrug, "Go on. I'll start bringing stuff out to the table."

I give him a quick kiss, then hurry over to where my cell phone is charging (my Happy Thanksgiving call to my parents had worn out my battery, since they'd forced me to speak to each of my sisters, their various children, and Grandma, too—who hadn't even wanted to talk to me, as doing so required taking her attention away from the episode of *Nip/Tuck*—"I just adore that Dr. Troy"—she was watching, *Dr. Quinn* apparently not being on yet).

"Uh, I'll be right back," I say to my guests. "I just have to run to the store to get some more, um, cream."

Mrs. de Villiers—the only one, besides Luke, who knows how very, very far it is from her apartment to any store that might be open and selling cream on Thanksgiving Day—looks at me in horror. "Can't we do without?" she wants to know.

"Uh, not if we want whipped cream with our pumpkin pie!" I cry.

And slip out the door. Fortunately, no one even seemed to notice I'm not wearing a coat. Or carrying my purse, for that matter.

As soon as I get to the door to the emergency exit, I start dialing. Inside the stairwell, it's cold . . . but private. And for once I get excellent reception. Shari picks up on the second ring.

"I don't want to talk about it right now," she says. She knew it was me from the caller ID. "Just enjoy your meal. We'll talk about it tomorrow."

"Uh, no, we *won't*," I say. "We'll talk about it right now. Where are you?"

"I'm fine," Shari says. "I'm at Pat's."

"Pat's? Your boss? What are you doing there? You're supposed to be here. Look, Shari, I know you and Chaz had a fight, but you can't leave me alone with all of them like this. Tiffany is wearing a suede BODYSUIT. With a zipper that goes from her throat to her crotch. You can't do this to me."

Shari is laughing. "I'm sorry, Lizzie," she says. "But you're just going to have to fend for yourself. I'm not leaving here."

"Come *on!*" I'm begging, but I don't care. "You guys fight all the time. And you always make up."

"It's not a fight," Shari says. "Listen, Lizzie, we're right in the middle of dinner over here. I'm really sorry. I'll call you tomorrow and explain, okay?"

"Shari, don't be this way. What did he even do this time? I can tell he feels terrible about it. He's already had three scotches, and he only just got here. Just—"

"Lizzie." Shari's voice sounds different. Not sad. Not happy. Just different. "Listen. I'm not coming over. I didn't want to tell you, because I didn't want you to freak out—I want you to enjoy your holiday. But Chaz and I didn't just have a fight, okay? We've broken up. And I moved out."

～ Lizzie Nichols's Wedding Gown Guide ～

Finding the perfect dress for your bridesmaids . . .

I know what you're thinking. You're remembering all the hideous dresses you were forced by your sisters and friends to wear at their weddings, and you want to get revenge by choosing something similarly frightening, and forcing them to wear it.

Well, stop right now.

This is your opportunity to be the bigger person . . . also, to accumulate some good bride karma (and let's face it, all of us can use a little of that).

It is impossible to find a dress that looks good on everyone—unless of course your bridesmaids are all Victoria's Secret models (but even then there are going to be issues over the color of the material. Not even covergirls look good in every shade).

But you can significantly reduce your bridesmaids' angst by:

Picking a dress that flatters the most figure-challenged person in the group. If it looks good on your size-eighteen niece, it will look good on your size-eight roommate. Or—and I know this is radical—give your bridesmaids a color that you know they all look good in (black is flattering to nearly everyone), and ask them to pick their own dresses. True, they won't all match completely. But neither do their personalities. And that's what you love them for anyway, not how they look.

If you really want them to all have the same dress, pick one that they can afford, or pay for all the dresses yourself. Yes, I know—they made you pay for yours when you were *their* bridesmaid, so why should you pay for theirs? But we are RISING above their level, remember? Asking your friends and family to spend three hundred bucks or more on a dress they will never wear again (DO NOT tell yourself that they will. Surrender the fantasy, they WON'T) is unreasonable. Pick one they can all easily afford—or pay for it yourself.

Alterations, alterations, alterations. A good seamstress can fix any number of problems with fit. Employ one. And make sure your bridesmaids get to her in plenty of time for her to make any necessary adjustments.

Your wedding is supposed to be a happy time. One reason some brides have a difficult time with it is because they refuse to be flexible and to think of anyone else's feelings save their own. DO NOT BE THAT BRIDE.

Your bridesmaids will thank you for it.

LIZZIE NICHOLS DESIGNS™

• Chapter 16 •

What you don't see with your eyes,
don't witness with your mouth.

—*Jewish proverb*

t wasn't any one thing," Shari is telling me over a bubble
tea break at a place near where she works called the Village Tea House. I wanted to meet at Honey's. But Shari
said she is over dive bars. Which I guess I can understand.

But I sort of prefer red vinyl booths to velvet throw pillows on
the floor. And diet Coke to herbal tea with tapioca on the bottom.
They don't serve diet Coke at the Village Tea House. I asked. They
only serve beverages with "natural" ingredients here.

Like tapioca is natural.

"We just . . . grew apart, I guess," Shari goes on with a shrug.

I am still having trouble processing all of this. About Shari and
Chaz breaking up, I mean, and her moving out . . . and missing my
Thanksgiving dinner, which, not to brag, turned out pretty darn well.

Well, except for the part where Mrs. de Villiers insisted we all
play charades after dinner, and her team of Luke, Tiffany, and herself creamed my team of myself, Chaz (who was so drunk he could
barely move), Monsieur de Villiers (who doesn't understand anything about how to play), and Raoul (ditto). Not that I am competi-
tive or anything. I just hate boring party games like that.

Oh, and the part where I had to drag myself to work this morning at Pendergast, Loughlin, and Flynn, even though practically no one called and I was the only one there, except for all the junior partners, of course. And Tiffany, who showed up hungover (of course), claiming she and Raoul went out after leaving my place and "got so wasted" drinking at Butter with a bunch of other models (I don't see how these girls can drink so many high-caloric cocktails, like mojitos and cosmos, and stay so thin).

"I don't understand how you could grow apart," I say to Shari, shaking my head, "when you were *living with* each other. I mean, Chaz's apartment is not all that big."

"I don't know." Shari shrugs again. "I guess I just fell out of love with him."

"It was the curtains, wasn't it?" I can't help asking gloomily.

Shari gapes at me. "What? The curtains you made?"

I nod. "I shouldn't have gone with Chaz's choice of material." Chaz had insisted I make their living room curtains out of a bolt of red satin he'd found in a Chinatown thrift shop. I wouldn't have agreed—I was thinking a muted sage linen—except that the material was embroidered with gold Chinese characters (the clerk at the shop had said they spelled "good luck"), and had such a deliciously kitsch look to it that I agreed with Chaz that it really livened up the place, and that Shari would get a kick out of it.

But when I'd come over to hang the finished curtains, Shari had asked me pointedly if I was trying to make their apartment look like Lung Cheung, the neighborhood Chinese restaurant where we used to eat as kids back in Ann Arbor.

"No, of course it wasn't the curtains," Shari says with a laugh. "Although with the gold couches, they do sort of make the place look like a bordello."

I groan. "We really thought you'd like it."

"Listen, Lizzie. It wouldn't have mattered what anybody did to that place. I was never going to like living there. Because I didn't like who I was when I was living there."

"Well, maybe this is a good thing, then," I say. I'm trying to put a positive slant on things, I know. But Chaz was so devastated by Shari's moving out, it's hard not to want to see him happy again . . . even if Shari doesn't look all that devastated herself. In fact, Shari looks better than I've seen her since we moved to New York. She's even got on some makeup, for a change.

"Maybe some time apart will help you guys to figure out what went wrong," I say. "And make you appreciate what you had more. Like . . . you two could start dating again! Maybe that's what went wrong in the first place. When you're living with someone, you kind of stop dating. And that can take all the romance out of the relationship." You know what else can take all the romance out of a relationship? Sleeping on a pull-out couch with your boyfriend's parents in the next room. But I don't mention this.

"But maybe if you guys are *dating*," I go on, "the fire of your love will be reignited, and you'll get back together."

"I am never getting back together with Chaz, Lizzie," Shari says, calmly removing her tea bag from her mug and laying it on the side of the earthenware plate we've been provided for this purpose.

"You never know," I say. "I mean, a little time apart might actually make you miss him."

"Then I'll just call him," Shari says. "I still want to be friends with him. He's an amazing, funny guy. But I don't want to be his girlfriend anymore."

"Was it all the cookies?" I ask. "You know, that he doesn't have a job, and had nothing to do all day except read and bake and clean and stuff?" Which actually sounds like a dream existence to me. With all the work I'm being saddled with—Monsieur Henri has me practicing ruching . . . like I didn't master the art of ruching in eighth grade, when I realized ruching hides a less-than-flat tummy. I'm getting a little tired of playing Sewing Kid to Monsieur Henri's Mister Miyagi—I barely have time to run the vacuum once in a while, let alone do any baking.

On the other hand, I *am* learning a lot. Mostly about the challenges of parenting teen boys in the new millennium. But also about running a bridal-design business in Manhattan.

"Of course not," Shari says. "Although speaking of jobs, I should be getting back to mine soon."

"Just five more minutes," I beg. "I'm really worried about you, Shari. I mean, I know you can take care of yourself, and all of that, but I still can't help feeling like this is all my fault. If I had just moved in with you and not Luke, like we were supposed to—"

"Oh, please," Shari says with a laugh. "Chaz and I breaking up had nothing to do with you, Lizzie."

"I let you down," I said. "And for that, I am so, so sorry. But I think I can make it up to you."

Shari's straw hits the tapioca at the bottom of her mug. "Oh, this ought to be good," she says, about my offer to make it up to her. Not about the tapioca. Although Shari has always loved stuff like that.

"Seriously," I say. "Did you know that there's an empty apartment just sitting above Monsieur Henri's?"

Shari keeps on slurping. "Go on."

"Now, I know Madame Henri wants two thousand a month for it. But I have seriously been doing so much work for them—they're totally dependent on me at this point. So if I ask them to let you live in the apartment at a reduced rate—say, fifteen hundred a month—they'll have to say yes. They'll just HAVE to."

"Thanks, Lizzie," Shari says, putting down her mug and reaching for her raffia slouch bag. "But I've got a place."

"At Pat's? Living with your *boss*?" I shake my head. "Shari, come on. Talk about taking your work home with you—"

"It's actually pretty cool," Shari says. "She has a ground-floor place in Park Slope, with an actual yard in the back, for her dogs—"

"Brooklyn!" I'm shocked. "Shari, that's so far!"

"It's actually a straight shot on the F," Shari says. "The stop is right outside where I work."

"I mean from me!" I practically yell. "I'll never see you anymore!"

"You're seeing me now," Shari says.

"I mean at night," I say. "Look, won't you let me at least talk to the Henris about you possibly moving into the place above the shop? I've seen it, and it's really cute, Shari. And pretty big. Considering. It's on the top floor, and the place below it is just used for storage. You'd have the whole building to yourself after work hours. And one whole wall is exposed brick. You know how much you love that look."

"Lizzie, don't worry about me," Shari says. "I'm good, really. I know this whole thing with Chaz seems like the end of the world to you. But it's not to me. It's really not. I'm happy, Lizzie."

And just like that, it hits me. Shari really *is* happy. Happier than I've seen her since we moved to New York. Happier, really, than I've seen her since college. Happier than I've seen her since those early days back at McCracken Hall, when she first started going out with (or sleeping with, basically) Chaz.

"Oh my God," I say, as reality finally sinks in. "There's someone else!"

Shari looks up from her bag, which she's digging through to find her wallet. "What?" She looks at me strangely.

"There's someone else," I cry. "That's why you say you and Chaz are never going to get back together. Because you've met someone else!"

Shari stops looking for her wallet and stares at me. "Lizzie, I—"

But even in the winter afternoon light, spilling in through the Village Tea House's less-than-clean windows, I can see the blush slowly suffusing her cheeks.

"And you're in love with him!" I cry. "Oh my God, I can't believe it! You're sleeping with him, too, aren't you? I can't believe you're sleeping with someone I haven't even met. Okay, who is he? Spill. I want all the details."

Shari looks uncomfortable. "Lizzie, look. I have to get back to work."

"That's where you met him, isn't it?" I demand. "At work? Who is he? You've never mentioned a guy at work. I thought it was all women. What is he, like the copier repairman or something?"

"Lizzie." Shari isn't blushing anymore. Instead, she's gone kind of pale. "This really isn't how I wanted to do this."

"Do what?" I stir the tapioca at the bottom of my mug. I am totally not eating it. Talk about empty carbs. Wait—does tapioca even have carbs? What *is* tapioca, anyway? A grain? Or a gelatin? Or what? "Come on. You've only been gone from work for like ten minutes. No one's going to die if you're gone five minutes more."

"Actually," Shari says. "Someone might."

"Come on," I say again. "Just admit I'm right, and that there's someone else. Just say it. I'm not going to believe you're really over Chaz until I hear you say it."

Shari, her lips set in a straight line, stabs at her tapioca with her straw. "All right," she says, her voice so soft I can barely hear her above the pan flute music they're playing over the speakers in every corner of the tea shop. "There's someone else."

"I'm sorry," I say. "I couldn't hear you. Would you mind repeating that a little louder, please?"

"There's someone else," Shari says, glaring at me. "I'm in love with someone else. There. Are you satisfied?"

"No," I say. "Details, please."

"I told you," Shari says, diving back into her bag and pulling a ten-dollar bill from her wallet. "I don't want to do this now."

"Do what?" I demand, grabbing my coat as she shrugs into hers and clambers to her feet. "Tell your best friend about the guy you just dumped your long-term boyfriend for? When would be a good time to do it? I'm just wondering."

"Not now," Shari says. She's picking her way past floor pillows on which our fellow tea-drinkers are sitting. "Not when I have to get back to work."

"Tell me on the way," I say. "I'll walk you back."

We reach the door and step out into the cold winter air. A semitrailer barrels by on Bleecker Street, followed by a stream of cabs. The sidewalk is crowded with busy shoppers taking advantage of the Black Friday sales. Somewhere in this city, Luke is being dragged in and out of museums by his father, and Mrs. de Villiers is having her clandestine meeting with her lover.

Apparently, she isn't the only one who's been up to clandestine meetings.

Shari is uncharacteristically silent on our walk back to her office. Head ducked, she keeps her gaze on her feet . . . which is actually important to do in New York City, what with so many of the side-walks being in such a sorry state of disrepair.

She's clearly upset. And I'm upset that I've upset her.

"Look, Share," I say, trotting along behind her. She's walking about a million miles an hour. "I'm sorry. I didn't mean to make light of the situation. Honest. I'm happy for you. If you're happy, I'm happy."

Shari stops walking so abruptly, I practically run into her.

"I'm happy," she says, looking down at me. She's standing on the curb and I'm in the gutter. "I'm happier than I've ever been. For the first time in my life, I feel like I'm living with purpose—like what I do has meaning. I'm helping people—people who need me. And I like that feeling. It's the best feeling in the world."

"Well," I say. "That's great. Could you let me up on the sidewalk, though? Because I'm afraid I'm gonna get run over."

Shari reaches down and pulls me by the arm up onto the side-walk beside her. "And you're right," she says. "I *am* in love. And I want to tell you all about it. Because that's a big part of why I'm so happy right now, too."

"Cool," I say. "So spill."

"I don't even know where to start," Shari says, her eyes shining—and not just because it's cold enough out to make them water.

"Well, how about a name?"

"Pat," she says.

"The guy you're in love with is named Pat?" I laugh. "How weird! That's your boss's name!"

"The girl," Shari corrects me.

"The girl what?"

"The *girl* I'm in love with," Shari says. "*Her* name is Pat."

Know your . . .
Wedding-veil lengths!

Shoulder—This veil just brushes—what else?—your shoulders. Remember, the taller the bride, the longer the veil should be. This length not recommended for petite brides.

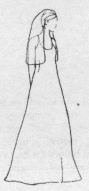

Elbow—This veil extends to just past your elbows. The more detailed your dress, the simpler you want to keep your veil.

Fingertip—The ends of this veil hit you just at mid-thigh, or fingertip length. The longer the veil, the more attention is taken away from the bride's midsection. So this length is recommended for fuller-figured brides.

Ballet—The ballet length veil extends to the ankles (presumably this veil got its name for being a longer veil that brides still needn't worry about tripping over).

Chapel—This veil sweeps the floor, and sometimes drags upon it. If you choose this length, please practice walking in it before the ceremony, to avoid any veil-snagging disasters.

Lizzie Nichols Designs™

• Chapter 17 •

There are a terrible lot of lies going about the world, and the worst of it is that half of them are true.

—*Winston Churchill (1874–1965), British statesman*

𝓘 can't sleep.

And it's not just the metal bar cutting into the middle of my back through the inadequately thin sofa bed mattress beneath me, either.

Or the fact that I can hear my boyfriend's father snoring, even though he's separated from me by several dozen feet and a wall.

It's not even the slight traffic noises I can hear through the double-paned windows overlooking Fifth Avenue.

It doesn't have anything to do with the incredibly rich meal I just had at Jean Georges, one of New York's premier destination restaurants for gourmands, which cost as much as twenty yards of dupioni silk . . . per *person*.

Or even with the fact that my boyfriend's mother came back from her day of Black Friday "shopping" loaded down with plenty of gift bags but looking oddly vital and glowing . . . especially for a woman who'd allegedly just slogged through the pre-Christmas hordes at Bergdorf Goodman. It wasn't just my imagination, either. Her husband kept looking at her and going, "What is different? You have done something different! Is it your hair?"

In response to which Bibi de Villiers merely called him an old goat (in French) and waved him away.

And it isn't even that my boyfriend and I are going to be on two different continents during our first New Year's Eve as a couple, missing that vital Happy New Year stroke-of-midnight kiss.

No. It's not any of those things. I know that. I know what's keeping me up—I know it perfectly well.

It's the fact that earlier today (or yesterday, I guess, considering it's well after midnight by now), my best friend announced that she's in love with her boss.

Her female boss.

And get this: her boss loves her back. Even asked her to move in. And Shari was happy to oblige.

Not that there's anything wrong with that. I mean, I love Rosie O'Donnell. That documentary about her gay cruise ship line totally made me cry.

And I think Ellen DeGeneres is a goddess, too.

But my best friend, who has always, by the way, liked GUYS? Not just LIKED guys, but has always SLEPT WITH guys—way more guys than me, I might add—and who has never expressed sexual interest in a woman the whole time I've known her?

Well, except for that girl Brianna in the dorm.

But Shari was really drunk that night and said she just woke up with Brianna in her bed and no idea how she got there.

Wait. Was that a sign? Because Brianna (and her boyfriend, actually) was always hitting on me. But I just told her I wasn't interested. Why didn't Shari just say she wasn't interested, like I always did?

Although Lord knows I've never drunk as much as Shari (she can afford the empty calories. I can't).

Still.

But wait. Shari always did like those foreign films at the Michigan Theater in Ann Arbor. You know, the French ones about young girls coming of age sexually, usually with another, older girl as their mentor, or whatever.

God. That was a sign, too.

And now that I think of it, there was that time Kathy Pennebaker—God. It always goes back to Kathy Pennebaker, doesn't it?—invited us over to a slumber party, then wanted to take a group bubble bath. I was like, "Um, aren't we a little old for a group bubble bath—at *sixteen*?"

But Shari, if I recall correctly, actually *joined* Kathy in her parents' bathroom, while I stayed downstairs to watch my then-crush, Tim Daly, on a *Wings* marathon.

God. I'd *wondered* what all that splashing had been about. I even yelled up the stairs for them to keep it down, because I couldn't hear what Tim was saying to Crystal Bernard.

Jeez. How embarrassing.

So, okay. I shouldn't have been so surprised.

And I guess, considering how much Shari has been talking about Pat, it isn't *that* surprising. I mean, we all knew she liked her. We just didn't know she LIKE liked her.

And what's not to like? Because, after Shari dropped her little bomb, and I stood there on the curb with my mouth hanging open like an idiot, Shari grabbed my hand and said, "Come meet her."

I was too stunned to resist. Not that I'd wanted to. I was completely curious to meet this person for whom Shari had dumped Chaz, the previous love of her life.

And, okay, Pat is no Portia de Rossi.

But she's a slender, vibrant woman in her early thirties, with a cascade of bright red ringlets going down her back, and skin the color of milk, with a quick laugh and bright, twinkling blue eyes.

She shook my hand and said she'd heard a lot about me and that she supposed hearing about her and Shari was a shock, but that she loved Shari very much, and, more important, her dogs, Scooter and Jethro, seemed to love Shari very much.

To which I didn't know what to say, except that I'd like to meet Scooter and Jethro someday.

So Shari and her new girlfriend invited me over to watch the Jets game next weekend.

I seriously don't know which is more shocking to me: that my best friend is in love with a girl, or that she's started watching professional football.

In any case, I said I'd be there. And then Shari walked me to the elevator.

"Are you sure you're okay about this?" Shari wanted to know, as we waited for the rickety two-person lift to arrive. "Because you look kinda . . . well, the way you looked that day Andy showed up at Luke's cousin's wedding."

"I'm sorry," I said. "Because I don't feel that way at all. I'm totally happy for you. That's all. I just . . . how long have you known?"

"How long have I known what?"

"You know. That you like girls."

"I don't," Shari said with a smile. "I like *some* girls. Just like I like *some* guys. Just like *you* like *some* guys." Her smile faded, and she added seriously, "It's about the person's soul, Lizzie, not the parts they have on the outside. You know that."

I'd nodded. Because that's true. At least, that's how it's supposed to be.

"I don't love Pat because she's a woman," Shari went on, "any more than I loved Chaz because he's a man. I love them both for who they are on the inside. It's just that I realized the one I'm most romantically interested in is Pat. Possibly because she doesn't leave the toilet seat up."

I stared at her until Shari nudged me. "That was a joke," she said. "It's okay for you to laugh."

"Oh," I said. And laughed. But then my laughter faded as I thought about something else.

"Shari," I said. "What about your mom and dad? Have you told them yet?"

"No," Shari said. "That's a conversation best saved for the next time I see them in person. Christmas vacation, I think."

"Are you going to take Pat to meet them?"

"She wants to go," Shari says. "But I'm trying to spare her. Maybe after they've gotten used to the idea."

"Right," I said. I tried to push down the spurt of jealousy I felt that Shari's girlfriend actually *wants* to meet her parents, whereas my boyfriend has expressed not the slightest iota of interest in meeting mine. There were much more important things to take under consideration, after all. Like, I couldn't even imagine how Dr. and Mrs. Dennis were going to react to the news that their daughter is in a romantic relationship with a woman. Dr. Dennis will probably head straight to his liquor cabinet. Mrs. Dennis will head straight to the phone.

"Oh God!" I'd stared at Shari, wide-eyed. "You know what's going to happen, don't you? Your mom is going to call my mom. And then my mom is going to find out I'm not actually living with you anymore. And then she'll know I'm living with Luke."

"She'll probably just be grateful," Shari said, "that you and I aren't a couple."

"Yeah." My shoulders sagged with relief. "You're probably right about that. Hey—" I glanced at her in some alarm. "We're not, are we? I mean . . . you never felt about *me* the way you feel about Pat, did you?"

Please say no, I was praying. *Please say no, please say no. Because I value Shari's friendship more than anything, and if it turned out she was in love with me, well, how could we be friends anymore? You can't be friends with someone who's in love with you if you don't love that person back the same way . . .*

Shari regarded me with an expression I might almost have called sarcastic.

"Yes, Lizzie," she said. "I have been in love with you since the first grade when you showed me your Batgirl Underoos. The only reason I'm with Pat is because I know I can't have you because you stubbornly refuse to love me and not Luke. Now come over here and kiss me, you little minx."

I blinked at her. And she burst out laughing.

"No, you idiot," she said. "Although I love you dearly as a friend, I have never been romantically interested in you. You're actually not my type."

I don't want to sound pejorative, but her tone seemed to imply that she couldn't understand why *anyone* would be interested in me romantically.

I didn't say so at the time, but I was kind of wondering the same thing. I mean, doesn't Pat realize that Shari is an inveterate blanket hog (as I discovered to my disadvantage when we were forced to share a sleeping bag at camp that time those mean girls threw mine in the lake) and has, to my knowledge, never once returned a book she borrowed? It was a miracle that Chaz, a known bibliophile, even put up with her as long as he did. I purposely never loaned Shari my clothing, because I knew I'd never see it again.

Of course Shari never asked to borrow any of my clothing. My style is just a little too retro for her, I guess.

But, whatever.

"You have a type?" I asked her with a raised eyebrow. "Because you seem to cover a pretty wide range—"

"Primarily," Shari interrupted, "I like people who can keep their mouths shut once in a while."

"Well, then, it's no wonder you and Chaz broke up," I said, just as the elevator, groaning with the strain, finally arrived.

"Ha ha," Shari said. Then, giving me a hug, she said, "Take care of him for me, will you? Don't let him slide into one of his funks where he stays inside all day reading Heidegger and never ventures out except to buy booze. Promise?"

"Like you have to ask," I said. "I love Chaz like the brother I never had. I'll make sure to get Tiffany to invite him out with her and some of her model friends. That should cheer him up."

"That ought to do it, all right," Shari agreed.

And the elevator doors closed and she was gone.

And that was that.

Well, except for the part where now I can't sleep a wink, because I keep replaying it all over and over in my head.

"Hey." The word, spoken so softly beside me, causes me to jump. I turn my head. Luke is awake, and blinking at me sleepily.

"Sorry," I whisper. "Did I wake you?" I hadn't been making any noise. Had I managed to wake him with my noisy thoughts? I've read that couples can become so close that they can read each other's minds. *Ask me to marry you, Luke. Luke, ask me to marry you. Luke. I am your father* . . . Oh no, wait—

"No," he says. "It's this damn metal bar—"

"Oh yeah. It's killing me, too."

"Sorry about this," Luke says with a sigh. "We just have to put up with them for one more night and then they'll be gone."

"It's all right," I say. I can't believe he's worrying about me when he has something so much bigger to worry about—his mother's secret affair, I mean.

Except of course he doesn't know about that. Because I haven't told him. How can I? He's so happy his parents are back together.

And something like that could totally sour him against marriage forever. I mean, what if he concludes, from his mother's catting about—not to mention Shari's recent abandonment of Chaz, and his own ex-girlfriend's leaving him for his own *cousin*—that women are incapable of fidelity?

And things between us have been going so well—familial visitations aside. Even having Tiffany and Raoul to Thanksgiving dinner didn't prove the disaster I thought it would, as they provided a welcome distraction for Chaz, who seemed to take great pleasure in watching Tiffany gad about in her thigh-highs and catsuit—I really think Luke might have forgotten all about that whole "people our age don't even know what love is" thing.

Maybe I'll even be getting an extraspecial present for Christmas. The kind that comes in a very small box.

Hey. You never know.

"Well," Luke says, his lips suddenly in my hair, "I think you're a trouper. You've gone above and beyond the call of duty. And hey—did I mention that turkey you made was delicious?"

"Oh," I say modestly. "Thanks."

Well? He doesn't need to know it came already cooked.

"I think you're a keeper, Lizzie Nichols," he says, his lips now moving lower than my hair, and toward some other parts of my body that can appreciate lips more than hair.

"Oh," I say in a different voice. "Thanks!" A keeper! Why, that's *practically* a marriage proposal. Calling someone a keeper is like saying you never want to throw them back into the dating pool for someone else to snatch instead. Right?

"And you're sure," he says, from down there, "that you and Shari never—"

I sit up and glare at him in the darkened room. "Luke! I told you! No!"

"Whatever!" he says with a laugh. "I'm just asking. You know Chaz is going to ask, too."

"I told you." I can't believe this. "You can't say anything to Chaz. Not until Shari's told him. I wasn't even supposed to say anything to you—"

Luke laughs—not very nicely, I might add. "*Shari* told you something and asked you to keep it a secret?"

"I *am* capable of keeping some things to myself, you know," I say indignantly. Because, seriously . . . if he only knew what I've been keeping to myself since I moved in.

"I know," he says with a laugh. "I'm just teasing you. Don't worry, I won't say anything to him. But you know what Chaz is going to say."

"What?" I ask, relenting—but only because he looks so handsome in the moonlight spilling in from the windows.

"That if Shari was going to decide to become a lesbian, why did she have to do it *after* they'd broken up?"

I yank the sheet up over the parts of my body he seems to be finding so interesting.

"For your information," I say, "Shari is not a lesbian."

"Bi, lesbian. Whatever. What's with this?" He tugs at the sheet.

"What's with the labels?" I demand, tugging back. "Why do people have to be defined by their sexual preference? Can't Shari just be Shari?"

"Sure," Luke says, looking taken aback. "Why are you being so defensive about this?"

"Because," I say. "I don't want people to call Shari my 'lesbian friend.' And I'm sure she doesn't, either. Well, actually, I'm sure Shari doesn't care. But that's not the point. She's just Shari. I don't call Chaz your 'heterosexual friend.'"

"Fine," Luke says. "I'm sorry. I've never had my best friend's girl-friend ditch him for another girl before. I'm a little confused at the moment."

"Welcome to the club," I say.

Luke rolls over to stare at the ceiling.

"Obviously," he says after a moment's silence, "there's only one thing we can do."

"What?" I ask suspiciously.

He shows me.

And, in the end, I have to admit—he has a point.

Which he makes—nice and emphatically, I might add.

~ *Lizzie Nichols's Wedding Gown Guide* ~

Feeling the glove . . .

Some brides opt for a more formal look by donning gloves on the big day. Gloves come in many lengths, and can be the perfect accessory for the fashion conscious or merely traditional bride. They have a practical use, as well—brides who wear gloves certainly needn't worry about their manicure . . . or smearing their own messy fingerprints on their pure white gown.

The most common types of bridal gloves are:

 **Opera Length**—These long white gloves stretch from the fingertips to the upper arm.

 **Elbow length**—Like the opera length, only these end just above the elbow.

 **Gauntlet**—These kinds of gloves are hand-and-fingerless, covering only the forearm.

Fingerless—Just like the lace ones Madonna used to wear. Or the woolly ones Bob Cratchitt is often pictured wearing.

Wrist—These gloves cover the hand only, like ski gloves.

Gloves should be removed for the ring part of the ceremony (it is considered ill-bred to wear rings OVER glove fingers. If your glove does not open at the wrist, cut a small hole beneath the wedding finger of your left-hand glove so you can easily wiggle your finger through to receive the ring) and of course while dining.

Brides with very muscular arms or those wearing long sleeves should avoid gloves altogether.

• Chapter 18 •

No one gossips about other people's secret virtues.

—Bertrand Russell (1872–1970), British philosopher

The Monday after Thanksgiving, we got slammed at the Pendergast, Loughlin, and Flynn reception desk. I don't know if there have ever been any official studies on this, but I would say, just judging from my own observations, divorce requests definitely go up after a long holiday weekend.

A sentiment with which I could actually sympathize, having spent mine with the de Villierses . . . who are all very charming people, but not without their annoying quirks. Like Mrs. de Villiers's annoying quirk of talking about Dominique, Luke's ex, and how happy she and Blaine, Luke's cousin, are. Apparently Dominique is doing a great job managing Blaine's financial affairs . . . and he needs the help, because his band, Satan's Shadow, is superhot on the indie metal circuit.

Another hot topic of conversation for Mrs. de Villiers is Blaine's sister's pregnancy. Vickie isn't even due until the spring and doesn't even know the baby's sex yet, but Luke's mother is already buying tiny onesies and booties and cooing over how much she can't wait to have a grandchild of her own, making Luke look extremely uncomfortable and putting back my woodland-creaturing of him weeks, possibly even months.

And Mr. de Villiers's annoying quirk wasn't much better. His was not looking where he's going and consequently putting his foot through my Singer 5050—which I purposely moved from the dressing table to the floor beneath my hanging rack, thinking no one would trip over it there, since there was a metal bar in the way.

And yet somehow Luke's father managed to destroy it . . . or at least the bobbin.

He apologized profusely and offered to pay for a new one. But I told him it was all right, that the machine was old and I'd been intending to get a new one anyway.

I swear I don't know where some of the things that come out of my mouth even come from.

Anyway, they're gone. They left Sunday afternoon, after much kissing and talk of all the fun they're going to have at Château Mirac over Christmas and New Year's. Of course, they pressured me to come along, but I could tell they didn't really mean it. Well, Luke did, of course. And maybe his dad did.

But his mom? Not so much? The smile she gave me as she said, "Oh, do come, Lizzie, it will be such fun," didn't go all the way up to her eyes. They didn't crinkle at the sides like they normally did when she smiles.

No. I know where I'm not wanted. And that's at the de Villierses' familial holiday celebration in France.

Which is fine. It is. It's totally cool. I explained I only had the long weekend off anyway, which I'd be spending flying home to see my parents, before returning to work on Monday.

I don't think it's my imagination that Mrs. de Villiers looked kind of relieved about that. I mean, that she was getting her son all to herself.

Which you would think she'd realize makes the grandchild production thing kind of difficult. But maybe she has other candidates in mind . . . ones who aren't working two jobs, one of them nonpaying, and the other hardly worth bragging to her girlfriends about. I mean, a receptionist? So not as glamorous, say, as an investment banker or market analyst . . .

Especially not the Monday after Thanksgiving, when everybody and their mother seems to want a divorce lawyer. Tiffany says the only busier time in the office is right after New Year's, which is when a lot of proposals take place, so people want to come in for their prenups.

I've said, "Pendergast, Loughlin, and Flynn, how may I direct your call?" so many times, my throat is getting sore, and I'm starting to rasp a little. Fortunately, Tiffany has come in early (as usual) to shoot the breeze, and is willing to spell me for a few minutes while I run to the ladies' room to spray a little Chloraseptic down my throat.

"So Raoul says he can get your friend Shari in to see his internist," Tiffany says, as she takes my chair. "You know, if she's still sick. Is she still sick?"

"She's not sick," I say, opening my drawer and pulling out my Meyers handbag—which barely fits in there, thanks to the back issues of *Vogue* which Tiffany insists on saving. "She and Chaz broke up."

"They did?" Tiffany swings her wide, blue-eyed gaze up at me. "Right before your party? God, no wonder he said she was sick. How totally embarrassing. So is one of them moving out? Which one? Oh my God, why didn't you *tell* me?"

Because I've been trying really hard not to mention anything about it to anyone—especially people like Tiffany who could conceivably say something to Chaz's father. Obviously Luke knows, but he's the only person I've told. I'm really trying not to be such a gossip these days. Shari asked me not to say anything to anyone until she'd had a chance to speak to Chaz about it—which I hope to God she has, because I don't know how much longer I can keep from saying anything to him when he calls the office to return his father's phone calls. Between that and the thing about Luke's mom, I am BURSTING with secrets.

And it's driving me mental.

"I don't know," I say. "Look, let me just go spray my throat and I'll be right back—"

Tiffany doesn't get a chance to reply, though, because the phone chirps and she has to grab it. "Pendergast, Loughlin, and Flynn, how may I direct your call?"

The ladies' room of the law offices is actually situated outside the lobby, by the elevator doors. To get in, you have to punch in a code. This is not to keep random tourists from wandering in off the street to use the Pendergast, Loughlin, and Flynn bathrooms, since for one thing random tourists can't even get into the building without an appointment and passing a security screening. I don't actually know why all the offices in this building keep the doors to their ladies' (and men's. The management of this building is not sexist) rooms locked, and require a code to enter.

In any case, one of the duties of the receptionist at Pendergast, Loughlin, and Flynn is to give the code to any clients or visiting lawyers who ask for it. The code is very easy to remember: 1-2-3.

And yet some clients (and lawyers) have to be given the code two, even three times before they retain it. This can be annoying to the receptionist, though of course we never show it. Still, it makes me wonder why we need the lock at all, since in all the time I've been using the ladies' room at Pendergast, Loughlin, and Flynn, no one has ever been in it at the same time I have. It's the most underused bathroom in all of New York.

The day I go in to spray my throat (and put on a little lipstick and fluff up my hair) is no exception. I'm alone in the very clean, very beige bathroom. I'm gazing at my reflection in the huge mirror hanging above the sinks, grateful that last night I finally got to sleep in my own (well, Luke's mother's own) bed, instead of on the pull-out couch, because the bags under my eyes from tossing and turning around so much are finally starting to fade. I swear, when I am a certified wedding-gown specialist with my own shop, and I finally have some money to spare, I am going to buy one of those Pottery Barn pull-out couches that don't have the metal bar across the middle, that are actually comfortable.

Well, first I'm going to buy my own apartment so I actually have a place to keep my stuff where it won't get tripped over and broken.

Then I'm buying the couch.

And I probably won't even have to worry about ever sleeping on it again, because the next time Luke's parents come to visit, they can just stay at Luke's mother's apartment, and not mine—

It's as I'm enjoying this lovely fantasy that I hear something. At first I think it's just the heel of my shoe on the tiles beneath me. But then I realize I'm not alone in the Pendergast, Loughlin, and Flynn ladies' room. The door to the last stall is closed.

I'm about to sneak away to give the person some privacy when I hear the noise again. It's kind of a whimpering noise. Like a little kitten.

Or someone crying.

I duck down to see if I recognize the person's shoes beneath the stall door. Instantly I realize I'm looking at the feet of Jill Higgins, New York's current most famous bride-to-be. Because on those feet are a pair of Timberlands.

And nobody wears Timberlands to Pendergast, Loughlin, and Flynn but Jill.

Who is apparently taking a break in the bathroom to cry for a while before her next appointment with Chaz's dad.

I know, as an employee of the firm, I should quietly leave the ladies' room, and pretend like I never heard what I'm hearing.

But as a not-yet-certified wedding-gown specialist—and more important, a girl who knows what it's like to be constantly ragged upon (as my sisters have ragged upon me for my entire existence)— I can't just turn and walk away. Especially since I know—I just *know*—I can help her. I really can.

Which would explain why I walk over to the door of her stall and quietly tap on it—although I'll admit, my heart was thumping. I really need this job, after all.

"Um . . . Miss Higgins?" I call through the stall door. "It's me, Lizzie. The receptionist?"

"Oh . . ."

I've never heard so much emotion piled into a single word. That "oh" is laden with fear—I guess about what I'm going to say or do, having caught John MacDowell's fiancée weeping in the bathroom. Am I going to call the press? Pass her a box of Kleenex? Run and get Esther? What?—regret, self-loathing, embarrassment, and even what sounds like a healthy dose of mortification.

"It's okay," I say through the door. "I mean, I sometimes feel like crying in here myself. In fact, most days."

This elicits a burble of laughter from the woman in the stall. But it's a tearful burble.

"Do you want me to get you something?" I ask. "Like tissues? Or a diet Coke?" I don't know why I thought she might want the latter. It's just that a nice cold diet Coke always makes me feel better. Except hardly anyone ever offers me one.

"No-oo-oo," Jill says in a tremulous voice. "I'm okay. I think. It's just—"

And before I know it, she's off—*really* crying this time, in big huge gasping baby sobs.

"Whoa," I say. Because I know what it's like to cry like that. I've been there. I've done that.

And I know there's only one thing that ever makes me feel better when I've got that big a crying jag going on.

"Hang on," I say to Jill through the stall door. "I'll be right back."

I run out of the bathroom. Then, so as to avoid Tiffany (who, after all, is probably wondering what happened to me. Especially since she doesn't technically start work for half an hour, and I've left her sitting in my chair, answering all the calls that I should be picking up), I zip through the locked back door to the office (code to get in: 1-2-3), and hurry into the Pendergast, Loughlin, and Flynn kitchen.

There, I seize an armful of items—under the watchful gaze of an intern on a coffee break—and hurry back to the ladies' room, where I find Jill still lustily weeping.

"Hang on," I say, setting my armful of pilfered treats down on the counter by the sinks. "I'm coming." I survey the assortment before me. I really don't have time to make a careful selection. I can see that urgent help is needed, and right away. I grab the first plastic-wrapped confection I see, and kneel down beside the stall to hand it through the gap beneath the door.

"Here," I say. "Drake's Yodels. Dig in."

There is stunned silence for a moment. I wonder if maybe I have just committed a huge faux pas. But hey, when I cry, Shari always gives me chocolate. And it makes me feel better *immediately*.

Well, maybe not immediately, but eventually.

But maybe Jill's problems are so huge that it's going to take more than just a Yodel to make her feel better.

"Th-thank you," she says. And the snack cake (although, really, if you ask me Yodels are more of a dessert than a snack) disappears from my hand. A second later I hear plastic crinkling.

"Do you want some milk with that?" I ask. "I have both whole and two percent. There was skim, too, but, well, you know. Also, I have a diet Coke. And a regular Coke, if you need the sugar."

More crinkling. Then I hear a tearful, "Regular Coke would be good."

I crack the can open for her, then pass it beneath the stall door.

"Th-thanks," Jill says.

For a moment there's no sound except soft slurping. Then Jill says, "Do you have any more Yodels?"

"Of course I do," I say soothingly. "And Devil Dogs, too."

"Yodels, please," she says.

I pass another one under the stall door.

"You know," I say conversationally. "If it's any consolation, I know what you're going through. Well, I mean, not *exactly*, but, you know, I work with a lot of brides. Most of them aren't under the kind of pressure you are, of course. But, you know. Getting married is *always* a little stressful."

"Oh, yeah?" Jill asks with a bitter laugh. "Do all their future mother-in-laws hate them the way mine hates me?"

"Not all of them," I say. I've helped myself to a Devil Dog. Just the creamy filling inside, though. It's less carbs than the cake part. I think. "What's up with yours?"

"Oh, you mean besides the part where she thinks I'm a gold digger out to rob her son of his rightful inheritance?" I hear more crinkling plastic. "Where do I start?"

"You know," I say. *Don't do it*, a voice inside my head is saying. *Do not do it. It's not worth it.*

But a different voice is telling me that it is my duty, as a woman, to help, and that I cannot let a girl who has suffered as much as this one has to continue to wallow in misery . . . especially when she doesn't *have* to.

"When I said I work with a lot of brides, I didn't mean here," I go on. "I mean, not *just* here. I'm actually a certified wedding-gown specialist. Well, *I'm* not. I mean, I'm not certified. Yet. But I work with someone who is. Anyway, my specialty is restoring vintage or antique gowns, and refurbishing them to fit modern brides. Just in case that information is at all helpful to you."

For a second, there is no sound from the stall. Then I hear some more crinkling. Then the toilet flushes. A second later, the stall door opens and Jill, looking red-eyed and pink-faced, her hair a blowsy mess, with Yodel crumbs all over the front of her woolly sweater, comes out, staring at me warily.

"Are you kidding me with this?" she demands, not in what you would call a teasing or even friendly manner.

Oops.

"Look," I say, straightening up from where I've been leaning against the bathroom wall. "I'm sorry. I just heard, you know, through the grapevine, that your future mother-in-law was trying to make you wear some dress that's been handed down in their family for generations or something. And I just wanted to let you know that—you know. I can help."

Jill is blinking at me, her expression devoid of any emotion whatsoever. She's not wearing any makeup, I notice. But then she's one of those healthy, outdoorsy girls who can get away with it.

"Not just me, I mean," I add hastily. "Lots of people can help, this whole town is filled with people who can help. Just don't go to this one guy, Maurice? Because he'll just charge you a lot and he won't actually fix it. The gown, I mean. Monsieur Henri—that's where I work—is the place to go. Because, you know, we don't use chemicals or anything like that. And we care."

Jill blinks at me some more. "You *care?*" she repeats, sounding incredulous.

"Well, yeah," I say, realizing—a little belatedly—how I must sound to her. Because it isn't as if she isn't hounded all day by people who want something from her—the press, for a quote or a photo; the public, for what it's like to be engaged to one of the richest bachelors in New York; even her beloved seals, the ones she's willing to throw out her back for, are probably always after her for fish. Or whatever it is the seals in the Central Park Zoo eat.

"Look," I say. "I know you're going through a rotten time right now, and it must seem like everybody and his brother wants a piece of you or whatever. But I swear that's not why I'm telling you this. Vintage clothing—it's my life. I mean, you can see what I have on, right?" I point at the dress I'm wearing. "This is a rare long-sleeved, kimono-style dress from the 1960s by the designer Alfred Shaheen, who was better known for his authentic South Seas designs—basically Hawaiian shirts—but who also made some hand-screened Asian prints as well. This dress is a fantastic example of his work— see the wide, obi-style belt? Which is actually a good look for me, because I have more of a pear shape, you know, so I want to emphasize my waistline and not my hips so much? Anyway, this dress was in pretty bad shape when I found it in the bottom of the dollar bin at the place where I used to work back in Ann Arbor, Vintage to Vavoom. It had this really gross stain on it—grape jelly, I think— and it was actually floor length because I think it was meant to be a hostess dress. And it was way too big for me in the boobs. But I just threw it in a pot of boiling water and gave it a good soak, then I dried it out, cut it off to mid-knee, hemmed it, redid the darts, and, boom."

I do a little pivot for her, the way Tiffany had taught me to.

"And now I've got what you see here. What I'm trying to say"—I pivot over to where she's standing, gaping at me—"is that I know how to take someone else's trash and turn it into treasure. And that if you want me to, I can do it for you. Because what would stick it to your future mother-in-law more than you walking down the aisle in the dress she's forced onto you, looking way, way better in it than she ever did?"

Jill shakes her head. "You don't understand," she says.

"Try me."

"That—that thing she wants me to wear. It's . . . hideous."

"So was this," I say, indicating the Alfred Shaheen. "Grape jelly. Floor length. Bullet boobs."

"No. This is worse. Way worse. It's got like—" Words seem to defy Jill. So she uses her arms to make a circle. "This hoop skirt thing. And there's . . . *stuff*. Hanging. It's got this plaid thing—"

"The MacDowell clan tartan," I say gravely. "Yes. Yes, of course it would have that."

"And it's like a million years old," Jill says. "And it smells. And it doesn't fit."

"Too big or too small?" I ask.

"Too small. Way too small. There's no way anybody could make it fit. I already decided." She tosses her head, her blue eyes glittering. "I'm not wearing it. I mean, she already hates me. What's the worst that can happen?"

"True," I say. "Do you have something else in mind?"

She looks at me blankly. "What do you mean?"

"I mean, do you have another dress in mind? Have you shopped for another gown?"

She shakes her head. "Oh, right. When would I have time to do that? In between manicures? What do you think? No, of course not. What do I know about any of this stuff? I mean, John, he keeps telling me just to go to Vera Wang or whatever, but it's like every time I even think about going into one of those places—you know, those designers—I get all short of breath, and . . . well, it's not like I've got girlfriends, or whatever, who are into that stuff. Everyone I know, they've got like monkey shit all over their shoes. *Literally.* What do they know from bridal gowns? Really, I was just thinking maybe I'd fly home and pick something up back at the mall in Des Moines. Because at least there I know what I'm getting myself into—"

Something cold and hard grips my heart. I recognize immediately what it is, of course. Fear.

"Jill." I reach for another Devil Dog. I need it. For sustenance. "Can I call you Jill?"

She nods. "Yeah, whatever."

"I'm Lizzie," I say. "And please, don't ever say that word around me again."

She looks at me blankly. "What word?"

"Mall." I shove a fingerful of delicious filling into my mouth and let it melt. Ahhhh. Better. "No. Just no, okay?"

"I know," she says, her eyes suddenly bright with tears again. "But seriously. What else am I gonna do?"

"Well, for starters," I say, "you're going to bring the MacDowell clan bridal gown, tartan and all, to me, here." I pass her one of my business cards from my purse. "Can you come this afternoon?"

Jill squints down at the card. "Are you serious?"

"Dead serious," I say. "Before we make any drastic decisions involving the mall, let's just see what we have to work with, okay? Because you never know. You may have something salvageable. And then you won't have to deal with the mall *or* the high-fashion boutiques. And it would be a really nice in-your-face to your mother-in-law if we could make it work."

Jill narrows her eyes at me. "Wait. Did you just say 'in-your-face'?"

I look at her guiltily over the second fingerful of Devil Dog filling I've just stuffed into my mouth. "Um," I say around my finger. "Yeah. Why?"

"I haven't heard anybody say that since eighth grade."

I pop my finger out of my mouth. "I was always kind of a late bloomer."

For the first time since coming out of the toilet stall, Jill smiles. "Me, too," she says.

And the two of us stand there grinning idiotically at each other . . .

At least until the door to the ladies' room swings open and Roberta comes in, freezing mid-step when she sees us.

"Oh, Lizzie," she says, smiling at Jill. "There you are. Tiffany just asked me to check on you because you'd been gone from the desk for so long—"

"Oh, sorry," I say, sweeping the remains of the junk food I'd looted from the kitchen into my arms. "We were just—"

"I was having a blood sugar issue," Jill says, reaching out to grab another Coke and a Yodels from the pile in my arms, "and Lizzie was just helping me through it."

"Oh," Roberta says, smiling even harder. Well, what's she going to do? Yell at me for sneaking the entire contents of the Pendergast, Loughlin, and Flynn snack closet into the ladies' room for one of their most high-profile clients? "Great. So long as you're both all right."

"We are," I say cheerfully. "In fact, I was just heading back to the desk—"

"And I have a two o'clock with Mr. Pendergast," Jill says.

"Okay, then," Roberta says. Her smile is practically frozen onto her face. "Good!"

I hurry out to the lobby, where Tiffany's eyes widen perceptibly when she sees who's following me. Esther, Mr. Pendergast's assistant, is waiting by the reception desk. She looks even more surprised than Tiffany to see Jill Higgins following behind me and Roberta.

"Oh, Miss Higgins," she cries, her gaze going straight to the Yodel crumbs on Jill's chest. "There you are. I was getting worried. The security desk called and said they'd sent you up some time ago—"

"Sorry," Jill says smoothly. "I stopped for a snack."

"I see," Esther says, darting a quick look at me.

"She was hungry," I say, indicating the snack cakes and sodas—and minicartons of milk—in my arms. "Want some?"

"Er, no, thank you," Esther says. "Won't you come with me, Miss Higgins?"

"Sure," Jill says, and starts following Esther out—only to fling me an enigmatic look over her shoulder as she rounds the corner . . . a look I am in no shape to interpret, since I'm getting ready to be yelled at by my boss.

But Roberta doesn't say anything except, "Well. That was, er, nice of you, to, er, help Miss Higgins."

"Thanks," I say. "She said she was feeling light-headed, so—"

"Quick thinking," Roberta says. "Well. It's past two, so—"

"Right." I dump the stuff from the kitchen onto the reception desk—causing Tiffany to make a small noise of protest and give me a dirty look. "Sorry, Tiff," I say. "But I gotta run. My shift's up for the day—"

And then I bolt out of there like a bike messenger with a clear shot up Sixth Avenue . . .

Lizzie Nichols's Wedding Gown Guide

A word on . . .

Shoes!

Of course you want to look your best on your wedding day, and higher heels can help emphasize a nice figure, and improve a less-than-perfect one. Keep in mind, however, that you will be spending a LOT of time on your feet on your wedding day. If you insist on heels, wear a pair at a height you are somewhat used to.

If your wedding heels are still less than comfortable by the time the big day rolls around, it's always a good idea to bring a second pair of shoes to wear during your "downtime," such as while you're waiting for the photographer to set up, et cetera.

One word on beach weddings: few things are lovelier than being married at sunset on a tropical beach. Keep in mind, however, that heels and sand do not mix. If you are being married on a beach, skip the shoes altogether. Just be sure to put some bug repellent on your ankles to ward off sand fleas or you'll be scratching throughout the ceremony.

LIZZIE NICHOLS DESIGNS™

• Chapter 19 •

If you reveal your secrets to the wind, you should
not blame the wind for revealing them to the trees.

—*Kahlil Gibran (1883–1931), poet and writer*

At five of six that day, I give up hope that Jill Higgins is
going to walk up and ring the bell to Monsieur Henri's.
I've been, I know, too presumptuous. Why would Jill
Higgins, who is marrying one of the richest men in Manhattan,
choose me—a woman she knows only as the receptionist at the law
firm where she is getting her prenup negotiated—as her certified
wedding-gown specialist?

Especially since I'm not even certified! Yet.

I haven't mentioned to Monsieur and Madame Henri that I've
given their name and address to one of the most famous brides-to-
be in the city. I don't want to get their hopes up. Business has not
been good, and there've been conversations (in French, of course,
so I won't understand what they're saying) about packing it up for
good when Maurice finally opens his shop down the street and
steals away the last of their customers. The Henris have mentioned
decamping for the cottage in Provence.

There would be a significant loss of income if this were to take
place, since they've taken out a second mortgage on the building in
order to pay for the boys' college tuition, and the home in which

they live in New Jersey has depreciated considerably with the current housing sales slump. Plus there's the small fact that the two boys, Jean-Paul and Jean-Pierre, adamantly refuse to move to France, or even transfer to colleges less expensive than New York University, to which they commute daily from home (when they aren't sneaking overnight stays in the apartment upstairs).

Of course, I have no doubt that if the decision to give up the shop is ever made, the boys will end up doing precisely as their mother insists. Money, not discipline, is what is lacking in the Henri family—at least if the way Monsieur Henri piles the work on me at the shop is any indication. For someone who claims his business is going under, Monsieur Henri certainly seems to have enough sewing for me to do, day in and day out. He's had me make so many lace ruffles—the same ones I'd admired in his shop window, months earlier, and swore to myself I'd learn to create on my own—that I can practically do them in my sleep. And I've completely mastered the art of the sewn-on diamond drop, for that all-over shimmer effect. And don't even get me started on ruching.

Madame Henri is fussing at her husband for him to hurry and pack up so they can leave, because the Rockefeller Center Christmas tree lighting—scheduled to take place tonight—makes the traffic so impossible that it takes an hour, practically, just to navigate out of the city, when the bell to the front door of the shop rings, and I look up to see a pale face, framed by a curtain of blond hair, peering at me urgently.

"What is this?" Madame Henri wants to know. "We have no appointments today."

"Oh," I say quickly, getting up and going to the door. "This is a friend of mine." I open the door to let Jill in . . .

. . . and only then notice that there is a chauffeured black Town Car with smoked windows parked with its motor running in front of the fire hydrant, and that behind Jill stands a tall, athletic man I immediately recognize as—

"Oh!" Madame Henri drops her purse and flings both her hands to her cheeks. She's recognized Jill's companion as well. Which, considering how often his face appears on the front page of the *Post*, isn't any wonder.

"Um, hi," Jill says. Her cheeks are very red from the cold outside. She's carrying a garment bag. "You said to stop by. Is this a bad time?"

"This is a perfect time," I say. "Come on in."

The couple step in from the slight snow flurry that has started up, lightly coating their hair and shoulders with drops that sparkle more than any crystal I've ever sewn onto anything. They bring with them the smell of cold and good health and . . . something else.

"Sorry," Jill says, wrinkling her nose. "That's me. I came straight from work and I didn't have time to change. We wanted to beat the tree traffic."

"That intoxicating odor," John MacDowell says, "that you're smelling right now is seal excrement. Don't worry, you get used to it."

"This is my fiancé, John," Jill says. "John, this is Lizzie—"

John sticks out a large hand, and I shake it.

"Nice to meet you," he says, seeming to mean it. "When Jill told me about you—well, I really hope you can help us. My mother—I mean, I love her and everything, but—"

"Say no more," I say. "We completely get it. And, believe me, we've probably seen worse. May I introduce you to my boss, Monsieur Henri? He owns this shop. And this is his wife, Madame Henri. Monsieur and Madame, this is Jill Higgins and her fiancé, John MacDowell."

Monsieur Henri has been standing nearby staring at the three of us with a stunned expression on his face. When I say his name, he takes a quick step forward, his hand extended. "*Enchanté*," he says. "I am very pleased to make your acquaintance."

"Nice to meet you, too," John MacDowell says politely. Madame Henri practically faints when he says the same thing to her. She hasn't been able to utter a sound since the couple entered the shop.

"Shall we see what you have here?" I ask, taking the garment bag from Jill.

"I'm warning you," John says. "It's bad."

"*Really* bad," Jill adds.

"We are used to bad," Monsieur Henri assures them. "That is how we came by our endorsement from the Association of Bridal Consultants."

"It's true," I say gravely. "The National Bridal Service has given Monsieur Henri their highest recommendation."

Monsieur Henri inclines his head modestly while at the same time moving behind Jill to help her out of her down parka. "Perhaps we can get you some tea? Or coffee?"

"I'm fine," John says, handing over his own parka. "We're . . ."

His voice trails off. That's because I've opened the garment bag. And now all five of us are staring at what I've revealed.

Monsieur Henri nearly drops the coats, but at the last second his wife darts forward to scoop them up.

"It's . . . it's hideous," Monsieur Henri breathes—thankfully in French.

"Yes," I say. "But it can be saved."

"No." Monsieur Henri shakes his head, like someone in a daze. "It cannot."

I can see why he might feel that way. The gown isn't promising, to say the least. Made of yards and yards of clearly valuable antique lace over cream-colored satin, it's a princess cut, with an enormous full skirt, made even bigger by a hoop sewn into the hem. The neckline is a typical Queen Anne style, with enormous poufed sleeves that end in tartan bows at the wrists. Draped along the skirt is more tartan, held in place with gold toggles.

It looks, in other words, like something out of a high school drama club's production of *Brigadoon*.

"It's been in my family for generations," John says apologetically. "All the MacDowell brides have worn it—with various degrees of alteration. My mother is the one who put in the hoop when she wore it. She's from Georgia."

"That explains a lot," I say. "What size is it?"

"A six," Jill says. "I'm a twelve."

Monsieur Henri says in French, "Impossible. It is too small. There is nothing we can do."

"Let's not be hasty," I say. "Obviously the bodice will have to go. But there's enough material here—"

"You are going to chop up the ancestral gown of the richest family in the city?" Monsieur Henri demands, again in French. "You've lost your mind!"

"He said other brides have altered it," I remind him. "I mean, come on. We can at least try."

"You cannot fit a size-twelve woman into a size-six gown," Monsieur Henri snaps. "You know it cannot be done!"

"We can't fit her into *this* gown the way it is now," I say. "But fortunately it's too long on her." I take the gown from the hanger it's on and hold it up to Jill, who stands with her arms at her side, looking alarmed. "See? If it were too short, I'd say you were right. But like I was saying, if we unstitch the bodice—"

"My God, are you mad?" Monsieur Henri looks shocked. "Do you know what the mother-in-law will do to us? She could even take legal action—"

"Jean," Madame Henri says, speaking for the first time.

Her husband glances at her. "What?"

"Do it," she says in French.

Monsieur Henri shakes his head. "I am telling you, it cannot be done! Do you want me to lose my certification?"

"Do you want Maurice to steal away what little business we have left when he opens his shop down the street?" his wife demands.

"He won't," I assure them both. "Not if you let me do it. I can. I *know* I can."

Madame Henri nods at me. "Listen to her, Jean," she says.

The issue is no longer up for debate. Monsieur Henri may wield the needle, but his wife wears the pants in the family. Once she has ruled, there is no more argument. Madame Henri's word is always final.

Monsieur Henri's shoulders sag. Then he looks at Jill. Both she and her husband-to-be are staring at us, wide-eyed.

"When is the wedding?" Monsieur Henri asks weakly.

"New Year's Eve," Jill says.

Monsieur Henri groans. And even I have to swallow hard against the soreness that has suddenly crept back into my throat. New Year's Eve!

Jill notices our reaction, and looks worried. "Does that . . . I mean, will you have enough time?"

"A month." Monsieur Henri stares down at me. "We have a *month*. Not that it matters, since what you are saying cannot be done in any amount of time."

"It can if we do it the way I'm thinking we should do it," I say. "*Trust me.*"

Monsieur Henri takes a final look at the monstrosity on the hanger.

"*Maurice,*" his wife hisses. "Remember Maurice!"

Monsieur Henri sighs. "Fine. We will try."

And I turn, beaming, toward Jill.

"What was that all about?" she asks nervously. "I couldn't tell what you were saying. It was all in French."

"Well," I start to say . . .

Then realize what she's just said.

I turn guiltily toward Monsieur and Madame Henri, who are both staring at me in horror. It's hit them at the same time as it's hit me: we've just had an entire conversation in their native language—which I'm not supposed to understand.

But hey. It's not like they ever asked.

I give the Henris a shrug. Then, to Jill, I say, "We'll do it."

She stares at me. "Okay . . . but how?"

"I haven't completely figured that out yet," I admit. "But I have an idea. And you're going to look great. I promise."

She lifts her eyebrows. "No hoop skirt?"

"No hoop skirt," I say. "But I'm going to need to take your measurements. So if you could just come with me back to the dressing room—"

"Okay," she says. And follows me past Monsieur and Madame Henri, who continue to stand there, looking stunned. I can see that they are going over in their heads every conversation they have ever had within earshot of me.

And that's a *lot* of conversations.

Behind the curtains that make up the walls of the dressing room, the smell of seal is stronger than ever.

"I'm really sorry," Jill says. "I'll totally change before I come the next time."

"That's okay," I say, trying to take only shallow breaths. "At least you know that guy must *really* love you, if he's willing to put up with *that.*"

"Yes," Jill says, with a smile that makes her normally merely attractive face stunningly beautiful for a moment. "He does."

And I feel a twinge. Not of jealousy, really, although there's a little of that in it, I guess. But mostly it's caused by the fact that I want what she has—not an engagement to the richest bachelor in Manhattan; not a future mother-in-law who is making it her single goal in life to ruin any chance at joy I might have on what is supposed to be the happiest day of my life.

But a guy who would go on loving me even if I smelled like seal poo. Not just go on loving me, but want to spend the rest of his life with me—although I'd settle at this point for coming to Ann Arbor for Christmas with me—and be willing to verbalize that desire in front of a room full of friends, family members, and sneaky members of the press who happened to worm their way into the church.

Because right now, that's something I'm pretty sure I don't have.

But hey. At least I'm working on it.

⌐ Lizzie Nichols's Wedding Gown Guide ⌐

Time to ask the age-old question: White, ivory, or cream?

Believe it or not, there are many different shades of white. Don't believe me? Check out the paint section of your local hardware store. You've never seen so many different names for what many people consider a single color—everything from Eggshell to Navajo to Blush.

The days of the traditional snow-white wedding gown are long gone, and many brides are opting to take advantage of this trend by picking out gowns in off-white, beige, pink, and even blues. To find the color that flatters your skin tone best, follow this easy guide:

Snow White—Dark of hair? Then traditional white really will look best on you. Whites with a blue or lavender tint will complement you as well.

Cream—Blond? Your light locks will best be set off by a cream-colored gown. The hint of gold will echo the tawny highlights in your crowning glory (your hair, not your tiara). Remember Princess Diana, on *her* special day . . .

Ivory—In between? Ivory looks good on nearly everyone. That's why it's used on so many walls.

• Chapter 20 •

To a philosopher all news, as it is called, is gossip, and they who edit it and read it are old women over their tea.

—Henry David Thoreau (1817–1862), American philosopher, author, and naturalist

where have you been?" Luke wants to know, when I finally stagger home later that evening, my arms loaded down with books.

"The library," I say. "Sorry, did you call? You're not allowed to have your ringer on there."

Luke is laughing as he comes over to take the books from my arms. "*Scottish Traditions,*" he reads aloud from the covers. "*Your Scottish Wedding. Tartans and Toasts.* Lizzie, what's going on? Are you planning a visit to the Emerald Isle soon?"

"That's Ireland," I say, unwinding my scarf. "I'm doing a Scottish bridal gown for a client. And you're never going to believe who the client is."

"You're probably right," he says. "Have you eaten? I've got some leftover turkey reheating in the oven—"

"I'm too excited to eat," I say. "Come on. Guess. Guess who the client is."

Luke shrugs. "I don't know. Shari? She's having some kind of lesbian wedding?"

I glare at him. "No. And I told you, don't—"

"Label her, yes, yes, I know," Luke says. "All right, I give up. Who's your client?"

I flop down onto the couch—my sore throat really *is* bothering me a little. It feels great to sit down—and say triumphantly, "Jill Higgins."

Luke has gone into the kitchen to pour some wine. "Am I supposed to know who that is?" he asks across the pass-through.

I can't believe it. "Luke! Do you even read the paper? Or watch the news?"

But even as I ask it, I know the answer. The only paper he reads is the *New York Times*, and all he ever watches are documentaries.

Still, I try.

"You know," I say as he comes forward with a glass of cabernet sauvignon in each hand. "That girl who works in the seal enclosure at the Central Park Zoo? And she threw her back out returning one of the seals to the enclosure? Because they jump out when the water level gets too high, you know, from excessive snow or rain." I am able to add this last bit because Jill just told me about it, in the dressing room while I was taking her measurements, when I asked her to tell me how she and John met.

"And while she was in the emergency room she met John Mac-Dowell—you know, of the Manhattan MacDowells? Well, they're getting married at like the biggest wedding of the century practically, and Jill asked *me* to fix her wedding dress for her." I am still so stoked, I'm bouncing up and down on the couch. "Me! Of all the people in New York! I'm doing Jill Higgins's wedding gown!"

"Wow," Luke says, smiling his beautiful, even-toothed smile. "That's great, Lizzie!"

It's clear he has no idea what I'm talking about. None.

"You don't understand," I say. "This is huge. See, the press has been savage to her, calling her 'Blubber' and stuff, just because she's not some skinny model, and works with seals, and she cries in front of them sometimes, because they won't stop hounding her, and her mother-in-law is making her sign this prenup and wear this hideous—you can't even imagine how hideous—wedding gown, and I'm going to fix it, and everything will be perfect, and Monsieur Henri will finally start getting some business, and then he'll be able to pay me, and then I can quit working for Chaz's dad, and do what I love full-time! Isn't that *great*?"

Luke is still smiling—just not as much as before. "That *is* great," he says. "But—"

"I'm not saying it's going to be easy," I interrupt, thinking I know what he's about to say. "I mean, we only have a month—less than a month now—to get the dress done, and it's going to take a *lot* of work. Especially if I'm going to do to it what I think I'm going to have to do to it, just so it will fit. So you're probably not going to see very much of me for a while. Which is just as well, since you have finals anyway, right? I'm seriously going to have to work late if we're going to pull this off. But if we do, Luke—just think! Maybe Monsieur Henri will let me run the shop! I mean, he's been wanting to retire and move to France . . . this way he could do it and not have to sell the place at a loss. Then I can start saving my money, and maybe—please, God—get some small-business loans or something, and eventually be able to *buy* the business—building and all—from him someday—"

Luke is looking distinctly nonplussed by all this. I know it's a lot of information all at once. But I can't help thinking he could be a *little* more excited for me.

"I *am*," he insists when I mention this (a little churlishly, I admit, but hey, my throat hurts). "It's just . . . I didn't know you were serious about this bridal-gown thing."

I blink at him. "Luke," I say. "Were you not there this summer, when all those friends of your parents were coming up to me, telling me I should open my own bridal-gown design business?"

"Well, yes," Luke says. "But I just thought—you know. That that would be something you'd do down the line. Maybe after getting a business degree."

"A business degree?" I screech. "Go back to school? Are you kidding me? I just graduated. Wait, I haven't *even* graduated yet! Why would I want to go *back*?"

"Lizzie, you need more to open your own business than just a talent for refurbishing vintage clothing," Luke says a little dryly.

"I know that." I shake my head. "But that's what I'm doing at Monsieur Henri's. Learning the ropes of running your own business. And, Luke, I really think I'm ready. To take it to the next level, I mean. Or I will be, depending on how this thing with Jill Higgins goes."

Luke looks dubious. "I don't see how one wedding dress can make such a huge difference."

I gape at him. "Are you kidding me? Have you *heard* of David and Elizabeth Emanuel?"

"Uh." Luke hesitates. "No?"

"They designed Princess Diana's wedding gown," I say, feeling a little sorry for him. I mean, really. He knows a lot about the principles of biology, which he's studying this semester. But not so much about popular culture.

But that's just as well, because really, which would you *rather* your doctor know about?

"And because of that one dress, they got superfamous," I go on. "Now, I am in no way putting Jill Higgins in the same category of fame as Princess Diana. But, you know, *locally* she's pretty well known. And when it gets out we're doing her dress, well, it's going to be very good for business. That's all I'm saying. And since she's getting married on New Year's Eve, there's a bit of a time crunch, so—"

"So you're not going to be around much," Luke says. "Don't worry, I understand. And you're right, what with my finals, you won't be seeing much of me anyway. Not to mention the fact that I leave for France in just three weeks. For a couple of people who live together, we sure don't seem to see each other much."

"Except when we're sleeping," I agree. "But, you know. Then we're unconscious."

"Well," Luke says. "I guess I'll just have to be happy with what I can get. Although I was kind of hoping you could spare a little of your precious time to go tree-shopping with me."

"Tree-shopping?" I stare at him for a few seconds before I realize what he's talking about. "Oh, you mean you want to put up a Christmas tree?"

"Well, yeah," Luke says. "Even though we won't be able to spend the real holiday with each other, I was still hoping we could have our own private celebration before we both take off to be with our families. And to do that, we need a tree . . . especially since I got you a little something special, and I need a place to put it."

My heart melts. "You got me a Christmas present? Ahhh, Luke! How sweet!"

"Well," he says, looking pleased by my reaction, but a little embarrassed as well, for some reason. "It's not really so much of a Christmas present, I realize now, as an investment in the future—"

Wait . . . did he just say what I *think* he did?

An investment in the *future*?

"Come on," Luke says, getting up abruptly, and going into the kitchen. "You've got to eat something. Your voice is sounding a little scratchy. We don't want you coming down with something. You have a wedding dress to design!"

The big send-off

Traditionally, wedding guests have been provided with tiny sachets of raw rice to open and then toss at the happily wedded couple as they leave the venue at which the wedding ceremony has taken place (usually a church). The rice represents fertility. Tossing it at the couple is supposed to represent your wish for them to have good luck and abundance in their future lives together.

In recent years, however, many churches and other buildings in which weddings are performed have banned the throwing of rice. The stated reason for this ban is that the uncooked rice is harmful to birds if swallowed. This is, in fact, an urban myth. Many species of birds and ducks depend on raw rice as a main staple of their diet.

The problem with the rice is that it actually poses a danger to humans . . . the hard granules are slippery beneath the feet, and many wedding sites choose to avoid a lawsuit by the banning of rice.

A popular substitute for rice these days is birdseed. However, this can pose just as big a risk to the health of your guests as rice, when it comes to creating a slippery surface.

Furthermore, rice, birdseed, and even confetti are extremely difficult to clean up, and for venues that perform multiple weddings per day, cleaning up after each bridal couple's departure (since no bride wants to step in the rice or confetti of a previous bride) is time-consuming and expensive.

That's why I always recommend bubbles as a wedding favor. Guests can create a pretty "canopy" of bubbles under which the newly wedded couple can duck on their way to their carriage or limo. And no one has ever filed a lawsuit from slipping on a bubble.

Just maybe from getting one in the eye.

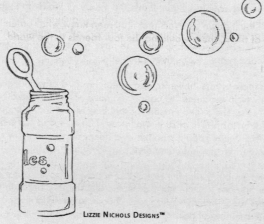

• Chapter 21 •

a n investment in the future?" Shari sounds dubious on the other end of the phone. "But that could be anything. Stock certificates. One of those World Trade Center coins from the Franklin Mint."

"Shari." I can't believe she's being so dense. "Come on. Luke is not going to get me something from the Franklin Mint. It's an engagement ring. It *has* to be. He's trying to make up for not going home with me to meet my parents."

"By buying you an *engagement ring*?"

"Yes. Because what better thing to give me right before I leave to go back home?" I'm a little giddy just thinking about it. "It's like, even though *he* can't be there, the *ring* will be, so everyone will know how serious it is between us. Oh, hold on." I press the hold button, then line 2. "Pendergast, Loughlin, and Flynn, how may I direct your call?"

I send the call to one of the junior partners, then hit the button to line 1 again.

"It makes sense," I say to Shari. "I mean, we've been going out for six months. We've been living together for four. It's not as if it would be completely out of left field if he proposed."

"I don't know, Lizzie." Shari sounds like she's shaking her head. "According to Chaz, Luke is the kind of person who, um . . . lacks follow-through."

"Well, maybe because of my careful tutelage," I say, recalling Chaz's not very charitable warning of several months earlier—which was just Chaz, being jealous of the fact that Luke has a girlfriend who actually likes him, and not her female boss, "he's changed."

"Lizzie." Shari sounds tired. "People don't change. You know that."

"They can change in small ways," I say. "Look how when you first started going out with Chaz, he had that thing, remember, where he ate pork chops and Rice-A-Roni every night? You totally weaned him off that."

"By telling him if we didn't have something else once in a while, I was going to stop sleeping with him," Shari says. "But when I'm not around, that's still all he ever eats."

"Ooooh," Tiffany chimes in, beside me, from over the top of the bridal magazine she's reading. Because I brought a bunch of them in to work, for inspiration. "When you and Luke do get married, you could totally have your company's PR person send out a press release, you know, to like *Vogue* and *Town & Country*, and they'll send reporters out to cover your wedding, and that will just get you *more* clients. And free publicity."

I stare at her. For someone who is so ditzy that she has, upon occasion, forgotten to lock the office door after closing for the day, Tiffany can be pretty savvy.

"That's good," I say to her. "That's *very* good."

"Hello," Shari says. "Are you talking to me? Or to Miss Hairspray for Brains over there?"

"Hey, now," I say. "Come on."

"Well, I'm trying," Shari says. "But seriously, Lizzie. I know you love Luke and all. But do you really see yourself with him fifty years from now? Even *five* years from now?"

"Yes," I say, taken aback by the question. "Of course. Why? What's wrong with him?" The other line chirps. "Crud. Hold on." I press line 2. "Pendergast, Loughlin, and Flynn, how may I direct your call? Mr. Flynn? One moment please."

A second later, I'm back with Shari. "Seriously. Why do you sound like you think Luke and I don't have a future?"

"Well, honestly, Lizzie," Shari says. "What do the two of you have in common? Except sex?"

"Lots of things," I insist. "I mean, we both like New York. We both like Château Mirac. We both like . . . wine. And Renoir!"

"Lizzie," Shari says. "Everybody likes that stuff."

"And he wants to be a doctor," I go on. "And help save people's lives. And I want to be a certified wedding-gown specialist. And help make brides look good. *We're practically the same person.*"

"You're making a joke out of it," Shari says. "But I'm serious. One of the reasons I realized Chaz and I were wrong for each other, and Pat and I so right, is that intellectually Pat and I are compatible. And I don't think the same could be said about you and Luke."

I feel tears sting my eyes. "You think he's intellectually superior to me, is that it? Just because he likes documentaries and I like *Project Runway*!"

"No," Shari says, sounding exasperated. "What I mean is, he likes documentaries and you like *Project Runway* . . . and yet you guys only ever watch documentaries. Because you're so busy trying to get him to like you, that you just do whatever he wants, instead of telling him what *you* really want to do. Or watch."

"That is not true," I cry. "We watch shows I like all the time!"

"Oh, yeah?" Shari lets out a bitter laugh. "I had no idea you were such a *Nightline* fan. I always thought you were more of a David Letterman type of girl. But hey, if *Nightline* is what floats your boat—"

"*Nightline* is a totally good show," I say defensively. "Luke watches it so he can stay abreast of world issues, since he often misses the evening news, being busy at the library, studying—"

"Face it, Lizzie," Shari says. "I know you think you've found your handsome prince—literally. But do you really think of yourself as the princess type? Because I sure don't think of you that way. And I'm pretty sure Luke doesn't, either."

"What is *that* supposed to mean?" I demand. "I'm totally the princess type! Just because I make my own clothes instead of waiting for a fairy godmother to come along and sprinkle me with fairy dust—"

"Elizabeth?" It's only then that I notice that Roberta has approached the reception desk. And that she does not look happy.

"Uh," I say to Shari. "Ihavetogobye."

I hang up. "Hi, Roberta," I say. Beside me, Tiffany has pulled her feet from the desk and is making herself look busy by pulling open a drawer and arranging bottles of her fingernail polish in rainbow order.

Expecting to receive a warning about making personal calls on the firm's time, I'm surprised when Roberta says, "Tiffany, it's nearly two. Would you mind taking over for Lizzie a few minutes early so I can have a word with her in private?"

"Sure," Tiffany says with a furtive glance at me that screams, *You are so busted!* And causes my stomach to twist into an immediate knot.

I follow Roberta back to her office, conscious of Daryl's—the fax and copier supervisor—pitying glance. He apparently thinks I'm busted, too.

Well, whatever! If Pendergast, Loughlin, and Flynn wants to fire me over one personal call, then they better fire everyone else at the firm, too! I've overheard Roberta on the phone with her husband plenty of times!

Oh, God. Please don't let me get fired . . . please . . .

I think I'm going to throw up.

It's only when I walk into Roberta's office and see that the *New York Post* is open on her desk to a large picture in the center of the second page that I realize this might not be about my using the firm's phone for personal calls. Because even though they're upside down, I can make out the words, "Blubber's New Mystery Pal." And I can see that the photo is of me walking Jill to her Town Car after her fitting the night before.

The knot in my stomach turns into something that feels more like a fist.

"Correct me if I'm wrong," Roberta says, holding the paper up. "But isn't this you?"

I swallow. My sore throat, which had been miraculously cured by Luke's "investment for your future" remark, comes back with a vengeance.

"Um," I say. "No."

Honestly, I don't know where the lie comes from. But once it's out, there's nothing I can do to stuff it back in.

"Lizzie," Roberta says. "It's obviously you. That's the same dress you wore to work yesterday. You can't tell me there's another one like that anywhere in Manhattan."

"I'm sure there are loads," I say. And I'm not lying this time, either. "Alfred Shaheen was a very prolific designer."

"Lizzie." Roberta sits down behind her desk. "This is very serious. I saw you talking to Jill Higgins in the ladies' room yesterday. And then, apparently, you met her somewhere after work. You know the firm takes the confidentiality of its clients extremely seriously. So I'm going to ask you again. What were you doing yesterday with Jill Higgins—and, if this photo is to believed, her fiancé, John Mac-Dowell?"

I swallow again. I wish I had a Sucrets. Also, that I didn't need this job so badly.

"I can't tell you," I say.

Roberta raises a single eyebrow. "I beg your pardon?"

"I can't tell you," I say. "But I can tell you that it has nothing whatsoever to do with the firm. Honestly. It has to do with a completely different business. But it's a business that also has confidentiality clauses. That I really can't violate."

Roberta's other eyebrow rises to join the first. "Lizzie. Are you telling me that this is you in the picture?"

"I can neither confirm nor deny it," I say, parroting the phrase Roberta herself told me to say whenever reporters call the firm, requesting information about people on whom they are writing stories.

"Lizzie." Roberta does not look amused. "This is very serious. If you are harassing or otherwise bothering Miss Higgins—"

"I'm not!" I cry, genuinely startled. "*She* came to me!"

"For what?" Roberta demands. "What other line of work are you in, Lizzie?"

"If I told you that," I say, "you'll know why she came to see me. And she hasn't given me permission to tell anyone that. So I can't say. I'm sorry, Roberta."

I can't believe that I'm doing this. I mean, actually NOT spilling a secret for a change. This is a real sign of my inner growth. I should totally be celebrating.

Too bad I feel so much like vomiting.

"You can fire me if you want to," I go on. "But I promise you, I am not bothering Jill. If you don't believe me, call and ask her. She'll tell you."

"She's *Jill* to you now?" Roberta says with more than a little sarcasm in her tone.

"She told me I could call her that," I say, wounded. "Yes."

Roberta looks down at the picture. She seems to be at a loss. "This is highly irregular," she says at last. "I honestly don't know what to say about it."

"It's nothing illegal," I say.

"Well, I should hope not!" Roberta cries. "Are you going to be meeting her again?"

"Yes," I say firmly.

"Well." Roberta shakes her head. "All I can say in that case is, try to be more careful not to get your picture in the *Post*. If one of the partners had seen this and recognized you—"

"I had no idea there was a photographer there," I say. "But I'll definitely be more careful in the future. Is that it? Can I go now?"

Roberta looks startled. "Well, you're in an awfully big hurry to get out of here. Christmas shopping?"

"No," I say. "I have to get to that business that I'm doing for Jill."

Roberta's shoulders slump. "Fine," she says. "But fair warning, Lizzie. This firm prides itself on its sterling reputation. Any whiff of impropriety on your part and you're gone. Understand?"

"Totally," I say.

Roberta looks down, dismissing me . . .

. . . and I bolt from her office. Heading back to the reception desk to get my coat and purse, I ignore Daryl's whispered *"Yo! What'd you do this time?"* and Tiffany's *"Oh my God, are you all right? You look like someone just told you that your Prada handbag is a fake."*

"I'm fine," I mutter. "I'll see you tomorrow."

"Seriously," Tiffany hisses, "call me and tell me what she said. I'm collecting Roberta stories to submit to the Smoking Gun."

I wave at her and hurry out, my heart hammering so hard in my chest, I'm afraid it's going to fly out and hit the wall. When the elevator doors open, I rush inside without even looking to see who else is in there before pounding the button for the lobby. It isn't until a voice beside me says, "Well, hello there, stranger," that I look up and see that Chaz is in the car with me.

"Oh my God," I cry. "Were you going up to see your dad? Why didn't you say anything? I'd have held the door for you—oh no, and now you're going down. I'm sorry!"

"Relax," Chaz says. "I wasn't going up to see my dad. I was coming to see you."

"Me?" I'm shocked.

"I was hoping I could take you for a drink," Chaz says. "And pump you for the information I need about my ex in order for me to start rebuilding my male ego so I can learn to love again."

I chew my lower lip. "Chaz," I say. "I am trying really hard not to talk about people behind their backs. It's this whole new thing with me. I have gotten in so much trouble in the past for being a big mouth, and I'm really trying to change. Because despite what *some* people think, people *can* change."

"Sure they can," Chaz says. The elevator has reached the lobby. "Come on. Let me take you for a beer at Honey's."

I'm about to say *I can't*. I know Chaz is hurting, but I have a dress to design. I'm about to say, *I have to get to the shop. We have this huge project—which is another thing I can't talk about—and I'm in a time crunch, so I'll see you later, okay?*

But then I look into his face and see that it's been a while since he shaved—and, as far as I can tell, changed baseball caps.

Which is how I find myself sitting across from him in one of the red vinyl booths at Honey's, a sweating diet Coke in front of me, listening to the dwarf sing "Dancing Queen," a not entirely unpleasant experience.

"I just need to know," Chaz is saying into his bottle of beer. "I know it sounds stupid, but . . . I mean . . . do you think I did something to . . . turn her?"

"What? Of course not," I cry. "Chaz! Come on. No."

"Well, what happened then?" he demands. "I mean, a person isn't straight one day and then gay the next. Unless maybe I did something to make her—"

"You didn't," I say. "Chaz. Trust me. You didn't. It's exactly like Shari explained to you. She just fell in love with someone else. And that person just happens to be another woman. It's no different than if she'd met some other guy she ended up falling for instead of you."

"Uh," Chaz says. "It's different."

"It's not," I say. "It's still love. Love does crazy things to people. You can't blame yourself. I know Shari doesn't blame you. She still loves you. She told you that, right?"

Chaz grimaces. "She mentioned it."

"Well, it's true. She does still love you. Just, you know. Not romantically anymore. It happens, Chaz."

"So you're saying," Chaz says slowly, "that I could, conceivably, fall in love with a guy sometime?"

"Conceivably," I say. Although to tell the truth I really can't picture Chaz in a homosexual relationship. Or, rather, I can't picture any of the homosexual guys I've known (and dated) actually wanting to be in a relationship with Chaz, seeing as how his fashion sense is less than minimal and he does have an alarming enthusiasm for college basketball and not much interest in home furnishings. I have a much easier time picturing Luke comfortably nesting with another man.

"Have *you*?" Chaz wants to know.

"Have I what?" I glance at the clock above the bar. I really need to get to the shop. I have about a million ideas for Jill's dress and my fingers are itching to get started on them.

"Ever been in love with a woman."

"Well," I say slowly. "There are a lot of women in my life I've really admired, and wanted to be like, and wanted to get to know better. But not, you know, *sexually*."

Chaz is scraping the label off his beer bottle with a thumbnail. "And you and Shari never . . . er . . . experimented?"

"Chaz!" I throw my coaster at him. "No! Ew! You and Luke are exactly alike. That's it, I'm leaving—"

"What?" he cries, looking truly alarmed as he catches my arm before I've made my way completely off the end of the bench. "I was just asking! I thought maybe, you know, all girls do that kind of stuff—"

"Well, they don't," I inform him. "Not that there's anything wrong with it. Now let go of my arm, I have to get to work."

"You just came from work," he points out.

"My other job," I say. "At the bridal shop. We have a really big new job, and I want to get started on it."

"You really like this wedding stuff, don't you?" he says as, over on the karaoke stage, the dwarf switches from Abba to a little Ashlee

Simpson, declaring that, despite what everybody thinks, he didn't steal my boyfriend. "You really believe in it . . . the happy ending, the rice . . . the whole thing."

"Yeah," I say. "Of course I do. And I know you're sad right now, Chaz—and you have every right to be. But someday it will happen for you—I promise. Just like it's going to happen for me, too." Maybe sooner than anyone thinks.

"Well, I hope you're not still counting on making it happen with Mr. Woodland Creature," Chaz says.

I stare at him. "Why shouldn't I be?" Then, when I see him rolling his eyes, I say, "Oh, come on, Chaz. Not your horse thing again. For your information, Luke is doing very well in his classes, and, furthermore, he seems ready to take our relationship to a new level."

Chaz raises his eyebrows. "Threesome?"

I smack him in the center of his baseball cap. "He's gotten me a Christmas present," I say, "that he says is an investment toward my future."

Chaz's eyebrows furrow in a rush. "What's *that* supposed to mean?"

"What else *could* it mean?" I ask. "It has to be an engagement ring."

Chaz frowns. "He hasn't told me about buying any ring."

"Well, he's hardly likely to," I say, "considering what he knows you've recently been through. Do you really think he's going to brag about getting engaged to me when he knows your girlfriend just left you for a woman?"

"Thanks," Chaz says. "You really know how to make a guy feel great."

"Well, you aren't exactly Mr. Charm yourself," I say, "with the whole Luke-not-being-a-horse-you-would-bet-on thing. But you're probably feeling differently about all that now, aren't you?"

"Truthfully?" Chaz shakes his head. "No. An investment toward your future could be anything. Not necessarily a ring. I wouldn't get your hopes up, kid. I mean—no offense—the two of you aren't even spending the holidays together. What does that say about your big happily ever after?"

"Chaz." I regard him steadily from across the booth before I slide out and leave. "I know Shari hurt you. I frankly can't believe she did that, although I know it really wasn't easy for her and she does feel super badly about it. But seriously. Just because your romance didn't work out doesn't mean all romances are doomed. You just need to get back out there, find some pretty philosophy Ph.D. candidate you can talk to about Kant or whatever, and you'll feel better about things. I promise."

Chaz just stares at me. "Someday you're really going to have to describe to me in more detail what life is like on the planet you live on. Because it sounds really great, and I'd like to visit there one day."

I give him a sour smile, and leave the booth, just as the dwarf breaks into his signature piece, "Don't Cry Out Loud."

I hope Chaz takes a cue from him.

Makeup

Many brides opt to have their makeup professionally done on their wedding day. This is often a good idea—if there is a professional doing it, then that's one less thing the bride has to worry about going wrong.

However, too many brides who opt for professional makeup on the big day end up looking as unlike their normal selves as relatives lying in a casket whose faces have been done over by a mortician. Make sure you and your cosmetic specialist are on the same page about color, amount, and shade . . . and make sure he or she uses a light hand. Yes, you want to look good for your photos—but you also want to look natural and pretty up close to your guests as well. A talented professional makeup artist can easily achieve both.

Some makeup tips to remember:

—Have your first meeting with your makeup professional four weeks before your event. That will give the two of you plenty of time to come up with a look with which you are both happy.

—Your makeup should not be so heavy that your neck and face are two visibly different shades. BLEND!

—You will be shiny on your wedding day from nerves and possibly the heat. Make sure you and your bridesmaids have plenty of blotting tissues on hand, as well as powder.

—Curling your eyelashes with a heated curler can create lasting oomph for the eyes.

—Be sure to use waterproof mascara—you *will* be crying. Or at least sweating.

—Under-eye concealer will hide any dark circles from a restless night's sleep.

—And lastly, opt for lipstick that stays on permanently—you will be using your mouth to kiss, eat, and drink throughout the day/evening, and you don't want to have to stop for constant reapplications of your favorite shade.

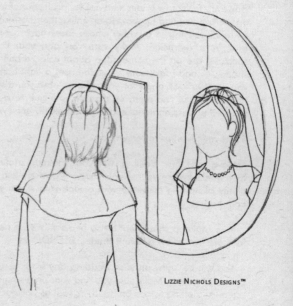

LIZZIE NICHOLS DESIGNS™

• Chapter 22 •

Foul whisp'rings are abroad.

—William Shakespeare (1564–1616), English poet and playwright

It didn't take long for the press to figure out where Jill Higgins was meeting her new mystery pal—though I managed to keep my own picture out of the tabloids by not walking her to her car anymore.

In no time word was out all over town that Jill Higgins, the bride of the wedding of the century, was using Monsieur Henri as her personal certified wedding-gown specialist. The next thing anybody knew, we were beating off the hordes of brides descending on the little shop demanding that we work on their gowns, as well. Jean-Paul and Jean-Pierre had to be employed as doormen/bouncers to keep the paparazzi out, and the brides coming in.

Any residual resentment the Henris might have felt toward me for not letting on that I knew French fell by the wayside when they realized they were booking so many appointments with desperate brides, they had to buy a two-year calendar.

Not that either Henri had laid so much as a finger on Jill's dress since she'd brought it in. Monsieur Henri had tried after I told him my plan, telling me that it could never be done and that I was going to get sued by John MacDowell's mother.

His wife, however, calmly lifted the gown from his fingers and handed it back to me, with a gentle, "Jean. Let her get to work."

Which I appreciated. Especially considering the "stupid" remark. She had evidently changed her mind, and now the dress—Jill's dress—hung on a special hook in the back of the workroom, where every day I flung back the sheet that covered it, took in what I'd done the day before, and what I needed to get done in the next few hours, freaked out, then got to work.

They say it's always darkest until right before the dawn. I've worked on enough projects to know how true this saying really is. A week before Christmas—I'd promised to have Jill's dress done by the day before Christmas Eve, so there'd be time for any last-minute alterations before the ceremony on New Year's Eve—I was sure the dress would never get done on time . . . or worse, that it would get done but look awful. It's no joke making a size twelve out of a size six. Monsieur Henri had been right to say such an undertaking was impossible.

Except it wasn't. Impossible, I mean. It was just really, really hard. It required hours of backbreaking seam snipping, even more of sewing, and the consumption of many, many, many diet Cokes. I was in the shop from two-thirty in the afternoon—as soon as I could make it there after my shift at Pendergast, Loughlin, and Flynn, still my only paying gig—until midnight, sometimes even one in the morning, at which point I would stagger home, fall into bed, and wake at six-thirty the next day to shower and dress and go back to the law firm. I rarely if ever saw my boyfriend, let alone anyone else. But that was all right, because Luke was just as busy studying for his finals. If he hoped to finish his postbac program in a year, he had to cram as many classes as he could into each semester, which meant he had four finals to worry about—basically the academic equivalent of making a size-six dress into a size twelve.

But even though I haven't seen much of my boyfriend in the past few weeks, I've seen plenty of the box he placed under the tiny Christmas tree he bought on the street—complete with a miniature stand—and put in front of the windows, so the twinkling lights he wrapped around it could shine down on Fifth Avenue. I saw it (the box, I mean) the minute I stepped through the door one night after a long, painful battle with the tartan on Jill's dress. It was kind of hard to miss—again, I'm talking about the box.

Because it's huge.

Seriously, the box is the size of a miniature pony. Or at least a cocker spaniel. It's almost bigger than the tree itself. It is definitely NOT a ring box.

But, as Tiffany said, when I mentioned this to her, "Oh, maybe he's one of those."

"One of what?" I asked.

"You know, one of those guys who don't like it when their girl-friend guesses what they're giving to her, so they put it in like a mil-lion different boxes inside of boxes, so she won't be able to shake it and guess."

This makes brilliant sense, of course. Luke knows perfectly well I can't keep a secret (though I've been doing pretty well since moving to New York. Really, I think I'm maturing). It's a short step from not being able to keep a secret to not being able to keep from snooping in one's Christmas presents. It's true I already accidentally snagged the silver foil wrapping paper on the box just a little by vacuuming too close to it the other night. But I stopped myself from peeling the foil back.

I know Tiffany's right, and that Luke is doing the box-within-the-box thing. That's just so like him.

Which is why I did the same for the sleek leather wallet I got him from Coach. The box I used to disguise the much smaller box the wallet actually comes in is a box Mrs. Erickson gave me that used to contain multiple bottles of dishwashing liquid that she bought two years ago during a trip to Sam's Club in New Jersey. It's taken her this long to get through enough bottles to throw out the box.

I just hope Luke doesn't take a big sniff of his gift. Because if he does he'll get a snootful of liquid Dawn.

And then, before I know it, it's the day before Christmas Eve, and I'm as nervous as a kid about to visit the Santa in the mall. Not about Luke's gift to me—although that has me plenty jittery—or about the fact that the two of us are about to spend over a week apart in totally different parts of the world, but about what Jill's going to think of her dress. Because—as these things do—it had finally come together a few days before, and now . . . well, even Madame Henri had looked at it, then at me, and said gravely, "Good. Very good."

Which, from her, is high praise indeed. But even more meaningful was her husband's critique, which included several scratchings of the chin . . . much pacing . . . two or three pointed questions about tartan ribbon . . . and finally a nod and a *"Parfait."*

Not the ice cream, but "perfect."

But he isn't the critic of whose opinion I'm most afraid. We still need to make sure Jill likes it.

She finally shows an hour after we've shut down the shop— shooed out the last appointment for the day, pulled down the blinds, and finally, switched off the lights in the front room, to make it look as if everyone had gone home. This is, of course, to throw off the paparazzi.

Then, when the doorbell rings at precisely seven o'clock, Madame Henri hurries to unlock the door, still not flicking on any lights. Two shadowy forms slip inside. At first I think Jill has brought her fiancé and I feel a burst of irritation with her—everyone knows it's bad luck for the groom to see the bridal gown before the wedding.

But then I remember how Jill had come to each fitting alone, looking so hounded, not just by the press, but by her own social isolation, seeing as how her family lives so far away, and her friends know no more about wedding gowns than she does.

And I'm glad she's brought John with her, because he's really done everything he could to make things easier for her—even recently intervening in the prenup negotiations, and demanding that Jill be given a fair agreement or his parents will be stricken from the guest list for the reception, a bold move that succeeded perfectly, and made Mr. Pendergast so giddy that he ordered an extra round of champagne for everyone at the firm's Christmas party at Montrachet (from which I'd had to duck out early to get back to work on Jill's dress, thus missing the highlight of the evening: Roberta getting so drunk, she was found making out with Daryl, the fax and copy supervisor, in the cloakroom—unfortunately by Tiffany, who took snaps of the event with her camera phone, and e-mailed them to all of us).

So that's why, when Madame Henri finally judges it safe to switch on the lights, I'm shocked to see that the person Jill has brought with her is not loyal, lovable John at all, but an older woman—almost an exact replica of her, as a matter of fact—whom she introduces as her mother.

My surprise is followed quickly by a rush of relief. *Yes.* Jill has an ally at last—one besides me and her husband-to-be, I mean.

"Lizzie, hello," Mrs. Higgins says, pumping my hand with the same heartiness her daughter habitually employs in her handshakes, as if she's unaware of her own strength, which in Jill's case is considerable, given the fact that she routinely lifts hundred-pound seals. "I'm so glad to meet you. Jill's told me so much about you. She says you practically saved her life . . . and that you're very generous with—what were they again, honey? Yoodles?"

"Yodels," Jill says, looking embarrassed. "Sorry, I had to tell her about that time we met, in the bathroom—"

"Oh, sure," I say with a laugh. "We have more in the back if you want some—" Given all the work I've been doing, the low-carb diet has completely fallen by the wayside. I have no idea how much weight I've gained recently, but it's not inconsiderable. And yet I find it really hard to care, I'm so excited about Jill's dress.

"No, that's okay," Jill says, laughing. "I'm good. So. Are you ready?"

"I'm ready if you are," I say. "Let's go."

And I take her into the back, while Monsieur and Madame Henri offer Mrs. Higgins a chair and some champagne.

My fingers are shaking as I lower the rich ivory folds over Jill's head, but I try to hide my nervousness by explaining, "All right, Jill, this cut is what we call an empire waist. It means the waistline falls just beneath the breasts, which on you is the narrowest part of your body. What this will do is allow the skirt to fall straight down your body, kind of flowing around it, which is what someone with your body type wants. The empire waist was made popular by Josephine, the wife of Napoleon Bonaparte, who adapted it from Roman togas she saw depicted on ancient art. Now, as you can see, we've gone off the shoulder, because you have such nice shoulders, we wanted you to show them off. And then this right here—this is the original tartan that was hanging off the old dress—and we're using it as a sash beneath the breastline, see? It emphasizes your tiny waist. And finally, here are some gloves—I was thinking above the elbow, so that they almost reach the dangling straps there . . . Well." I've steered her in front of a full-length mirror. "What do you think? I was thinking hair up, with maybe some curly tendrils hanging down, to sort of complete the Grecian urn look . . ."

Jill is staring at her reflection. It takes me a minute to realize that her silence isn't disapproval. Her eyes are as wide as quarters and just as shiny. She's holding back tears.

"Oh, Lizzie" is all she seems able to say.

"Is it terrible?" I ask nervously. "It's all the original dress. I just took out the seams . . . well, pretty much *all* the seams. It was hard, but I really think this style suits you. You have sort of classic proportions, and there's nothing more classic than Grecian urns—"

"I want to show Mom," Jill says in a choked voice.

"Okay," I say, hurrying behind her to lift the four-foot train I've attached to the back of the gown. "This hooks up, you know, into a sort of drapy bustle off the back for when you're dancing. I didn't want it to get in your way. But I wanted you to have some presence, you know, because St. Patrick's Cathedral is so huge—"

But she's already tearing out of the back room and into the front of the shop, where her mother and the Henris are waiting.

"Mom!" Jill cries when she bursts through the curtain separating the shop from the back room. "Look!"

Mrs. Higgins chokes on the champagne she is in the act of swallowing. Madame Henri wallops her on the back a few times and the woman is finally able to recover enough to say, her eyes glistening as much as her daughter's, "Oh, honey. You look gorgeous."

"I do," Jill says, sounding shocked. "I do, don't I?"

"You really do," Mrs. Higgins says, hurrying over to get a closer look. "That's the dress she gave you? The old battle-axe—I mean, John's mother?"

"This is the dress," I say. I feel funny inside. I can't really explain it. But it's like a combination of excitement and joy at the same time. Really, the only appropriate way to describe it would be to say it feels like someone's opened up a bottle of champagne—*inside* me. Or, as Tiffany would say, up my cootchy. "Obviously, I modified it a bit."

"A bit!" Jill echoes with a giggle. Yes! A giggle! From Blubber! This is big. *Really* big.

"It's just so lovely," Mrs. Higgins coos. "She looks like . . . well, like a princess!"

"Speaking of which, we need to talk headpieces," I say. "I was telling her she should wear her hair up, with just a few curly tendrils hanging down in back. So maybe a tiara isn't a bad idea. I think it would look really pretty against her hair—"

But it's clear no one is listening to me. The two Higgins ladies are staring at Jill's reflection in the shop mirror, murmuring softly to each other, and giggling. To look at them, it would be hard to imagine that just weeks ago the bride had been weeping in a ladies' room and often showed up for her fittings smelling of seal poo.

"Well," Madame Henri says to me, when I walk over to join the couple, since it's clear neither client nor her mother is listening to me. "You did it."

"I did," I say, still feeling a little bit dazed.

Then Madame Henri does something that surprises me. She reaches down and clasps my hand in hers. "For you," she says with a smile.

Then Madame Henri slips something into my hand. I look down and see a check. With a lot of zeroes on it.

A thousand dollars!

When I look up again, I see that Monsieur Henri is looking embarrassed but pleased.

"Consider it your Christmas bonus," he says in French.

Touched, I rush over to hug him—and his wife—spontaneously. "Thank you!" I cry. "You're both just—*fantastique!*"

"So, you're coming, right?" Jill asks me later as I'm carefully helping her out of the dress. "To the wedding, right? And the reception? You know you're invited. You and a guest. You can bring that boyfriend of yours I've heard so much about."

"Oh, Jill," I say, smiling. "That is so sweet of you. I'd love to come. Only Luke won't be able to make it. He's going to France for the holidays."

Jill looks confused. "Without you?"

I make sure my smile stays in place. "Sure. To visit his parents. But don't worry. I wouldn't miss your wedding for the world."

"Great," Jill says. "So I know I'll have at least one friend. Besides my family and the guys from the zoo, I mean."

"I think you'll be finding out soon that you have a lot more friends than you know," I say, meaning it.

Walking home that night, I feel as if I'm floating on a cloud. The thousand-dollar check and wedding invitation are the least of it. The fact that she'd liked it—*really* liked it!—is all I can think about.

And she'd looked so good! Just like I'd known she would. Mrs. MacDowell was going to DIE when she saw Jill coming down the aisle. Just die. She had given her future daughter-in-law that dress to humiliate her, because she didn't approve of her son's choice.

Well, who was going to be humiliated now, when "Blubber" turned out to be the most beautiful bride of the season?

And I was going to be there to watch it all take place! Honestly, I have the best job in the entire world. Even, you know, if it doesn't pay what you'd call a regular salary.

I'm still floating as I head into our building and up the elevator to our apartment. I'm still floating when I unlock the door and find Luke inside, with the Christmas tree's lights lit, holding a bottle of wine and going, "There you are! Finally!"

"Oh, Luke!" I cry. "You won't believe it. But she loved it. Absolutely loved it. And Monsieur and Madame Henri gave me a Christmas bonus, and Jill invited me to her wedding—too bad you're going to miss it. But the important thing is, she really, really loved the dress. And she looked great in it, too. No one will be calling her 'Blubber' ever again."

"That's great, Lizzie!" Luke has poured us each a glass of wine. It's only then that I realize the lights are off—all except the Christmas-tree lights and a few candles. He's set up a cheeseboard and some bowls of snacks he knows I like—spicy nuts and candied orange peel. It's so festive—and romantic.

Then he says, as he hands me one of the glasses of wine he's poured, "I couldn't have picked a more perfect gift for you then. Do you want to open it now?"

Couldn't have picked a more perfect gift for me? Because everything else is going so perfectly and proposing to me will just make my evening that much better? That's the only thing I can think of that he could mean.

"Of course I want to open it now," I cry. "You know I've been dying to ever since you put it there!"

"Well, have at it," Luke says. Which is a strange thing to say to someone you're about to propose to under a Christmas tree. But whatever.

Taking my wineglass with me, I go to sit on the parquet beside my gift and wait until he's seated by his.

"Do you want to go first?" I ask, thinking that my gift to him is really going to be a letdown after the tears of joy that are going to follow his to me. But he says, "No, you first. I'm so excited to see what you think," so I shrug and dig in.

When I peel off the wrapping paper to find beneath it a giant box that says "Quantum-Futura CE-200" on it, I begin to lose my happy, floaty feeling. But when I see that the picture on the box is of a sewing machine, the floating feeling goes away entirely.

And when I look up questioningly and see Luke beaming at me from across his wineglass, not looking at all like he's about to propose, I actually start feeling . . . well. Pretty bad.

"It's a sewing machine!" he cries. "To replace the one my dad broke. But this one is way better than the one he kicked. The lady at the store said it's the top of the line. You can do all sorts of embroidery and stuff with it. It comes with a minicomputer inside!"

I blink down at the gigantic box. An investment for my future. That's what he'd said.

And that's what he'd given me, all right.

And before I know what's happening, I'm crying.

~ Lizzie Nichols's Wedding Gown Guide ~

Weddings are supposed to be a happy time. That's why no one, least of all the bride, ever wants to admit that sometimes—well, weddings just don't happen. Maybe the groom gets cold feet. Maybe the bride does. Maybe the couple decides the timing isn't right after all. Maybe a beloved family member passes away, making everyone uncomfortable with the idea of holding a celebration during a time of mourning. In any event, things happen.

That's why the savvy bride purchases wedding insurance. Like travel insurance, wedding insurance will guarantee that you don't lose the entirety of your deposits on things like venues, cakes, photographers, food suppliers, wedding limos, flowers, honeymoon, even your gown . . .

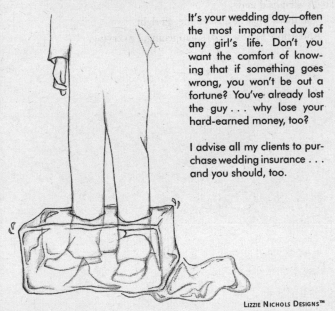

It's your wedding day—often the most important day of any girl's life. Don't you want the comfort of knowing that if something goes wrong, you won't be out a fortune? You've already lost the guy . . . why lose your hard-earned money, too?

I advise all my clients to purchase wedding insurance . . . and you should, too.

LIZZIE NICHOLS DESIGNS™

• Chapter 23 •

Love and scandal are the best sweeteners of tea.

—Henry Fielding (1707–1754), English writer

hat's the matter?" Luke cries, watching me break down. "What . . . did I get the wrong one? Why are you crying?"

"No—" I can't believe this. I can't believe I'm crying in front of him. I can't believe I don't have better control of myself. This is ridiculous. It's not his fault. It's my fault. I'm the one who got the ridiculous idea that when he said my gift was an investment for my future, that he meant . . . that he meant . . .

"That I meant what?" he asks bewilderedly.

And then, to my horror, I realize I've been speaking out loud. No! I've been so good! I've been so careful! I've laid out so many tiny bread crumbs for him to follow! I can't bash him over the head with a mallet now. Not when he's come so close—

"That you were giving me an engagement ring," I hear myself sob, "and that you were going to ask me to marry you!"

There. I've done it. It's out. It's floating out in the universe now, for anyone to hear—even Luke.

And, just as I'd known, deep down—just as I'd always known, somehow, even before Shari and Chaz tried to warn me—he's horrified.

"*Marry* you?" he bursts out. "Lizzie . . . I mean, you know I love you. But . . . we've only been going out for six months!"

Six months. Six years. It doesn't make any difference. I realize that now. There are some woodland creatures that, no matter how many bread crumbs you leave out for them . . . no matter how patiently you wait . . . are never going to be yours. They'll never let themselves be tamed. Because they prefer to run wild and free in the forest.

And that's what Luke is. Everyone else could see it. Just not me. I'm the only idiot who refused to acknowledge the truth. That he's happy to live with me now. But not forever. Six months. Six years. He's never going to let himself get tied down.

At least not by me.

"I thought we were having fun," Luke is saying. He appears to be genuinely upset. "I love living with you, it's been great—but marriage. I mean, Lizzie, I can't even see where I'm going to be next year, let alone four years from now, when I'm finished with medical school—if I even get into medical school! Which I don't even know if I will! How can I ask you to marry me? How can I ask *anyone* to marry me? I'm not even sure—I mean, I can't say for sure if I'll *ever* get married. I don't know if marriage is something that will *ever* even be on my radar."

"Oh," I say quietly.

Because what else can I say to this? Obviously, this is a conversation we ought to have had some time ago. I mean, if he isn't even sure marriage is something he wants down the line . . . not just with me, but with *anyone* . . .

Except that maybe he might have realized it was something he wanted if I'd played it cooler. But of course now I've ruined everything by opening my big mouth. If I had just hung on for a bit longer . . .

But no. A year from now . . . two . . . he'll still be saying the same thing. I can see that by the panic in his eyes. It's completely different than what I see in John MacDowell's eyes when he looks at Jill. Or even what I used to see in Chaz's eyes when he looked at Shari.

How could I have been so blind? How could I not have seen that that look was never in Luke's eyes?

"It's okay," I say gently. I'm so tired. So, so tired. I've been working so hard. And tomorrow I have to get on a plane and fly home.

Thank God. All I want, at that moment, is to be home and in my mother's arms . . . the way Jill flew to her mother's arms, only for a different reason. Jill's was joyful.

Mine? Not so joyful.

"God, Lizzie," Luke is saying. "I feel so terrible. If there was ever anything, anything I did to make you think—but I mean, you told me that thing, about how you want to open your own shop. So I just assumed you felt the same way. That marriage wasn't even in the equation. Because supposing we get married and I get into medical school out in California? You'd have to give up the shop! You wouldn't want to do that. Give up your business, for me? Of course not. Or supposing after I graduate, I get some job in like Vermont or something . . . Would you want to go to *Vermont* with me?"

The answer, of course, is yes. Yes, actually, I would. I would go anywhere, Luke. Anywhere. And give up anything. As long as we could be together.

But clearly he doesn't feel this way about me.

"I just . . ." Luke is going around, turning on the lights. I blink in the sudden brightness. "Lizzie, I'm so sorry. Oh God. I've really fucked everything up, haven't I?"

"No," I say, shaking my head, and using the back of my wrist to dry the tears from my cheeks. "No, you haven't. I'm sorry. I'm the silly one. I just have weddings on the brain, or something. A hazard of the profession. It's just—"

"It's just what?" he asks, coming up to me and putting his arms around my waist. "Lizzie—what can I do to make this right between us? Because I want to. I want to keep having fun, like we were—"

"Yeah," I say. I'm about to shrug it off. Because what's the point, really?

But somehow this time . . . I can't. I just can't. Maybe because of the joy I'd just seen on Jill's face. Maybe because I'm realizing I'm not actually going to get to casually reply, when one of my sisters asks if that's an engagement ring on my finger, "Why, yes. Yes, it is," when I go home tomorrow. I don't know.

But it's time, I realize, to be honest. With Luke. And with myself.

"Fun's great," I say. "But, you know, Luke . . . I *want* to get married someday. I really do. And if you don't . . . well, what's the point of even being together? I mean, don't you think it'd be better for us to break up, so we can get back out there and try to find the person we *can* picture a future with?"

"Hey," Luke says, pressing his lips to my hair. "Hey, don't talk like that. I didn't say I can't picture a future with you. I'm just saying that right now I can't picture a future for myself—let alone with anyone else! So how can I presume to put you in it, as well . . . much as I might like to see you there?"

I rest my cheek against his chest. I can feel the crisp starch of his white button-down, and smell the light scent of the eau de cologne he wears as aftershave. It's a smell I've come to associate with sex and laughter.

Until now.

"I know," I say, gently pushing him away. "And I'm really sorry. But I have to go."

And I turn and head into the bedroom, where my suitcase for tomorrow's trip sits. The only thing I haven't packed yet is my toiletries. I go into the bathroom to do that now.

"You're kidding me with this, right?" Luke's followed me. "This is a joke."

"It's not a joke," I say, slipping my toothbrush and facial soap into my Luscious Lana toiletries bag. I can barely see what I'm doing, because my eyes are so filled with tears. Stupid eyes.

I brush past him to stuff my toiletry bag and cosmetics bag into my suitcase. Then I wrench up the little pull handle and begin dragging my bag to the door.

"Lizzie." Luke darts in front of me. His expression is anxious. "What is the matter with you? I've never seen you like this—"

"What?" I demand, a little more sharply than I mean to. "You've never seen me angry before? You're right. That's because I've been trying to be on my best behavior with you, Luke. Because I've been trying to prove to you that I'm worthy of you. Worthy of being with a guy as great as you. It's like . . . it's like this apartment. This beautiful apartment. I've been trying to act like the kind of person who would live in a place like this . . . a place with a little Renoir girl on the wall. But you know what I figured out? I don't *want* to be the kind of person who would live in a place like this. Because I don't *like* the kind of people who live in places like this—people who cheat on their husbands and lead girls to believe they've got a future together when they don't because they're not interested in marriage, only in having fun. Because I think I'm worth more than that."

Luke blinks at me. "Who's cheating on their husband?" he asks, puzzled.

"Ask your mother who she met for lunch the day after Thanksgiving!" I say before I can stop myself. Inwardly, I groan. Okay, that's it. I have to get out. Now. "Good-bye, Luke."

But Luke doesn't take the hint and get out of my way. Instead, he sets his jaw.

"Lizzie," he says in a different tone from before. "You're being ridiculous. It's ten o'clock at night. Where do you even think you're going?"

"What do you even care?" I demand.

"Lizzie. I *care*. You *know* I care. How can you just walk out like this?"

"Because," I say. "I can't do for now. I need forever. I *deserve* forever."

I shove past him, unlock the door, and pull my suitcase out into the hallway, stopping only to grab my coat and purse along the way.

It's sort of hard to make a superdramatic exit like that, though, when you have to stand there and wait for the elevator to come. Luke leans in the doorway, staring at me.

"You know I'm not going to run after you," he says.

I don't say anything.

"And I'm leaving for France tomorrow," he goes on.

I stare at the numbers above the door of the elevator as they light up, one by one. They're a bit blurry, because of my unshed tears.

"Lizzie," he says in his infuriatingly reasonable tone. "Where are you going to go, huh? You're going to find a new place over Christmas vacation? This city shuts down the week between Christmas and New Year's. Look, let's just use this time apart to cool off a little, okay? Just . . . just be here when I get back. So we can talk. Okay?"

Thankfully, the elevator finally comes. I get on it. And, not caring that the uniformed elevator attendant is listening, say, "Good-bye, Luke."

The elevator doors close.

∼ Lizzie Nichols's Wedding Gown Guide ∼

The party's over . . .

What to do with your gown now that your wedding is through?

Well, many women choose to save their wedding gown for their future daughters or granddaughters to wear at their own weddings. Others may choose simply to store their wedding gowns for the sake of posterity.

Whichever you choose, it's important to have your wedding gown cleaned after its final wearing, as even hidden stains, such as those from champagne or perspiration, can discolor the delicate material over time.

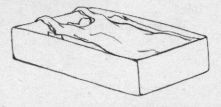

But some women, once their dress has been cleaned and placed in a preservation box, may find that it no longer holds the sentimental value for them that it once did. Perhaps their marriage ended in divorce, or even the death of their spouse.

While it may hold painful memories for you, don't throw your wedding gown away—donate it to Lizzie Nichols Designs™ or any one of numerous 501(c)(3) charities that exist to help impoverished brides have the wedding of their dreams—501(c)(3) charities are fully tax deductible, so you'll be making your accountant happy, too.

You'll be helping a fellow bride in need, and you'll be replacing possibly unhappy memories with new, joyful ones. Try it . . . you won't be sorry!

LIZZIE NICHOLS DESIGNS™

• Chapter 24 •

There is only one thing in the world worse than being talked about, and that is not being talked about.

—Oscar Wilde (1854–1900), Anglo-Irish playwright, novelist, and poet

I t's my fault," I say.

"It's not your fault," Shari says.

"No," I say. "It is. It *is*. I should have asked him. Back in France, I should have just asked him how he feels about marriage. You know? I could have avoided all of this if I hadn't played that stupid woodland creature game. For once, if I actually *had* opened my mouth, I might have spared myself a lot of pain and hardship."

"Yes," Shari says. "But you wouldn't have gotten laid as much."

"True," I say with a tearful sigh. "So true."

"Better?" Shari wants to know as she presses the cool washcloth against my forehead.

I nod. I am stretched out on her girlfriend Pat's futon couch, in their nice big living room in their Park Slope apartment. On either side of me is a large Labrador retriever. Scooter, on the left, is a black Lab. Jethro, on the right, is a golden.

Even though we've only just met, I love them both very, very much.

"Who's a good boy?" I ask Jethro. "Who?"

I see Pat look uneasily at Shari. Shari says, "Don't worry. She'll be all right. She's just had a bit of a shock."

"I'll be fine," I say. "I'm just going back home tomorrow to visit my family. But I'll be back. I'm not staying in Ann Arbor. New York didn't chew me up and spit me out. Not like it did Kathy Pennebaker."

"Of course you're coming back," Shari says. "We're coming back on the same flight on Sunday. Remember?"

"Right," I say. "I'll be back, and I'll be fine. I'll land on my feet. Because I always do."

"Of course you do," Shari says. "We're going to go to bed now, all right, Lizzie? You stay out here with Scooter and Jethro. And if you need anything—anything at all—don't be shy about coming to wake us up. I'll leave the hall light on, just in case. Okay?"

"Okay," I murmur as Jethro licks my hand in long, steady strokes. "Good night."

"Good night," Shari and Pat call. And turn out the light and leave the room.

I hear Pat whisper to Shari, "Wait . . . did he really give her a *sewing machine*?"

"Yes," I hear Shari whisper back. "She'd convinced herself he was getting her a ring."

"Poor thing," Pat murmurs.

Then I can't hear them anymore, because they go into their bedroom and close the door.

I lie there, blinking in the semidarkness. I'd come out of Luke's mother's building, hailed a cab, and instructed the driver to take me to Park Slope. I'd had to call Shari to get the exact address. She'd been able to tell by my tone that it was an emergency and had instructed me to come right over without even asking for details. That's what best friends do for each other, after all.

Pat's place is very pretty and pleasant, a basement apartment with a lot of wainscoting and sage-colored walls and spider plants hanging in baskets from the ceiling. There are pictures of ducks on the walls. The blanket Pat put over my shoulders when I came, weeping, through the door, had a mallard duck on it.

There is something very comforting about ducks used as an item of decor. I personally wouldn't want a duck motif in my house, but I am heartened by the fact that someone does.

Maybe, I think, as I lie there between Jethro and Scooter, whose hot, stinky breath I find almost as comforting as the ducks, *Shari and Pat will let me move in here with them.* Just until I can find a place of my own. That would be nice, three girls against the world. The world of men. Men who aren't sure they see marriage in their future . . . or at least, not marriage with a girl like me.

"It's my fault" was what I'd kept telling Shari, when I first came through the door. "I mean, how can I expect him to know he wants to marry me when he only met me six months ago?"

"Well, even if marriage isn't important to him," Pat had said crisply, "he might have realized it'd be important to a girl who earns her living making wedding dresses."

"I don't actually earn my living that way," I'd informed her.

"The guy is a rat fink," Shari had replied. "Here, drink this."

The whiskey helped. Hearing Shari call Luke a rat fink didn't. Because deep down inside, I know he's not a rat fink. He's just a guy who, up until a few months ago, didn't know what he wanted to do with his life. Or rather, he knew . . . he was just afraid to take the risk and try it. Until I came along and encouraged him.

Maybe that's his problem with marriage. Maybe he's just afraid to take the risk and admit that there might be a girl out there with whom he could picture spending the rest of his life. Obviously that girl isn't me. But maybe that's just because, despite everything I've been telling myself for the past six months, Luke and I aren't right for each other after all. Maybe I haven't even met my soul mate yet. Or maybe I have, and I missed him.

Or maybe, like Chaz is always saying, you make your own soul mate.

Maybe the truth is that getting married isn't the be-all and end-all of the universe. Lots of perfectly happy people aren't married. They don't sit around crying about it. In fact, they'd probably laugh at the idea of ever getting married. There's nothing wrong with being single . . .

. . . which is what I keep telling my mother and sisters when I get back to Ann Arbor the next day. Because of course they can all tell by my reddened, weepy eyes that something is wrong.

"Luke and I broke up," I tell them. "He wasn't ready for a commitment, and I was."

And Rose and Sarah have a few snarky things to say about it. Rose: "I knew it wouldn't last. I mean, you met him while you were on vacation. Vacation flings never last." Sarah: "Guys never want a commitment. That's why you should have just let yourself get pregnant. Once he knows there's a bun in the oven, he commits fast enough. I mean, when his mom finds out she's about to be a grandma, anyway."

But I don't want to get my husband the way Rose and Sarah got theirs. Because that's as dishonest as my whole woodland creature strategy.

And look how that turned out.

Fortunately Shari's Christmas Eve announcement to her parents about her new girlfriend takes all the attention off me, and is soon the talk of the neighborhood, thanks to Mrs. Dennis's speed dial. Dr. Dennis, I later learn, responds to the news with a mere tightening of the lips and a trip to his liquor cabinet.

But Mrs. Dennis has soon appointed herself the community spokeswoman for PFLAG. "It stands for Parents, Families, and Friends of Lesbians and Gays," Shari's mother proudly tells mine over Christmas Day dinner. "It's the national organization for promoting the health and well-being of gay, lesbian, and bisexual persons, as well as their families and friends."

"Well," Mom says. "How nice."

"Would you like to join?" Mrs. Dennis asks. "I have a pamphlet right here."

"Oh," Mom says, putting down her forkful of Yorkshire pudding. "I'd love to."

Shari winks at me from across the table. *Did he call?* she mouths. Because Shari is convinced that, despite what I think, it's not over between me and Luke, and that he's going to call me, and we'll talk things out, and everything will be fine.

Shari lives in a fantasy world. Possibly due to all the ducks.

Christmas Day is always a zoo at the Nichols household, because Mom hosts all of her children and grandchildren, in addition to Grandma and the Dennises and the occasional graduate assistant of my dad's who can't afford plane fare home for the holidays, and so comes over with a dish from their native country to share (which is how our holiday meals often consist of beef Wellington with a side dish of malai koftas and a basket of fresh-baked poori).

There is no escape from the shrieking of the under-six set, and the relentless cheer of Mom's caroling with the Muppets record, and Dad's grad student's patient explanation to everyone at the dinner table that the defocusing effect of the radial field gradient is compensated by ridges on the magnet faces which vary the field azimuthally, and Rose's breakdown because her latest EPT showed two blue lines instead of the one she expected, and Sarah's fury because she asked for white gold diamond stud earrings, and her husband, Chuck, got her yellow gold instead ("I mean, is he *color blind*?").

And through it all I clutch my cell phone in my hand, occasionally thinking I feel it jump—but it's only my own heartbeat I feel, I guess, because he doesn't call, not even to wish me a merry Christmas.

And I don't call him because—well, how can I?

It's when I'm seeking some kind of relief from the stream of tears and chatter of the rest of the house that I stumble across Grandma in the basement rec room, perched in front of the television in the La-Z-Boy she demanded my parents buy her, watching *It's a Wonderful Life*—the original, not colorized, version.

"Hey, Gran," I say, sinking down onto the couch. "Jimmy Stewart, huh?"

Grandma grunts. I don't miss the bottle of Bud in her hand. It's one of the special ones Angelo, Rose's bohunk husband, prepared for her, filled with nonalcoholic beer instead of the real thing. Not that it makes any difference. Grandma will act drunk later anyway.

"That's when they knew how to make *real* movies," Grandma says, gesturing toward the screen with her beer bottle. "This one. What's that other one, with that Rick? Oh, right. *Casablanca*. Those were real movies. Nothing blowing up. No talking monkeys. Just smart talk. Nobody knows how to do that in movies anymore. It's like everyone in Hollywood got retarded."

I think I feel my phone vibrate. But it's nothing. A second later, I have to bow my head to hide my tears.

"This guy's good," Grandma goes on, indicating Jimmy Stewart with her beer bottle. "But I like that Rick, who owned the café in *Casablanca*. Now, he was the real deal. You remember when he helps the girl's husband win the money, so she doesn't have to sleep with that Frenchie to get it? That's a real man, for you. What does Rick get for going to all the trouble? Not a thing. Except peace of mind. I don't want that Brad Pitt phony baloney. What'd he ever do, except take his shirt off, and adopt a lot of orphans? Rick never takes his shirt off. He doesn't need to! We don't need to see him naked to know he's a real man! That's why I'd take Rick over that Brad Pitt any day. Because he's such a real man, he doesn't need to take his shirt off to prove it. Hey. What're you crying for?"

"Oh, Gran," I choke. "Everything—everything is so awful!"

"What're you, pregnant?" Grandma wants to know.

"No, Gran, of course not," I say.

"Don't of course not me," she says. "That's all any of your sisters ever do. Get knocked up right and left. You'd think they'd never heard there's a population crisis. So what's the matter with you, if you're not pregnant?"

"Ev-everything was going so well," I sob. "In N-New York, I mean.

I think I might really be able to make something out of this wedding dress rehab thing. I can figure out which way is First Avenue and which way is First Street. I finally found a place I can afford that does good highlights . . . and then I had to go and cry when Luke gave me my Christmas present, because I thought I was g-getting an engagement ring, and he g-got me a . . . sewing machine!"

Grandma takes a meditative sip of her beer. Then she says evenly, "If your grandfather had ever given me a sewing machine for Christmas, I'd have hit him over the head with it."

"Oh, Gran!" I can barely see, I'm weeping so hard. "Don't you see? It's not the gift. It's that he doesn't want to get married—ever! He says he can't look that far into the future. But don't you think if you love someone, Gran, even if you can't see where you'll be or what you'll be doing twenty years from now, you'd still know you want that person to be there?"

"Well, of course," Grandma says. "And if he said he didn't know, well, you were right to give him the old heave-ho."

"It's more complicated than that, Gran. I mean, don't tell Mom, but Luke and I—we've been l-living together."

Grandma snorts at this information. "Even worse. He's had a taste, and he's still not sure he likes you well enough to make a permanent go of it someday? Tell him toodleloo. Who does he think he is, anyway—Brad Pitt?"

"But, Gran, maybe some guys really do need longer than six months to know whether or not a girl they like is the one for them."

"If he's a Pitt, maybe," Grandma says with a snort. "But not if he's a Rick."

It takes a few seconds for me to digest this. Then I say, "If I move out, I'm going to have to find a whole new place to live. I'll probably have to pay even more in rent than I am now. Because I got the girlfriend deal on my current place."

"Which would you rather have," Grandma asks, "money? Or your dignity?"

"Both," I say.

"So? Find a way to have both, then. You're up to the challenge. You're the one who was always going around, claiming you could fix anything with a glue gun and a needle and thread. Now go open your grandma another beer. And make it a real one this time. I'm tired of this nonalcoholic crap. It's just empty calories for *nothing*."

I get up and take Grandma's empty beer bottle from her. Her gaze is glued back to the screen. Jimmy Stewart is running down the street, wishing Mr. Potter a merry Christmas.

"Gran," I say. "How come you like Sully on *Dr. Quinn* so much, but you hate Brad Pitt? Isn't Sully always taking his shirt off, too?"

Grandma looks up at me as if I've lost my mind. "That's *television*," she says. "That isn't *movies*. That's completely different."

~ Lizzie Nichols's Wedding Gown Guide ~

You did it! You're married at last! All that hard work, all those grueling hours . . . now it's time to head to the reception and PARTAY!

But wait . . . do you have your wedding toast ready?

Not just best men and fathers of the bride are standing up to say a few words at wedding receptions anymore. These days, more often than not, the bride herself is paying a hefty portion of the cost of the wedding. So why shouldn't she take a moment to say a few words?

The best bridal speeches include a little bit of everything—humor, warmth, and yes, even some tears. But here are some absolute musts:

Thank guests who've traveled a long way to get to the ceremony/reception, or otherwise have gone out of their way to be with you.

Thank everyone for their gifts and generosity (this does not preclude your having to write thank-you notes later).

Thank any of your friends who have put up with you during the wedding preparations. This includes any members of the bridal party who have gone above and beyond for you (of course, anyone who agrees to stand up with you at your wedding is going above and beyond for you, so you should probably include them all).

Thank your mom and dad. Especially if they're paying. Even if they're not, acknowledge any special role they might have had in your courtship/ceremony.

Thank your future husband for putting up with you. A funny story about how you met or fell in love would also work.

Finally, toast your guests, and thank them again for coming to help you celebrate your special day.

Then get wasted. Only not so much that you mess up your dress.

• Chapter 25 •

a sewing machine?" Tiffany looks shocked. "No. No way."

"It's not the sewing machine," I say to her. "I mean, that was the catalyst for the conversation in which I later realized he doesn't feel about me the same way I feel about him."

"But a *sewing machine?*"

It's the Monday after Christmas, the first day back at work, and my second day back in New York. I'd spent what was left of Sunday scouring the want ads, trying to find an apartment that—unlike the empty one sitting over the shop, which Madame Henri wanted two thousand bucks a month for—I could afford.

But it was hopeless. The only places I saw for a thousand dollars or less a month were roommate shares. In Jersey City. And urged potential sharers to keep an open mind.

It was especially depressing to be sitting in Luke's mother's Fifth Avenue apartment, with the Mirós on the wall and the steps to the Metropolitan Museum of Art right outside the double-paned windows, looking at ad after ad that stated *hombres de preferencia*.

Hombres? I don't want to live with a bunch of hombres. I just wanted *one* hombre . . .

And he still hasn't called, much less left me a note. I came back to find the apartment exactly as I'd left it . . . clean, my sewing machine still in its box, sitting next to the now completely dried-out little Christmas tree. The box I put Luke's present in is beside it, still wrapped. He hadn't even bothered to see what I'd gotten him.

I wonder if I can take both gifts back and exchange them for cash. It's not like I don't need the money.

"So it's not even like a *present*," Tiffany points out. "Because his dad BROKE your sewing machine. So he got you something he actually OWED you. Not even something, like . . . *new*. Something you already have that he *broke*."

"Right," I mutter. "I know. Okay?"

"But I mean . . . what kind of present is THAT? If Raoul broke something of mine—or God forbid his DAD came to visit and broke something of mine—I would expect him to replace it, and not try to pass the replacement off as a CHRISTMAS PRESENT. Because he still owes you a PRESENT."

"I know," I say, and am relieved when the phone rings. "Pendergast, Loughlin, and Flynn, how may I direct your call?"

"Lizzie." I'm surprised to hear Roberta's voice on the other end of the line. "Is Tiffany there yet?"

"Yes," I say. Tiffany had come into work early, as usual, to ask how my Christmas had gone, and tell me all about hers, which had been spent at Raoul's godmother's estate in the Hamptons, where they'd made drunken love on a polar bear skin rug, and Raoul had gifted her with a canary diamond cocktail ring and a fox stole, which she is wearing inside because, as she says, "It's part of my OUTFIT," of snakeskin pants and a silk blouse.

"Good," Roberta says. "Could you ask her to take over the desk while you come back here and see me please? And kindly bring your coat and purse with you."

"Oh. Okay." I hang up slowly, feeling all the blood in my body dropping to freezing temperature.

Tiffany must read from my expression that something is wrong, because she tears her attention away from her ring for a moment and goes, "What?"

"Roberta wants me to come back to her office," I say. "Right now. And she wants me to bring my purse and coat."

"Oh, shit," Tiffany says. "Shit, shit, shit. That fucking bitch. The day after Christmas, too. Talk about a fucking Grinch."

What did I do? I'm wondering, as I stand up and reach for my coat. I was so careful. *No one saw Jill and me together after that one time. I'm sure of it.*

"Listen," Tiffany says, sliding into the chair I've just vacated. "Just because we won't be working together anymore doesn't mean we can't be friends. I really like you. You invited me to Thanksgiving dinner. No one else in this fucking place ever invited me anywhere. So I'm going to be calling you. Do you hear me? We'll hang. If you want to go to the shows during Fashion Week, whatever . . . I'm here. Got it?"

I nod dumbly and start for Roberta's office. I can see that someone is in there with her already. As I get closer, I can see that the someone is Raphael, from the security desk downstairs. What is Raphael doing up here? I wonder.

"You wanted to see me, Roberta?" I say, stepping into her office.

"Yes," Roberta says coldly. "Come inside and close the door, will you, Lizzie?"

I do as she asks, glancing nervously at Raphael, who is looking nervously back at me.

"Lizzie," Roberta begins, not even bothering to invite me to sit down. "You recall a conversation we had a few weeks ago about your having been photographed by the press in the company of one of our clients, Jill Higgins, don't you?"

I nod, not trusting myself to speak, because my throat has gone dry with terror. Why is Raphael here? Have I broken the law? Is he going to arrest me? But he isn't even a real cop . . .

"You assured me at that time that your relationship with Miss Higgins had nothing whatsoever to do with this office," Roberta goes on. "So kindly explain to me why I opened the *Journal* this morning to find this."

Roberta hands me a copy of the *New York Journal*, open to the second page ...

... on which there is splashed a huge black-and-white photo of Monsieur Henri and his wife, standing in front of the shop and grinning ear-to-ear beneath the headline "Meet the Designers of Blubber's Wedding Gown!"

The first thing I feel is a bubble of outrage burst inside my chest. Designers! They aren't the designers of Jill's dress! That's me! I am! How dare they try to pass themselves off—

But then as my gaze skims the article, I see that the Henris haven't tried anything of the sort. They are extremely upfront about the fact that Elizabeth Nichols—"an exceptionally talented young woman," according to Monsieur Henri—is the one who refurbished Miss Higgins's wedding gown, after having met Miss Higgins "at the law offices of Pendergast, Loughlin, and Flynn, where Miss Nichols works as a receptionist, and where Miss Higgins sought representation for the handling of her prenuptial agreement with husband-to-be John MacDowell."

And then—grainy but still recognizable—is a picture of me, hurrying through the doors to the lobby of the very building in which I'm standing now.

And all I can think is, *Gray Cords! It was Gray Cords! I knew he was trouble the first minute I saw him!*

Also, *Why, oh, why, did the Henris have to open their mouths about me and how Jill and I met? True, I never told them it was a secret—but why did I tell them anything about it at all? I should have just said she was a friend. Oh God. I'm such an idiot!*

"You know how much we here at Pendergast, Loughlin, and Flynn pride ourselves on keeping our association with our clients private," Roberta is saying. I can hear her voice only dimly through the roaring in my ears. "You were warned once before. You know I have no choice now but to let you go."

I look up from the newspaper article, blinking rapidly. The reason I'm blinking so much is that my eyes have filled with tears.

"You're *firing* me?" I cry.

"I'm sorry, Lizzie," Roberta says. And she actually looks as if she means it. Which helps. Kind of. "But we talked about this. I'll make sure your last check gets mailed out to you promptly. I'll just need your office key. Then Raphael will escort you out."

My cheeks burning, I dig around in my bag until I find my key chain. Then I remove the key to the office doors from it and hand it over. The whole time, my brain searches feverishly for some kind of response to the charges laid against me. But there's really nothing I can say. She *had* warned me. And I didn't listen.

And now I had to pay the price.

"Good-bye, Lizzie," Roberta says, not unkindly.

"Bye," I say. But a bubble of spit, brought on by the fact that I am weeping openly now, prevents me from saying more. I let Raphael guide me with a hand on my arm through the office—conscious of everyone staring, although of course my vision is so blurred I can't actually see whether or not they really are looking at me—and to the elevators. We ride down to the lobby in silence, because there are other passengers on board with us.

When we reach the main floor, Raphael continues to guide me through the lobby, because I still can't see. At the doors to the outside he stops and says a single word to me: "Bummer."

Then he turns around and heads back to the security desk.

I push open the lobby doors and head outside into the bitter Manhattan cold. I have no idea where I'm going, really. Where *can* I go? I have no job, and soon, I'll have no place to live. I have no boyfriend, either, which is really, you know, freeing, on top of the just-getting-fired-and-having-no-place-to-live thing. I feel, in fact, just like Kathy Pennebaker probably did, when she finally admitted that New York City—that big, gutsy, glittering town—had beat her to a pulp and sent her packing.

I'd actually seen Kathy while I'd been home for Christmas. She'd been at the Kroger, pushing a cart in the produce section, looking so washed out and wan, I hardly recognized her.

Is that going to be me someday? I'd wondered, as I'd stared at her from my hiding place behind the nut and dried fruit bins. Will I cease to care what people think of me and go to the grocery store in an overlarge ALL STATE 400 AT THE BRICKYARD SUMMER RUMBLE NASCAR T-shirt and cropped cargo pants (in the winter)? Will I start dating a guy whose mustache is yellow from nicotine, and who is stocking up on cold medicine—so much so that he can only be planning on mixing up a batch of crystal meth for the weekend? Will I ever actually buy radishes? I mean, for a salad or even just to use as garnish?

And then, hurtling down the street with tears streaming down my face, trying not to slip in the slush beneath my feet, I realize something.

And not just because I've suddenly found myself standing in front of Rockefeller Center, its ice-skating rink and gold statue of a man lying down iconic to New York City's image—the more so with the glittering, towering Christmas tree behind.

No. No, I realize. That will *not* be me. That will *never* be me. I would *never* wear cargo pants in public. I don't think I could bring myself to date someone who has a yellow mustache. And radishes are only good on tacos.

I'm not Kathy Pennebaker. And I will never be Kathy Pennebaker. EVER.

My resolve thus strengthened, I turned around and found a cab—on my first try! At Rock Center! I know! It was a miracle—and gave the driver the address of Monsieur Henri's.

When he pulled up in front of the building, I opened my purse to find I had no cash—except the ten-dollar bill Grandma had given me.

But what choice did I have? I handed over the bill, told the driver to keep the change, and barged into the shop, where I found Monsieur and Madame Henri chuckling over the copy of the *Jour-*

nal with steaming mugs of café au lait in their hands and a plate of madeleines in front of them.

"Lizzie!" Monsieur Henri cried delightedly. "You are back! Did you see? Did you see the story and photo? We are famous! Because of you! The phone won't stop ringing! And the best news of all—Maurice! Maurice is closing his shop down the street and moving it to Queens, instead! All because of you! All because of that story!"

"Yeah?" I unwind my scarf, staring at both of them with fury. "Well, I got fired because of that story."

This wipes the smiles off their faces.

"Oh, Lizzie," Madame Henri begins.

But I hold up a single finger.

"No," I say. "Not a word. You're going to listen to me. First off, I want thirty thousand a year *plus* commissions. I want two weeks' paid vacation, full medical *and* dental. I want at least one sick day per month plus two personal days per year. And I want the upstairs apartment, rent free, all utilities paid for by the shop."

The couple continue to stare at me, openmouthed in surprise. Monsieur Henri is the first one to recover.

"Lizzie," he says, sounding wounded. "What you ask, of course, you deserve. No one is suggesting otherwise. But I don't see how you can ask us to—"

But Madame Henri silences him with a *"Tais-toi!"*

While her husband looks at her with surprise, she says to me, clearly and concisely, *"No dental."*

I practically feel my knees give beneath me, I'm so relieved.

But I don't let on. Instead, I say, with all the dignity I can muster, "Done."

And then I accept their invitation to join them for café au lait and madeleines. Because when your heart is broken, carbs don't count.

Aaahhhh! You're home from the honeymoon! Time to start enjoying wedded bliss, right?

WRONG. You have work to do. Get out your stationery—maybe you've sprung for the thank-you cards that match your invitations; maybe you're merely using your new monogrammed note cards—and your favorite pen, and *start writing.*

If you were smart, you didn't wait until after the honeymoon to begin the thank-you process, but started writing and sending out thank-you cards *as you received each gift.* If, however, for some horrible reason you chose to wait, you have your work cut out for you now. At the very least, you ought to have been saving each gift tag, with a note scribbled on the back as to what the gift actually was. If this is the case, you have it easy: just jot a thoughtful note—MENTIONING THE GIFT RECEIVED BY NAME—to each giver, signing it cordially with both spouses' names.

If you have not kept track of who gave you what, start doing some investigating. Because you can bet that even if you haven't been paying attention, someone has. And that someone—usually a mother or mother-in-law—can tell you exactly what you received from whom.

The reason you must mention the name of the gift received in your thank-you note is so that the giver knows for certain that you received their gift, and that it was acknowledged in some thoughtful way. Writing "Thank you so much for the gift" is neither polite nor satisfying to the giver . . . and in general will guarantee that when the baby shower comes around, you will not be receiving anything from that person.*

Yes, you must handwrite each card. No, you may not send a photocopied or even printed letter of thanks to your guests.

*Exception: If a guest gave you a gift of money, it is not necessary or polite to mention the amount in your thank-you note. Call any amount "a generous gift."

• Chapter 26 •

I cannot tell how the truth may be; I
say the tale as 'twas said to me.

—Sir Walter Scott (1771–1832), Scottish novelist and poet

Wait," Chaz says. "So he said he couldn't picture a future with you in it?"

I'm carting the second-to-last armload of clothes up the narrow staircase to my new apartment. Chaz, behind me, has the last one.

"No," I say. "He said he couldn't picture the future, period. Because it's too far away. Or something. You know what? The truth is, I don't even remember anymore. Which is fine, because it doesn't matter."

I reach the top of the stairs, turn left, and I'm in my new apartment. MY apartment. And no one else's. Clean, furnished in shabby chic, and featuring faded pink wall-to-wall carpeting and cream-colored wallpaper with pink roses in every room save the bathroom, which is tiled in plain beige, it features floors that slope even worse than the ones in Chaz's place; only four windows—two that look out onto East Seventy-eighth Street from the living room and two that look out into a dark courtyard from the bedroom; a kitchen so tiny only one person can enter it at a time.

But it also boasts a full-size tub in the bathroom, with a scorchingly hot shower, and two tiny, but highly decorative, fireplaces—one of which by some miracle actually works.

And I love every inch of it. Including the queen-size, lumpy bed, in which I've no doubt many unspeakable acts have been committed by the younger two Henris, but which a proper airing and a fresh set of sheets from Kmart ought to cure, and the tiny black-and-white television with rabbit ears, that I intend to replace with a color set as soon as I have enough money saved.

"That sounds like Luke, though," Chaz says, coming into the bedroom where we've assembled the hanging rack along one wall. "You know. That whole follow-through thing we were talking about."

"Yeah," I say. It's been a little over a week since Luke and I broke up—if, indeed, that is what happened that night in the hallway of his mother's apartment building. I haven't heard a word from him.

And the pain is still too raw for me to talk about it very much.

But Chaz seems to be unable to speak of anything else. It's a small price to pay, I suppose, for his helping me to move—he borrowed a car from his parents and everything. He seems to feel it's the least he can do, considering his best friend is responsible for my broken heart and his father's company for my current state of pennilessness.

But I've pointed out that the latter, at least, has turned out to work to my advantage, since it galvanized me into finally demanding the compensation I deserved from my "real" employers. Even Shari was stunned by what she called my "sudden development of *cojones*."

"Free rent *and* a salary? Good job, Nichols," was what she said over the phone, when I called to tell her the news.

Although, if you think about it, all of this really is Shari's fault. She's the one who went out with Chaz, who was the one who invited us all to Luke's château last summer. In fact, the whole thing could be construed as Chaz's fault. Chaz is the one—as he pointed out on the stairs a little while ago—who told Luke how much I love diet Coke, thus prompting Luke to buy me diet Coke that day in the village, and making me fall in love with him, because of his thoughtfulness.

And Chaz is the one who got me the job at Pendergast, Loughlin, and Flynn that I later lost.

Of course, if he hadn't invited us to France, I'd never have met Luke. And if he hadn't told Luke about my loving diet Coke, I'd have never fallen in love with Luke. And if I hadn't fallen in love with Luke, I probably wouldn't have moved to New York. And if I hadn't moved to New York, I wouldn't have gotten the job at Chaz's dad's firm, and then I never would have met Jill, and thus made my dream of being a certified wedding-gown refurbisher a reality.

So. Everything really is all Chaz's fault.

Which is why it's only fitting he help me move.

"Well," Chaz says, as I take the last dress from him, and slip it onto the hanging rack. "That's it. You sure that's everything?"

Even if it's not, I can't go back now. I left the key to Luke's mother's apartment with the doorman, along with a note—brief but cordial—thanking Luke for the use of the place, and asking that he get in touch with me about any outstanding bills or issues concerning the place.

There is no way I can ever go to the Met again. I'll be too nervous about running into him. Though I'm going to miss poor Mrs. Erickson, for whom I'd also left a good-bye note, since she's spending the holidays in Cancún, and doesn't even know I've moved out. I even stood in front of the Renoir girl, and wished her a fond farewell. I hope Luke's next girlfriend—whoever she is—appreciates her.

"I'm sure," I say to Chaz.

"Well, then I guess I better run the car back," he says. "I don't want to deal with holiday parking and all that."

"Oh, right," I say. I'd almost forgotten that it's New Year's Eve. I've got Jill's wedding to go to in a few hours. Which reminds me. "What are you doing tonight, anyway? I mean, with Luke still out of town, and Shari—well, with Pat. Do you have any plans?"

"They're having a party at Honey's," Chaz says with a shrug. "I figured I'd hang out there."

"You're going to spend New Year's Eve in a karaoke bar with strangers?" I can't keep the incredulity from my voice.

"They aren't strangers," Chaz says, sounding wounded. "The dwarf with the bow staff? That bartender who's always yelling at her boyfriend? Those people are like family to me. Whatever their names are."

And suddenly I'm taking his arm.

"Chaz," I say. "Do you own a tux?"

Which is how, nine hours later, I find myself standing beside Chaz in the Grand Ballroom at the Plaza Hotel (now the Plaza Luxury Condominiums), a glass of champagne in one hand, and the clutch that matches my 1950s pink silk Jacques Fath evening gown in the other, as Jill Higgins, now MacDowell, standing on top of the ballroom's grand piano, prepares to throw her bouquet.

"Here," Chaz says. "Give me that stuff. You better get up there."

"Oh," I say. Despite my reservations—once I'd made sure that Jill's dress looked perfect (which it did) and that her mother-in-law's eyes bulged out when she saw her in it (they did), I'd been reluctant to stay long at the reception. It's weird to be at a wedding where the only people you know are the bride and groom, who certainly don't have much time to spend with anyone but family on the big day—I was having a pretty good time. Chaz declared that there was no way he was going home before twelve ("I'm not getting into a monkey suit just to change into jeans before the ball drops"), and the truth was, he was right. Jill's friends from the zoo were hysterically funny, and as out of their element as I was. And John's friends weren't anywhere near as snooty as I'd expected—the opposite, in fact. Just about the only person, in fact, who didn't seem to be having that good a time was John's mother, and that, apparently, had to do with the fact that someone overheard Anna Wintour say that Jill's gown was "cunning."

Cunning. The head of *Vogue* called something I made—well, rehabbed—*cunning*.

Which actually is no surprise to me, because I think it's pretty cunning, too.

In any case, it's clear Jill will be Blubber to the press no more, and that seems to have depressed John's mother . . . so much so that she's currently sitting with her head in one hand at the head table, shooing away solicitous waiters who keep coming by with ice water and aspirin.

"Everybody," Jill is yelling from on top of the piano. "Get ready! The person who catches it is the next one to tie the knot!"

"Go on," Chaz encourages me. "I've got your bag."

"Don't lose that," I say. "It's got all my needles and emergency sewing kit and everything in it."

"You sound like a nurse," he assures me with a laugh. "I won't lose it. Just go!"

I hurry to the front of the room where the bridesmaids and assorted female zoo employees are gathered before the grand piano, thinking to myself bemusedly that for someone who habitually wears nothing but jeans and a baseball cap, Chaz cleans up *very* nicely. My heart actually skipped a beat when I opened up the door and saw him standing there in his "monkey suit," ready to escort me.

Then again, I suppose *all* men look handsome in tuxedos.

"Okay," Jill calls. "I'm going to turn around and do it so it's fair. Okay?"

I reach the front of the room, and jostle in with all the other girls. I see Jill notice me. She smiles and winks before she turns around. What does *that* mean?

"One," Jill calls.

"ME!" shrieks the woman beside me, whom I recognize as one of the other seal keepers at the zoo. "THROW IT TO ME!"

"Two," Jill calls.

"No, ME!" another woman screams, leaping up and down in her festive though aggressively bright charmeuse satin pantsuit.

"Three!" Jill says.

And her bouquet of white irises and lilies soars through the air. For a moment, it's silhouetted against the warm gold lights from the ceiling. I lift up my arms, not expecting much—I've never caught a ball on the fly before in my life—and so am shocked when the bouquet falls neatly into my outstretched hands.

"Whoa," Chaz says, when I run up to him triumphantly a little while later, to show off my bounty. "If Luke saw you with that, he'd probably pass out."

"Look out, bachelors of Manhattan!" I yell, brandishing my bouquet. "I'm next! I'm next!"

"You're drunk," Chaz says, looking pleased.

"I'm not drunk," I say, blowing some of my hair from my face. "I'm high on life."

"Ten," the people around us suddenly start chanting. "Nine. Eight."

"Oh!" I cry. "New Year's! I forgot it's New Year's!"

"Seven!" Chaz joins the chanting. "Six!"

"Five," I yell. Chaz is right, of course. I *am* drunk. Also, cunning. "Four! Three! Two! One! HAPPY NEW YEAR!"

The people who managed to remember to hold on to their wedding favors—New Year's horns—blow on them, hard. The band launches into "Auld Lang Syne." And above our heads, a net is released, and hundreds of white balloons tumble softly down, like snowflakes, to land in piles around us.

And Chaz reaches for me, and I reach for him, and we kiss happily as the clock strikes midnight.

～ Lizzie Nichols's Wedding Gown Guide ～

Here is a bona fide cure for any postwedding-reception hangover:

Pour 5 ounces of tomato juice into a tall glass. Add a dash of lemon (or lime) juice and a splash of Worcestershire sauce. Sprinkle in 2 or 3 drops Tabasco sauce, then add pepper, salt, and celery salt to taste. If you're feeling adventurous, add some ground horseradish. Add ice, then garnish with celery stick and lime wedge.

Finish off with 1.5 ounces of vodka.

Enjoy.

LIZZIE NICHOLS DESIGNS™

• Chapter 27 •

I wake to pounding.

At first I think the pounding is just coming from inside my head.

I open my eyes, not recognizing where I am for a few moments. Then my vision clears, and I see what I had originally taken for big pink blurry blobs floating before my eyes are actually roses. And they're on the walls.

I'm in the bed in my new apartment above the bridal shop.

And, I realize when I turn my head, I'm not alone.

And someone is knocking on the door.

These are far too many realizations to have at once. Any one of them would be confusing enough all on its own. But considering the fact that they all occur to me simultaneously, it takes me a minute to process what's actually going on.

The first thing I notice is that I'm still in my Jacques Fath evening gown—rumpled now and stained with chocolate cake. But it is very firmly on . . . as are my Spanx beneath it.

Which is good. *Very* good.

I notice furthermore that Chaz is fully dressed as well. That is, his tuxedo pants and jacket are still on, but he appears to have lost his tie, and his shirt is more than halfway unbuttoned, the studs—his grandfather's onyx and gold studs, I remember him telling me—gone, as are his shoes.

I rack my poor, addled brain, trying to remember what happened. How did Chaz—my best friend's ex-boyfriend; my ex-boyfriend's best friend—end up sleeping, even if fully clothed, in my new bed?

And then, as I take in other facts—such as that Jill's bouquet is sitting on my bedside table, looking wilted but really not worse for wear, and that my shoes appear to have vanished—I begin to recall the chain of events that led to this startling early-morning discovery: Chaz and I sharing a New Year's kiss that started out as merely a friendly peck . . . at least, that's how I'd intended it to be.

But then Chaz was throwing his arms around me and turning it into something more.

I'd pushed him away—laughingly—only to realize he wasn't laughing. Or at least, not as much as I was.

"Come on, Lizzie," he said. "You *know*—"

But I'd laid a hand over his mouth before he could finish whatever it was he'd been about to say.

"No," I'd said. "We *can't*."

"Oh, why the hell not?" Chaz had demanded against my fingers. "Just because I met Shari first? Because you know if I'd met you first—"

"*NO*," I'd said, pressing my hand down even more firmly. "That's not why, and you know it. We're both feeling very vulnerable and alone right now. We've both been hurt—"

"Which is all the more reason we should seek solace in each other," Chaz said, taking my hand in his and moving it away from his mouth—so he could kiss it! "I really think you should take all your frustrations over Luke out with me. Physically. I promise to lie very still while you do it. Unless you want me to move."

"Stop it," I'd said, wrenching my hand away. How could he make me laugh so much during what was supposed to be such a serious moment? "You know I love you—as a *friend*. I don't want to do anything that might jeopardize our relationship . . . as *friends*."

"I do," Chaz said. "I want to do things that might jeopardize our relationship as friends a *lot*. Because we're *always* going to be friends, Lizzie. No matter what. I really think it's the whole physical part of our relationship that needs a lot more work."

"Well," I'd said, still laughing. "You're just going to have to be patient then. Because I think we both need time to grieve for what we've lost . . . and to heal."

Chaz, not unsurprisingly, made a disgusted face at this—both the idea of it as well as the way I'd put it seemed to displease him. But I'd continued, undaunted, "If, after a suitable amount of time, we're both still interested in taking our friendship to another level, we can reevaluate."

"How much time are we talking about?" Chaz had wanted to know. "I mean, to grieve and heal? Two hours? Three?"

"I don't know," I'd said. It had kind of been hard to concentrate, considering the fact that he still had his arms around me, and I could feel those studs of his grandfather's pressing through the silk of my dress. That wasn't all I felt pressing through it, either. "At least a month."

He had kissed me again after that, as we swayed back and forth to the music.

And I don't think it was just the champagne that made me feel as if it were raining gold stars all around us, instead of white balloons.

"Well, at least a week," I'd said, when he'd finally let me up to breathe.

"Deal," he'd said. Then he'd sighed. "But it's going to be a long week. What have you got on under there, anyway?" His hands were at the waistband of my panties, which he could feel beneath my dress.

"Oh, those are my control-top Spanx," I'd said, deciding in that moment that in this and all future relationships, I was going to be ruthlessly, even brutally honest—even to my own disadvantage—such as by admitting to a guy that I wear control-top panties. Not just panties, either, but basically bicycle pants.

"Spanx," Chaz had murmured against my lips. "Sounds kinky. I can't wait to see you in them."

"Well," I'd said, welcoming yet another opportunity to be brutally honest. "I can tell you right now it's not going to be as exciting as you might expect."

"That's what you think," Chaz had said. "I just want to let you know that when I look into my future, I see *nothing* but you." Then he'd whispered, *"And you're not even wearing Spanx."*

And then he'd dipped me, so that suddenly I was giggling up at the ceiling, from which the last of the balloons were still falling, in fat, lazy arcs.

The rest of the night was a blur of more kissing, and more champagne, and more dancing, then more kissing, until finally, staggering out of the Plaza just as fingers of pink light were beginning to stretch across the sky above the East River, we tumbled into a waiting cab, and then somehow, into my bed.

Only nothing had happened. Obviously nothing had happened because (a) we're both fully clothed, and (b) I wouldn't have *let* anything happen, no matter how much champagne I might have had.

Because this time, I'm going to do everything the *right* way, instead of the Lizzie way.

And it's going to work, too. Because I'm *cunning.*

I'm lying there thinking about how cunning I am—also about how untidy a sleeper Chaz is, considering the fact that his face is all smushed against one of my pillows, and that, even though he isn't a drooler, like I am, he's definitely a snorer—when I realize that the pounding sound I'd thought was actually my hangover is coming from the door.

Someone is knocking on the outer door to the building—which actually has an intercom, but it's broken (Madame Henri swore to me it would be fixed by the end of next week).

Who could be pounding on the door at—oh God—ten in the morning on New Year's Day?

I roll out of bed, then climb unsteadily to my feet. The room sways . . . but then I realize it's only the slanting floors that make me feel as if I'm about to fall. Well, the floors and my severe hangover.

Clinging to the wall, I make my way to the door of my apartment and unlock it. In the narrow—and chilly—stairway to the ground floor, the pounding is louder than ever.

"Coming," I call, wondering if it could be a UPS delivery for the shop. Madame Henri had warned me that by taking occupancy of the apartment on the top floor of the brownstone, I'd be responsible for signing for all after-hours deliveries.

But does UPS even deliver on New Year's Day? It can't possibly. Even Brown must give its workers the day off.

At the bottom of the stairs, I struggle with all of the various locks, until finally I can pull the door open—though I've kept the security chain on, just in case the person outside is a serial killer and/or religious fanatic.

Through the three-inch crack between the door and frame, I see the last person in the world I ever expected.

Luke.

"Lizzie," he says. He looks tired. Also annoyed. "Finally. I've been knocking for hours practically. Look. Let me in. I need to talk to you."

Panicked, I slam the door shut.

Oh my God. Oh my God, it's Luke. He's back from France. He's back from France, and he came to see me. Why did he come to see me? Didn't he get my brief but cordial note in which I gave him my new address so he'd know where to forward my mail, but instructed him not to contact me there?

"Lizzie." He's pounding on the door again. "Come on. Don't do this. I flew all night to get here to say this to you. Don't shut me out."

Oh God. Luke's at my door. Luke's at my door . . .

. . . and his best friend is asleep in my bed upstairs!

"Lizzie? Are you going to open the door? Are you still there?"

Oh God. What am I going to do? I can't let him in. I can't let him see Chaz. Not that Chaz and I did anything wrong. But who would even believe that? Not Luke. Oh, God. What do I do?

"I'm . . . I'm still here," I open the door to say. I've thrown back the chain, but I don't move to let Luke step inside—even though it's freezing, standing there on the stoop in my evening gown, with the bitter cold seeping in around. "But you can't come in."

Luke looks at me with those sad dark eyes. "Lizzie," he says, apparently not even registering the fact that I've obviously slept in my clothes. And not just any clothes, either, but my Jacques Fath evening gown that I've been saving for years for an event fancy enough to wear it to. Not that he would know that. Because I never told him.

"I've been a total ass," Luke goes on, his gaze never straying from mine. "I'll admit, when you brought up . . . well, the marriage thing last week, you really threw me for a loop. I wasn't expecting it. I really did think we were just hanging out, you know. Having fun. But you made me think. I couldn't *stop* thinking about you, as a matter of fact, though I tried. I really tried."

I stand there blinking at him, shivering. This is what he flew all the way back to America—apparently spending his New Year's Eve on a plane—to say? That I ruined his holiday, even though he tried not to think about me?

"I even talked to my mother about it," he says, the winter sunlight bringing out the bluish highlights in his ink-dark hair. "She's not having an affair, by the way. That guy she met the day after Thanksgiving? That's her plastic surgeon. He does her Botox. But that's beside the point."

I swallow. "Oh," I say. And realize, belatedly, that that's why Bibi's eyes hadn't crinkled when she'd smiled at me while issuing her invitation to join them in France for the holidays: she'd just had Botox injected into them.

Still, this doesn't change anything. It doesn't, in fact, change the part about how Luke chose to spend the holidays with his parents instead of going with me to the Midwest to meet mine.

I remind myself of this because I'm trying very hard to keep my heart steeled against him. Because, of course, the hurt is still fresh. Like I'd said to Chaz, we're both still grieving.

But seeing Luke, looking so tired and vulnerable, on my doorstep isn't helping.

"Mom is the one who told me what an idiot I was being," Luke goes on. "I mean, even though she was kind of pissed about the whole thing where you thought she was having an affair. She was trying to keep the Botox from my dad."

I'm finally able to pry my tongue from the roof of my mouth long enough to say, "Dishonesty in a relationship is never a good thing." As I know, only too well.

"Right," Luke says. "That's why I realize how lucky I am, Lizzie, to have you." He reaches out and takes my hand in his icy cold, leather-gloved fingers. "Because even if maybe you do have a reputation for talking too much, there is one thing about you: you do always tell the truth."

Nice. Also, true. Well, mostly.

"Did you come all this way to insult me?" I ask, trying to sound haughty—though of course the truth is that I just feel like crying. "Or is there a purpose to all of this? Because I'm standing here freezing—"

"Oh!" he cries, dropping my hand, and hastily whipping off his coat, which he then drapes gently around my shoulders. "I'm sorry. This would be a lot easier if we could just go in—"

"*No*," I say firmly, grateful for the coat. Although now my stocking feet are like ice.

"Fine," Luke says with a little smile. "If that's the way you want it. I'll just say what I came here to say and then let you go."

Yes. Because of course that's the kind of thing princes do. Fly thousands of miles just to say good-bye.

Because whatever else they might be, princes are unfailingly polite. Good-bye, Luke.

"Lizzie," Luke says. "I've never met a girl like you before. You always seem to know what you want and exactly how to go after it. You aren't afraid to do or say anything. You take risks. I can't tell you how much I admire that."

Wow, this is a very nice good-bye speech.

"You came into my life like a . . . well, a tsunami or something. A good one, I mean. Totally unexpected, and totally irresistible. I honestly don't know where I'd be now if it weren't for you."

Back in Houston with your ex, I want to say.

Only I don't. Because I'm sort of curious to hear what he's going to say next. Although mostly I just want to run back upstairs to bed.

Except I can't, I remember belatedly. Because there's a snoring man in my bed.

"I'm not the kind of person who's good at going after what I want," he goes on. "I guess I'm more cautious. I have to weigh all the possibilities, calculate each and every risk involved—"

Yes. I know.

Good-bye, Luke. Good-bye forever. You'll never know how much I loved—

"That's why it took me so long to realize that what I really want to say to you—" He's fumbling in the front pocket of his charcoal wool trousers now. And I can't help thinking, Why is he doing this . . . what's he doing? Is he just trying to torture me? Does he have no idea how hard I'm trying not to throw myself at him? Why can't he *just go away*? "What I think I've *always* wanted to say to you, since the day I met you, on that crazy train, is—"

—*get out of my life, and never contact me again.*

Only that's not what he says. That isn't what he says at all.

Instead, for some reason, he's sunk down onto one knee, in front of the closed bridal shop, and the lady across the street walking her dog, and the guy in the minivan looking for a parking space, and the entire population of East Seventy-eighth Street.

And though I can't believe what I'm seeing, and I'm positive my tired, hungover eyes are playing tricks on me, he's pulled from his pocket a black velvet box, which he opens to reveal a diamond solitaire that glistens in the morning light.

No. No, that's really what he's doing. And there are words coming out of his mouth. And those words are:

"Lizzie Nichols, will you marry me?"